Reap the Wind

>—I—◦—I—<

A CASSIE PALMER NOVEL

KAREN CHANCE

A SIGNET BOOK

SIGNET
Published by New American Library,
an imprint of Penguin Random House LLC
375 Hudson Street, New York, New York 10014

This book is an original publication of New American Library.

First Printing, November 2015

Copyright © Karen Chance, 2015
Penguin Random House supports copyright. Copyright fuels creativity, encourages diverse voices, promotes free speech, and creates a vibrant culture. Thank you for buying an authorized edition of this book and for complying with copyright laws by not reproducing, scanning, or distributing any part of it in any form without permission. You are supporting writers and allowing Penguin Random House to continue to publish books for every reader.

Signet and the Signet colophon are registered trademarks of Penguin Random House LLC.

For more information about Penguin Random House, visit penguin.com.

ISBN 978-0-451-41907-1

Printed in the United States of America
10 9 8 7 6 5 4 3 2 1

Penguin
Random
House

"YOU DEFINITELY NEED TO CHECK OUT THIS SERIES."
—Literary Escapism

Praise for the Cassie Palmer Novels

Tempt the Stars

"An action-packed romp through the Cassandra Palmer universe." —All Things Urban Fantasy

"Stellar.... Chance has done a fantastic job weaving everything into a fantastic story that sucks you right in." —A Book Obsession

"The best of the series." —The Demon Librarian

"Cassie is the ultimate poster child for heroines having to learn to roll with the punches and stay on their feet. Per usual, you can count on the awesome Chance delivering a story that hits the ground running and never looks back." —*RT Book Reviews*

Hunt the Moon

"This isn't just urban fantasy—it's storytelling at its best." —SFRevu

"I am as surprised as anyone to have book five of a series stand me on my head and dazzle me, and even more so as I realize I could pick up *Hunt the Moon* and these characters would do it again and again and again." —All Things Urban Fantasy

"A fascinating world.... The author has reinvented her writing style for the series and raised the bar of expectations high. Her story transcends mere urban fantasy and veers toward epic fantasy." —LoveVampires

Curse the Dawn

"A truly riotous ride.... Chance adds plenty of twists and obstacles to her first-person series that blends time travel, magic, vampires, and more. The pace is rapid, and the exploits are wild. Chance aces another one!" —*RT Book Reviews*

continued ...

"The urban fantasy equivalent of a summer blockbuster ... quite the satisfying urban fantasy adventure."　—SF Site

"Outstanding. The characters pull you into their world and won't let you go.... The dialog is funny, the story is fast-paced, full of intrigue with really hot sex scenes."
　　　　　—The Romance Readers Connection

"A dark theme tempered with humor, action, and romance comes alive in *Curse the Dawn*, one of the best of the Cassandra Palmer series."　—Romance Reviews Today

"Chance is outstanding in her punchy delivery.... Swift action sequences, tight plotline, a memorable cast, some rather steamy and heart-thumping scenes ... are all reasons to love this book and indeed this series."
　　　　　—The Truth About Books

Embrace the Night

"Cassie is a well-rounded character, and the intensity and complexity of the plot puts her through her paces physically, emotionally, and psychically."　—*Publishers Weekly*

"If you thought *Touch the Dark* and *Claimed by Shadow* were action-packed, well, buckle your seat belt.... Lara Croft would have a hard time keeping up."　—SFRevu

"Quick pacing and imaginative use of some old mythologies blend into a captivating read that will leave readers clamoring for more."　—Monsters and Critics

"Ms. Chance continues to expand her well-built world with time travel, fantastical beings, steamy romance, and the nonstop action her wonderful series provides. This is a fast-moving read that's hard to set down."　—Darque Reviews

"A wonderfully refreshing step away from the cookie-cutter regime of the usual vampire novels ... this novel has it all. Believable characters, descriptive settings, and thrills and chills kept this reader on the edge of her seat."
　　　　　—Roundtable Reviews

Claimed by Shadow

"A nonstop thrill ride from beginning to end, a wildly entertaining romp with a strong, likable heroine." —Rambles

"Ms. Chance is a master.... [A] series well worth getting hooked on." —Fresh Fiction

"A great writer of supernatural fantasy that is on a par with the works of Kim Harrison, Charlaine Harris, and Kelley Armstrong." —*Midwest Book Review*

"Magic aplenty populates this fast-moving, rather dark tale of power, corruption, double-dealings, and painful attractions as Cassie comes to grips with her new role in this follow-up to *Touch the Dark*." —Monsters and Critics

Touch the Dark

"A grab-you-by-the-throat-and-suck-you-in sort of book with a tough, smart heroine and sexy-scary vampires. I loved it—and I'm waiting anxiously for a sequel."
—#1 *New York Times* bestselling author Patricia Briggs

"A really exciting book with great pace and a huge cast of vivid characters. This is one of my favorite reads of the year."
—#1 *New York Times* bestselling author Charlaine Harris

"Exciting and inventive." —*Booklist*

"Fast and heavy on the action, *Touch the Dark* packs a huge story.... A blend of fantasy and romance, it will satisfy readers of both genres." —Fresh Fiction

"A very promising start to a new series, and an exceptionally entertaining first novel." —*Locus*

"A wonderfully entertaining romp with an engaging heroine. Here's hoping there's a sequel in the works!"
—*New York Times* bestselling author Kelley Armstrong

"Karen Chance takes her place along with Laurell K. Hamilton, Charlaine Harris, MaryJanice Davidson, and J. D. Robb to give us a strong woman who doesn't wait to be rescued.... The action never stops.... Engrossing." —SFRevu

"Combines humor, action, and the paranormal into a scintillating story that will leave readers begging for more."
—Romance Reviews Today

Books by Karen Chance

THE CASSIE PALMER SERIES

Touch the Dark
Claimed by Shadow
Embrace the Night
Curse the Dawn
Hunt the Moon
Tempt the Stars
Reap the Wind

THE MIDNIGHT'S DAUGHTER SERIES

Midnight's Daughter
Death's Mistress
Fury's Kiss

THE MIRCEA BASARAB SERIES

Masks

ACKNOWLEDGMENTS

To the crew at Penguin—thanks for the hard work and patience as this monster came together.

Chapter One

Okay, this was going to be easy.

That wasn't something I said very often, because my life is a lot of things, but easy has never been one of them. My name is Cassie Palmer, and I used to be a down-on-my-luck clairvoyant who made ends meet by reading tarot in a bar. But then stuff happened. A lot of stuff. A lot of hair-raising, spine-tingling, unbelievably crazy and potentially deadly stuff. As a result, I was now a down-on-my-luck Pythia, the chief seer of the supernatural world.

Yeah, I don't know how that happened, either.

But my no-good luck was about to change. Because my partner, who was currently lost in time, and who I'd been searching for for what felt like *forever*, was right across the room.

And this time, nothing was going to go wrong.

"This time, nothing is going to go wrong," I said into my beer.

The should-have-been-handsome-but-wasn't-because-he-was-an-ass who was propping up the wall next to me didn't answer. His shirt was open and he was poking at something on his stomach—presumably a bruise. I clenched my hand on my beer mug so I wouldn't be tempted to add a few more.

"Did you hear me?" I demanded softly, trying not to call attention to us. Not that that seemed likely. The little dive in Amsterdam where we'd washed up was loud, and an especially raucous group had just blown in through the door. Along with a blast of cold air and icy slush that numbed my toes even through thick leather boots and added another layer of frost to my eyelashes.

Apparently, central heating was not a thing in the 1790s.

The smart people were over by the fire, which had managed to melt the slush around a small ring of chairs and a few stool-type things that I guess were supposed to be tables. Or beer holders, anyway. But we couldn't join them and try to thaw out. Because the bar was by the fire and a half-demon war mage named Pritkin was by the bar.

He'd glanced around a few times since we'd come in, but hadn't picked me out because my strawberry blond curls were hidden under a dark brown glamourie. The same one that had changed my tip-tilted nose into a pug and fattened my already plump cheeks into chipmunk territory. It was not a great look for me, but since my reluctant partner had provided it, I'd decided it could be worse.

I was sort of surprised he hadn't given me warts.

I wasn't surprised that he hadn't bothered to answer. Rosier might be Lord of all Incubi, the demon race known for being smooth, suave, and charming, but I didn't get to see that side of him. No, I saw this side. The side that was poking at his hairy abdomen with a frown, as if the ring of bruises there was potentially life-threatening.

If only, I thought, and kicked him.

That won me a glare out of a stranger's black eyes, because Rosier was wearing a glamourie, too. Normally, he shared the green eye color and rugged blond good looks of his son and our elusive target. And nothing else. The stubborn sense of honor, the brutal honesty, and the iron discipline of the man I knew must have all come from Pritkin's human side, because I'd yet to see a shred of them in his reprehensible father.

"Why are you asking me?" the creature demanded, glowering at me from under greasy dark brown bangs. "I wasn't the one who screwed up last time."

"You got mugged last time!"

"You shouldn't have left me alone," he complained. "London is a dangerous city, doubly so in the Victorian age—"

"You're a *demon lord*! How the hell you managed to get beaten up—"

"A demon lord without magic."

"—by a handful of street thugs who didn't even have— wait. What?"

He scowled at me. "Why do you think I'm carrying this?" he slapped the side of the leather man purse he'd brought along, because I guess incubi are more secure in their sexuality than most guys. Or maybe there was another reason.

He'd pulled the little patch out of it that had provided my glamourie earlier. I hadn't stopped to wonder about it at the time, being too busy already wondering how to get into my multilayered Victorian outfit. But now it occurred to me that maybe a demon lord shouldn't have to carry around his magic.

And shouldn't have the crap beaten out of him quite so easily.

"In their infinite wisdom, the demon council decided to put a dam on my power," he confirmed bitterly. "They worried about what I would do to some of them, back in time with both foreknowledge and magic intact. Not being able to deprive me of the former, they restricted the latter— something that becomes a problem when one is set upon by six huge brutes!"

I didn't waste time pointing out that it had been three the first time he told that story, because deflating his ego could wait. Something else couldn't. "Then what about the counterspell?" I hissed.

Rosier and I were putting up with each other because we had a common goal: to save his son from obliteration. Pritkin's twenty-first-century body was back where it belonged, and in decent shape despite being hit by a deadly curse. But only because it hadn't been the target. His soul had. The demon spell had sent his spirit sliding back through the eras of his life, and would destroy it once it reached the beginning of what had been, thankfully, a very long existence.

At least, it would unless we put the countercurse on him first.

But that wasn't my job. I'd done my job—flipping us

through time after the wildly careening soul, which didn't have anything like a steady, predictable path. It jumped here and there, like a piece of flotsam in the rapids, catching only occasionally on some bit of time's shoreline before being snatched off again a few minutes later.

And now the one person who could stop it was telling me he couldn't cast the damned spell?

"Of course I can," Rosier said acidly, when I pointed this out. "They had to leave me that much, or what's the use in my coming?"

"Nothing as far as I can—"

"But that's the only one."

I stared at him as his meaning sunk in. "You mean *that's the only spell you can do*?"

He gestured at his bruised ribs. "Obviously."

"But . . . but what if we run into trouble?"

"Well, you're a witch, aren't you?"

"No! No, I am not a witch! How many times do I have to—"

A hand reached around my shoulders and clapped over my mouth. "Keep your voice down! That is not a popular word in this era."

I shut up, because he was right. And because I didn't have a choice. And, eventually, Rosier decided to let me breathe again, but just so he could interrogate me.

"What do you mean, you're not a witch?"

"I mean, I don't do witch stuff," I whispered. "I do Pythia stuff. That's why I have bodyguards!" Only there was a limit to how many people I could take along on my jaunts through time, since every person added to the already considerable strain. So I'd left my guards at home, assuming that a demon lord could protect me.

Only to find out that he couldn't even do that for himself.

"What do we do if we're attacked?" he demanded.

"That's what I just asked you!"

"You couldn't have mentioned this before?"

"You told me to get us here and you'd take care of the rest!"

"That was before I knew I was dealing with someone without even rudimentary—" He abruptly cut off.

"What is it?" I glanced around nervously. But it wasn't a

witch-hunting posse coming for me with torches blazing. In fact, nothing of interest appeared to be happening at all. Just the bar's alcoholic tabby winding around a few legs, looking for handouts, more icy rain lashing the windows, and a couple guys arguing over a game of dice.

And Pritkin chatting up one of the barmaids.

I did a double take at that, because it wasn't the sort of thing you saw every day. Or ever. The asshole beside me had seen to that.

About a century ago, Rosier had had one of his intermittent bouts of fatherly enthusiasm, during which he usually managed to screw up his son's life in a major way. That time, he'd decided he wanted Pritkin back in hell on a permanent basis. Not so much for the pleasure of his company as to use him as a pawn in his little power games.

The fact that incubi gain power and influence through sex, and that this plan had therefore involved whoring his son out to the highest bidders, wasn't thought of as a problem. Or probably thought of at all, since incubi have to feed to live anyway. So obliging other demons merely meant a two-way power exchange for them, with a little added influence for the pimp-in-chief.

At least, it did unless you were Pritkin. Who, as half human, could live off pizza like the rest of us. And who'd had this weird idea that there might be more to life. Long story short, he'd ended up being allowed to stay on earth, but only for as long as he could handle complete abstinence — something that, for most incubi, was considered the same as constant torture. Rosier assumed he'd have his son back inside a month.

He was still waiting.

As a result, when I met the stubborn cuss known as John Pritkin, he'd been that strangest of strange creatures: a celibate incubus. So it was more than a little odd to watch him flirting with a buxom blonde who was trying her best to fall out of a low-cut blouse. It looked like barmaids dressing for tips wasn't a new concept, I thought, scowling.

And then a mug was shoved in my face. "Here," Rosier told me abruptly. "I need a refill."

"So? What do you expect me to do about it?"

"Get me another!"

"With what? You were mugged, remember?" He'd

charmed the first round out of the other barmaid somehow,
but that sort of thing wasn't in my repertoire. Besides, I still
had beer.

"Do you usually pay for your own drinks?"

"No, but that's in—what are you doing?" I demanded,
as he started unbuttoning the top of my prim little shirt-
waist.

"Advertising."

I slapped his hand away. "Advertise yourself!"

"I'm not his type."

"His—" I stopped, staring at Rosier.

"We need to get him alone," the demon said impatiently.
"And distracted. Can you think of a better way?"

"I can't think of too many worse ones," I said, clutching
my top to stop Rosier from looking down my shirt. "And
anyway, that sort of thing doesn't work on Pritkin."

"Doesn't work on your version," he corrected, wiping
something off my cheek. "But this isn't the man you know,
and this one didn't come in here for a drink. He came in for
a meal."

"But this place doesn't serve—" I broke off at the look
Rosier was sending me. "Oh."

That type of meal.

"Hurry," Rosier said, stealing my beer. "It looks like he's
already found the first course."

I looked back at the bar to see that, sure enough, Pritkin
was being led off somewhere by the blonde. I felt my face
flush. I thought he'd have better taste.

And then Rosier gave me what could only be called a
shove, sending me stumbling into the middle of the room.

I might have returned the favor, but he was right, damn
him. We couldn't just de-hex Pritkin from across the bar,
however nice that sounded. That's what had tripped us up
in London.

I'd left the poor, unprotected demon lord at the mercy
of the city's murderous brutes in order to play damsel in
distress. Or at least damsel in need of some directions. Pritkin had gone sauntering by the alley where we'd popped in,
and I'd run after him to lure him back so Rosier could zap
him, although not with the counterspell.

We'd planned to knock him out and wait—until his eyes
glowed neon green with a double dose of soul energy be-

hind them. We'd showed up in London to get ahead of the hexed spirit, because hitting him with the counterspell before it arrived wouldn't help. And, knowing Pritkin, would probably get us hit back. So unconscious it had had to be.

Or distracted, although that sort of thing was more daunting for me than for a horny demon lord.

I looked back to see Rosier shooing at me, with an expression of utter disgust on his face. Whatever. I started winding my way through the low, bench-like tables, nervousness gnawing at my gut.

Sure, Rosier wouldn't have a problem seducing somebody into doing what he wanted. It was practically his job description. But it wasn't mine, and the whole thing was uncomfortable in ways I didn't want to think about right now.

Like some of the things Pritkin had said recently, after he'd had his father's prohibition lifted, but before he'd gotten zapped with the curse. Things I had probably misinterpreted. Things that, even if I hadn't misinterpreted, weren't going anywhere, because my personal life was even more complicated than my job.

And wasn't that saying something?

I stopped in front of a tattered curtain leading to what I guessed was the back of the bar. And then just stayed there, chewing my lip and trying to come up with a better plan. Because this one wasn't going to work.

I wasn't one of Rosier's succubi, some experienced femme fatale. Hell, I wasn't even a femme slightly nauseous. I was a time-traveling, ghost-whispering, somewhat clumsy clairvoyant, with an upturned nose, too many freckles and cheeks nobody would call defined even without Rosier's idea of a disguise. I wouldn't have been competition for Dolly Parton in there on my best day.

But I had to come up with something. Enough to keep Pritkin in sight, at least. Otherwise, if his soul came and went while he was in the back, we might never know it. And that would be a problem, since we were fast running out of time before—

And then I *was* out.

The curtain was abruptly thrown back and the blonde emerged with a giggle and a wink, tucking something down the front of her front. Wow, I thought, faintly disappointed. That hadn't taken long.

And then I was being jerked through the door by a furious war mage. "You!"

"What?" I asked stupidly.

And then three things happened at once. The outer room went suddenly silent, a knife blade bit into the skin of my throat, and the barmaid came back through the curtain, smirking at me. And then continued doing so as she toppled over, stiff as a blond-haired mannequin. And hit the floor, bouncing on her considerable padding off to the side.

Pritkin and I stared down at her for a moment, at her glassy eyes and messy hair and still-leering face. Which was more than a little creepy, since she was now leering at my left boot. And then we looked at each other.

"What did you do?" we demanded, at the same time.

"What?" we said again.

And then "Stop that!"

And Pritkin did. But only so he could grab me and snarl: "It's here, isn't it?"

"Wh-what's here?" I asked, as he backed me into a wall with no effort at all. Because I've always found a knife over my jugular to be really persuasive.

"Don't play games," he hissed.

I started to swallow and then stopped, afraid I'd push the blade in more. Of course, that might not matter. Since one glance at the frozen girl told me I had bigger problems than a pissed-off war mage.

There are spells that can render a person unconscious just that fast, but they wouldn't leave her with one hand raised, adjusting a bit of material over the assets between her assets. Or cause her skirts to be stuck in a swirl, like around moving legs. Or make stray bits of her hair stay suspended in air that was no longer flowing.

She looked like someone had called her name right after she'd come out of the back, and she'd turned toward them, professional grin already in place. Only to freeze halfway through the motion and come tumbling back in here. She looked like a frame cut out of a movie, which would have been weird if I hadn't seen that sort of thing before.

"You know," I told him nervously, "I've never felt less like a game in my—"

"What you stole from me!" he yelled, making me flinch.

And freak out, since I wasn't sure I hadn't just slit my own throat.

And then a voice came from the outer room. "In back! Check it out."

Pritkin and I froze, stiff as the girl on the floor. I don't know what his reasoning was, but mine ran something like: crap. That command had been in English, which was weird enough considering where we were. But not as much as hearing it in imperious female tones, in a place where women were tolerated only if they were with a man or serving drinks.

It can't be, I told myself sternly. You're just being paranoid. Even your luck isn't that—

And then the curtain was flung back and Pritkin let go of me to face off with . . . two little girls?

That's what they looked like at first glance, two teenagers wearing long, white gowns, their red and brown curls held back with ribbons from their innocent faces. But I knew the drill, I knew the goddamned *uniform*, and innocent they weren't.

"Oh, *shit*," I said, causing the brunette's head to jerk up.

Her hand followed the motion a second later, but I'd expected that and already thrown myself at the floor, jerking Pritkin down with me. As a result, the time wave she threw rippled overhead, missing us by inches. And hit something to our rear that collapsed in a cacophony of rusty metal and shattering glass that I didn't see because I was busy.

Freezing two Pythian acolytes in place before they could do the same to me.

It was lucky I was already on my hands and knees, because the power drain of stopping time was immediate and terrible, especially after flipping through the damn stuff all day. If "day" even meant anything anymore, which I wasn't sure it did, I was just sure I was going to throw up. And then Pritkin grabbed me again.

"Where is it?"

Dear God, he was single-minded, I thought, trying to crawl off. I'd forgotten that, somehow. Although I was remembering as he dragged me back to my feet and shook me.

I caught sight of myself—red face, tumbled blond curls,

startled blue eyes—in some brass platters hanging on the wall. And damn Rosier! He must have taken off the unflattering glamourie when he sent me after his son, and hadn't bothered to mention it.

Well, that explained my reception, anyway.

My Pritkin might not be here yet, but this one . . . well, we'd met before. To be precise, we'd met in 1793 on one of my previous time jaunts, which had been barely a year ago from his perspective. It was why I'd needed the glamourie.

Okay, and because the last time we'd met, I'd made like one of Rosier's street toughs and mugged him.

It hadn't been intentional—all right, it had been, but it was for his own good. He'd been looking for something he absolutely couldn't be allowed to find, and he'd had a map on him to its location, and, well, I'd had no choice but to take it.

And strip him and steal his clothes.

And get him beaten up by a vampire.

And then there was the small matter of burning the only map that led to the location of his most prized possession, so, yeah, I probably wasn't his favorite person just now. But I had one big advantage. "I'm n-not t-trying to k-kill you," I told him, pointing at the girls. "They are!"

It wasn't a lie.

Because the frozen barmaid, and the time wave, and the girls' prim little outfits all added up to one thing. One very, very bad thing. And if there was about to be a time battle in here, I didn't want him anywhere near it.

"You have to go," I told him frantically, when he finally stopped shaking me.

But Pritkin didn't go. He just stood there, looking bemused, as I tried my best to push him out the back door. "Why?"

"Because . . . there are some . . . people . . . after me and . . . goddamnit!" The guy weighed a freaking ton.

Green eyes narrowed. "Perhaps we could work out an arrangement—"

"No! No, we can't!"

"Give me what I want, and I will help—"

"You can't help me with this. It's . . . new magic," I said, thinking fast. "Really new. Like super new."

Pritkin frowned, but he didn't call me on the lie, maybe

because he couldn't. This Pritkin wasn't the spell master of my day, when there were few enchantments he didn't know or hadn't invented. This one was just back from an extended jaunt in hell, and was therefore out of the loop as far as magical theory went.

Way out. It was why he'd lost the property he was trying to recover from me to a couple of low-end scam artists who didn't have as much magic in their whole bodies as he did in his little finger. But knowledge is power, and they'd known stuff he didn't.

I could almost see the thoughts running through his head, but he still wasn't moving. And that was a problem since he was half again as heavy as me and most of that was muscle. But I was determined, because we didn't have a lot of time.

And then we had less, when he glanced at the curtain and then at me, and I suddenly found myself up against the wall again.

But this time, the knife was nowhere in sight.

"No, see —" I managed to say, right before a hard mouth came down on mine.

Chapter Two

"This . . . is no time . . . for a snack!" I gasped furiously when Pritkin let me up for air. Only to have him scowl in a very disturbing impression of his father.

All the more so because the next thing I knew, a knee was spreading my thighs, hard hands were gripping my hips, and he was nuzzling my neck with little growling sounds that sent shivers all the way to my belly.

And put a crease in my forehead, because this was so typical.

Not the sexy stuff, although there'd been a few moments. . . . But moments were all they'd been, because of the whole no-sex rule and because, well, it was complicated. But the stubbornness. The arrogance. The absolute certainty that he knew better than me about *every damned thing*, yeah, that was familiar.

The last time I'd seen him, other than for that glimpse in London, had been the moment he was cursed. And just after, when I was sure I'd lost him for good. It had felt like a punch to the gut. It had felt like the end of the world. I'd thought, if only we had one more minute . . .

And now that we did, all I wanted was to give him a swift kick.

But instead, my hands were finding their way under his shirt, my fingers were ghosting over his ribs and nipples, and my palms were enjoying the feel of springy chest hair under my hands.

And then he pushed me against the wall and kissed me again.

And damn it, I knew what he was doing, I thought, returning the kiss furiously. He was trying to use incubus abilities on me, and it wasn't going to work. Because he could feed anytime—I broke off to bite on a luscious lower lip—when we weren't—and to suck on his chin—in the middle—and along his jaw—of a damned crisis! I bit an earlobe and heard him inhale sharply. Served him right, I thought, worrying it, and wondering how I was supposed to face a Pythia at full power when I was barely able to stand up on my own.

And then suddenly I wasn't.

A single hand curved under my butt, lifting me, another captured my hands, shoving them over my head, and a body pressed against mine, holding me helplessly against the wall. I couldn't touch him, I couldn't *move*, except to wind my legs around his waist, skirts and all, and try to hold on. But he could, and he took full advantage, with little vibrations of his hips against mine that quickly had me gasping and groaning and staring at some cobwebs on the ceiling like I had no idea what they were.

And then he was groaning, too, and talking into my neck.

I couldn't understand a word because it wasn't English, at least I didn't think so. But it was hard to tell with all the white noise suddenly roaring in my ears. Along with the ebb and flow of labored breathing, which might have been mine but I wasn't sure because he was kissing me again, hot and hard and hungry, almost desperate. And his hips were moving more, pounding me into the wall until he forgot to hold my hands and they found his shoulders and I just hung on. And every time he did that *grind* again, the white noise ramped up and my heart sped up and my breathing became sobs became groans became cries until I was just screaming and thrashing and—

And . . . and . . . *oh*.

I held on as wave after wave of sensation crashed through me, like a hurricane slamming into a beach. Hurricane Pritkin, I thought deliriously, as the vibrations hammered at me, wild and tumultuous and demanding. And then softer, gentler, sweeter, but no less strong for all that. I finally surfaced to find his body still pressed against mine, his breathing uneven and his fingers trembling on my jaw. A piece of my hair was stuck to his cheek. I brushed it off, panting slightly, feeling drugged and delirious and golden warm wherever our skin touched.

And then someone cleared a throat.

It wasn't Pritkin.

I looked up, blinking. And saw a short, stout, middle-aged woman in a frilly Victorian frock framed in the doorway. She had a head full of improbable violet sausage curls and was carrying a cherry-covered parasol. The frock had cherries on it, too, big red ones on a white background, and small, round, purple glasses were perched on the end of her nose.

She looked totally nuts.

She also looked confused, although not half as much as I was.

"Are you finished?" she finally asked, politely.

I just looked at her.

"Yes, I remember," she said, a little nostalgically. "Take a moment, girl."

I took a moment.

And then I took another one.

"Who the hell are you?" I finally asked.

"My very question."

I opened my mouth, and then closed it again. Then I looked at the two girls in white, who were still imitating statues on either side of the door. "Yours?" I asked carefully.

"Quite."

I slumped back against the wall in sheer relief. "Oh, thank God."

Brown eyes that were shrewder than the outfit would suggest narrowed. "You were expecting another answer?"

"I—well, to tell the truth, I've been having a little trouble with some of my . . . associates . . . lately."

I'd almost said "acolytes," since that's who I'd assumed the girls were. I was a new Pythia, and not everybody from my predecessor's court was exactly on board with the change of command. Five especially had decided that they could do without me, preferably permanently. And since they were on the loose at the moment, it had been a logical conclusion that some or all of them had hunted me down.

Logical but, apparently, also wrong.

Unless my acolytes had adopted one hell of a new dress code.

"Some trouble?" A slender eyebrow went up.

"They sort of want me dead." It was one of the messes I was going to have to deal with as soon as I got Pritkin back.

Cherry red lips pursed. "Understandable. A rogue is a serious problem."

"I'm not a rogue."

That did not appear to go down well. "Whatever you are, you do not belong here."

"Neither do you," I pointed out. That outfit was pure Victorian excess.

She smiled gently. "Had you remained in London a little while longer, I would not have had to be."

Well, that explained that. It looked like the nineteenth-century Pythia had taken exception to my romping through her turf; why, I didn't know. Nobody had ever said anything before.

"Isn't the usual procedure to, uh, ignore that sort of thing?" I asked hopefully.

The eyebrow ratcheted up another notch. "Ignore a powerful demon lord intruding into areas he oughtn't?"

Crap. I should have known. Rosier.

He was just the gift that kept on giving, wasn't he?

"But no matter," she told me. "I do enjoy a bit of a chase. But I'm afraid this one is over now."

I swallowed. Under other circumstances, she'd have been right. I'd have gone back to Victorian Britain without a fuss, on the assumption that I'd be able to talk my way out of this sooner or later. But right now, I didn't have that option. Even if I could eventually convince her that I wasn't a dangerous rogue, that Rosier wasn't currently a powerful anything, and that we should therefore be allowed to go on our way, it wouldn't matter.

It would still be too late for Pritkin.

The demon who had cast the spell had boasted that it had been selected with my abilities in mind, to make rescue unlikely. As a result, Pritkin's cursed soul would only pass through each era of his life once. No matter how many times I came back to this year afterward, it would never be here again. And shortly beyond this point, his past became a lot more difficult to navigate, with a lengthy time spent in hell where my power didn't work well, if at all, and then . . . an early life at a point too far back in time for me to reach.

My hands clenched on his arms. I was drained from a day of time-shifting, demon-sitting, and now Pritkin's idea of a late-night snack. I was in no shape to challenge a Pythia who, presumably, had a lot more experience on the job than me and had two members of her court with her. Each of whom was like an extra battery pack, giving her a major advantage even if I'd been at full strength.

If I challenged her, I was going to lose.

But I didn't have a choice. I *had* to catch Pritkin here. And based on how fast his soul had been going, it could arrive anytime.

Only, looking into the woman's sharp brown eyes, time wasn't something I thought I had.

And then Pritkin's hands clenched back.

I looked up at him, surprised, but couldn't read his expression. But he didn't leave me wondering for long. "One kiss before you go," he rasped.

I blinked at him, not sure I understood, and then at my counterpart. Who sighed and rolled her eyes. "Get on with it, then."

He got on with it.

But this wasn't a normal kiss. I knew it as soon as our lips touched, because I'd felt something like it before, although the memory had faded somewhat. Until a spine-tingling, thrumming, heady rush coursed through every cell in my body, and I remembered.

Oh God, yes, I remembered, I thought, groaning and grabbing on to his hair, his shoulders, his butt, trying to crawl up his body as he filled me with life and energy and power, to the point that I found myself laughing against his lips, the feeling so giddy, so effervescent, so light, that it simply had to come out somehow.

"All right," the other Pythia said dryly. "I think that's quite enough."

I didn't answer, being too busy giggling and holding helplessly on to Pritkin.

"Come along, girl," she said impatiently.

"No." It was strangled, because I was desperately trying to keep a straight face.

I failed.

Brown eyes narrowed. "You don't want to test me, my dear."

"You know," I gasped, "I kind of think I do."

And then I froze her.

The expression on her face as she toppled over really set me off, but Pritkin was already towing me through the door and back into the bar. Where people were starting to move sluggishly as her time spell unraveled. And that included one extremely odd-looking demon lord who scowled in slo-mo when he saw me run through with his son, still doubled over with laughter and strange euphoria and utter disbelief that I'd just done that.

Oh God, I was so dead, I thought hysterically.

And then a sheet of rain slapped some sense back into me.

Pritkin had pulled open the door, which almost resulted in us getting blown off our feet. It looked like the other Pythia's time bubble extended only as far as this room. Because outside, nature was taking its course in the form of a gale of wind and sleety rain that was only slightly lessened when Pritkin jerked me around the corner and up against the side of the building.

There was intermittent cover under the eaves and the spreading arms of a tree. But unlike the dark shadows along a nearby canal, it was way too close to a window for my liking. A haze of golden light speared the darkness from between the gaps in a pair of old wooden shutters, highlighting random bits of war mage: a cheekbone, a stubbly jaw, one violent green eye.

And a pair of thin lips that opened to say: *"Where is it?"*

"Where is what?"

"My property!"

Oh, right. He wanted his damned map back. "We don't have time for that," I told him, sobering up slightly. "We have to get . . . somebody . . . and then get out of here—"

"Give me what I want and I will let you go!"

"I can't give you what I don't have," I told him, distracted, because the gaps in the shutters were from warped boards, not slats, and I couldn't see much inside. That was worrying, since Pythias weren't affected by time spells like other people. What I'd flung at her would have bought me fifteen minutes, maybe more, with anyone else. With her . . . I honestly didn't know how long we had.

But I was betting it came under the heading of not long enough.

Annnnnnd now Pritkin was shaking me again. "I helped you!"

"Yes, after m-mugging me," I pointed out. Although in fairness, it felt like I'd gotten back more power than I'd given. Like, a lot more.

Which was weird, because he was looking kind of energized himself.

Along with pissed.

"I b-burnt the map," I reminded him quickly. "You w-watched me—"

"But you'd memorized it, hadn't you?"

"Look, can we t-talk about this another—"

"You'd memorized it"—low and furious—"and you saw something in there that brought you here!"

"And you know that h-how?"

"Don't play dumb!"

"Trust me, she doesn't have to," came a cynical voice.

Pritkin's head jerked up at sight of the specimen that had just joined us. Fortunately, Rosier was still unrecognizable. Unfortunately, it was because he'd somehow managed to fall onto my leftover glamourie.

And I guessed it wasn't advisable to try to use two at the same time. Because the usually polished demon lord now looked like Popeye, with one bulging eye and one regular, a swollen chipmunk cheek, a bulbous nose, and a couple of shaggy brown things above his eyes that resembled fuzzy caterpillars. Caterpillars that pulled together when Pritkin grabbed his satchel.

"Does nobody in this benighted place have any respect for private property?" Rosier demanded.

I didn't know what kind of dangerous stuff Rosier was carrying, but Pritkin took one glance at the contents and his already fearsome scowl grew exponentially. He grabbed me around the neck, facing off with Rosier, the bag held tight in the hand that wasn't busy choking me. "Any closer and she dies!"

"Oh no, stop," Rosier said lazily.

"I'm not bluffing," Pritkin snarled. He looked down at me. "And now you're going to tell me what that thing was."

"What thing?" I asked, confused. "Look, we don't have time for—urp."

"I traced the thieves' movements," Pritkin told me, quietly vicious. "I discovered that they'd gone from England, where they stole my property, to Paris, where they sold it, via Amsterdam. I came here suspecting that they might have preferred to hide it well away from the auction site. And what do I find on the very day I arrive? My chief competitor—"

"You have to admit, it does sound damning," Rosier murmured.

"—trying to eavesdrop on my conversation with their sister!"

"Their—you mean the barmaid?" I asked, strangely relieved. Although that may have been because he'd finally realized he was choking me and loosened his grip slightly.

"Or were you distracting me while your accomplice searched the place?" Pritkin suddenly stared around, as if he thought his prize was about to drop from a tree or something. "That's it, isn't it? It's here!"

"No, I—"

"Then tell me where it is if you want to live!"

And, okay, things suddenly weren't so funny anymore. Because Pritkin wasn't kidding. I knew him well enough to know his don't-fuck-with-me expression when I saw it. Just as I knew I couldn't give him what he wanted. The map he'd lost had led to something called the Codex Merlini, a book of spells that needed to molder away exactly where it was, since some rather delicate events would later hinge on that. Some delicate, potentially world-ending events.

But I somehow didn't think that trying to explain that was going to go over well.

And then I didn't have to.

Half of the wall we were standing against suddenly crumbled in a cascade of rocks and dust and, oh, *crap*. I got a half-second glimpse of an incensed Pythia standing backlit amid the billowing clouds, parasol at the ready and chin tilted determinedly, and then I panicked. And since there weren't a whole lot of options, I did what I usually do when terrified and defenseless, and shifted.

But not me.

The power that allows me temporal shifts also permits spatial ones, to a limited degree. Limited in that I have to know where I'm going, which I didn't, and can see where I'm landing, which I couldn't. I also couldn't leave Pritkin with the cursed soul due to arrive any minute, and it's not like I had a lot of time to think about it and—

And so I shifted her.

"Was that supposed to *help*?" Rosier demanded, staring at the sight of a waterlogged Pythia rising from the dark and, okay, faintly slimy canal, lavender curls hanging dispiritedly around a by now truly furious face.

For a split second, I just stared back in horror. I'd been aiming for the opposite bank, but I couldn't see shit and—and damn.

"Run," I squawked. Only to find out that I couldn't. Because Pritkin wasn't letting go, not having managed to follow all of that.

But Rosier had and he grabbed his satchel back and took off. Leaving me behind, because nobody had ever accused him of being noble. But for once, I thought he had the right idea.

"You want . . . the Codex?" I asked Pritkin, panting from lack of air and utter, utter terror. "Because you just let it get away. *He* has it!"

And, okay, that worked, I thought, as Pritkin started after the fleeing demon lord. Sort of, I amended, as he jerked me along for the ride. But that was okay; that was good, even. I just had to keep them close and keep him from killing Rosier and keep an eye out for the damned soul while I was at it.

Well, and one other thing, I amended, as the gnarled old limbs of a tree exploded into flower as we passed.

I turned around while still running, watching through pelting rain as the massive trunk shrank, old bark became new, twisted limbs straightened and flowered and hung heavy with life. It would have been beautiful, except for the knowledge that a blast of reverse time like that wouldn't do me the same good. Would, in fact, age me right out of existence.

Good thing she couldn't see me any better than I could her, huh, I thought, right before something like the sun suddenly flooded the area all around us. Something exactly like, I realized, staring up at the darkened sky. And at a patch of icy slush the size of a house that had just been replaced by clear blue skies and fat, happy-looking clouds.

Damn, I didn't know we could do that, I thought, as the light of another day shone down around us, out of some type of time portal I didn't understand because I didn't understand much about this job. But if the idea was to turn a searchlight on us, it was doing okay, I thought, and jerked Pritkin into the shade of a nearby bridge.

"What the—" he began, staring upward at the shimmering beam that was sparkling off the water, and throwing moving shadows of tree limbs onto snow-covered streets as it started moving around, looking for us.

"New magic?" I said weakly. And received a frown in return, because Pritkin isn't stupid.

But before he could work it out, something like a speed-boat tore out from under the bridge, drenching us with freezing spray.

I hadn't seen who was driving it, but I guess Pritkin had. Because he swore and dragged us down a rusty ladder into a small dinghy, which seemed kind of useless since it had no form of propulsion that I could see. Outboard motors didn't exist in 1794.

But magic did. At least, I assumed there was some sort of spell involved when we zipped out into the canal, so fast that it sent me tumbling into the stern and had the prow of the boat leaping out of the water, barely touching the waves. But we were doing better than Rosier, who I saw when I scrambled back to my feet, just ahead of us.

He was in another speeding boat, courtesy of his big bag o' tricks, I supposed, but whatever he was using must not have come with instructions. Or steering. Because he was weaving back and forth along the narrow waterway, his boat hitting other boats and the high brick walls of the canal and basically anything and everything in his path, making his frantic face and waving arms kind of superfluous.

Yes, I knew he was in trouble.

But then, so were we.

Because the makeshift searchlight was now chasing us, flowing along the sides of the canal like bright water. The portal looked like an oval of colored film imposed over the black-and-white landscape around us, some avant-garde cinematography about youth and age. Behind us, skeletal trees became green, snow melted into leaf-strewn streets, people strolled along the shore enjoying a bright spring day.

And then stopped to stare through the portal at us, including one guy who ran into a tree.

I stared back as time boiled along a line just behind us, bisecting day and night. And summer and winter. And the bottom of our boat, sending me scrambling frantically into the front and Pritkin cursing and somehow increasing our speed.

It worked, sort of. We jumped ahead, all but flying now, with a sound like the crack of a mighty whip. Or, I realized a second later, like half a boat splintering and breaking and falling away.

I stared behind us through my wildly flying hair as what had been the back of our boat was swallowed by that other day, bobbing and listing and then sinking in bright spring sunshine. And realized that we weren't going to be any better off soon. Half a boat doesn't float well, and only our crazy speed was keeping us momentarily above water.

I looked around frantically, trying to spot Rosier, planning to shift us onto his vessel, which at least was still in one piece. But it was dark ahead, even without the glow from behind obscuring my vision. And the sleety half rain, half snow was coming down harder now, making it almost impossible to—

And then Rosier made it easy by crashing headlong into the back of a barge.

It sent him hurtling out of his craft and through the air, and I grabbed Pritkin and shifted even before he landed. We ended up right beside him, which would have been impressive—if I'd remembered to leave our broken craft behind. But we were still clinging to the sides, so our boat had come, too, and for a second there, it was skipping along the long, unladen surface of the barge, right beside a falling, cursing, and rolling demon lord. And then Pritkin reached out and grabbed his father. And I shifted us again, about a second before we would have plowed into the back of the captain's cabin.

So we plowed into one of the small bridges that spanned the canals instead.

That actually wouldn't have been so bad, since our little half craft had managed to land on top. But then we kept right on going. I screamed and grabbed Pritkin, who was clutching Rosier in a death grip but manfully keeping silent. Unlike the elegant demon lord, who was yelling right along with me as our momentum carried us across the narrow span, which was little more than a brick arch sans railings.

And off the other side.

And into a patch of bright sunlight and the front of a larger boat being guided along by a still-dripping Pythia.

"Well, hello," she said, smiling at me evilly, as I looked up from a pile of demon.

"Well, good-bye," I gasped, and kicked her into the canal.

Our tiny boat shuddered and shook as Pritkin got control of it again. And then abruptly detached itself from the Pythia's stately barge. And skittered off down the canal, through the early-morning sunlight of that other day that had now engulfed us, with Rosier clinging to the bow, Pritkin holding on to him, and me drowning along behind, my body half in the water as I gripped an oar I'd snared at the last second and hung on for dear life.

I tried to pull myself up, which would have been easier without all the kicking and scuffling feet in my face. And without being slung back and forth wildly, because no one seemed to be driving this thing. But then I forgot about all that; I forgot about everything.

Because I'd just looked up.

And seen a new form of light shining out of a pair of brilliant green eyes.

My throat closed up for a moment in sheer, unadulterated relief. And then opened so I could scream, "Hex him! *Hex him!*"

That won me a glare but nothing else, because Rosier was in a stranglehold and couldn't speak the damned words. And I could barely hold on, much less help him out.

And then the little boat got even more crowded when the triple-damned Pythia shifted in next to me with a snarl.

That would have been bad—really bad—if our craft hadn't suddenly sped into darkness again. And not because we'd passed under another bridge. It fell all around us, like night arriving in a moment, all but blinding after the glare. And then just as abruptly we hit something.

Hard.

We were thrown into the high front of the boat, all of us landing in a wad of thrashing limbs and screaming faces. And then we bounced off the prow and fell out the nonexistent back, because our craft was suddenly not budging. I realized why a second later, when my butt hit something hard and ice-cold.

Which was a good description since it was, in fact, ice.

More was spread out all around us, and had frozen the boat in place, which explained why we weren't moving.

I stared around at dim moonlight reflecting off a long ribbon of solid canal and felt dizzy and confused. First we'd been in a sleet storm, then in a sunny spring day, and now where were we? If we'd somehow escaped the other Pythia's time portal, or whatever the heck that had been, shouldn't we be back where we started? But there was no driving rain, no sleet, no boiling dark clouds to be seen. Just a quiet midnight scene, an icy canal, and a stooped figure on a bridge overhead, silhouetted against a harvest moon.

It was a tiny woman with a black cloak billowing in the breeze. And a wispy bun of white hair. And a pissed-off expression.

Rosier and Pritkin were wrestling over to the side, thrashing around in a way that threatened to break through the ice. I desperately wanted to go and help, but I didn't. Because the patch of sunlight had stopped just behind us, as if it was afraid to come any closer.

Like my counterpart of the dripping cherries, who wasn't looking so confident, suddenly.

"Lydia," Cherries said nervously. "I—I can explain."

"What?" The old woman scowled at her.

"It's me, Gertie." It was louder this time.

"What?"

"Ger—oh, for goodness' sake. Your horn."

"Speak up, why can't you?"

"Your horn! Put in your *horn*!"

"Give me a moment," the old woman said querulously. "I've got to put in me horn."

She pulled an old black ear horn out from under her cloak and held it to the side of her head. "What?" she demanded again.

"It's me," the other Pythia repeated, loud and slow. "Gertie. And I know we're out of place—"

"Demmed right, ye're out of place!"

"Yes, I know. But—"

"Always breaking the rules, you were. And now ye're consorting with the likes of him!"

"Consort..." Gertie puffed up. "I am doing no such thing—"

"Knew I should have trained your sister," the old woman muttered.

"I'm trying to get him back where he belongs!"

"Oh, I'll get ye back," the old woman said ominously.

"No! No, Lydia, you must listen—"

But listening didn't appear to be Lydia's strong suit. And a second later, there was no more Gertie. Who, I assumed, had just been sent packing to the 1880s.

By her 1794 counterpart.

It was getting crowded with Pythias around here, I thought blankly, as the old woman turned her attention on me. I smiled weakly. And then I shifted to the boys, not even waiting to get a good grip on them before shifting us all through the rapidly closing time portal behind us.

To my surprise, it worked. We landed in daylight, which was good. And in the middle of a canal that was no longer solid, which was bad. But that was still okay.

Until my damned useless partner sank like a stone.

I dove after him, grabbed him by the collar, and dragged him back to the surface, where he flailed and spluttered and tried to drown me.

"I thought your kind were supposed to float!" I said, smacking him upside the head.

"That's ... witches," he gasped, but calmed down slightly.

Until we looked around for Pritkin. And almost got run over by a canal boat full of tourists, instead. A Japanese guy in an "I got high in Amsterdam" T-shirt hung over the open side of the boat, snapping pictures of the waterlogged crazies, while Rosier cussed and flailed and swore and sank. And I stared around in confusion at a few hundred bicycles, a bunch of tiny cars, and no Pritkin, cursed or otherwise.

And all right, then, I thought, letting the water close over my own head.

Maybe this wasn't going to be as easy as I'd thought.

Chapter Three

For a number of strange-but-they-make-sense-in-context-I-swear reasons, home base for me is a penthouse in a Las Vegas hotel. It's usually pretty crowded, which is why I don't just shift inside anymore. I have enough problems without appearing in the middle of one of the vampire bodyguards who live with me and who already have a tendency to scream at odd moments. So I've learned to show up in the marble-floored foyer, which is usually pretty deserted, instead.

Usually, but not today.

I hit the ground from a good five feet up, because I'd forgotten I was swimming, in a rain of dirty canal water and a hail of tiny silver fish. And a soggy demon lord who almost fell on my head. And then a vampire screamed and pointed a gun at me.

A second later, he screamed again and pointed it at the floor. I thought that was a bit excessive until I blinked brackish water out of my eyes and realized that it wasn't the vamp who was screaming. It was the wards.

The spells that protect the suite must have been recalibrated to hate-demon mode while I'd been gone, which, considering some of the stuff that had happened lately, wasn't real surprising. But it was annoying. Like earsplittingly annoying.

The caterwaul went on and on as I coughed up half the

contents of the canal and tried to remember how to breathe. Which left me a little too busy to understand what the vamp was saying, much less try to answer back. I settled for sprawling there and gasping at him instead.

Rosier was less reticent, but luckily, the wards drowned him out, too. Even when he was pounced on by five large guards who tore out of the suite and proceeded to pummel the problem. I watched them for a moment, and then I scooped something I really hoped was seaweed out of my cleavage and started trying to get up.

It didn't go so great.

I felt like one of the tiny fish: beaten up, exhausted, and gasping for breath I still wasn't getting because of the damned corset that came with my outfit. I was also wearing about fifty pounds of waterlogged wool, half of which had managed to wrap itself around my legs, leaving me about as mobile as a beached seal. But I managed to get to my hands and knees anyway, and did an inchworm impression in the general direction of the front door.

Which opened the same moment I reached it, to show me a pair of overlarge Cerutti loafers.

They were black and had a nice gloss to the leather. That was good. Because suede wouldn't have handled the miniature tide that rolled over them nearly as well.

I looked up to see their owner mouthing some not-so-gentlemanly words and glaring at me. And then at the ruckus over my head. And then back at me again as I pointed and gesticulated and tried to convey over the din that I didn't actually want Rosier beaten up.

You know, *that* badly.

And then I found myself being lifted by two ham-sized hands, which brought me face-to-face with my chief body-guard, a swarthy giant named Marco.

It also left my feet dangling off the floor, because I am five foot four and Marco is not. But I didn't worry about giving him back strain. He could hold me there all day if he wanted, soggy wool and all. The ferocious package nature had provided had been upgraded centuries ago with a pair of fangs he didn't need, because who was going to jump Lou Ferrigno's big brother?

Unfortunately, I managed to strain him in other ways, like at the moment, judging by the frown that creased his forehead. And by the way he tucked me under one massive arm after a final glance at the chaos. And by how he carted me inside like a soggy sack of potatoes.

"I can walk," I protested breathlessly as the wards abruptly cut out. The combo of corset and Marco's idea of a gentle grip had left me with maybe half an inch of inflatable lung room.

Marco didn't answer. That was bad, since informing me of my various failings is Marco's favorite way of releasing tension. It was when he got quiet that you had to worry, so I was.

And that was before I was lugged through a living room filled to the brim with strangers.

Female strangers. All of whom looked like they were attending a Victorian-era tea party. Some appeared to be as young as two or three, others maybe ten years older, although it was hard to tell with the bows in their hair and the old-fashioned, infantilizing outfits they had on and—

And crap.

No wonder Marco wasn't happy.

"What are you doing?" One of the girls demanded, jumping off the sofa and hurrying up. "What is happening?"

She was a cute brunette, probably the oldest of the lot, and her name was Rhea. She was a member of my court, like the rest of them, although not one of the ones who wanted me dead. At least I didn't think so, although her expression was pretty fierce.

But then, she wasn't looking at me.

"Your mistress is back," Marco told her grimly.

"What are you doing with her?" she demanded. "Is she injured?"

"Not yet."

Judging by Rhea's expression, she didn't like that answer. It was almost funny, since people did not scowl at six-foot-five vampires with vicious tempers. Sane people, anyway. But Rhea had proven to have weird ideas about who was scary, and she actually seemed more intimidated by me than by my suite full of fanged monsters.

"Put her down!" she demanded, not that it did any good.

Marco just continued wading through the sea of girls, all of whom were now staring at me, some with their mouths hanging open.

So much for making a good first impression.

Not that it mattered. Next to my predecessor, the perfect and all-knowing Agnes, I already looked ... well, I mostly tried not to think about how I looked. I sighed and let my head droop onto Marco's brawny forearm.

Might as well get the lack-of-dignity thing out of the way early.

But Rhea didn't seem to think so. She followed us across the living room, through the lounge, and into the hall that led to the bedrooms. Which was harder to navigate than usual because it was piled high with folded cots. And then she kept on following us into my room, which had pallets all over the floor and pillows and blankets slopped around because, yeah.

My court needed somewhere to sleep, didn't they?

It was one of those things I probably should have thought about before running off with Rosier. But then, I hadn't expected to be saddled with a troupe of young girls I'd never met and didn't know what to do with. And time had been of the essence.

And thanks to his utter, utter ineptitude, it still was.

"About ... the guy ... I came in with?" I said breathlessly, catching myself at the last moment.

I didn't get an acknowledgement. I did get tossed onto the bed, though, instead of dropped on the floor, so I supposed that was something. I landed facedown on a nice brocade bedspread that was going to need changing after this, groaned, and flopped over. And watched as a pissed-off vampire tried to figure out how to remove my boots.

Considering that it had taken me fifteen minutes to get the damned things on in the first place, and that was before the laces got waterlogged, I didn't give much for his chances. But I should have known better. Marco had skills. And a sharp pocketknife, which I guessed was okay since it wasn't like I was going back to the 1880s again anyway.

"I need him. Alive," I clarified, because around here, you never knew.

Marco still didn't say anything.

I glanced at Rhea. She was standing at the ready, looking as if she was contemplating beaning an ancient vampire over the head with something, and wasn't that all I needed? "Can you give us a minute?" I asked.

She curtsied and bit her lip. But she didn't go anywhere. One of my boots did, though, squelching off and releasing a small tide of filthy water onto the carpet.

"It's okay," I told her as Marco tackled the other one. "He's . . . We need to have a chat."

"No, we needed to have a chat *yesterday*," Marco said, his voice low and venomous.

"We need to have an argument," I corrected. "Profanity may be used."

"I don't care," Rhea said staunchly, glaring at him. "I need . . . that is, I would like to request an audience."

"With who?"

She looked at me.

"Oh. Right." I wasn't used to being referred to like some kind of royalty. And didn't plan to get used to it, either. But that could wait. "In a little while."

Rhea curtsied again, and then just continued to stand there.

"He isn't going to hurt me," I assured her, and she finally left, still shooting Marco evil looks. And a second later the other boot came off.

The rug promptly went from filthy to unsalvageable, but I didn't care. I lay back against the bed with something between a sigh and a groan and wriggled my poor toes in relief. Along with his other failings, Rosier had gotten my boots two sizes too small.

"Oh God, that feels good," I said fervently.

The door slammed shut.

Uh-oh.

I didn't bother getting up. Experience had shown that I could be yelled at lying down just as easily. Of course, I didn't need to get up, I thought sleepily. I needed to get *back*. But even assuming that Pritkin's soul hadn't already flitted off somewhere, that the various Pythias had dispersed, and that we could get close enough to lay the spell without getting hexed, it still wouldn't do any good.

Because I was pooped.

And a jump of more than two centuries was tough enough even when I wasn't.

Marco's handsome, if alarmingly large, face appeared in the space over mine. "If you fall asleep on me, I may trash the room," he warned.

"Too late."

And look, it seemed like I could sit up, after all, I thought, as I was jerked back to the perpendicular. I would have protested, but Marco was busy relieving me of some of the godawful wool, so I didn't. "I don't suppose this could wait?" I asked as he stripped off the high-necked jacket.

"You know, that's funny," he told me, slinging it across the room, where it squelched wetly against the wall. "That's what I said to myself, just this morning. 'She's sleeping. Let the kid get some rest. There's plenty of time to find out what the hell happened last night!'"

"Last night?" I was fuzzy on last night. Maybe because, for me, it had been several nights ago. Or days. Or . . .

Time travel was hard.

"I can take my own skirt off," I told him, although not for modesty's sake. Being undressed by Marco was akin to being stripped by a rabid wolverine.

Might as well have saved my breath. But at least I had on four layers of petticoats, or crinolines or whatever the right term was, under there. Hell, I could outfit a whole house.

Which might be just as well, since I didn't see any luggage.

"Where'd you put the girls' stuff?" I asked, after Marco rolled me out of the skirt and almost off the bed.

"They didn't have any."

"They didn't have—"

"They said," he told me viciously, "that it was blown up!"

Oh, right.

That last night.

"Um. Well, see—"

"No," he said, crouching down beside the bed, getting on my level.

"No?"

"No." Dark brown eyes stared humorlessly into mine. "No lies. Not this time."

"I don't lie."

"Or evasions. Or tricky answers. I swear you're as bad as the master."

Considering who his master was, I decided to take that as a compliment. "Thank you?"

"Damn it, Cassie! I want to know what the *hell* is going on."

"Yes, well—"

"And when I want to know, is now!"

I licked my lips.

It wasn't that I liked keeping things from Marco. He was actually a very good bodyguard. Or he would have been for anybody else. I sometimes felt pretty bad for him, since he was the type who liked to think he was on top of things, that he had everything under control, that the world was sane and all was in its proper place.

Boy, had he gotten the wrong job.

But even if I'd been willing to spill secrets that weren't really mine, the fact was that Marco *didn't* want to know what was going on.

He didn't want to know that the reason he had a living room full of Pythian initiates was because a handful of their number had just tried to kill them by blowing up the old Pythian Court. Not because they hated them, but in order to set a trap for me. One that had almost worked.

He didn't want to know that the acolytes responsible were still out there somewhere. Or that the abilities they'd received from the old Pythia before she died had never been rescinded. Meaning that they could technically pop in here at any moment.

I didn't actually think they would. I was a lot more vulnerable elsewhere, and it was me they were after. But still. I didn't think Marco wanted to know that all the wards, guns, and vampire skills in the world might not be enough to deal with those girls' power if they decided to risk it.

"Well?" he demanded.

"I'm thinking."

"Damn it, Cassie!"

"Can you help . . . with this thing?" I asked, gesturing at the corset, which was the kind that laced up the back.

I wasn't stalling for time; I really was having trouble breathing. All that water had tautened the strings, as Marco found out when he flipped me over and tried to loosen them.

He muttered something and pulled out the knife again. "I can't keep you safe if I don't know where you are!" he told me, hacking away. "Or who you're with. Or what the *hell* you've been up to!"

"Exactly," I muttered into the mattress.

Marco also didn't want to know that I'd been hanging out with Satan's good buddy, only no. Satan, assuming he existed, probably had better taste. So did I, but I was stuck, at least for the moment.

And damn it, we'd been so *close*!

"You're not going to tell me a damned thing, are you?" Marco asked, flipping me over again.

The corset was in shreds, allowing me to take my first deep breath in what felt like days. For a moment, I just lay there, exploring the wonder that was oxygen. And staring up at Marco, who, despite current appearances, was a good person and a good friend. He deserved better than the insanity that was my life these days.

Of course, for that matter, so did I.

"You ought to ask for a transfer," I told him honestly.

Thick brows drew together into a frown. "It's that bad?"

"Isn't it always?"

He sat on the edge of the damp bed. "With you? Pretty much."

"I don't try to be a disaster," I told him, feeling my throat tighten up.

He sighed and took my hand, interlacing his fingers with my own. Since his were the size of sausages, that left mine spread uncomfortably wide, but I decided I could live with it. "You don't have to try," he told me. "It's a gift."

"You could always shoot me," I offered weakly.

"I've considered it. But then I'd have a few dozen time-traveling little girls on my ass."

"They can't all time-travel." At least, I really hoped not. "When did they get here?"

"You don't remember?"

I shook my head.

"You missed quite the scene," Marco said, letting go of my hand so he could lean back against the bedpost. And level exasperated dark eyes at me.

"Do I want to know?"

"No. But I'm going to tell you anyway," he said pleasantly.

I threw my arm over my face.

"So, you come back from hell. Big swirly portal thing coughs you up onto the rug after all but wrecking the living room. But okay. At least you're back.

"Only no. A couple minutes later, you're gone again. No explanation, no good-bye, no nothing. One second you're there, watching the news about that old house in London blowing up, and the next you're not. For a minute, I thought you'd jumped back through the damned portal!

"But then I realized that the witches were gone, too."

"The witches" in this case were a group of coven leaders who had volunteered to help me rescue mine. My coven, that is, since that's what the Pythian Court apparently was. Since I'd never considered myself a witch, the idea of having a coven took a little getting used to.

Not as much as the concept of changing time, though.

But I hadn't had a choice. I'd returned from my rescue attempt gone wrong only to find out that Agnes' mansion in London had just been bombed. I'd sat around on the living room sofa for a few minutes, watching a magical news feed showing mountains of still-burning rubble and rows of tiny body bags and clumps of stunned-looking war mages. And tried to absorb that.

And then I'd taken the witches and gone back in time to fix things.

I wasn't supposed to. The whole point of having a Pythia in the first place was to keep people from mucking about in the time stream, not to do it myself. But those little girls were my court now, even if I hadn't had a chance to meet them yet. And they'd died because of me. And it had only been fifteen minutes. . . .

Anyway, I'd done it. It probably made me a lousy Pythia, but then, what else was new? And I wasn't sorry, I thought defiantly.

Guilty, yes; sorry, no.

"And, uh, then what happened?" I asked, because I didn't know.

I guessed the witches had gotten my court out, since it was here now. And that the demons had done the same for me, after I'd stayed behind to cover everyone's retreat. And passed out from the strain of slowing down the battleground's worth of spells that my acolyte's dark mage friends had been throwing.

Because one had been waiting on me when I woke up, back here in my bed.

Not a spell—a demon. His name was Adra, head of the demon council, and incidentally, also the person who had cursed Pritkin. But he'd had a change of heart, or so he said, after seeing me risk my life to save my court.

I didn't know why that should matter to the council, but maybe they weren't as bad as I'd been told. Or maybe that had belatedly decided they might need some help with the gods, and I'd do. If, you know, they hadn't just wiped my friend out of existence!

But I'd had no chance to find out before Rosier was throwing a pack at me filled with old-fashioned clothes, and we'd left right afterward, with my head still spinning.

Marco narrowed his eyes. "You tell me. The next thing I know, the windows start shaking and the floor starts moving, and it feels like about a six on the Richter scale. And then that damned portal activates again and there you are, stumbling out along with three battered witches and a couple dozen freaked-out little girls!"

I bit my lip. "Sorry?"

"And then you take two steps and fall over, and I think you're dead. But no, turns out you're just exhausted. So I carry you off to bed. And the next morning, when I think I'm finally going to get a damned explanation, what happens?"

I didn't say anything that time.

"So I've had a day," Marco said grimly. "You were gone and the girls wouldn't tell me shit, and that damned mage kept calling—"

"You mean Jonas?" I asked worriedly.

"Who else?"

We were talking about Jonas Marsden, the head of the Silver Circle, the world's chief magical authority and my ... well, colleague, technically, although he acted more like my boss. And of course, he'd been there to see all of this. My luck practically demanded it.

"What did he want?" I asked, pretty sure I already knew.

"To talk to you. He had a fit when you disappeared last night, and a worse one when you came back. He wanted to carry you and the girls off somewhere, but Rhea wouldn't budge until she talked to you, and he didn't have enough mages with him to force the issue. Not with the witches yelling about 'Pythian sovereignty,' whatever the hell that is, and me threatening him with a couple dozen masters—"

I winced. And was suddenly profoundly grateful that I'd been unconscious.

"—but it wasn't pretty. For a while there, I thought I was going to have to call for reinforcements. But he finally agreed to go if I promised to have you call him as soon as you got up. But, of course, by this morning you'd skipped out—*again*—with no explanation—*again*. And I had to tell him you'd gone on an errand!"

"I owe you," I said fervently.

"Oh no. No, we're not even *there* yet."

I swallowed.

"So every half hour: is she back yet, is she back yet?" Marco gave Jonas' voice a high-pitched whine it in no way possessed. "And then the girls needed food and a place to stay—"

"I'll see if I can—"

"And then the press got word about your court blowing up, and they somehow got our number—"

"Not again. How do they keep—"

"—and then the boss called."

I swallowed. And, once again, everything else suddenly felt trivial. Manageable. Easy, by comparison. "The ... boss?"

"Yeah, you know." Marco smiled evilly. "Your husband?"

Chapter Four

Mircea Basarab was a lot of things. Handsome—beautiful, really, if you could use that word for a man—in that stunning way that movie stars are and the rest of us aren't. Only Mircea didn't need a great wardrobe and the right lighting. Mircea could make women swoon naked and in the dark.

Especially naked and in the dark, come to think of it.

It wasn't surprising, since he'd had five hundred years to refine his seduction technique, which he now used as the chief negotiator for the dreaded North American Vampire Senate. It controlled the country's vamps far more strictly than the Circle did its mages. And speaking of mages, the Senate was heartily tired of them monopolizing the Pythias, which they had done for centuries as the traditional Pythian bodyguards.

Right up until a Pythia ended up sort-of-kind-of-but-not-exactly married to a senator, that is.

Like I said, my love life is complicated.

Or it had been until recently, when Mircea had all but vanished from the scene. I hadn't heard from him in more than a week, not since he'd gone off to handle some crisis in New York. That had been a little disappointing, because, okay, he was busy, but would a phone call have killed him? But it had also been a relief, because we had things to talk about, oh yes we did, and they were things that I'd just as soon postpone until I fixed the immediate crises of a demon curse and a homeless court and a bunch of homicidal acolytes.

"What did he say?" I asked Marco casually.

Marco cocked a thick eyebrow at me. "Think you'd better take that up with him. He wants you to call."

He held out a shiny black phone.

I bit my lip and saw an unhappy-looking reflection do the same. Yes, Mircea and I needed to talk. Yes, we needed to do it soon. And not just because of personal issues. We were also allies in a war, the same war my dear acolytes had decided to join on the other side, and he might need something.

"Did he say it was urgent?"

Marco looked at me.

"Well, did he?"

"He didn't say it wasn't."

I felt my back muscles unclench slightly. Mircea was a diplomat, but if it was life or death he would have said so. And Marco would be looking a lot more than just exasperated right now.

Of course, ignoring this was only going to dig me in deeper, and I had a feeling that I was in over my head as it was. But I just couldn't deal with another problem right now, especially not a tall, dark, and handsome problem with wicked eyes and a knowing smile who played me like a violin even when I wasn't exhausted. And starving.

"I'm hungry," I told Marco plaintively.

He narrowed suspicious eyes at me but didn't argue. Because a hungry Pythia was a vulnerable Pythia. The energy of the office might be all but inexhaustible, but that wasn't true of the people who had to channel it. And out of fuel for me meant out of power.

He put the phone away. "What do you want?"

"Anything. And lots of it," I added as my stomach woke up to inform me that half a beer was not an adequate daily intake. "And I need to see ... uh, the guy. That I brought with me."

"The demon, you mean?" Marco asked dryly, because yeah. He knew the wards, too.

But a moment after he strode out, a bedraggled, beaten-up, sopping-wet demon staggered in, sandwiched between two vamps. Someone had given him another pop eye to match the glamouried one, which oddly made him look better. Or at least more symmetrical.

It didn't appear to have done anything for his temper.

"It's okay. You can leave him," I told the guards, more for their sake than his. Rosier might be temporarily powerless, but he wouldn't stay that way forever. And he struck me as the vindictive type.

They exchanged glances, but they didn't argue, either. Because we all knew it didn't matter. Which was why I jumped up and clapped a hand over Rosier's indignantly open mouth as soon as they'd gone. Vampire hearing ensured that they could eavesdrop equally well from the living room—of a suite on the other side of the building.

They didn't do it on purpose, exactly. It was just that, with superhuman senses and living in one another's brains half the time, vamps had about the same understanding of privacy as the NSA. And that was before getting orders to keep me safe or else.

So I put a finger to my lips while Rosier glared at me some more. But he stayed silent when I let him go so I could lean over and turn on the TV. Sumo wrestling, of course. Vegas only had about ten channels of the stuff. But I flipped around until I found a loud telenovela and blasted it, and then turned on the clock radio for good measure.

"What are—" Rosier demanded.

"Shhh!" I grabbed his hand and led him to the French windows on the other side of the room, which opened onto a balcony. It was a tiny trail of a thing, little more than a lip clinging to the side of the building. Because there are penthouses and then there are *penthouses*, and mine was of the low-rent variety.

I'd had a nicer one once upon a time, before the head of the Senate decided to move in and kick me out. It had a big balcony, with lots of room and a pool. I looked up and scowled; I bet she didn't even swim.

"What are you doing?" Rosier asked as I climbed out.

"I need to talk to you."

"And we can't talk inside?"

"Not unless you want to be overheard."

"I don't give a damn," Rosier said flatly. "And why do you live with a horde of bloodsucking fiends you can't talk in front of?"

"They're family," I snapped. "Now get out here."

"I'll pass," he told me, eyeing the twenty-something-floor drop without pleasure.

"Don't tell me you're afraid of heights!" I'd raised my voice a little, but it didn't matter because the wind out here was something else. It came whipping around the side of the building like a banshee every few moments, carrying everything before it—including sound. But there was a railing, and it was sturdy.

Not that Rosier seemed to think so.

"Of course not," he told me haughtily.

And stayed right where he was.

"Oh, for crying out loud!" I said. "You're afraid of water and you're afraid of heights. Anything else?"

"I'm not afraid."

"Then what, exactly, is the problem?"

"Prudence. I might not survive a fall from that height. And while I could make another body, it would take time."

"You're not going to be falling—"

"I know that. Because I'm not going to be out there."

"We don't have time for this," I hissed.

Rosier pried his hand loose from mine and began using it to strip off the double glamourie. The bulbous nose went first and then the fake pop eye. The real one had to stay, however, which meant that his looks didn't improve much.

Or maybe that was down to his expression.

"On the contrary, we have plenty of time," he said sourly, trying to pry off the shaggy left eyebrow, which had somehow become stuck. "Now that you've inexplicably brought us back to the present!"

"I did no such thing—"

"Then I was hallucinating the boat that almost drowned me?"

"You were doing that well enough on your own," I snapped, not feeling charitable toward the guy who'd had *one* job and managed to screw it up. Just like he was managing to broadcast our conversation to every damned guard in the place.

At least, he was until I shifted him outside with me.

That elicited enough screeching and caterwauling to have brought every vamp in the hotel running. Except that I'd anticipated it and shut the door firmly behind him. And then put my back to it so he couldn't dive back in, because I wasn't going to be pulling that trick twice.

As it was, my knees felt wobbly.

"Why didn't you hex him?" I demanded, to cover my reaction.

"Why did *you* shift us out of there before I could?" he returned savagely, whirling on me from where the shift had left him, half draped over the balcony railing.

"For the last time, I didn't shift us! That other Pythia must have done that. The old one," I clarified. "She . . . co-opted Gertie's portal . . . used it to send us back to our own time. Or something." It wasn't a great explanation, but I actually wasn't sure what had happened.

I'd been trying to shift us into the bright spring day that had been following us around like a panting puppy. It wasn't a long-term solution, but it hadn't needed to be. I'd just needed to buy a couple of seconds so Rosier could do his thing before Tweetie's grandma followed us through the portal.

But she hadn't given me the chance, hitting us with a time wave even as we dove. So instead of traveling half a year, or whatever it had been, we'd traveled two hundred, right back to our own time. And, somehow, she'd also managed to snatch Pritkin away in the process.

I didn't know how she'd done that, either. Or how she'd known that he belonged in that other time instead of with us. But it was lucky considering the huge amount of trouble that would have been caused if she hadn't.

I shivered a little. Removing Pritkin from the time line would have also removed me—from life, since he'd saved mine maybe a dozen times in the last few months. It was the same thing I was trying to do for him, if my damned counterparts would stop interfering! Especially with graduate-level Pythia stuff I didn't know how to deal with because I was barely out of kindergarten.

Maybe I should have felt lucky just to have survived. But what I mostly felt was pissed. As if this wasn't hard enough already!

And now Rosier was scowling at me again.

"She's from the *past*," he pointed out. "Yet she sent us back here? You're telling me your kind can manipulate the future now?"

"No." At least, *I* couldn't. I wasn't so sure about the rest of them.

"Then how did she do it?"

"I don't know. But that doesn't matter right now, does it? All that matters is that we have to get to Pritkin. And for that I have to eat—"

"Eat all you want. Sleep. Take a holiday!" He threw out a hand. And then quickly replaced it on the railing as another gust came roaring by. "What difference does it make?" he yelled. "By now, his soul is back in the demon realm—"

"So?"

"So we can't reach it there, little girl!"

Damn it! I glared at Rosier because I *knew* this was going to happen! It was why I'd been so desperate to catch Pritkin in Amsterdam. Since, shortly before that, he had spent what had seemed to him like fifty years or so in the demon realms, only to return to earth to find that more than a thousand years had passed.

Rosier had first snatched his son away sometime in the sixth century, when he was about my age, and the next time Pritkin saw earth, it was the late 1780s. Thanks to a much longer life span from his demon blood and the different time stream operating in hell, he hadn't changed all that much. But earth . . .

It must have been a damned wrenching experience, coming back Rip van Winkle–like to find that everything he knew was gone and everyone he cared about was dead. Just one of the hits his psyche would take from the curse of having Rosier for a father. But it wasn't much better for us, since our failure in the icy canals meant that our next stop was likely to be a whole lot warmer.

But impossible, it wasn't.

"My power may not work in hell all that well, but it doesn't need to," I reminded Rosier. "I can take us back in time on earth, and then you can take us into the demon realm. It amounts to the same thing—"

"It is not the same thing! It is not remotely the same thing!" The fake eyebrow had come loose and started slapping his face as he talked, like a trapped moth. He reached up and ripped it off, taking half of his own brow along with it. The suave demon lord was getting kind of hard to see right now.

But I didn't laugh.

He looked seriously demented.

"I had planned to catch Emrys *on earth,*" he informed me, using Pritkin's hated demon name. "Not in hell!"

"But the hells are your home ground—"

"Yes! Yes, exactly!"

"And that's a problem because?" I asked carefully.

"Do you have any idea how many enemies I have?" he demanded. "How am I supposed to go *without magic* into an area where I walk with caution even now? Why do you think the council has guards to protect us? For their looks?"

He was being funny, I assumed, since the demon council's guards didn't have faces. Or much of anything else. It didn't stop them from being deadly, however.

"So we'll . . . catch him when he goes to your court," I said, thinking fast.

Pritkin had spent much of his time away in the Shadowland, a minor demon realm that served as a gateway to the vast array of worlds that made up the hells. I didn't have fond memories of it, but Pritkin had apparently preferred it to Rosier's domain, where a large number of jealous incubi wouldn't have minded improving their rank by knocking off the royal heir. But he had been at court for a while, at least, and if we could catch him there—

"Oh yes. That would be better." The sarcasm dripped.

"It's your court!"

"Which is why I know it as well as I do," Rosier said grimly. "And entering it as a demon, fat with power and with no protection, wouldn't be foolhardy, it would be suicide."

"He's your *son*! And you're a council member. Get the guards to protect you if you're so worried about your precious neck!"

"I'm a council member *now*," he said, gingerly feeling the raw skin over his eye. "He is a council member *then*."

"He who?"

"Me who."

"What?"

"Me—the other me," he said impatiently. "The Rosier of that time. The one I would be assumed to be impersonating. An offense, I might add, that is punishable by death."

"Damn it! There has to be a way—"

"There is." I looked at him. "We wait."

"For what?"

"For Emrys' soul to enter earth again, natur—"

He broke off, possibly because he'd just been grabbed. And it looked like I wasn't as tired as I'd thought. Because the next second I was slamming the rat fink against the windows hard enough to dislodge an avalanche of dust from the crevices above. It came down in a reddish brown billow, coating us and partly obscuring Rosier's outrage.

It had nothing on mine.

"The devil is wrong with you?" he choked—literally, since his mouth had been open when the deluge hit. "You utterly insane—"

"Pritkin will be *twenty-four* by the time he reenters this world," I ground out. "We're supposed to let hundreds of years slip by and try to catch him in a *few decades*? Knowing that, if we miss, that's *it*?"

And it would be. The damned demon council had known my abilities when they cursed him, and had used the one spell that would be the hardest for me to counter. His soul would only pass through each period of his life once, and then never again. I couldn't go back to Amsterdam and try to get him again, because Pritkin's body might be there, but his soul, the modern, precious, cursed version I had to save . . .

Would not.

It was gone forever, tumbling backward through his life into the period he'd spent in the hells. And if we couldn't catch it there, with a millennium of time to work with, how were we supposed to manage it in a few short years on earth? How were we supposed to manage it before Pritkin literally aged right out of existence? And how was I supposed to even get us there to *try* it?

"We'll be waiting for him when he emerges," the damn demon was saying, because he still didn't get it. "We'll catch him the moment he—"

"No, we won't."

"And why is that?"

"Because I can't go back that far!"

I suddenly found our positions reversed, and myself backed into the glass door, forcefully enough to leave bruises on my bruises. And, okay, I thought, staring up into a truly devilish face, Rosier was looking more the part now. "What the *hell* does that mean?" he hissed.

"What I said!" I snapped, too angry to be intimidated. "The farthest back I've ever been was four hundred years—and that was without a passenger! What you're talking about would kill me. It also wouldn't work," I added, because Rosier didn't look too upset at that idea.

"Then why do the rumors say your kind can travel at will, even back to the ancient world?"

"I don't know! Like I know anything about this damned office. But I'm telling you I can't do it!"

"And I am telling you that you have to."

"I don't have to! We'll find him in the hells—"

"We aren't going to the hells," he said, and then raised his voice to talk over me when I tried to interrupt. "Even if I lost my mind and decided to risk it, it wouldn't work, girl. By the time you could recuperate enough to get us there, he'd already be gone."

"Don't be ridiculous! He was there for ages! We have plenty of—"

"Ages of *your time*. Earth's time. But he wasn't on earth, was he?"

I stopped, staring at Rosier. "What?"

"The hells are on a different time line—you know that." He sounded annoyed. "And the spell isn't on the time line, it's on *him*. It follows him. And where he was, perhaps fifty years passed."

It brought me up short. All the more so because I'd known that. I'd known it, but I hadn't wanted to think about it, hadn't wanted to acknowledge even to myself how close to the end we were getting. But suddenly, my hands were shaking.

I wanted to argue with Rosier, wanted to scream at him, to tell him that no, no, no, he wasn't right, he couldn't be. Pritkin was from *earth*. He was on *earth time*. . . .

But not when he was away from it.

Which meant that our window of opportunity had just been shortened by something like a thousand years.

I tried to process that, but I didn't have the strength. That last outburst had left me feeling weak and wobbly, with a brain that was having a hard time keeping up. Everything was coming too thick and too fast, and all I could think was the same thing, over and over.

"Then we've failed," I whispered, feeling dizzy. And lost. And very, very cold.

"Like hell we've failed." I looked up to find Rosier glaring at me again. "I'm going to see Adra," he said, brushing himself off. And talking about the head of the demon council.

"Why?"

"Because he laid the damned spell! He's the only one who can track it. He should be able to tell us approximately when Emrys' soul will enter earth again."

"What difference does it make?" I demanded shakily. "I can't shift again, probably not for hours . . . and even if I could, Pritkin was born in the *sixth century*—"

"I know when he was born."

I shook my head violently, because he didn't know. He didn't understand. "You're talking about *fifteen hundred years*. Even if we had more time, I *can't*—"

"You can and you will," Rosier said, his voice a whip crack. For a moment, he sounded exactly like his son giving me an order in the middle of a fight. It was enough to snap my head up, enough to bring me back from the brink. I blinked stupid tears away.

"How?"

"That's for you to discover. But the spell gets weaker as it moves along, losing power as the magic behind it gives out. It starts out lightning fast, but nearer the end, it slows down considerably. We *have* time."

"How much time?"

"That's what I intend to find out." The voice was hard. Like the hand that suddenly gripped my arm, possibly because I'd started to sway a little.

I looked up and met Rosier's green, green eyes. They were so like Pritkin's that, for a moment, I almost thought I saw a spark of compassion in them. And then the grip turned painful.

"Eat. Sleep. Do whatever you have to do. And then find us a way back there!"

Chapter Five

I woke up to a soft bed, cool sheets, and the feel of warm skin sliding against mine. It felt good; it felt better than good. Like the unmistakable thickness that pressed hard against me.

I smiled and stretched, pushing back into a strong embrace. Enjoying the feel of hard muscle and the quiver of anticipation that shivered from me into the body behind me. Or maybe it was the other way around; maybe he was the one shivering. I couldn't tell, didn't care.

An arm encircled my stomach, pulling me abruptly back. And the weight against me suddenly grew larger. A rough hand began to wander, exploring the jut of a hip bone, the curve of a rib, the dip of a navel. And then smoothing up my stomach, pushing my shirt along with it, up and over the swell of a breast.

A sound escaped my lips at the combination of chilly air and warm flesh. The latter began exploring my softness, but slowly, teasingly. Deliberately ignoring the tightly furled tip.

I moaned again, louder, and pressed into his grasp. But the gentle torture continued unabated, until I was gasping and sweating, shivering and desperate. Such a little thing, to leave me completely undone. Such a silly little thing . . . but it had, and I was, and I wanted . . .

And finally, finally, practiced fingers found the tender nub, rolling it expertly, making my breath catch in my throat.

I pushed into the hand, trembling and aching. And it tightened for a moment possessively before sliding back down my stomach. All the way down, past the silky scrap of my thong.

Until it grasped other things.

My breath sped up and my legs moved apart automatically. The grip tightened, rough calluses against delicate skin, and I writhed, almost in pain now. His breath sped up, too, ruffling the hair on the back of my neck as his fingers found a new nub to torture. And the desire that had been building and building suddenly caught fire, flaming out of control.

But I was trapped, caught between sinuous movements from behind, where his body still cupped me, and sure, sweet strokes from in front, those talented fingers both caging and bringing me to the brink in moments. Until the deep throb of desire blotted out everything else. A hand gripped my thigh, pulling it farther up. Leaving me open and aching as he slid slowly against me from behind, huge and hard and . . .

"Take me already!" I gasped, and heard him chuckle.

"Are you asking or demanding?"

"Either. Both." I barely knew what I was saying as that wonderful heat kept. Missing. The target. "Can't you find it?" I asked desperately, after another few seconds, because I was losing my mind.

"I think I can manage." The voice was amused, but the words were punctuated by a full-length glide against me. "But I don't take orders well."

"Neither do I!" I told him, pushing back.

"I've noticed" was hissed in my ear as the wonderful, hateful pressure slid against me again. And again. And—

"Damn it, Pritkin! Don't tease!"

Abruptly, the movements stopped. And the hands on my body tightened. And a familiar voice growled in my ear. "Pritkin?"

And then somebody knocked on the door.

I jerked awake with a little scream, staring around in confusion and instinctively grabbing for the sheet. That was lucky, because the door burst open a second later, spilling two well-armed security guards into the room. Along with a small vampire clutching large white paper bags.

The vampire's name was Fred. He was looking a little

bewildered. Possibly because of the scream, or because I was staring at him like he had two heads.

I clutched the sheet a little higher and did it anyway. My heart was in my throat, my hair was everywhere, and my nipples were hard as rocks. It was a little difficult to think clearly at the moment.

"Sushi?" he blurted out.

"Wh-what?" I stared at him some more.

"Or Indian?"

He thrust out the bags, so I stared at them instead. They looked like the kind you get at takeout places, and one of them had a greasy bottom that was about to leak through the waxed paper. It smelled wonderful.

My brain finally woke up enough to inform me that I must have fallen asleep while waiting for dinner, and that I was now freaking out Fred. And the other guards, one of whom had a hand on his gun. I licked my lips and retreated from heart attack territory, although I didn't lower the sheet. I couldn't because my shirt had ridden up. Had ridden suspiciously up, I thought, glancing around again.

But there were no phantom lovers in sight, and I knew from phantom. Just soft darkness, a dim haze from the nightscape outside the windows, and the air conditioner tossing the sheers around. I pushed sweaty hair out of my face and told myself to calm down.

It had been a dream, that was all—just a vivid dream.

Really, really vivid.

I swallowed, and turned my attention back to the small vamp.

He was silhouetted in the brighter wedge of light from the hall, a short, somewhat dumpy figure in an ill-fitting suit. It showed off his love handles but matched his large, myopic gray eyes. He had wispy brown hair that he'd let grow a little long to try to cover a bald patch, a tie that always ended up everywhere except where a tie was supposed to be, and a nose that looked like it was missing the glasses he chose not to wear because he thought they made him look weak.

I hated to tell him, but it really didn't matter. Scary, Fred was not. However, we all have our gifts. And right then, he was holding bags from two of the local eateries that had received the Fred seal of approval. Which meant that they specialized in greasy, sugary, spicy, or fried foods, or preferably all of the above.

My mouth started to water.

"Suuuushi, or Innnndian?" he asked again, recovering slightly. And wafting the bags around.

"What . . . what kind of Indian?" I managed to say, without drooling on myself.

"Tikka masala. And tandoori chicken, just out of the oven. They had some leftover stuff in the warming pans, but I made 'em give me the fresh."

"Poppadums?"

Fred drew himself up. "What am I, an animal? And garlic naan."

I nodded. "Okay."

"Do you want to know about the sushi?"

"No." After a chase through an ice storm and a dunk in frigid water, cold fish didn't appeal.

Fred shrugged philosophically. "More for me."

He ambled over and switched on the lamp beside the bed, while the other two vamps looked around. Probably wondering what I'd done with Rosier. They apparently decided that I'd either shifted him somewhere or thrown him off the building, and neither seemed to worry them overly much.

They left.

Fred started divvying up food.

I went to get a couple of towels—for hygiene's sake; the bedspread was already done for—and to check out the bathroom. But all I found was a mountain of extra linens and a plastic bag of the tiny toiletries the hotel gave out, for the girls, I guessed. But no phantom lovers.

Sometimes a dream is just a dream, I told myself, feeling a little embarrassed. And a lot hungry. I grabbed some towels off the heap and went to claim my share of the bounty.

And discovered that Fred—good old Fred—had outdone himself. I helped him lay out the picnic, then climbed into the small amount of space left by the headboard, my stomach insisting that I was starving the whole time. I must have looked it, too, because Fred generously donated a tempura shrimp roll to my plate, although he was stingy with the wasabi.

He saw my face and rolled his eyes. "Don't pout. Anyway, this place makes their own. None of that fake shit."

"Fake?"

"Didn't you know?" He plopped a much larger portion on his own plate, which he totally didn't need because vampire senses are stronger than humans'.

"Know what?" I asked, with my mouth full.

"That the wasabi in most sushi places isn't real. It's horseradish they've doctored up with green food coloring and some mustard."

"The bastards."

"Tell me about it. But this place has the genuine article, and it's hot. So be careful."

I was careful. It was delicious. I happily ate my way through the tempura with a burning tongue and watering eyes before starting on the bright red tandoori. It was good, too, falling-off-the-bone tender and oniony and spicy and . . . *yum*.

I came out of a food-induced haze a few moments later to find that something else had appeared on my plate. It wasn't chicken tikka. "What?" I asked, around a mouthful of awesomeness.

"Samosa."

I poked at the little fried ball with a fork. Some nasty green stuff oozed out through a break in the breading. And, okay, ewww.

"It's peas," Fred told me impatiently.

"Peas?"

"You know, small and green? They're these things called vegetables."

"Very funny." I pushed the pea thing over to the side of my plate.

Fred pushed it back. "Eat it."

"I don't want to eat it."

"It's good for you."

"Then you eat it."

"I don't need veggies."

"You don't need tikka masala, either," I pointed out, although a bunch of it had ended up on his plate. Along with most of the naan. I stole a piece back.

"There's plenty left," he said indignantly. "And you have to eat it."

"Why?" I eyed the pea thing suspiciously. I wouldn't put it past Marco to drug me. He wasn't supposed to, since it interfered with my ability to access my power. But after the last few days, I could see him deciding that it was the lesser of two evils.

But apparently I was being paranoid, because Fred looked heavenward. "Because I'll get The Look if you don't!"

"What look?" I asked, shoveling the rest of the cumin-infused basmati rice onto my plate and pouring on the remains of the tikka. This place Fred had found made it right, with lots of cream in the tomato sauce and big, tender chunks of chicken and large, fluffy rounds of naan and—

And I almost forgot what we'd been talking about.

Until I looked up. And encountered a credible imitation of my former governess's patented Look of Disapproval. It was so good, I felt a surge of the old, familiar guilt, despite the fact that I hadn't done anything.

Except picnic on the bed, which would have been enough for a Stern Talking-To, at the very least.

"Who is giving you The Look?" I asked, confused.

"Who do you think?"

"I have no idea." And I didn't. Because living in a penthouse full of guys, even vampire guys, was sort of like hanging out at a frat house.

The kitchen never had food but always had beer. The living room was filled with full ashtrays, cast-off suit coats that nobody had bothered to hang up, and the latest sports event on the TV. But the salon was where people mostly lived because it had the pool table and the newly installed poker table and the dartboard that someone had made out of a picture of Casanova's face.

He was the casino manager, and yes, usually looked pretty constipated, at least when he was around me. But he didn't have The Look. As far as I knew, nobody did.

"Rhea," Fred said, glancing over his shoulder, like he was afraid he might find her standing there.

"Rhea?"

"Yes, Rhea. Your acolyte. Or whatever she is." Fred looked like he might have some suggestions for other titles.

I frowned.

"What's wrong with her?"

"That's what I'd like to know," Fred said, and started on a local specialty, the Rock and Roll roll. It had spicy barbecued eel and creamy avocado and crunchy cucumber, and toasted sesame seeds sprinkled all over the top of—

"Stop it," he told me.

"Stop what?'

"Stop lusting after my roll. And start figuring out what to do about your court."

"Didn't they eat?" I asked, feeling guilty again. I hadn't thought—but then, I wasn't used to having to feed anybody but me. Which was hard enough around here.

"Oh, they ate," he said heavily. "I told them they could call up for pizza or whatever from room service, but no. Rhea wasn't having it."

"Then what did they have?" I asked. Because I was pretty sure that the only food in the fridge was a few stale beer nuts and some ketchup.

And I wasn't sure about the ketchup.

"Stuffed chicken. Roasted potatoes. *Broccoli*." Fred made a face.

"Where did they get that?" Vegas was not known for home cooking. You could get everything from a twenty-four-ounce prime rib topped with goat cheese and lobster, to a ninety-nine-cent shrimp cocktail that might or might not give you Mobster's Revenge. But stuffed chicken?

Fred mumbled something around a mouthful of eel.

"What?"

He swallowed. "I said, she got it at the grocery store."

"What grocery store?"

"The one she made me go out to. In the middle of the day." He shuddered. "She decided that, since we have a double oven, she'd cook."

"We have a double oven?"

"I know, right?" He munched cucumber. "Who knew?"

"So she sent you to the grocery store," I said slowly, because I was trying to imagine a girl who'd just narrowly escaped death deciding that what she really needed right then was a stuffed chicken.

And because of something else.

Rhea wasn't just some teenager. She was a member of the Pythian Court, and one who'd been handling the weird-

ness a lot longer than I had. If there was a way for me to go
back fifteen centuries without turning inside out, she ought
to know.

Well, maybe. I'd gotten the idea that she'd mostly
worked in the nursery, taking care of the little kids we
seemed to have a bunch of for some reason, instead of doing crazy time leaps. In fact, I seemed to remember her saying that she wasn't really an acolyte at all, just an initiate,
although I wasn't totally clear on the difference.

But still, she might know something.

"—lettuce. Spinach. *Bean sprouts*," Fred was saying,
with the air of someone pronouncing unfamiliar curse
words.

"Is she awake?"

He looked up from corralling an unholy mix of masala
and wasabi with some naan, and blinked. "Who? Rhea?"

I nodded.

"No, she's asleep. They all are. You were out almost two
hours. Why?"

I thought about waking her up, but then I'd have to explain why. And I couldn't explain why. I couldn't risk anybody else finding out that I was planning a jump like that.
Jonas would have a fit, and Marco . . . well, then I really
would be getting drugged.

I shrugged. "She said something about wanting to talk
to me."

"Probably about Jonas." That was Marco's voice, from
the doorway. I looked up to find him lounging against the
jamb, eyeing the spread on the bed.

"What about Jonas?" I asked, as he strolled over and
snared a piece of the roll Fred had lined up for a chaser.

And promptly turned white.

"What the hell?" he gasped, teary-eyed.

Fred grinned. "Teach you to steal a man's food."

"You don't need food! And what the fuck is in there?"

"Ghost pepper," Fred said, looking satisfied. "It's called
a roulette roll. All the pieces are pretty normal, except for
the one that has—hey!" That last was in response to Marco
stealing his beer. "I'm drinking that!"

"Not anymore," Marco told him, and downed it in a
couple of gulps.

I grabbed my bottle protectively. "What about Jonas?" I repeated.

"Just that they really got into it when he called earlier," Marco said, and went to the bathroom for some water.

"Got into it . . . about what?" I called after him.

He came back in carrying both courtesy glasses filled to the brim, and downed them before answering. And then went back for a refill. "Don't know."

Wuss, Fred mouthed.

"I heard that."

"You don't know?" I asked skeptically, because of course he did.

But Marco shook his head. "Silence spell. Guess she didn't want us knowing court business."

"Rhea can do a silence spell?" I asked enviously.

"Guess so. By the way, Jonas knows you're back."

"How?"

Marco came back in still scowling, although whether at me or at the lingering effects of the pepper, I didn't know. "Don't look at me like that. You were the one hanging off the side of the damned building because God forbid anyone should know what you're up to. And you know he has spies everywhere."

"Some people need to learn to mind their own business," I said, scowling.

"Couldn't agree more," he agreed, without a shred of irony.

Because, of course, I *was* his business, from a vampire point of view. Keeping the family safe was a Very Big Thing in the vamp world. Any master who couldn't do it lost face—possibly literally—very soon, because he'd be viewed as weak. As would any servant be who let down said master, which Marco clearly had no intention of doing.

Good, I thought evilly. "Tell Jonas I died," I told him.

"He'll want to see the corpse."

"Then tell him I left!"

Jonas was in my black book anyway. Only, unlike Mircea, I wasn't too afraid to talk to him. I was too pissed. He'd forbidden me to go back in time to rescue my court, and despite the fact that he probably didn't remember it because of the whole time-change thing, he'd still done it. Not to mention keeping from me the tiny fact that a bunch of my acolytes were bat-shit crazy and possibly homicidal. And what was his reason?

That I already had enough on my plate to worry about.

Yeah, like getting assassinated by enemies I didn't know I had, Jonas!

Of course, he thought the Circle could protect me. He *always* thought that. Only the kind of things that came after me weren't always things the Circle had seen before.

Jonas was smart, but he didn't think I was, and I was getting tired of being treated like a witless wonder. No, I hadn't been Pythia very long; yes, I was scarily ignorant of some parts of my job. But I was doing my best to remedy that in between planning rescue trips into hell and trying to stay alive! And so far, I'd proven a fairly quick study. If someone had been around to train me, I might have been doing even better.

Someone like my damned court, for instance.

But then, I wouldn't need the Circle so much in that case, now would I?

Marco's lips were twitching at whatever emotions had been running across my face. "What's so funny?" I asked.

"Nothing."

"Don't lie. You suck at it almost as much as I do."

"That's why I'm the muscle," he told me.

"I'd like to be the muscle sometimes," I said wistfully, only to have him reach out and pinch my sad excuse for a bicep.

"I'm thinking no," he said, grinning now. "But don't worry; I'll deal with Jonas."

He appeared to be looking forward to it.

"Was there something else?" I asked when he just stood there.

"The girls?"

"Shit." I didn't know what to do about the girls.

Marco nodded in agreement. "They slept in the living room, in the lounge, in your bed, and in the spare room last night, and we still didn't have enough space. We were tripping over cots—"

"And then they needed baths," Fred said darkly. "And we didn't have enough of those, either. By the time they finally finished, the whole apartment was steamy. And they left their stuff everywhere—"

"They don't have stuff," I pointed out.

"—bobby pins and ChapStick tubes and those little things that hold ponytails—what're they called?"

"Ponytail holders?" I asked.

He frowned at me.

Marco didn't, but he leaned against the bedpost and crossed his massive arms. Which was code for I'm-not-leaving–until-we-get-this-sorted, although I was damned if I knew what to do about it. Except the obvious, of course.

"This is a hotel, isn't it?" I asked peevishly. "Tell Casanova to find rooms for them."

"I tried, but nobody's seen him all day. And anyway, you know what he'll say."

Yes, I did.

If I hadn't known that Casanova was a vampire, I would have suspected Ferengi. He loved money like no one I'd ever seen, which meant he hated me because I didn't have any. But I assumed the Pythian Court was better off. It was a three-thousand-year-old institution that people regularly paid for a glimpse into the future, or at least, it had been once. I didn't know what it did for money now, but it had to have some, right? And either way, we were going to have to work something out, because this was not doable long-term.

"I'll talk to him," I promised.

"That should be fun," Marco said. But I guess it was good enough, because he left.

Fred didn't.

He pushed the pea thing over at me again. "Eat it. That way I can tell Rhea you had a vegetable."

"A deep-fried vegetable."

"The best kind."

I gave up and ate it. It was okay. Kind of bland.

"Well?" Fred asked curiously.

"I prefer my vegetables in salad form, preferably covered with Ranch dressing," I told him. "Or Caesar."

"Caesar's good," he agreed, bundling the remains of our feast into the damp bedspread and pulling it off like a bag. "By the way, when's that Pritkin guy getting back?"

"Why?"

"'Cause having another mage around might help with

the girls. They, uh, they don't seem to like vamps too much."

"Soon," I said. Because it was soon or never.

"Good to know." Fred hoisted his bag like a greasy-faced Kris Kringle. Then he reached over and impulsively messed up my hair. "Get some sleep, Cassie."

Chapter Six

Get some sleep. Sure. It was what I needed, but the aches and pains in my body and the burn of a wasabi-seared tongue said sleep wasn't in my immediate future. So I dragged myself off to get a bath instead.

And dear God, it was worse than I'd thought.

My clothes were stiff with brine, my skin was caked with salt and dust, and then I pulled a dead fish out of my bra. And freaked out and flung the thing into the trash, where it lay, staring back at me out of one fishy eye. I stared back, having one of those moments. You know the ones—where you suddenly get confronted by something so bizarre that makes you reexamine what you're doing with your life.

I'd had a dead fish in my bra.

I'd had a dead fish in my *bra*.

It was only one of the small silver ones that had hitch-hiked back from Amsterdam, little more than a sardine, but still. Other people had lipstick-smeared tissues in their trash. Or empty nail polish bottles. Or napkins with cute guys' phone numbers scribbled on them.

What did I have?

A dead, possibly time-traveling fish.

I threw a tissue over the tiny corpse and got in the shower.

I bet Agnes had never brought back a fish-filled bra. I bet Agnes wouldn't even have been in Amsterdam in the first place, because she'd have grabbed Pritkin in London. I bet Agnes would have known what to say to Jonas.

Too bad I wasn't Agnes.

But, somehow, I was going to have to find a way to deal with him anyway. And to figure out what to do with the coven I'd somehow ended up with and didn't want. And how to handle a bunch of rogue acolytes, and a pissed-off demon lord, and to *get Pritkin back*—

And I was. I was going to do all of it. But not right now.

Right now, I was going to wash my hair.

And I did, and it was glorious. Twenty minutes of soaping away salt and dirt and God-knew-what made me feel a lot better. And reek a lot less of whatever had been in those canals besides water. I even did the girlie stuff I never had time for anymore, the shaving and the plucking and the moisturizing, and felt almost human again by the time I got out and wrapped myself in a big white bath towel.

And swiped a hand across the bathroom mirror. And, despite everything, burst out laughing. Because guess who was scaly now?

Glamouries, the kind you bought out of a box anyway, had two parts: a base coat, which you spread over your face like lotion, and the control to tell it what to do. Rosier had removed the control when he wiped off the little patch, letting the real me shine through, because he knew a nemesis would get Pritkin's attention better than any femme fatale. But the base of the spell had remained, and was now flaking off in pieces like week-old sunburn.

Or like dried fish scales.

I shuddered a little and started peeling them off in strips, revealing the pale, freckled skin below. It was weirdly therapeutic. Or it would have been, if I'd been able to Zen out. But of course not. I decided that maybe my breakneck pace lately hadn't been such a bad thing. Too much free time and I started to think about all the stuff I didn't know how to deal with.

Like that dream earlier.

Because what the hell?

It was no big deal, I told my reflection. Just exhaustion mixed with the remnants of a powerful incubus' spell. That sort of thing was *supposed* to get a person hot and bothered, so the incubus could feed. Or in this case, so he could donate some energy to someone he needed to keep around a little longer.

Pritkin had wanted his damned map back, and if I ended up getting fried by an angry witch, that wasn't going to happen. But he couldn't fight her off and be sure of success, because he didn't know enough about modern magic. So he'd fed me some energy so I could do it for him. And he'd fed me a lot. It wasn't surprising that it had had some ... lingering effects.

Like the perma-hard nips it appeared to have left me with.

I peered down the front of my towel, in case I was imagining it, but no. Things were definitely perky down there. Really perky. Uncomfortably perky.

"Stop it," I told them.

Nothing. Except two happy little nubs that shouldn't be there because it wasn't cold in here. Was exactly the opposite, in fact, after my marathon shower, but that didn't appear to matter to a body that was having incubus flashbacks.

And wasn't that just all I needed?

"Seriously, cut it out," I said, frowning.

And then frowned some more, when they listened to me about as much as anyone did. And, okay, this was starting to piss me off. Along with everything else I couldn't control, I had to include my own body now?

"Damn it!" I said, feeling ridiculous and not caring because there was no one around to see me anyway. "I mean it. Cut it out right—"

"Cassie?"

I jumped, because the voice came out of nowhere, and not from outside the door. It sounded like it was right on top of me, loud and strong and echoing in the small, tile-lined box. I whirled around, staring at the soggy bath mat. And the wet floor. And the walls running with condensation.

And then, slowly, down at my own chest.

"Cassie—"

"Auggghh!" I jumped back, because I could swear that the voice had come from me. And yes, for a second there I was getting *Total Recall* flashbacks, and that's not something you need when you have a life as freaky as mine.

"Cassie!"

Quaid, start the reactor, I thought hysterically, and grabbed my boobs.

"Cassie!"

"Auggghh! Auggghh! Augg—"

And then the door was kicked open by a horde of monsters.

Only, thank God, these were monsters I knew.

Things got a little crazy after that, with a dozen vamps flooding into the small space, guns drawn and faces grim. And then confused. And then looking at me like I'd lost my mind.

And maybe I had, because there was no obvious threat. Just me with my tits in my hands, my hair everywhere, and pieces of used glamourie spotting my body. I looked like a zombie stripper.

I swallowed.

"What?" Marco demanded.

I swallowed again. "I—thought I heard someone's voice."

"Someone's?"

"It . . . it sounded like—"

"There!" somebody shouted.

And then glass was shattering and bullets were firing— or maybe that should be the other way around, but who could tell while being knocked to the ground? And then, while reaching back up and grabbing the shooter's arm, trying to force it down, because the idiot was firing right through the mirror. And on the other side was—

"Hold!" Marco bellowed, before I could.

Suddenly, there was silence.

My ears were ringing so badly, it actually sounded like the vamp was still firing. But although the gun was up, it was pointed at the floor, which appeared to be intact. As opposed to the wall which had held the mirror. And which now held a few shards and a lot of holes.

A lot of holes leading to the hall.

A hall that led to—

"The girls," I breathed. And then, through the echoing in my ears, I heard cries of alarm coming from the living room.

I shoved a bunch of vamps aside and ran through the

bedroom to the hall. Only to stop short at the sight of a dozen spears of light crisscrossing the darkness, where the brightness of the bathroom was leaking through the bullet holes. And highlighting floating dust motes and ruined wallpaper and a bunch of similar wounds on the other side of the hall—which also happened to form one wall of the living room.

And while no expense had been spared on the décor around here, the same couldn't be said for the drywall. I hiked up my towel and ran across a minefield of plaster and glass, hoping that the bar on the living room side had been enough to stop what the wall hadn't. And ran into Rhea, coming the other way. She looked as grim as I'd ever seen her, as grim as the night she'd dragged a bunch of little girls out of a house full of homicidal dark mages, while three witches and a clueless Pythia tried to hold off Armageddon.

And then she saw me.

And I don't think I've ever seen more relief on a human face. For a second, I honestly thought she was going to faint. So I grabbed her on my way past. And then we were through, into the lounge and then the living room, where—

Where I sagged against the messed-up wall, feeling kind of dizzy myself, because they were okay.

They were okay.

But only by sheer luck.

I took in the sight of a couple bullet-riddled paintings, a smashed clock, and more wallpaper that was going to need replacing—again. And that was on the far wall of the room by the stairs, which now had a new pattern of lead slugs imbedded in it. Most of them were chest high on me, meaning that they'd missed the girls only because it was night and everybody had been lying down on a forest of cots. And were now sitting up, staring at me and Rhea with wide eyes.

But they weren't screaming. They weren't saying anything, after those first, startled cries. Just like they hadn't last night, even with a house coming down around their ears. But they were pale, and some of the littlest had their faces buried in the nightgowns of the older girls. And I felt my skin prickle with something I didn't try to define as I whirled around, meeting Marco coming out of the hall.

"Are they ..." He stopped short at the sight of them, looking relieved.

"Barely!" My voice was shaking. "Who the *hell*—"

"A half-wit. But he said he saw something—"

"Saw something where?"

"In the mirror."

Anywhere else that would sound really strange. But this was Dante's, which redefined normal on a regular basis. And while I hadn't seen anything, I had sure as hell heard.

"Cassie!" That was Fred's voice, raised to carry. I grabbed the robe and slippers a vamp was holding out and shrugged into them on my way to the kitchen.

And found Fred just standing there, staring at the side of our brand-new fridge. The last one had had an accident, and been replaced with a shiny new stainless steel model. It was usually pretty boring, since none of the kitschy Dante's magnets they sold downstairs would stick to it. It was a lot more interesting now.

Because there was a man peering out of it.

A man with watery blue eyes, cheeks pinker than mine, and fluffy white eyebrows. Really fluffy, like tiny sea anemones had somehow managed to attach themselves to his face. And a mass of white hair that wafted about like a merman's in the air currents of the room behind him—a room that didn't form any part of my suite.

And despite the fact that I'd expected it, despite the fact that there weren't a handful of people in the *world* who could bypass the wards on this place and pull something like this, I still stared at him in disbelief.

"Jonas?"

"Cassie. I do apologize for the inconvenience—"

"Inconvenience?"

"I did try calling the usual way," he said, and actually sounded annoyed. Like this was all my fault somehow. "But your ... associates ... continued to insist that you were away—"

"I was away!"

"Yes, and we need to talk about that—"

"We need to talk about this!" I told him, throwing out an arm. "You almost got my court killed!"

Vague blue eyes suddenly sharpened. Jonas liked to play the doddering old man when he thought it would get him anywhere, but I knew him a little too well for that now. And it seemed that he wasn't in the mood anyway.

"I did nothing of the kind. Your vampires overreacted—"

"Something war mages never do," Marco said heavily, coming up behind me.

"—which should not be surprising considering that they were trained as a vampire's bodyguards—"

"Like Lord Mircea needs the help."

"—and to guard his home, not the Pythian Court. They have no experience—"

Marco snorted. "'Cause the mages guarding the court in London did such a great job."

"Will you please tell your servant to stay out of this?" Jonas asked me sharply.

"Marco isn't my servant. And he belongs here!"

"Yes. But you do not. Members of the Corps are on their way to move you and your court to—"

"Move?"

"—temporary quarters until we can determine—"

"I'm not going anywhere!"

"—where would be best for . . ." Jonas stopped, and his pink cheeks suddenly became a little pinker. "I beg your pardon?"

"Marco is right," I told him, furious. "You had guards on the court in London. Guards we found dead when we arrived! They didn't keep anybody safe—"

"When you arrived?" Jonas asked archly.

But I was in no mood to play games. "You know what happened! You've figured it out, or you wouldn't be here—"

"It was not too difficult to figure out. And the coven leaders you chose to take with you were happy to inform me in any case. Any excuse to deride the ability of the Circle to protect—"

"With reason! Your guards didn't protect anybody!"

"There were no more than a handful on duty," Jonas said, frowning. "And most were nearing retirement. The post was a sinecure, an easy assignment for those wounded in battle or with failing magic—"

"Failing?"

The frown grew. "They were there as a courtesy, Cassie. An honor guard. The court wasn't in danger—"

"The court was just blown up!"

The frown was edging into scowl territory. "A court is useless without a Pythia," he told me sharply, "and you were not there. Without you, there was no earthly reason to believe that anyone would wish to imperil the lives of a group of little girls—"

"No earthly reason," I said, trembling, but not with cold. "But there was an *un*earthly one, wasn't there? And you didn't tell me."

"You knew what we are facing; I briefed you on it myself—"

"You told me the old gods were trying to return. You told me I was in danger from them. You didn't tell me my court was!"

"They shouldn't have been!" Jonas snapped, suddenly angry. "Those girls were not in jeopardy—until they became bait in a trap for you. Something that would not have been the case had all of you been in our custody from the start!"

"Your custody?" The trembling was worse now. "Your *custody*? The Circle was trying to kill me for most of the last three months!"

"Under my predecessor. One of many lapses in judgment on his part, which is why he was removed. And afterward, I felt some . . . consideration . . . was due you, in light of your initial introduction to us. That you should be given time to understand that there are reasons why we are the traditional defenders of the Pythian—"

"The Pythian Court is defended by the Pythia!" Rhea said, rushing into the kitchen with a child in her arms. She looked at me wildly. "Lady—"

"What's going on?"

"They're coming in!"

"Who's coming in?" Marco asked, face darkening.

And then one of the vamps cursed, and suddenly, Rhea and I were alone in the kitchen.

"The Circle," she breathed. "They wanted to take us before. I should have told you, but you were so tired, but I should have told you—"

"And I should have expected it," I said, and ran to the living room.

Chapter Seven

The door to the foyer was open, and the doorway was full of men in leather dusters that made them look like action movie heroes. Which wasn't that far from the truth. The coats, ridiculous as they were in August, were needed to conceal the metric ton of weaponry that the Circle's power-houses carried around. None of which could be used tonight, because there were children in this damned apartment.

I pushed my way into the crowd of vampires, half of whom had guns out. "Put them away," I said harshly. Rico, one of Mircea's Italian masters, hesitated, then holstered his weapon so fast it looked like it had simply disappeared. It was a subtle indication to our guests of how fast it could be back in his hand.

Not that it mattered; war mages weren't big on subtlety. And anyway, the rest of the vamps were ignoring me and still had theirs out. And then Marco decided to make it worse.

"Looks like you boys found backup," he told them, from in front of the line of vamps. "At least that'll make this interesting."

"It isn't going to be interesting!" I said, coming up beside him. "It isn't going to be anything. They're leaving."

The mages didn't reply, didn't move. Neither did the vampires. But what the Circle's men—and Jonas, damn him—didn't understand, was that the vamps *couldn't*.

Vamps might have started out human, but they weren't anymore. They hadn't been for hundreds of years in some cases. And their society never was.

Okay, yes, sometimes they acted like it; sometimes they ate and drank and laughed right along with the little human they'd been ordered to guard. *But they weren't human.* The war mages might act crazy by most people's standards, might take insane risks, might even be a little touched in the head—I'd certainly thought so often enough. But given a bad enough situation, they would back down. They would wait for a better opportunity. They would live to fight another day.

The vamps wouldn't.

Even if I was willing to go along with Jonas' plan, they couldn't. Because they couldn't protect me if I was out of their sight. And that was what their master, the font of their wealth and position and strength and *life*, had ordered them to do. So they would stand their ground, would die to a man if they had to. Or more likely would kill every single war mage here and start a possibly irreparable breech with the Circle, and Jonas *didn't get that.*

I just hoped someone else did.

"Marco—" I said tightly.

"Tried," he told me, without turning around. "Master's phone don't work."

"Why not?"

He shrugged slightly, and it looked like massive boulders shifting under the thin cotton of his shirt. I saw one of the war mages in front, a dark-haired guy with a cleft chin, notice.

He had no idea. Marco didn't need his size. Marco could rip the man's blood out of him through the air, in particles too small to see, without even breaking the skin. He could drain him from across the room until the idiot turned ghost white and fell off the steps, a shriveled husk who'd never had time to realize that these were not the low-level vampires he was used to. These were senior masters, and of Mircea's family line.

Which meant they could also do it in seconds.

But then, the mages had their tricks, too, and these weren't the doddering old pensioners the Circle had left to guard my court. Not if the amount of power prickling over my arms was anything to go by. Jonas might have expected my cooperation, but he hadn't been sure of Marco's. He would have sent men he could trust.

So this . . . could be very bad.

And then Fred came up beside me. "Mircea's probably at the consul's," he told me.

"The consul's?" I looked upward briefly, in the direction of my old suite, hoping that what Mircea had wanted to talk to me about was a quick trip to Vegas.

But of course not. "No, no," Fred said. "Her place in up-state New York. She's got a house. . . . Anyway, they're doing a thing out there this week, choosing some new senators."

"What does that have to do with Mircea's phone not working? He told me to call him—"

"That was before."

"Before *what*?"

"Before they shut the place down," Fred said, sounding way too calm. Maybe too inexperienced to read the atmosphere that had Marco's hand flexing against his thigh. "There's a bunch of bigwigs on hand, consuls and such, and you know how many enemies they have. So our consul ordered the main wards brought online for the duration. And phones don't work through them."

"Then contact him mentally!"

"We already did. But it's hard to send complex stuff across that kind of distance. I mean, maybe not for senators, but for the rest of us—"

"Fred," I said through gritted teeth. *"Did you get through?"*

"Yeah, well, sort of. I think the idea that you're in trouble was understood okay, but some of the details might have gotten muddled."

"Meaning?"

"That." Fred nodded at the door. Where another mass of master vamps had just appeared behind the group of mages. Half of whom suddenly whirled to face them.

"The Circle isn't the only one who has backup," Marco told them gently.

The mages still didn't reply. They didn't have to. Because their boss had just appeared like a reflection in the windows leading to the balcony.

They were the same ones where the magical news feed had been projected last night, showing the destruction of Agnes' court. The same ones where I'd seen a dozen tiny body bags being lined up on a rain-drenched street. The same ones Jonas had been facing when he forbade me to go back and try to save them.

My vision started to pulse at the edges.

"I wanted to give you time," he told me now. "But we are out of it. The war has seen to that. And recent developments have clearly shown that you need guidance—"

"Guidance like you offered Agnes?" I asked hoarsely. It was below the belt—the two of them had been lovers, and her death had hit him hard. But right then, I didn't care.

No way would he have tried this with her.

No way.

"Agnes was an experienced Pythia," he told me crisply. "You are not—"

"I seem to be gaining it quickly."

"Agnes had years of training; you do not—"

"You don't get to decide when I'm ready for an office you have nothing to do with."

"And Agnes would have been in our care in the first place, instead of in the clutches of—"

"Agnes would be ashamed of you!"

That last hadn't come from me. Rhea pushed through the crowd, eyes wild, face flooding with a dark stain. And still carrying a little girl who couldn't have been more than two.

"You left them to die. You left her!" Rhea thrust out the child in her arms. What the hell someone that young had been doing at court, I had no idea. But right at the moment, she was staring at Jonas out of big brown eyes, confused and afraid, because loud noises had just woken her up, and big people were shouting, and she wasn't at her home, in her bed.

Because those of us who were supposed to protect her had failed.

"Look at her!" Rhea demanded. "Look at who you would have condemned! Look at who you would have left—"

"That's enough," Jonas said sharply.

But Rhea apparently didn't think so. In the past twenty-four hours, she'd seen her home destroyed, had been almost killed herself, and had been trying to project some sense of normalcy for a probably panicked group of girls. All while surrounded by creatures most people viewed as monsters.

I suddenly thought I understood that chicken better.

But it didn't look like it had been enough, and now Jonas was being told.

"Look at them all!" Rhea yelled. "You're sworn to protect us, but you didn't. You didn't! You left us to die, and now you dare to come and say we must go with you? For what? The only one to care about us is here!"

"Yes, she cared," Jonas said, low and vicious, his eyes glittering into mine. "She cared enough to violate the whole purpose of her office, to go back in time, to risk her life—and thereby to endanger all of ours!"

"It was *fifteen minutes*," I told him, jolted out of some of my anger by the rising tide of his. Rhea's little speech seemed to have shaken something loose, and he was looking . . . I didn't know for sure how he was looking, but I didn't like it.

"I didn't change much of anything," I told him, more quietly. "I got the girls out of the building before it exploded, that's all. It still went up on schedule; everything else stayed the same. The time line couldn't have been that—"

"I don't care about the damned time line!"

"Then what are we talking about?" I asked, honestly confused.

"We are talking about *you*!"

He looked from me to Rhea to the girls spread out on the cots, some clutching pillows and, in a few cases, stuffed animals for comfort. And staring at Jonas with wide eyes. He met them unflinchingly.

"I would have saved you had I known ahead of time," he told them. "Would have sent an entire battalion to your aid had I had any inkling. But once you were dead, I would have left you so. For I could not have saved you then without risking that which I valued more."

It was an unbelievable speech. Even more so, several of the older girls were nodding, as if they agreed with him.

What kind of brainwashing bullshit had Agnes been teaching them?

"My life is not worth more than theirs!" I snapped. "I am not—"

"You are *Pythia*!" he shouted, rounding on me with blue eyes blazing. "You are the only one we have left! And we are facing a possibly world-ending war! So, yes, I would have left them to their fate. I would leave ten thousand more lying dead on the ground before I would risk you. For if we lose you, we lose the war. We lose *everything*."

He wasn't pink anymore; he was white, almost as much as his hair. I'd never seen him like this. Never seen him remotely close.

But I finally understood what all this was about.

I finally understood that Jonas was afraid.

It seemed incredible. He'd been a daredevil in his youth, racing insane flying cars through the ley line system, the massive rivers of metaphysical power that flowed over and around our world and which the more lunatic mages used for transport. It was a game that left competitors dead even more often than NASCAR, but Jonas had seemed to revel in it. And then in old age, he'd engineered a dangerous coup that had ousted his much younger counterpart and returned him to preeminent power in the Circle. To say that he was not a man who rattled easily was the understatement of the century.

But he was sure looking like it now.

And that I *didn't* understand.

Yes, we were facing a possible invasion. Yes, it was by creatures out of legend, creatures who should have stayed there, because they were far too much for humanity to handle. And yes, it was scary as hell, because our main defense, a wall of energy once erected around our world by one of the gods themselves, had recently been proven to be less than the perfect barrier we'd always thought it was.

Which was even more of a problem than it normally would have been, because the being battering at the gates right now was the worst possible scenario for a world already torn by war: the god who personified it.

I got that.

I got all of that.

What I didn't get was what Jonas thought I could do about it.

"Do you expect me to fight Ares for you?" I asked, bewildered. It sounded incredible just saying it.

But Jonas apparently didn't think so. "You defeated a god once before—"

"I *helped* defeat *Apollo*. And he was mostly dead already."

He'd been the first one to breach the barrier, and had ended up the godly version of crispy fried for his trouble. He might still have been okay, if he'd taken time to heal, but of course he hadn't. Godly pride had made him assume that he was still more than a match for us pathetic humans. And that plus some really amazing good luck on our part had left us alive and him . . . well, we all hoped he was dead.

Nobody had heard from him since, anyway.

But that was Apollo. Known for lyre strumming and nymph chasing, if the old legends were to be believed. This was *Ares*. I'd recently fought his half-human kids and barely survived, and that was with help I wouldn't have again. But the god of war himself?

"You are a demigod," Jonas pointed out, causing several of the war mages to flick me quick glances, as if they didn't believe it.

Of course, sometimes neither did I. And with my hair hanging limp and dripping around my face, my body wrapped in an old gray bathrobe, and my feet in fuzzy pink slippers, I didn't look like someone whose mother had been a goddess. But then, I didn't look like it all dressed up, either. I was a five-foot-four blonde with skinny legs, out-of-control curls, and freckles.

Imposing I was not.

Mom had been more so, and had been the one, in fact, to erect the wall that was still keeping out her kind, thousands of years later. But Mom was dead, and I was what we were stuck with. And I was not going to be enough.

"You have abilities even the gods do not possess," Jonas argued, as if he was trying to convince himself.

I hoped he was succeeding, because he wasn't doing a damned thing for me.

"Like what?"

"You can stop our time stream—"

"Which helps us how?" I asked, bewildered. "You know how long that lasts, and that's against *humans*. I don't even know if it would work on a god. But even if did, it would give you what? A few minutes? What kind of damage can you do in a few minutes?"

"More than you think." It was grim.

"Not enough," Rhea said hollowly, because she'd been the one to receive the vision of Ares' return, not me. And even in memory, it was enough to blanch her skin, to flood her eyes. Because she hadn't just seen Ares return.

She'd seen us fail.

More specifically, she'd seen the Circle fail, seen Ares mopping the floor with them, news that had apparently hit Jonas harder than I'd realized at the time. So, okay, if ever a man had reason to panic, he did. But I still didn't see what he expected me to do.

It was one reason I'd been working so hard to get Pritkin back. I didn't know how to fight gods, didn't even know where to start. So rather than sitting around, wringing my hands over what I didn't know how to do, I'd been concentrating on what I did. And not just for personal reasons.

Yes, I cared about him. Yes, I owed him my life many times over. But it was also a fact that he'd forgotten more magic than Jonas ever knew. He'd been hiding out under the name of John Pritkin for centuries, but it wasn't the one he'd been born with, the one history knew him by, the one he'd desperately kept hidden because of the myth, the magic, the aura that still encircled the name of the greatest mage of them all.

Merlin.

That's who I was after, that's who I'd been desperately chasing through time, that's who I'd gone to hell and back for—literally. But if Pritkin was to have any chance at a normal life after this was all said and done, I couldn't tell anyone. I couldn't tell Jonas that I *was* working on a way to deliver us from Ares, the only one likely to work: by bringing back the most dangerous mage of them all.

If anybody could come up with a way to defeat a god, it was Pritkin.

I didn't just want him back; I *needed* him back.

And I didn't have time for this.

"I've never refused to help you," I reminded Jonas. "I've

done everything you asked. I'll help you in the future, too, however I can. But this . . ." I gestured at the mages. "This is not helping! It's the opposite, in fact: it's endangering the alliance between the Circle and the Senate—"

"We don't need the Senate," Jonas said, dismissing one of the most powerful supernatural groups on the planet with a wave of his hand. "We need you. That is what the prophecy foretold. If we are to successfully resist Ares, we need you and your mother—"

"My mother is dead."

"But she helped you to defeat Ares' children, did she not? Perhaps that was her part of the journey. The rest, you must walk, but not alone. The Circle will—"

"Be leaving now," Marco said flatly. Because his eyes had never left the mages, and he must have noticed something I hadn't. Some escalation in power that had put up a red flag to vampire senses.

"Yes, we will be," Jonas said curtly. "With Cassie."

I swallowed, trying to think. I had a little power saved up, thanks to some food and a couple hours' sleep, but not enough. Not that I knew what I'd have done even at full strength. Freeze time so Marco and company could kill everyone more efficiently? Because we were supposed to be on the same side!

Something nobody else seemed to remember.

And then Rhea grabbed my hand.

And, suddenly, it felt like it had when Pritkin gave me energy. Okay, not *exactly* like, but there was a definite power boost. She met my eyes.

"You're risking a lot for an old prophecy," I told Jonas, taking the fussy child from her.

And feeling another, smaller hit of power flow through me.

"We've seen its worth," he argued, because he didn't want this to end in bloodshed, either.

"We've seen what could be coincidence," I told him, pushing through the vampires toward the other girls, as if taking the fussy child back to her bed. "You said it yourself: myths have to be interpreted."

"And how else would you interpret this one?" he demanded. "There were to be three gods, according to legend, and three champions to help you fight them. Apollo was the first, and as foretold, he was injured by contact with the ouroboros spell that hedges our world, before you finished him off."

"That doesn't prove anything," I argued, handing the girl to a plump initiate with chocolate skin and ringlets. And then sitting down beside them on a cot, in the midst of several others. "Anyone coming into our world would have to get by that spell."

"It nonetheless followed the pattern that was foretold. As did your defeat of Ares' sons. Your mother was to be your champion there, and I think disposing of four out of the five qualifies!"

"But the Spartoi weren't Ares, and my mother is now gone," I pointed out. "If Ares does come through, I won't have her help."

"It doesn't matter. You're stronger than you know."

"You think I can defeat the god of war, yet you send a squad of mages to kidnap me?" I looked over at them, and saw that several were now openly watching me, instead of the mass of master vampires. It would have been funny, under other circumstances. Them with their ton of weapons and me with my fuzzy slippers. Only I wasn't feeling like laughing.

"I think you can defeat him *with guidance*," Jonas said. "Which you are not getting here—"

"That's not your call."

"I am making it mine, until you are old enough—"

"I'm twenty-four."

"And I am one hundred and seventy-nine!" he said angrily. "When you are my age—"

"I'm not likely to get to your age." At this point, I'd settle for seeing my next birthday. "But even if I do, I won't agree to put the Pythian power under the control of the Circle."

"As opposed to leaving it in the hands of the vampires? They do nothing that is not self-serving!"

"And this isn't?" I asked as more and more of the girls gathered around, as if for comfort. "Breaking with the vampires, just when we need them most, pressing your rights beyond anything tradition allows, destroying any chance of Pythian neutrality—"

"There is no neutrality in war!"

"There must be, Jonas. We need the others—all the others. I can't defeat Ares on my own—neither can you. Rhea's vision showed you that. If you try to do this alone, prophecy or not, you'll fail. And then we *all* fail."

"I do not intend to do this alone," he told me. "That is rather the point." I felt Rhea grab my hand again, felt the girls press close, felt a surge of power hit me, everything they had, even as his voice said: "Take her."

I didn't wait to see the group of mages move, didn't even wait for the words to finish leaving his lips. I threw out a hand, and with it went everything I had left, and everything my court could give me. I held nothing back—and I still didn't think it had been enough.

But I couldn't tell. Because a second later, I was on my knees, retching and half blind from a power loss I couldn't afford. And hands were grabbing at me, and the room was spinning and Rhea was yelling something I couldn't hear over the roaring in my ears and the frantic beating of my heart. But through swimming eyes I saw half a dozen master vampires sprawled in the floor in front of the door, having jumped in that one split second—

For men who were no longer there.

Chapter Eight

I woke in a puddle of drool, facedown on a soggy bit of squishiness that I finally identified as one of the sofa pillows. It had little jewels in the embroidery that a fumbling hand told me had left pockmarks all over my left cheek. And a crease in my face from some decorative cording that was definitely not rated for sleeping.

I groaned and tried to sit up, but it didn't work. And I couldn't see why, since my hair was in my eyes and my lids were half stuck together. And something was slapping me softly in the face.

Finally, I managed to pry my eyes open enough to realize that it was the sheers that were usually hanging demurely beneath the drapes framing the balcony. And which were now all over the place because the doors were open and the wind was blowing them around. I knew this because it was blowing across me, too.

And the sofa I had apparently passed out on.

And the kid who was asleep on my butt.

And something with hard bits that was wedged up my—

I fumbled around underneath me until I found a stuffed werewolf that had been getting way too personal. And then I pried my body off the sofa and shoved the pillow under the little girl's face, soft side up. And stepped off the couch.

And froze.

Because my foot had just crunched glass.

It was everywhere.

Everywhere.

I suddenly realized that the balcony doors weren't open, they were *gone*, without even any shards left around the edges. Which probably explained why there was a guard out there, every two feet, smoking and drinking and testing the weight-bearing limits of Dante's architecture.

Considering who had built this place, I'd have been worried if I were them. But if they were, or if they were freaking out about the events that were just beginning to edge back into my consciousness, they didn't show it. Rico even winked at me, through a haze of smoke.

I tried winking back, but my eyelid was still gummy and it got stuck.

I sighed. And pried it up. And glanced around to see what else had changed.

Annnnnd it was a lot.

The coffee table was gone, too, with its glass top. And the pictures with their metal frames. And the sconces with their mirrored backs. Even the recessed lights were different, their shiny rims now covered in black duct tape.

I blinked at them for a minute, swaying a little because my butt was still asleep. The clock had been obliterated, so I couldn't see the time, but it felt like the middle of the night. Looked like it, too, with nothing but darkness and the distant glow of neon visible beyond the balcony. But somebody was cooking, nonetheless, and it smelled . . . oh so good.

I retrieved my slippers from beside the couch and shuffled my way into the lounge.

And discovered that it had been visited by the mad redecorator, too.

The TV was gone, and so was the light over the card table. The nice glassware on the portable bar had been replaced by red Solo cups, upping the I-live-in-a-frat-house ambience to something approaching 100 percent. But the real showstopper was the pool table.

Each of the little balls had been stuffed into somebody's socks, I guess because they were glass and kind of reflective.

"Don't you think this is a bit much?" I asked, toting one into the kitchen.

Rhea, who was at the sink, gaped at me for some reason.

"No," Marco said, not turning from the stove, where he was cooking something in a cast-iron skillet. It matched the black duct tape on everything from the stove knobs to the drawer pulls to the sink faucets. And coordinated with the heavy taupe and black zigzag blanket someone had affixed to the front of the fridge.

"Don't worry; she always looks like that in the morning," Fred told Rhea, looking up from chopping a slab of bacon on the cutting board.

"I do when I sleep on the sofa," I said, vainly trying to pat down my wayward hair. "By the way, why was I on the sofa?"

"Because you wouldn't let us move you," Marco told me, finally turning around. And giving me the once-over before shaking his head.

"I wouldn't *let* you?" I repeated. Marco didn't usually bother to ask for permission.

"The girls wanted to keep you with them, and when I tried to cart you off to bed anyway, you flailed at me."

"I did not."

"You did." He rolled up the sleeve of his golf shirt to show me a massive bicep and a nonexistent bruise.

"You'll be telling Mircea I abuse you next."

"I already tell him that."

I snorted. And opened my mouth to give him the reply he deserved. But then something was shoved into it. Something wonderful.

"What—" I asked, after chewing and swallowing.

"Tochitură moldovenească." Marco rolled the sounds over his tongue lovingly, even though that wasn't Italian.

"And that's what?"

"This," Marco said, handing me a flimsy paper plate.

And a plastic spork.

"Oh, come on!"

"It's only temporary, until I can get somebody in to upgrade the wards."

"When will that be?"

"Couple hours. We had someone do a hatchet job last night, just in case Jonas managed to find—hup," he said, and quickly put another few paper plates under the first one, which was quickly soaking through.

"Just in case he managed to find . . . what?"

"Not what. Who," he corrected. "His boys. Who you shifted . . . where?"

I had a vague recollection of a bunch of angry, half-drowned war mages thrashing their way up a familiar, pebble-strewn beach. Bet it hadn't been a fun swim with all that hardware, I thought evilly. And then looked up to see Marco cocking a thick black eyebrow at me.

"Lake Mead."

"Ha!" Fred said.

"It isn't funny," I told him, trying not to grin. And it wasn't, really. This thing with Jonas wasn't likely to go away just because we changed the wards. Or sent his boys for a surprise midnight swim. I needed to talk to him, right after I figured out what the heck to say.

I sighed and put it on my list.

"You going to eat that, or admire it?" Marco asked me.

I looked down at my plate. There were thick, crispy bacon, lovely meaty sausage, eggs fried in what might be bacon grease if I was lucky, polenta, and some weird white crumbly stuff I couldn't immediately identify. But overall, an easy nine out of ten.

"Eat it," I said, and found a stool at the bar.

The crumbly white stuff turned out to be some kind of delicious cheese. Which went really well when mixed with everything else in a gooey mass of heart-attack-inducing awesomeness. I started shoveling it in.

"What did you say this was again?" I asked after a heady few minutes.

"Moldavian breakfast of champions."

"And you know how to make it why?"

"Horatiu taught me," Marco said, referring to Mircea's oldest servant. "It's from the old country."

"Old country my ass," a redheaded charmer named Roy said, coming in. "That's Southern cooking."

"Southern Romanian, maybe."

"Moldavia's actually to the north," Fred piped up.

"I don't care where it is," Roy said, bending over my plate. "That's bacon, eggs, and cheese grits. Half the South eats that for breakfast every morning."

"Well, I learned it from an old Romanian, and I'm pretty sure they had it first," Marco said, in his don't-argue-with-me-I'm-the-boss voice. And then he looked down, and his face changed. From hard-ass master vamp to . . . well, I didn't know exactly what that expression was. But it was soft and he was smiling.

At the barefoot cherub in a crumpled white nightgown who was tugging on his pants leg.

"Phoebe!" Rhea said, quickly coming around the table. "Don't bother the . . . the man. He's cooking."

She reached for her, but the little girl had already been swept up into Marco's arms, looking impossibly tiny next to my giant of a bodyguard. Whose bicep was bigger around than her whole body. He showed her the contents of the pan. "You want some bacon and eggs?"

She nodded enthusiastically.

"I—was going to make oatmeal," Rhea said, looking between the two of them.

Marco and the girl wrinkled noses at exactly the same moment, causing me to burst out laughing. And to almost swallow my damn spork. Rhea looked back at me in alarm.

"I don't think she wants oatmeal," I told her.

"It . . . it's just . . ."

"It's just?"

"That isn't very healthy," she blurted, looking at my plate. And then stood there, apparently stricken. And confusing the heck out of me.

Rhea seemed to have some kind of split-personality thing going on that I didn't understand. One minute, she was telling off dangerous master vampires and the head of the Silver Circle, and the next she was freezing up into Little Miss Meek Voice when she had to talk to me. It was disconcerting. It made me feel like Godzilla. It was also going to be a problem if she didn't get over it.

I decided to push her a little.

"So you think I shouldn't be eating this?"

"I . . . No." She looked startled. "No, I wouldn't presume to . . . I mean, what the Pythia eats is, of course, her own—"

"But it's not healthy."

"It's . . ." She looked at my plate unhappily. "It's just . . . well, there's no vegetables . . ."

"No vegetables in oatmeal, either," Fred pointed out.

"No, but it's a whole grain," she said, glancing at him.

And looking relieved to have someone she could actually argue with.

"Polenta's whole-grain—"

"And oatmeal isn't cooked in bacon grease!"

"We could add a vegetable," I said, bringing her attention back to me. "Couldn't we, Fred?"

He looked at my plate thoughtfully. Vegetables were not Fred's strong suit. "Well, I guess I could chop up an onion—"

"An onion doesn't count!" Rhea told him severely.

"Or put half a tomato on the side," I said, thinking of all the breakfasts I'd seen Pritkin eat. He was supposed to be a health-food nut, and most of the time he lived up to it. But on Sundays he splurged on the most god-awful breakfasts on the face of the earth. I'd kind of gotten the idea that, lately, he'd been making them deliberately horrible just to mess with me.

"The court was in London," I added. "That's what the kids are probably used to."

"Yeah, the Brits got great breakfasts," Fred enthused. "With that nice thick back bacon—"

"And fried mushrooms—" I added.

"—and fried eggs—" Fred agreed happily.

"—and fried sausages—"

"—and fried bread—"

"You do realize that everything you've mentioned is *fried*?" Rhea asked him.

"—and scones swimming in butter," I said, piling it on.

"Oh, don't even go there," Fred told me. "'Cause then you're gonna need your strawberry jam and your orange marmalade and your clotted cream—"

"Clotted *cream*?" Rhea said, looking horrified.

"And cheesy Welsh rarebit," he said dreamily. And grinned at me, as if he thought he'd won.

As if.

"Baked beans and toast," I told him smartly.

"Toad in the hole," Fred shot back, the light of challenge in his eye.

"Fresh kippers—"

"Scotch eggs—"

"—deviled kidneys—"

"—faggot—"

" —bubble and squeak—"

" —crumpets!" Fred said, starting to look a little worried.

I grinned, because Pritkin was Welsh, and the Welsh eat scary, scary things. "Laver bread," I said smugly. Nothing like seaweed first thing in the morning.

"Marmite!"

"Kedgeree—"

"Pancakes!"

"Pancakes are American."

"Shit, shit!"

"Give up?"

"No! No, I—"

"Ticktock, Fred."

"Marag freaking Dubh!" Fred said, looking desperate. And then hopeful, when I hesitated.

And then laughed in his face. " —and fried potatoes!"

"Bullshit!" Fred pointed at me. "Bullshit!"

"What?"

"We already said that!"

"We did not."

"Yes, we did! We must have! You don't get to win on fried potatoes!"

"Mmm. Fried potatoes." I rubbed it in.

"Bullshit!"

"Fried potatoes do not count as a vegetable!" Rhea snapped.

And then suddenly clapped her hand over her mouth, in the realization that she had just yelled at the Pythia. She stared at me for a split second, in something approaching horror, and then ran out of the room. I sighed.

That hadn't exactly been the response I'd been hoping for.

"What?" Fred asked me. "She wasn't even playing."

"See that the kids get fed something," I told him, and went after her.

I found her in my bedroom, making up the bed. Which seemed kind of a waste, considering the state it was in. "I was going to have the bedspread changed," I began, only to have her rip it off. "Rhea, it's okay."

She shook her head, sending dark curls flying. "It's not okay! It's dirty. They should have changed this al—"

"Rhea—"

"—ready, in case you woke up and wanted to—"

"Rhea."

"—change beds or have a nap or—"

"Rhea!"

She abruptly stopped, clutching the awful bedclothes to her chest and staring at me.

"I don't need a maid," I pointed out.

And saw her face crumple. "Then I'm no use to you!"

"No use? You had the vision about Ares."

"And maybe I was wrong! I don't know anymore!"

"You weren't wrong."

"I don't—" She caught herself. "Yes, Pythia."

"Don't do that!"

She jerked, and flushed guiltily. "I-I'm sorry," she told me, gray eyes huge, although I doubted she had any idea what she was apologizing for.

"Or that," I said, moderating my voice. "I don't need an apology when you haven't done anything wrong."

"But you said—"

"That I don't want a *yes, Pythia* or a *no, Pythia* if that's not what you really think. I need someone who tells me the truth. Especially now." I glanced at the door, because no way everybody in the damned apartment couldn't hear us.

This whole lack-of-privacy thing was really starting to be a bitch.

"The truth is, I don't have visions," Rhea blurted as I looked back at her. "I don't have anything. I was supposed to be a seer—they tested me, and I passed. I passed, and you know they don't let you stay at the Pythian Court unless you score very high. But then—"

"No, I didn't know that," I said, sitting on the edge of the bed, trying to slow her down. "I wasn't brought up there."

"No," she agreed, casting a nervous glance at the door. "You grew up with *them*."

"Well, not with *them*, exactly. I grew up at the court of another vamp, a guy named Tony."

"He—he must have been good to you," she said, obviously trying for diplomacy.

"Tony? Tony wasn't good to anybody. Tony was a bastard."

Rhea seemed taken aback by this information.

"Vamps are just people," I told her. "Good ones and bad ones and really irritating ones, just like anybody else."

"But . . ." She looked at the door again, and then did something in the air that I really hoped was a silence spell. And I guessed so, because she was suddenly a lot less tactful after it clicked into place. "They're not like anybody else!" she said fervently. "They can kill you—"

"A mage can kill you. A nonmagical human can kill you—"

"But they won't . . . they don't . . ."

"They don't what?"

"They don't *eat* you!"

I laughed. This didn't seem to go down well, either. "I'm sorry," I told her. "But Fred mostly eats tacos."

"But they have to feed on us," she hissed, in an undertone, despite the spell. "They can't live otherwise."

"No, they can't."

"So the children . . ."

I blinked. "You're worried about—no."

"But they're *here*. And they're so vulnerable. And I can't protect them if—"

"Rhea!" She stopped, face pale, arms still grasping the pillow. And looking oddly childlike herself. It made me wonder how old she was.

So I asked.

"N-nineteen, Lady."

"Nineteen?" I'd have guessed older. Maybe because everyone else seemed to defer to her.

"I know." She looked chagrined. "It's old. But they needed someone in the nursery, and I didn't have anywhere else to go, and—"

"Since when is nineteen old?"

"For the Pythian Court it is, if you're not selected."

"Selected?"

"To be trained as an acolyte. They assist the Pythia, advise her, help her on her missions—"

"Good. Because I could really use some of that." I put a hand out. "Congratulations. You can be my first acolyte."

And, okay, that didn't go so well, either, I thought, as Rhea jerked back, and started shaking her head violently. "No, no, no!"

"Rhea—"

"You don't understand! It doesn't come to me! It doesn't! I've tried and tried and—"

"What doesn't come to you?"

"Anything!" she said passionately. "That's why I take care of the nursery! It was the only thing they found I could do. I was good with the little ones, but everything else . . . I *can't*—"

"Rhea!" I put some power behind my voice, because the girl was wigging out. "Listen to me. I don't know what else you were supposed to do, but you've already done the stuff I need, okay? You've already done it."

"I haven't done anything."

"Okay. Then I was imagining you at the coronation? You weren't there?"

"No. I mean—I was there. I saw what you—"

"We're not talking about me. Why were you there?"

"To—to tell you about the acolytes. I'd had a vision—at least I think I did; I don't have visions—"

"But you saw something that time," I prompted.

She nodded.

"And the acolytes noticed and asked you about it. And you realized that they were happy at the thought of the god of war returning and kicking all our butts."

She nodded some more. She was starting to remind me of a Pythian bobblehead.

"So you figured they'd joined the other side. And since Agnes was dead, you managed to get invited along to the big party for her successor so you could do what? Eat appetizers?"

"No! To warn you! To tell you what I'd seen—"

"So . . . to assist and advise me?"

She had been about to say something, but at that she abruptly shut her mouth. And then opened it again after a minute. "No."

"No?"

"I wouldn't dream of advising the Pythia," she said primly, and I couldn't help it. I lay back on the bed and laughed again.

God, I was losing it.

"My Lady—"

"Stop it." I told her when her concerned face appeared above mine.

"Stop . . . ?"

"Stop calling me that. My name is—"

"Lady Herophile."

"Bullshit." I decided to borrow Fred's word.

"What?" Rhea blinked. I guessed Pythias didn't swear, either, although I was pretty sure I'd heard Agnes on more than one occasion. . . .

"That was the title Apollo gave me, when he was trying to make me into his stooge," I told her. "I chose Lady Cassandra—"

"I'm sorry! No one told—"

"—but I don't like that, either. Call me Cassie."

She just looked at me. But there was suddenly a stubborn tilt to her jaw that hadn't been there a moment ago. But which had been in full evidence when she'd been putting Fred in his place.

"You're not going to call me Cassie, are you?" I asked.

"I will call you whatever you like, of course, Lady," she said, and then seemed offended when I laughed at her again.

"Okay, look. We need to get a few things straight," I told her. "One. The vampires around here aren't going to eat you—or the kids. When they're not here babysitting me, they have courts of their own, with plenty of followers more than happy to provide them with whatever sustenance they need. In fact, Mircea—that's their master; he's . . . kind of the big boss, you know? Over the whole clan?"

She nodded.

"He regularly turns away would-be servants because he has too many already."

"He—people *want* to get bitten?" She seemed appalled. She'd obviously never met Mircea.

"Yeah," I settled for. "Some people do. But you don't, and they know that, so you don't need to worry, okay? They are here to defend us. They would have died last night defending us, if need be."

Rhea looked troubled by that, as if she wasn't sure what to think. But she didn't question it. I'd bet the boys were going to get peppered with questions later, though.

Good; give them something to do.

"Second," I told her, and sharpened my voice. "You are

my acolyte. As of now. Later, if you hate it, we'll see about changing that. But for right now, I need somebody who understands the Pythian position better than I do. And that's you."

She nodded, eyes wide and startled, and maybe a little terrified.

Welcome to the club, I thought.

"And third . . ."

"Third, Lady?"

"Third, how the heck do I jump back fifteen hundred years?"

Chapter Nine

"So these were Agnes' private rooms." I didn't switch on a light, although there was a panel by the door. But a couple of sconces on the walls were set on low, plus the city-at-night haze outside of a set of floor-to-ceiling windows gave enough brightness to see by.

And there was plenty to see. Like plush carpets on highly polished floors, what looked like genuine old masters on the walls, and chandeliers overhead, softly chiming in the air-conditioning, of the kind that often cost more than the houses they decorated. And the whole was brought together by a color scheme in pale beige and blue, which along with the dim lighting had a very calming effect.

Or it would have, if we hadn't been trying to burgle the place.

"Very private," Rhea agreed softly, coming in behind me and quickly shutting the door. "No one came here except honored guests. And the acolytes, of course."

The acolytes. Great. "Let's hope we don't see any of those tonight."

"We won't. They're at the coronation."

Yeah, that was the plan. We were a little more than a week back in time, on the night the acolytes were at my coronation in Washington State, watching me duel a demi-god. Meanwhile another, later me, was here trying to rob their old boss. My life was weird.

And possibly also short, if they came back early.

"Any ideas?" I asked, glancing at Rhea, who looked like she belonged here in her formal, high-necked white gown. I, on the other hand, looked like a tourist that had somehow wandered in off the street, in jeans shorts and a tee with a picture of the blond Powerpuff chick on it. It showed her lifting weights and declared proudly that I was "Powering my Puff into Tuff." Of course, it had been a present from Pritkin.

A very, very optimistic present. Especially now, when I wasn't feeling tuff so much as gnawingly anxious. Being places where I'd almost died tended to do that to me.

I'd better get over that, I thought randomly.

Or my vacation spots were going to start getting really limited.

Rhea shook her head. "It could be anywhere. But she was using a lot, near the end. There should be some . . . somewhere."

She looked around a little helplessly. Maybe because Agnes had basically had her own apartment on the upper floor of the London mansion that used to be the Pythian Court. There was a bedroom, visible through a doorway to the left; a sitting room, which we had entered into from the hall; and an office on the opposite wall to the right. And those were just the parts I could see.

"Take the bedroom," I told her. "I'll check in here."

She nodded and hurried off, and I started searching the lounge.

It wasn't easy. There was a massive three-sided sectional with about fifty pillows facing a fireplace. And a wall of shelving with a lot of drawers. And a bar with even more drawers and a ton of glassware. And what we were after was smaller than the average perfume bottle.

I just hoped Rhea would know it when she saw it, because I wasn't sure I would.

I'd only seen it once before, back when I was just some tarot reader the Senate needed to run an errand for them. They'd suspected that some of the Pythian power had come to me, since the old Pythia was dying and my mother had once been her heir. But Mom had been disgraced, I'd never been trained, and they hadn't been sure that whatever Agnes was leaking would be enough to do the trick.

So they'd sussed out a potion, called the Tears of Apollo, to help me out.

I'd all but forgotten about it since I'd ended up inheriting the whole shebang shortly thereafter, and hadn't needed it again. But I should have wondered—why have a potion if the Pythia didn't need it? I guess the answer was: because sometimes she did.

Rhea thought it was possible that we'd find some here, since Agnes had been knocking the stuff back like water the last year or so she lived. She'd been using it to augment her failing strength and allow her to still shift. And if it could boost a dying woman back to something like full power, Rhea thought there was a good chance it could turn me into super Pythia, bestrider of centuries.

Or at least, get Rosier and me back to the sixth century without ripping my guts out.

So I checked every damned pillow, only pausing occasionally to glance at the gorgeous curtains draping the windows. Or the dazzling rock crystal on the bar. Or what looked like one of van Gogh's sunflower paintings glowing in a splash of moonlight on the living room wall. But the only thing I found was a good start on an inferiority complex.

The place looked like it could have come out of the pages of a magazine. Like the house downstairs, with its formal reception areas and opulent everything. It was impressive when you first walked in, but what would it have been like to live here? With not a thing out of place and even the folds of the drapes impossibly perfect?

I thought back to the cheerful mess at Dante's, with the overflowing ashtrays and the zigzag fridge and the wine stain on the carpet that nobody had ever bothered to clean up because they were waiting for the next Apocalypse. This place smelled vaguely floral. Mine smelled like Marco's cigars, takeout, and vampire feet. This place was quiet, serene. Mine was chaos on a daily basis. This place was . . .

Oh, hell. This place was Agnes, elegant and intimidating and flawless. It fit her.

It would never have fit me.

I wasn't a champagne sort of girl. I was more the Bloody Mary type, specifically the kind they served in one of Dante's bars, with fifteen olives, a bunch of chicken fingers, a cheeseburger, a fistful of onion rings, and a freaking pep-peroni pizza, all stuck on skewers on top. It wasn't elegant, but it got the job done.

Like me, usually.

Usually, but not tonight, because I couldn't find a damned thing, in either the living room or the adjacent office-of-a-thousand-drawers.

I finally gave up and went to see if Rhea had had better luck.

And immediately felt bad for complaining. Because she was having to go through every pocket in every outfit in a walk-in closet as big as my bedroom. Maybe bigger, I thought, staring down a mirror-lined length of plush white carpeting to a tufted ottoman the size of a couch.

In front of a massive dressing table full of more freaking drawers.

"Shit," I said, with feeling.

Rhea looked up. Her dark hair was frazzled and lint-filled, and her eyes were red from all the fibers floating around in the air. She looked like she wanted to agree with me.

But, of course, that wouldn't be ladylike.

Since I'd given up on that a while ago, I said it again.

"Lady Phemonoe had a lot of clothes," she agreed, as I made the long walk to join her.

"And makeup," I said, staring at the dresser top. Damn; I knew drag queens at Dante's who had less than this.

"She used a good deal of it, that last year," Rhea said quietly. "I saw her without it once, when I brought up some tea. She was . . . haggard."

"But she couldn't afford to look like it."

"The Circle expects . . . a certain standard." *Even from a dying woman* remained unsaid.

"Yeah, well, the Circle can go . . ." I caught myself just in time, remembering Rhea's more refined sensibilities.

But she didn't seem to mind. If anything, she seemed curious. "You don't fear them."

"No."

"Everyone else does."

"Everyone else didn't spend weeks getting chased by them all over creation," I said, kneeling in front of the be-hemoth. "They spent the first few months of my reign at-tempting to kill me."

"But they failed."

"Not from lack of trying."

"And then you helped Mage Marsden retake control and become Lord Protector again," she said, as if reciting.

"It seemed the best way to get the bounty off my head." And to get Saunders, his corrupt, homicidal, son-of-a-bitch predecessor out of office.

And goddamn, there were a lot of drawers!

"But he couldn't have done it without you."

"I don't know about that."

"He couldn't have!" she said, suddenly vehement. "He didn't move until he had the Pythia on his side. He wouldn't have done half the things he's known for without the Lady's help, and yet he treats her successor like—" She stopped abruptly and pressed her lips together.

And then she went back to furiously sorting coats.

I looked at her for a minute but didn't say anything. It felt weird to be defended, to have someone else act like maybe there was something wrong in how I was treated. I'd thought that way myself at times, but everyone else acted like things were fine and I was the one with the problem. Everyone except Rhea.

She actually sounded more offended for me than I was for myself, hence the weird.

But it was a nice weird.

I got busy, too, but the only interesting thing I found was a strip of paper tucked into the lining of a drawer. It was a group of pictures, actually, old and black-and-white and all in a row, the kind photo booths give. And while the faces staring back at me were familiar, they were so changed from the ones I knew that I barely recognized them.

Agnes had freckles; I'd never noticed them before under the war paint. And Jonas . . . I grinned in spite of everything, even in spite of last night. Because who could be furious with *that*?

He was standing behind Agnes, as if they had both barely fit in the little booth. And while she was trying to look prim and proper and posed for the camera, he was making a face behind her head. And with his shock of crazy hair even crazier than usual and his Coke-bottle glasses making his already large eyes huge . . . it was pretty damned funny.

Agnes caught him in the second pic, and grabbed him by the towel he had slung around his neck, as if threatening to strangle him.

Or not, I thought, grinning. Because the third image showed that his face had been dragged down to hers, abruptly enough that his glasses were half askew. And yet he didn't seem to mind.

"Who knew the old guy could kiss like that?" I asked Rhea, passing her the picture.

She stared at it, as if needing to adjust her mental image. I didn't have the same problem, since there hadn't been much there to start with, at least not about Agnes. All I really knew for sure was that she'd been the perfect Pythia and had dated Jonas for decades.

It suddenly occurred to me that maybe I ought to know more than that.

"Where was she from?" I asked.

Rhea looked up. "Lady Phemonoe?"

I nodded.

"Pittsburgh."

"Pittsburgh?"

"Yes, why?"

The Pythia from Pittsburgh. "Then why did she have an English accent?"

"She was trained here. The previous Pythia was British, and had her court here. When Lady Phemonoe was identified, or Agnes Wetherby as she was known then . . ." She broke off at my expression. "Is something wrong?"

Agnes Wetherby, the Pythia from Pittsburgh. "Nothing."

Rhea gave me a little side-eye, but then she continued. "She was brought here as an initiate, at the age of six—"

"Six?"

"Yes, it was very late," Rhea said, agreeing with a point I hadn't been making. "But her parents were somewhat influential and fought the process. They managed to hold it up for more than two years."

"Fought it?" I looked down at the picture in her hand, which suddenly seemed less happy. "You mean girls like Agnes are forced to be here?"

"It's considered an honor to be selected," Rhea said carefully.

I shot her a glance. "Did you look at it that way?"

She didn't answer.

I went back to looking at the photo, trying to imagine what it would have been like to suddenly lose everything so young. To leave your family, your home, your friends. And come to a place where everything was different, from the food you ate to the clothes you wore to the people ...

"It's better than the alternative," Rhea said, after a moment.

"The alternative?"

"The schools the Circle operates. The ones for magical humans with dangerous powers. They call them—"

"I know what they call them."

I also knew what they really were. The "education centers" were little more than prisons for people with abilities the Circle didn't like. People like my father, who had been a necromancer but had somehow managed to avoid them. People like me, because I'd inherited his power, not with dead bodies but with spirits. Which were dangerous only to my sanity, when a passel of bored ghosts wouldn't *shut up already*. But which would have been enough to have me locked away, possibly for life.

Only it seemed like that might have happened anyway.

"But clairvoyants aren't dangerous," I pointed out. "And I've seen plenty on the outside, hanging around, doing readings—"

"You've seen plenty of charlatans, Lady," Rhea corrected gently. "Real clairvoyants are rare, and those powerful enough for the court rarer still."

"But we're not *dangerous*," I repeated. "We're not firestarters or jinxes or dark mages—"

"Knowledge is always dangerous, and there are always those who fear it. The Circle worries about what we might know about them—their numbers, abilities, plans—and what we might tell others. Unless ..."

"Unless you're brought up to think that the sun shines out of their ..." I caught myself, but Rhea nodded, ducking her head so I wouldn't see her smile.

I didn't smile back. She didn't know it, but she'd just added another problem to my growing list. A big one. Or more accurately, a bunch of little ones that added up to a big one, because I hadn't actually planned on keeping my court.

I'd intended to talk to Casanova about getting the girls some rooms, yes, but that was temporary, so they'd have real beds to sleep in and enough bathrooms while I figured out what to do with them. And so they'd be away from me. Because shit happened to me.

Shit happened to me all the time.

But even without the safety thing, the plain fact was that I managed to screw up my own life on a regular basis; I didn't have any business being in charge of anyone else's. Especially in the middle of a freaking *war*. Peacetime, sure, run Cassie's school for talented tots or whatever, but now?

Uh-uh. They needed to *go*. They needed to go back to their families, as soon as I figured out who they all were. They also probably needed major therapy after the last couple days, but that could be dealt with once they were safely away from me.

Or that had been the plan, anyway. But now I learned that I wouldn't be sending them home, I'd be sending them to jail, and I somehow didn't think Jonas would be willing to talk parole right now. And damn it, I didn't need this!

"The initiates are free to go at sixteen if they don't choose to accept an acolyte's position," Rhea said, watching me.

"And until then? Are their families allowed to visit?"

"It's . . . thought better if they don't."

Yeah, might interfere with the brainwashing.

But at least I knew why Agnes had so many little girls hanging around. She'd probably felt bad turning any of them away, figuring they'd be better off at court than with the Circle. And she was probably right. But that had been before the war broke out and the court ended up at ground zero and, God, the Circle pissed me off!

Sure, take a bunch of little kids away from their families, treat them like some kind of freaks, lock them up where they don't want to be, and then get surprised when some of them turn on you!

Only my acolytes hadn't just turned on the Circle, had they? They hadn't ended up becoming dark mages like some of the kids who escaped those prisons. No. They'd gone for the big-time, planning to bring back the freaking *gods, w*hich, yeah, would screw the Circle over nicely but would also manage to kill off the rest of us.

So this was a problem. And I couldn't even rely on Jonas to help me with it, because he was busy. Trying to lock up another clairvoyant who was out of his control!

And who was going to stay that way.

"Lady, is . . . is something wrong?" Rhea asked, and she was back to that meek voice again, the one I was really starting to hate. But just because right now I hated everything.

"No. So that's how they met," I said, looking down at the photo. "Agnes was at court, and Jonas was Lord Protector."

Rhea shook her head. "He wasn't Lord Protector then. And they didn't meet here. They met—"

"Yes?"

"I—I'm not sure. It was a long time ago."

And yet the only picture of him had been crumpled in an old drawer. There weren't any others that I'd seen—of him or anyone else. And I suddenly realized what was bugging me about this place.

Where were the snapshots? The napkins with silly doodles on them? The theatre ticket stubs? Where were the stupid stuffed animals he'd won for her at a fair, the crappy "silver" rings bought from a vendor that turned her finger green, the postcards, the tacky souvenir shot glasses, the love notes? This place looked like it was already up for sale and somebody had cleared all the personal stuff away so a buyer would be able to see themselves in it.

And maybe they could have, but I couldn't see her.

I couldn't see Agnes.

"Did you find any more photos?" I asked, because maybe she kept the private stuff back here. But Rhea shook her head.

"She . . . wasn't usually sentimental." Her fist clenched tight enough to wrinkle the photo for a moment, but then she held it out to me.

"Keep it," I told her. "You knew her better than I did."

Her look of gratitude was swift, but it lit up her whole face. She'd be really pretty, I thought, if she ever got out of grandma's nightgown. I wondered if she even had other clothes.

"And take whatever else you want," I added. "If anything fits . . ." I broke off at her look of alarm. "What?"

"I—this is what we wear," she told me. "The ini—the acolytes," she corrected. "It's tradition."

It's ugly, I didn't say, because she was clutching the neck of the thing like I planned to rip it off her. "Agnes didn't wear that," I pointed out.

"The Pythia wears what she chooses, of course."

"But you don't."

"I—it's part of the discipline—"

"You're not in the marines."

"—and tradition," she repeated. Like maybe I hadn't gotten it the first time.

"But somebody changed the tradition at some point, right? That's old, not ancient."

She looked down at the nightgown. "Lady Herophile VI designed it. In 1840—"

"It looks it."

Rhea's lip twitched; I saw it. "It's better than the previous one."

"Do I want to know about the previous one?"

"Grecian robes. They weren't at all practical—Lady Herophile said," she added, before I got the idea that she might have an opinion on something. "She wrote that she felt like she was in a costume all the time, and when she went out, she either had to wear an all-enveloping cape, or sneak out in normal street wear and break the rules. She was always breaking the rules—until she became Pythia, of course."

"Of course."

"Afterward, she was quite a proper Pythia," she added quickly.

Why did I doubt that? "Her name wouldn't happen to have been Gertie, would it?"

"Gertrude, yes," Rhea said, looking surprised that I'd know that.

Cherries. Figured—she'd looked like someone who liked clothes. I got a sudden image of her sneaking out of a window of the Pythian mansion in a Grecian gown, with a pack of normal clothes thrown over her back. I could totally see it.

And I didn't blame her one bit.

"The 1840s was a long time ago," I pointed out.

"I—yes. Yes."

"That looks scratchy," I added, looking at the lace around the high neckline.

"Sometimes . . ."

I glanced around. There was everything from fringed flapper dresses to buttoned up forties-era coats to wide-legged sixties trousers to even wider-shouldered eighties power suits. And everything in between. Too bad it was all going up in smoke in a week or so.

"Did Agnes have heirs?" I asked, and then wished I hadn't. Because Rhea had just reached out a hand to touch a glittering purple and gold evening dress, which was brushing the floor beside her.

She abruptly snatched it back.

"It's yours. Everything is yours," she told me hurriedly.

I looked at her, a little exasperated. "Would you please stop doing that?"

"Doing . . . what?" Her eyes started darting around, like maybe her body was doing something she wasn't aware of.

"That," I told her. "Stop acting like I'm a cross between Attila the Hun and the Second Coming! Or you're going to be in for a real disappointment."

"I—I'm not—"

"Because I'm not Agnes, okay? I'm not perfect. I make mistakes—"

"Perfect?"

"—I make a lot of them. And if you keep on jumping every time I do, you're going to get whiplash or some—"

"Agnes wasn't perfect," she blurted out. And then looked appalled, although whether because she'd dared to use a Pythia's first name or because she'd said something less than complimentary, I didn't know.

"I meant, in comparison to me," I clarified.

"In—in comparison to—"

"And if I'm her heir, then you can have whatever you want. So, what do you want?"

Rhea looked like she was trying to keep up, which was crazy since we were only talking about clothes.

"If you could wear whatever you want, what would it be?" I asked impatiently. It was an easy question. Although maybe not for her. She glanced around again, at the bewildering mass of colors and materials and choice. And then her eyes focused on a prim little skirted suit that might as well have been the updated version of the nightgown.

"Don't lie to the Pythia," I reminded her sternly.

She bit her lip and looked at me. "Jeans?" she finally whispered.

"Good answer," I told her, and threw her one of Agnes' spare pairs.

Chapter Ten

An hour later, Rhea was looking like a whole new woman in jeans and a pink peasant blouse. Well, the jeans were more like capris, since she was taller than Agnes, and the top was loose enough to show too-sharp collarbones. But overall, she looked good.

Unlike me. I was hot, sweaty, and had discovered a heretofore unknown allergy to whatever the heck old clothes give off. My back was killing me, my knees were sore from crawling around on the carpet, and my nose was running. I decided I needed a break and settled down cross-legged on the floor with Agnes' huge old sewing kit.

She did embroidery. Who knew?

"And they weren't just powerful seers," Rhea was saying, because she'd come out of her shell when she came out of the dress, which was good. But then she'd decided I was woefully ignorant about Pythian lore, which was bad. Because she was trying her best to educate me.

I didn't like to complain. It wasn't like I couldn't use it. But I was tired and my head hurt, and worse, we still hadn't found anything.

I was trying not to look at my watch, but it was getting harder. Rosier could be back anytime, and I had to be there, and I had to have the Tears. But we'd been through almost the entire closet, and so far—nothing. Except for an old lipstick, a couple folded handkerchiefs, and a few spare coins. And I was beginning to believe there wouldn't be anything else, because Agnes was freaking meticulous about her clothes.

This wasn't going to work.

"Lady?"

I looked up to find Rhea's dark gray eyes on me. They looked concerned. I blanked my face, because panic was probably number 847 on the list of things Pythias weren't supposed to do. "Yes?"

"I was saying that the Pythias were more than famous seers. They were also some of the most powerful and knowledgeable women in the ancient world."

I nodded.

"Themistoclea I, for example, was the tutor of Pythagoras, the father of philosophy, who said that he learned much of what he knew from her."

"Really?"

"Yes. And Lady Phemonoe I, the first prophetess at Delphi, is credited with inventing hexameter verse. The sort used in ancient epics," she added when I looked at her blankly.

"Oh."

"And Perialla VI discovered the ley line system—"

"Bet that was a shock."

Rhea nodded, looking glad to see me show some interest, however vague. "She shifted into the middle of one by accident, and was almost roasted before she could get back out! But it led to the exploration of the whole system thereafter. That was in the thirteenth century, and then in the fourteenth . . ."

She kept talking, but it was getting harder to pay attention, because I didn't care about Pythian history right now. I cared about exactly one thing, but a potion used by a single person isn't exactly easy to come by. And my options if this didn't work weren't looking good.

I'd used up the Senate's bottle on their errand, and I doubted they had any more, since their weapons cache was currently a glass slick in the desert. And, according to Rhea, only the Circle's potion masters knew the recipe, so I couldn't just go out and buy some. And Jonas wasn't likely to help me do something so dangerous, which was why I was having to hope for some of Agnes' leftovers.

Only there didn't appear to be any.

They never showed this part on TV, I thought vehemently. Searches were supposed to take a couple of minutes. You walked in, checked a few obvious places, and then whatever you needed jumped into your hand.

Only so far, nothing was jumping.

Except for the needle I'd just stuck halfway through a finger. Damn it!

"They were political powerhouses, too," Rhea was saying. "Consulted by world leaders on occasions of war and strategy, treaties and diplomacy. Pythias told the Greeks how to defeat the Persians, told Philip of Macedon how to defeat the Greeks, and predicted the rise of Alexander—"

I looked up. Finally, a name I knew. "As in, the Great?"

"Yes. One of the few to ever dare lay hands on a Pythia."

"He assaulted her?"

Rhea nodded. "He'd visited another sybil, who had flattered him by telling him he was divine—a son of Zeus, who had supposedly visited his mother Olympias one night—and he wanted the Pythia to confirm it. She chose to say nothing, rather than to enrage him with the truth, but it didn't help. And his army had surrounded the temple complex, and she knew she couldn't fight them all, and she feared for her people. . . ."

"Well? What did she do?" I asked when Rhea trailed off.

Her lips twitched, and, okay, yeah. She'd hooked me. "She told him what he really wanted to hear: that he was unbeatable."

"Oh." I felt irrationally let down.

"She didn't tell him that he would die of poison before he had a chance to enjoy any of his conquests."

I perked up. "Well, he should have been nicer."

Rhea laughed. "Yes. He should have been! Like the Emperor Nero, who was thrown out of the temple by a later Pythia because he'd killed his mother. *Go back, matricide! The number seventy-three marks the hour of your downfall!*"

"Damn." I'd have liked to have seen that. By all accounts, Nero had been a murderous little snot. "But living to seventy-three doesn't seem so bad."

"That's what Nero thought. Until he was killed a few years later by a general named Galba—who was seventy-three at the time!"

"Sweet."

"Pythias are even said to have commanded the gods. Well, demigods," she amended. "Xenoclea I ordered Hercules to be sold into slavery for a year, to compensate for killing a man while a guest under his roof. His sale price was to go to the children of the slain."

I started to protest that Hercules was only a myth, but considering my life lately, I just went with "Really?"

She grinned. "She even decided who he would be sold to."

"And that's funny because?"

"Because she selected Queen Omphale of Lydia, who was known for having a sense of humor. The queen took away his lion skin and weapons, and dressed him in women's clothes. And made him stand around holding a basket of wool while she and her handmaidens did their spinning!"

"For a *year*?"

"For a year." Rhea looked satisfied. Probably because this Xeno-whoever couldn't have come up with a better torture for a musclebound he-man.

"Why haven't I heard any of this before?" I asked.

Rhea's smile faded. "I don't know," she said, her brows drawing together. But she threw it off in a minute. "And it was a Pythia, Aristonice IX, who helped to broker the treaty between the Circle and the vampires that still holds today."

"She must have really been something," I said, wondering how she'd managed to balance those two groups, who usually loathed each other. And if the current consul remembered her.

Guess she would, considering she was old as hell.

I sighed.

"No," Rhea said, a little fiercely.

"No?"

"No!" She shook her head, sending a storm of fuzzies into the air. "We have to learn Pythian history growing up, and she's taught because of the treaty. But other than that, there was nothing unusual about her. She didn't go about battling gods, for instance!"

"Well, maybe she didn't have any to battle."

"No." She was tugging little pockets inside out so fast I was afraid she was going to rip something. "None of them did. None of them had to face what you face. They didn't have to elude Circle assassins or battle demigods or face Apollo himself—"

"I had a little help with Apollo."

"—or any of it! Yet they had more support than you've ever been given! The only people to help you are the Senate, and they ..." She threw up her hands. "They don't know anything!"

"Don't tell them that," I said, thinking of the consul's reaction.

"I would never tell anyone anything you didn't want me to," she said, looking faintly shocked. "But you shouldn't have to live like that. You should have *support*. You should have *help*; you should have—" She cut off abruptly.

I was about to ask why when I heard it, too. A sound. A sound like a door opening outside.

Rhea and I looked at each other, and then we scrambled for the closet entrance.

I grabbed her arm, in case I needed to shift us away, but there was a chance it was just someone in to do the housekeeping. Only I didn't think so. Who does housekeeping at ten o'clock at night?

And then I knew it wasn't.

Because a sliver of the living room was visible through the mostly shut bedroom door, and those didn't look like maids.

There were maybe half a dozen, but I couldn't be sure since my inch of visual space didn't give me much to work with. Just the backside of some dark leather trench coats, the kind only war mages and Nazis thought of as a fashion statement. But it was a woman who spoke.

"Did you leave a light on in the bedroom?"

"No." Another woman.

"You're sure?" The voice sharpened.

And *shit*. Before even waiting for a reply, the coats were coming this way. I had a split second to see the door start to swing open, and then we were landing somewhere darker and a whole lot more cramped.

Rhea gasped, maybe because her stomach had come into contact with the side of Agnes' desk when I shifted us into the office. But she clapped a hand over her mouth the next second, and then I jerked her down, out of line of sight. We hit the ground, staring out across the darkened living room through the legs of a sofa table, at almost the same time that a man's voice called from the bedroom.

"Looks like someone was searching the place."

"*We* searched the place!" *You idiot* went unsaid but implied.

"Don't take that tone with me." A big, dark-haired man stuck his head out of the bedroom door. "And I said searching, not searched. Someone was just in here."

"Oh, so you're psychic now?" the woman asked sarcastically. I adjusted my position slightly, until I could see something other than legs. Past a lamp and a Lucite spill of fake flowers, I saw a model-pretty face, long auburn hair, dark slacks, and a light-colored tank under a leather jacket.

Looked like someone else had decided the dress code was bullshit.

Acolyte? I mouthed at Rhea, who nodded grimly.

"I leave that mumbo-jumbo to you," the man replied. "I deal in facts—"

"And what facts are those?" the acolyte asked witheringly.

"That a damned rush of magic just slapped me in the face!"

"Probably the wards," another man piped up. "They've been itching me since we got here."

"It's not the wards. I know wards—"

"You don't know these," the woman cut in. "They're not the pissant things you're used to dealing with. The Circle's top wardsmiths made them—"

"The Circle!" one of the other coats said contemptuously. "They're not as good as they think they are."

"Neither are you."

"Then it's too bad we're the best you got," the dark-haired mage said, coming back into the living room. "And I'm telling you, someone just did a spell."

"And I'm telling you, it was the wards," the smaller man

argued. He was Asian, bald, and looked uncomfortable in his skin. "These things don't like us."

The tall acolyte looked like she agreed with the wards. "They won't hurt you as long as you're with us. Now get the safe open."

"Where is it?" the small man asked, taking something out of his coat.

I glanced at Rhea and mouthed, *Silence spell?* Because I had a few burning questions. But she shook her head. Apparently, it was powerful enough that they might pick up on it, too.

"Do you know the combination?" I whispered.

She shook her head again, looking guilty. "I only saw it opened once, and that was years ago. I'd forgotten it was even there."

So much for the idea of shifting back a couple hours and beating them to it. But I suddenly had a serious need to get in that safe. Luckily, it looked like they were going to be nice enough to open it for me.

Or not, I thought, as the smaller mage went to the sunflower painting and jerked it open, revealing a steel-colored block. That promptly shocked the hell out of him as soon as he touched it. "Shit!" He jerked his arm back, and I swear I thought I saw it steaming.

"Looks like it's warded, too," the bigger mage said.

"Of course it's warded!" the tall acolyte told him. "What did you expect? Get it open!"

"You get it open," the small mage said, still clutching his arm. "It likes you."

"I don't crack safes!"

"Is there anything you *do* do?" the bigger mage asked, and one of the others laughed.

It didn't appear to faze her. "Yeah. I communicate with the master on a regular basis. And guess what I'm going to tell him next time?"

The big man's grin faded. "Get it open," he told the smaller mage.

"I can't get it open! The damned thing won't let me near it!"

"You heard the man," he told the acolyte, who looked like she was wondering why she'd been cursed with incompetents. "You're gonna have to turn the wards off."

"Why didn't I think of that?" she asked. "In case you hadn't noticed, there are a dozen Circle mages downstairs who would notice if I do!"

"Old men." A third mage scoffed. "Useless bastards."

"Maybe. But those useless bastards could have another fifty war mages here in minutes if anything goes wrong. You think you're up to dealing with that?"

The big mage didn't answer. "What's so important in there, anyway?" he asked instead, eyes narrowing. "Must be something valuable."

"More than you know."

"Like what, exactly?"

"Like this." The woman held up something I couldn't see all that well but that had Rhea stiffening beside me.

And then I was stiffening, too, when the mage said: "A potion? That's it?"

The acolyte started to reply, and then stopped. "Yes," she told him. "That's it. We want the potion; anything else you find is yours."

The mage said something else, but I didn't hear, because my heart was suddenly pounding in my ears. It looked like we were after the same thing. But what did an acolyte want with the Tears?

"It doesn't just help with shifting," Rhea whispered, before I could ask. "It helps with everything."

"Everything meaning . . . ?"

"Everything. The power becomes easier to access, so anything you want to do with it becomes easier, too."

I stared at her for a moment, stunned at the very thought. The wonderful, wonderful thought of being able to use my power without wanting to throw up afterward. Or being so exhausted I was staggering. Or getting killed because I was tapped out at the wrong time.

Like when someone's life hung in the balance.

"They probably want it to even the score," Rhea said softly. "They're not as strong as you. Or even as strong as Myra," she added, talking about Agnes' former heir, who, thankfully, was no longer a problem.

Unlike this group.

"So how strong are they?" I whispered, my eyes on the bottle in the acolyte's hand. "Like right now, for instance?"

"I don't know." She bit her lip. "Without the Tears, probably all five wouldn't even equal Myra's abilities."

"And with them?"

She didn't say anything.

Yeah, okay. Now I *really* wanted that potion. Not that that was looking too likely.

"You're war mages," the redhead was saying. "Figure it out! Or I'll be sure to tell the master exactly who it was who let him down."

"Stop threatening me," the big mage warned.

"Then stop giving me a reason! Open the safe and you'll get what you deserve. Fail . . . and the same is true."

The big mage said a bad word. And then he looked at the smaller one. "Go get that son of a bitch."

"Which one?"

"What do you mean, which one?" He gave him a shove. "The one we left in the stairwell!"

"What are you talking about?" the acolyte said sharply.

The mage shrugged. "One of the old bastards they got guarding this place was going out when we were coming in. He saw us, so we had to put him out of commission."

"Put him . . ." The acolyte looked dumbfounded. "What am I supposed to do when someone notices he's missing?"

"That's your problem—"

"I'm making it yours!"

"What do you care? You have to get out of here soon anyway. New sheriff in town, isn't there?"

One of the other women cursed, but the redhead stayed on point. "We can't leave yet! We won't have everything in place until the end of the week!"

"Then say you don't know. Say he went somewhere. Or don't say any damn thing at all and let them figure it—"

The door slammed back open. "Will somebody fucking help me already?" the smaller mage gasped. "He weighs a ton!"

He was also fighting, a gray-haired old man with blood on his face and a great well of it blooming on his left side. He could barely breathe, but he was fighting.

Until one of the mages hit him in his wound, and he suddenly went white and limp.

Rhea gripped my arm when I jerked. "Lady—"

"I'm not going to do anything stupid," I whispered harshly.

Rhea didn't look like she believed me. "Part of an acolyte's training is how to pull out of time freezes," she told me grimly.

And yeah, I needed to work on my poker face.

"—not with war mages," the big guy was saying. "They're trained to resist that kind of stuff."

"They're trained not to give you the combination, too!"

The mage looked at her sardonically and then jerked the old man up. "Hadn't planned to ask for it."

He dragged his captive over to the wall, and I tried desperately to think. I could stop this—literally—but for how long? I didn't know, because I didn't know what the acolytes could do. And then there was the problem of what happened to me after I stopped time if I didn't have Pritkin around to recharge my batteries. I did have Rhea, but one acolyte wasn't likely to counter the massive drain of a Pythia's greatest weapon, not when it had taken my whole court to power me up for a much easier spell. And if even one of the acolytes managed to pull out with me sitting on empty . . .

"What are you doing?" the redhead demanded as the mage shoved the painting out of the way again.

"There's one way around any ward. Wear it out."

"No. No!" The old mage had come to and was struggling again—and he was struggling hard. But the third mage got a spell off before he could, freezing him in place.

"Can't you just use a chair or something?" the acolyte asked dryly.

"Wards can tell the difference," the big man told her. "Maximum output demands maximum threat."

"You're the expert." She shrugged and leaned against the wall.

The two mages hoisted the stiff body up, and the air forced out through his lungs sounded like a scream. My hands sank into the carpet in front of me as I fought to keep them still. We're in the past, I told myself harshly. It's done. It's over.

But it wasn't over. It was happening *right now*. And they were going to kill him, and then they were going to get the safe open, and if there were Tears in there . . . but there were four acolytes and five dark mages in the room and I couldn't freeze them all, and—

And maybe I didn't need to freeze them.

Maybe I didn't need to do anything to them.

"Stay here. Stay low," I told Rhea, who was watching me out of huge eyes.

"What are you going to do?"

"Something stupid."

Chapter Eleven

The strain hit like a fist, immediate and terrible. Followed by the feeling of power pouring out of me, like blood out of the old man, only faster. This wasn't going to last.

So I *moved*, jumping to my feet and then over the couch, praying that the time bubble I'd just thrown over myself would go, too.

Which it did, speeding up time inside the spell and my movements along with it, while it stayed normal everywhere else. But normal isn't frozen, and I was spotted before I'd even cleared the sofa. The nearest mage jumped for me, probably lightning fast from his perspective—

And not nearly as slow as I'd have liked from mine.

I dodged him, but it was like avoiding someone strolling down a sidewalk when you're running. Easy but not effortless, and there wasn't just one of him. And all five had spotted me now.

I jumped over the remaining part of the sofa between me and the old man, hit the ground, and rolled like a hero in an action movie. Only they don't usually end up running into someone's boot, which was moving faster than I'd expected. But I managed to pull back at the last moment, jerking aside in what probably looked to him like a blur of motion, and turned a crushing blow into just another bruise.

Just as well I didn't have that swimming pool, I thought vaguely. I'd look like hell in a bikini.

And then they were everywhere.

I twisted to avoid another boot, this one headed for my head, grabbed it as it passed and jerked, causing the owner to fall backward into another mage. That gave me enough time to get to my feet but not to get away, because the small Asian guy lashed out with a move worthy of Bruce Lee, fast enough to get an elbow in my ribs and hard enough that I almost lost breakfast. Instead I pulled away, bounced off the back of the sofa and sprang past him—

Into a flurry of fists that came at me all at once. The only thing that saved me was the fact that none of them were clutching weapons. I didn't understand why for a second, but then it hit me.

The wards were up.

Wards that disliked weapons' fire of any kind, magical or otherwise. Wards that were probably designed to hate it in the lady's own chambers. Wards that could save my ass if I could only manage to—

Shit.

The mage whose weapon I'd been reaching for pulled away, although that wasn't the problem since I was much faster than him. I just wasn't faster than the bolt of something that sprang from the hilt of his gun when I got a finger on it. A finger that promptly went dead, along with the rest of my hand and my chances of setting the wards off, because I needed a damned weapon for that!

Or, as it turned out, an acolyte.

Rhea started earning her new status a second later, when the guy with the gun spun and grabbed me around the neck. And tried his best to wrench my head off. But he hadn't quite managed it when she threw a bolt of something that sent him flying back against the wall like he'd been bitch slapped by the Hulk.

It was a less-than-perfect solution, since I went, too, slamming against delicate embossed wallpaper hard enough to leave me reeling. But I considered it worth it. Because the jolt caused his grip to loosen and I jerked away, and he got pissed and pulled a gun.

"Noooooooooo!" I heard someone yell, the time bubble distorting it into a single epic syllable.

That wasn't epic enough. The mage let off a barrage of

bullets that were still traveling too fast for me to see. But not, it seemed, for the wards.

Because the slugs incinerated midair, in a line of red heat against the dim light of the room, the last exploding right in front of my face like a miniature firework.

I was still staring at the glowing green aftereffects, still feeling the tiny stings of powder burning my cheeks, still cross-eyed and breathing hard, when the real fireworks began.

Little red dots suddenly appeared everywhere, at the ends of dozens of tiny streams of light crisscrossing the gloom, targeting anyone with a weapon. The mages cursed and shielded, except for the guy with the gun. Who took half a second to realize what was going on and to drop it.

It was half a second too long.

I flung myself back to the floor as a bolt of fiery orange painted the air above my head. There was a crack like thunder. There was a surprised yelp. And then there was a burning, shrieking mage.

His coat must have offered some kind of protection, because on fire or not he was still able to run. So he did, jumping and flailing and stumbling across the room toward the French windows—why, I don't know. Maybe because it had started to rain, and in his panic he thought that the whisper-soft mist falling outside was going to put out a magical fire that burned like phosphorus and was already eating through his coat.

It didn't.

He screamed out on the balcony, a wail of pain and fury that was cut off when another bolt hit him. And ripped him off his feet, sending him hurtling backward through the air, toward the line of buildings across the street. It was a weirdly beautiful sight as his coat flamed up around him, a bloodred ember among all that falling rain.

And then someone kicked me in the head.

It wasn't a mage. They were huddled lumps under their shields, being wailed on by the bolts, which were hitting down everywhere now. It also wasn't a ward, none of which appeared to be aiming for me. But the same couldn't be said for the acolytes.

The wards were avoiding them, since they belonged here.

Which was a good thing, as otherwise Rhea would have been toast. And a bad thing, because I was about to be.

Because this had just become a time battle, and oh, *shit*.

The auburn-haired acolyte was the first to show off and send a time spell my way. It was small and iridescent and flimsy-looking, like a kid blowing a soap bubble, and I dodged it easily. But then her buddies, a couple of brunettes and a blonde, got in on the act, and suddenly the air around me looked like the kid had been joined by a dozen friends.

And while I ducked and dodged and avoided most of them, it only takes one, doesn't it?

I saw it coming, the tiny harbinger of doom, no larger than a tennis ball, that one of the girls had managed to conjure up. But I was powerless to avoid it with another one streaming by on the other side. And I couldn't duck because I had just been thrown to the floor again courtesy of the smallest mage.

And it looked like I'd been wrong; one of them *had* lost his weapons fast enough. And was quickly proving that he didn't need them. He grabbed me from behind in some martial arts move I didn't know and wouldn't have time to learn because he was about to strangle me to death.

I tucked my chin as Pritkin had taught me, and beat him to the punch. But he still had hold of me where I couldn't hit him. And speed doesn't do a lot of good against strength when strength has you by the neck.

Until he suddenly started screaming. I jerked away and twisted back around in time to see his skin browning and shriveling up, his eyes being sucked back into their sockets, and his lips pulling away from his teeth. And then disappearing altogether, like his scream, which cut off when his vocal cords dried up and dusted away. But I could still hear it echoing in my ears as I scrambled back.

But not fast enough. Not to avoid the small, flimsy bubble that floated out of his open mouth a second later, and into my spell. And popped them both with a sound I didn't hear, because I was suddenly hearing everything.

Furniture was crashing, glass was shattering, people were screaming. Including one of the brunettes, who was yelling: "I'm out! I'm out!"

It looked like that damned bubble had taken everything she had.

Luckily, that wasn't true for me. Because she spied the flying mage's dropped weapon a second later, and grabbed it. But nothing grabbed her back, because the wards still weren't targeting the acolytes! So I had to—with a shift that sent her out the same window as the burning man, only she wasn't burning.

She was falling.

Because Agnes' rooms were three stories up, and she hadn't managed to grab the balcony in the half second she'd been beside it.

I was still staring after her, panting with effort and disbelief, when Rhea started screaming. "Lady! *Lady!*"

My head jerked around to see her holding on to the slumped body of the old war mage, trying to drag him toward me and to wrestle with the auburn-haired acolyte at the same time. It wasn't working, because the mage appeared to be a dead weight. And because the acolyte had just gotten a knife against Rhea's throat.

Suddenly, it seemed like everything quieted down. It didn't; my peripheral vision still showed me cowering mages and shooting wards and acolytes keeping their distance, because they didn't know how much juice I had left. For that matter, neither did I, but it was going to be enough. It was going to be enough to age her out of existence if she didn't let go of my acolyte right fucking now.

And then the door slammed open and what looked like a whole platoon of war mages ran in, and I guessed they were ours. Because the auburn-haired witch looked from me to them to the mages in between. And made the executive decision to cover her ass.

"Kill them! They *attacked* us!" She pointed at her former allies, who had a half second to realize they'd been sold out before the war mages did what war mages do best.

And then Rhea got shoved at me, along with the old man she was still supporting. I didn't understand why, until the redhead smiled. And tossed the knife even as I grabbed for them, a casual arc of silver in the low light, traced by the bright flash of a ward that didn't know me, didn't know me at all. Except as someone unfamiliar who was about to have a weapon.

Only I didn't.

Because by the time it landed, we were sprawling in the middle of my foyer at Dante's, me and Rhea and an old man pouring blood from a wound held together only by his own gory hand. While the other was pressing something hard and blood warm into my palm, something I couldn't see because the gnarled fist had captured mine, the grip surprisingly strong. "Don't let them—"

"It's all right," I said, clutching him, my head spinning from the shift, while Rhea scrambled to her feet and ran for help that was already bursting out of the suite. "You're safe—"

"No! No one's safe. Don't *let* them . . ." He cut off, blood filling his mouth and choking off his voice.

"Get Marco," someone said.

"He's asleep—" Someone else.

"I know that! Go *get* him!"

The old mage grasped the front of my shirt, pulling me down. "Don't—"

"Get him up. Get him off her," someone said.

"Leave him alone." That was Rhea.

"We need to get him to a doctor—"

"No, we don't," she said softly.

I stared down into watery blue eyes. The man was fading, and he knew it. His hand slid down my shirt, falling to the floor, but his eyes never left mine, although I doubted he could see me anymore.

"Get back," I told the circle of staring men. "Trust me," I told the mage, trying to sound confident when my hands were unsteady and my breathing was labored, and when I went to wipe the sweat off my brow, I streaked myself with his blood like war paint.

"Cassie—" Someone gripped my shoulder.

I looked up and spied Rico in the doorway. "Get them back."

He didn't ask why. But he must have done something. Because a moment later, I and the old man were alone in a widening stain of red, vividly bright against all that cool marble.

I laid him gently on the floor. "It's all right," I told him. "I've done this before."

I don't know if he heard, much less believed me. But the

time bubble I summoned popped into existence around him a second later, as pure and perfect as I could have wished, something that had my breath going out in a trembling sigh. Because I hadn't half believed it myself.

But it had worked. And like a similar one I'd accidentally conjured up a few days ago, it almost immediately began to have an effect. Gray hair lightened with streaks of red, papery skin turned firm and blushed with health, gnarled finger bones straightened and lengthened, back to more youthful versions, age spots receded into nothingness.

And blood continued to pour from the wound in his side, just as warm, just as terrible.

"Why isn't it working?" I asked, looking up at Rhea, who was staring down at the man in shock, as if she'd never seen him before. And she probably hadn't, not this version anyway, since instead of ninety he now looked about sixty, maybe younger. Younger, but no better. "Rhea!" my voice snapped. "What am I doing wrong?"

She looked at me, startled, and then her expression softened. "Nothing."

"But he isn't *healing.*"

She shook her head. "No. We—we can manipulate time, but not bodies. We still need healers—"

"But this worked on a vampire just a few days ago!" And it had. Jules, one of my bodyguards, had stumbled into a battle-strength curse that had done its best to erase him right out of existence. Instead, I'd erased it, by taking him back to a time before the spell was laid, making it as if it had never happened at all.

So why wasn't it working now?

"Vampires aren't human." That was Marco's voice, from behind me. I turned my head to see him, still half dressed, pulling one of the golf shirts he liked over the mat of hair on his chest. "And Jules was cursed, not stabbed," he added, pushing a vamp out of the way and crouching down beside me.

"That shouldn't matter! I'm making him younger. I've already taken him back before it happcned!"

"You're applying power to him; you're not sending him back through his life," Rhea said, looking at me sadly. "You can make him younger or older, but he will still be what he was when you began."

And what he was, was dying, she didn't add.

Because she didn't have to.

"But *Jules.*" I gripped Marco's arm.

"Way it was explained it to me, you can't go around changing the components of a spell and expect it to work," he told me. "And once that curse was cast on him, Jules became a component. But the spell had been cast on Jules *the vampire*, and when he became Jules *the human*, it unraveled. Or whatever magic does, I don't know."

"But . . . but he was human when he became a vampire, and I removed *that*—"

"You may have had some help there," he told me gruffly.

"Mircea." Marco gave me a nod I didn't need, because I should have known. Mircea was a five-hundred-year-old senior master with a talent for healing. His power mixed with mine . . . Who knew what it could do? "Then can he—"

"He's too far away."

"He was just as far with Jules!"

"But Jules was his—his Child, his blood. This guy ain't. And none of us has his skill."

I stared from him to the mage and back again. And read the truth in Marco's black eyes. He'd been a gladiator once; he knew battle wounds. Both the kind you survived, and the kind you didn't.

No. *No.*

The bubble snapped, as useless as the one who'd made it, and the mage touched my arm. I stared down at him, furious and hurting. But I didn't see any recrimination on his face. Only desperation to tell me something. I bent over him to hear the whispered words. "Heard them talking—"

"The dark mages?"

He shook his head slightly. "Acolytes. Before—" He cut off, choking.

"The acolytes want the Tears."

A nod.

"What are they planning to do with them?" I didn't get an answer, and his eyes were starting to go vague.

"His name is Royston," Rhea told me, kneeling on his other side. "Elias Royston."

"Mage Royston. What are they going to do?"

He tried to tell me, but the only thing that came out of

his mouth was a gout of blood. It splattered my cheek; I could taste it on my lips.

"Get her away . . ." One of the boys started forward; I didn't see who. But Marco held him off.

"Elias. What are they planning to do?"

"To bring him back. *Don't let them.* . . ."

"To bring who back?" I asked, afraid I already knew. "*Elias.* Who are they—"

"The old ones. One of the old—"

He went limp in my arms.

"Gods," I whispered.

Chapter Twelve

Someone had cleaned up the glass in my bathroom, leaving just a new, blank backboard ready for a mirror that hadn't arrived yet. I was oddly grateful that I couldn't see what I looked like, couldn't see the expression on my face. Couldn't see anything but the bottle the old man had given me, gripped so tightly in my hand.

It was thick, brown, pitted glass, with little ripples I could feel under my fingertips. I held it up to the light and something moved inside, something dense and syrupy, something that didn't quite obey the laws of physics. It was a little too sluggish here, a little too quick over there, climbing the sides of the container in ways a liquid shouldn't.

But it had plenty of room, because the bottle was almost empty.

Maybe an eighth of the contents remained, answering one of the questions I'd had: why had the acolytes wanted the potion so badly if they already had it?

Because they didn't have enough of it.

They'd searched Agnes' rooms, just as Rhea and I had, but unlike us, they'd found something. Something that had whetted their appetites for more, so they'd called in their dark mage associates to get it for them. And they hadn't cared what methods they used to do it.

I put the potion down and ran some water in the sink, scrubbing at the drying blood on my hands and face.

"Did I tell you how I lost my daughter?"

I looked up to find Marco standing in the bathroom door, his bulk almost filling it. It took me a second to register what he'd said, because it was so unexpected. And because my brain didn't seem to be working so well right now.

"No."

"You remind me of her. Thought so first time I ever saw you. Not in looks; she was dark . . . but in something. Some stupid sense of optimism, maybe."

It felt like a slap. My body was bruised, but my nerves were worse. I didn't need this.

"Then I ought to be reminding you of her less every day," I said, and reached for a towel.

And had my arm caught halfway.

"No. You're exactly like her. That's the way she was, too. Never believed it could happen to her; never believed what men can do—"

"I'm more worried about women right now."

"You're not worried about anybody! Not enough!" It was savage.

"So where do you want me, Marco?" I asked, pulling away. And grabbing the damned towel because I was dripping all over everything. "Cowering under the bed? Praying that the big bad god of war doesn't find me? Because I don't think that'll work."

"And this will? Running around exhausting yourself, barely making it back—how many times are you going to try this shit?"

"Until the job's done."

"Are you doing your job? Jonas was right about one thing. You're the only Pythia we got. Putting yourself in danger for no good reason—"

"It's a good reason."

"We both know what it is, or should I say 'who'?"

I'd been drying my face, but at that I looked up.

"Everybody knows what you've been doing," he told me.

"I doubt that."

"Not the particulars, maybe, but the main point—yeah, I think we got that."

"Good for you." I pushed past him and went into the bedroom.

Marco followed. "Listen to me. You lose people in war, all right? You need to come to grips with that."

I jerked open a dresser drawer. "*I* need? I'll ask you the same thing I asked Jonas: what the hell are you saving me for? To trot me out when Ares shows up, and say hey, here's our champion? Because that's not going to work. I'm not humanity's get-out-of-jail-free card!"

"I never said—"

"You implied it. Everyone's always implying it."

"Everyone is trying to keep you safe!"

"I'm not safe!" I turned on him. "None of us are safe! We're all in this together, and if the gods come back, vampire or mage or Pythia or whatever isn't going to matter!"

"*If* they come back. We don't know—"

"We know. Rhea *saw*. She saw him come back, and not half dead like Apollo—"

"Rhea saw," he repeated. "Why didn't you see? You're Pythia, not her."

"I don't know. I don't see much anymore. Maybe the power is used up with all this shifting."

"Or maybe there's nothing to see. Maybe she's wrong—"

"And if she's not?"

"All the more reason for you to stay here, and not waste yourself—"

"I can't stay here!" I slammed the drawer shut.

"You need to calm down."

"I am calm! I just want to know what you or Jonas or anybody thinks I'm going to do for you if Ares comes back. Here's a clue—I'm going to die, just like everybody else. Keeping me in reserve is no different from . . . keeping a queen in reserve on a chess board because you're scared to lose her? Know how best to lose her? Lose the game!"

"We're not playing a game," Marco said as I started back for the bathroom.

"No, we're not. But life involves risk."

"Yeah, but maybe I don't want to risk you."

"Maybe it's not your call."

"Maybe I don't want to see another girl I love lying bloody and broken in the damned road!"

I turned toward him and saw the agony on his face. Like it had just happened. Like all those years hadn't mattered at all.

"She was eight," he told me.

"You don't have to do this."

I might as well not have spoken. "I was away on a training exercise with the troops. She and her mother were back home, on the farm with my brother. He had a gimp leg and couldn't serve, but he could wield a sword—I'd taught him that.

"And stupidly believed it would be enough.

"I still don't know what happened. Never did. Just came back to a burnt-out farmhouse and the crisped body of my brother, still clutching that damned sword. And my wife and daughter in a ditch across the road, as if they'd been running away but hadn't made it. And neither of them had been spared."

"Marco—"

"Do you understand what I'm telling you? They were dead and worse than dead, and there was nothing left for me but burying the bodies! I don't want to bury yours!"

"You won't." I barely got the words out.

"No, I won't. I won't have it. I won't be there. You'll die in some damned other place, in some other time, where I can't reach you—"

"I'm not an eight-year-old child, Marco—"

"And you're not your mother, either!"

It stopped me again, but not because of the violence. "I know that."

"Do you?" He grabbed me, so lightning fast my eyes couldn't track the movement. And the next thing I knew, I was over by the closet, facing the full-length mirror on the inside of the door. And a wild-eyed barbarian with tangled hair, blood-flecked skin, and a clenched fist.

It took me a second to realize it was me.

The stomach of my T-shirt was completely drenched, parts of it were singed, and there was a bloody handprint on one shoulder. I stared at it, at the deep impressions where Mage Royston had gripped me so hard at first. And then at the elongated marks trailing down the front, as his strength failed.

A pulse started pounding in my head.

"Four months ago you were answering phones and making copies at a travel agency." Marco grated. "I don't care whose blood you have; you're *twenty-four*. An untrained magic user with a damned tenuous grip on your power. And a sitting duck if you run out of it!"

For a moment, I saw myself through his eyes. Saw that girl I'd been for so long, small and weak and alone, huddled in the dark so the big bad things didn't find me. Marco was right. That was who I'd been, who I'd been my whole life.

But it wasn't who I was.

I wasn't my mother, and I never would be. But I wasn't that girl anymore, either. I looked in the mirror, and my own eyes stared back, but they weren't the ones I was used to. They should have been clouded with fear, with uncertainty; should have been darting around, looking for the nearest exit, getting ready to run. Instead, they were angry, steady, defiant.

I wasn't my mother.

I wasn't even Agnes.

But I was Pythia.

I heard Marco curse. And slam out of the door a second later, because he could read expressions, too. He almost ran into Rhea coming in.

She flattened herself against the door frame, getting out of his way, and then stayed there, as if unsure whether she should come the rest of the way in or not. And yeah. I guess even human ears had been able to pick up that little discussion.

Right then, I didn't care.

"I can't use my power where I want," I told her bitterly. "I can't save who I want. What exactly *can* I do?"

She raised her eyes from the bloody bottle I was still holding up to mine. "Make an old man's last moments free from torture? Give his death meaning? These are not small things, Lady."

I stared back at her until her face started to blur. "Then why doesn't it feel like enough?"

But Rhea didn't have an answer for that.

"Did you want to see me about something?" I asked, after a minute. And turned back to the bureau to jerk on a fresh tee.

She nodded. "The children. They're . . . I think it would do them good to see you. That you're all right, I mean."

I glanced at the bloody pile of clothes on the floor. Yeah. Maybe should have thought to shift to the bedroom.

"Mage Royston was popular," she said, following my gaze. "He used to do magic tricks for the girls."

"A Circle member would be good at that."

She shook her head. "He was terrible. His magic . . . It wasn't very strong anymore, so he did the human kind."

"You mean the fake kind."

She nodded. "Card tricks mostly . . ."

"And the girls liked that?"

"They liked trying to figure them out."

Too bad I didn't know any.

I finished dressing and followed Rhea back into the living room. The door to the foyer was closed now, but the girls were still staring at it. And looking grim, anxious, shocked, and stoic by turns, depending on their natures. But none of them was looking all that great—or that well cared for.

They'd had enough to eat; I knew Marco well enough to be sure of that. But their clothes were starting to look grubby, which I guess wasn't surprising since they'd been wearing the same things for two days now. And damn it, this was no place for children!

I had a brief moment to wonder if they wouldn't have been better off with Jonas, before the first one noticed me. And the look of joyous relief on her face made me feel ashamed. These girls had been brought up to have their whole lives revolve around the Pythia, only to have her abruptly snatched away from them. And then to almost die when her acolytes tried to kill them. And then to get dragged off here, into the midst of a bunch of what they probably thought of as monsters, in the service of another Pythia they didn't know and who was never here anyway.

If I were them, I'd have hated me.

But instead, they pushed past the vampires to get to me, a wave of grubby white gowns and reaching hands, touching me, pressing around me, worried about *me* instead of what had happened to them. And what, from their perspective, was still happening. The knot of shame in my breast grew exponentially, but so did something else. The same something that had flared when that damned acolyte grabbed Rhea. A fierce, almost frightening possessiveness.

They were mine, this ragtag group of girls, and I wasn't

turning them over to Jonas. Wasn't seeing them broken apart, wasn't having them sent off to those damned schools the Circle ran, wasn't giving them into the care of people I didn't know and sure as hell didn't trust. I was going to take care of them; I was going to figure it out. They were my court, and . . . and that's all there was to it.

But I couldn't tell them that.

Suddenly, I couldn't seem to say anything.

And then Fred came to the rescue.

"No, no, no, I got this," he said, jogging in from the lounge, and talking to someone over his shoulder.

"Got what?" I asked warily as he turned to me and grinned. And shoved out a fistful of floppy.

It took me a second because of the color. "Balloons?"

"Picked 'em up at the grocery store," he told me proudly. "Thought they might come in handy."

"The grocery store?"

"Yeah, they had a sale. Practically giving them away. Don't know why."

Because they're depressing, I didn't say, since he was only trying to help. But honestly, who bought black balloons? Fred, apparently, and now he was blowing them up.

"Trust me . . . I used to do this . . . all the time," he told me in between breaths. He soon had a cluster of long, skinny tubes, which he then proceeded to tie together using vampire speed. One second, there was a depressing bunch of cylinders, and the next . . .

It was worse.

The kids were glancing at each other, like they didn't know what to make of it, either. But Fred looked hopeful. And then he started moving his creation up and down, so that the tortured appendages hanging off either side flopped about in a dying-bird sort of way. One of the littlest girls made a sound and hid her face.

"Fred," I began, trying to figure out how to say *please stop* without hurting his feelings.

And then one of the guys solved the problem for me. "What the fu—uh, heck?"

"Leo," Roy said, frowning at him from beside the bar.

"What? I said *heck.* And look at that thing."

"What is it?" another guy asked. "A spider?"

"A bat, obviously," Fred said. And flapped it about some

more, on the theory, I assume, that he just hadn't been vigorous enough the first time.

"Freakiest thing I ever saw," the vamp mumbled.

"Freakiest?" Roy dropped ice into a glass. "You haven't been here long enough."

"Then why does it feel that way?"

"I have more," Fred said, finally realizing that his distraction was not a hit. "A lot more. I used to make these all the time—well, the pig bladder kind—"

"But were any of them any good?" Leo asked.

Fred stopped to glare at him, while Roy assessed his latest attempt. "What is that?"

"It's a clown!"

"Oh, demonic clown. Great choice."

The little girl started sobbing softly.

"Hang on a minute," I said, rooting through a side table and pulling out a pack of battered old tarot cards.

They were grubby and creased and kind of pathetic-looking, and I should have replaced them years ago. But they'd been a gift from someone I cared about, so I just never had. Plus, they had a charm on them I thought the girls might like. It had proven oddly accurate at reading the atmosphere around a situation and giving advice in the form of a pertinent card.

And sure enough, practically as soon as I touched them, one popped up.

A black one.

A black one with a leering devil on it.

Well, shit.

I tried to stuff it back in the pack before it made a bad matter worse, but it was slick and my hands were fumbling and it got a good start on its speech first: *The devil card signifies that the querent feels stuck or restricted in life, bound like the figures in chains on the card's surface. But while these bonds may seem unbreakable, a closer look shows that the chains are in fact quite loose, and that the querent therefore has it in his power to slip free of them whenever he chooses. The people on the card are not bound by real chains, but by fear, lack of hope, and lack of belief in their own abilities. The devil card teaches that, as long as you are willing to allow others to exploit and restrain you, they can and will. But no one has power over you unless you give it to them. And what you give, you can take back again.*"

The card went on, burbling happily about the history of the tarot and the card's reverse meaning and God knew what else. I wasn't listening anymore. I was staring at the devilish figure on the front, and feeling like the clue bat had just smacked me across the head.

"Cassie?" someone said, and I looked up to see Rhea staring worriedly at me. Along with the vamps. And the kids, except for the one who was still sobbing quietly, because I hadn't done jack about that, had I?

And I still didn't. Because a moment later, Fred was being muscled aside, and Marco knelt in front of the crying child. And pulled a playing card out from behind her ear.

She blinked at it, and then at him, and then went back to crying. But she was still watching through her fingers when it suddenly went up in flames. Several of the vamps took a rapid step back, causing Marco to sneer at them. And to let it burn down almost to his fingertips before he threw it into the air, where it disintegrated into powder.

Only to pull it out from behind the girl's ear again, whole and new and not even singed.

Her mouth made a perfect O of astonishment as she looked from him to the air and back again. Marco sat back on his heels, looking satisfied. Until she reached over and pulled the original card out of the pocket of his shirt.

He met my eyes.

"Magical children," I said.

"Yeah. They always surprise you."

"Marco—"

"Do what you gotta do," he told me bitterly. "Just come back, all right?"

I nodded and pulled Rhea into the hallway.

Chapter Thirteen

The plaster had been vacuumed up—mostly. The guys didn't let housekeeping in when we were under siege, I guess afraid of a mage posing as a cleaning lady, so they'd taken care of it themselves. Which explained why the corners were still white and glass shards glittered here and there on the Berber.

But Rhea wasn't looking at them.

She was looking at the bullet holes.

Yeah, she'd had a baptism by fire these last few days, hadn't she? I knew what that was like. But I wasn't about to make it any better.

"Would it work?" I asked.

"Lady?" Her eyes moved back to mine.

"Could the acolytes shift Ares here, from beyond the barrier?"

"I . . . What?"

"Elias said they were trying to bring back the gods, and we know they were after the Tears. I'm asking if they could be connected."

She shook her head. "I . . . don't think so."

"Are you sure? Even if they all worked together?"

She shook her head, harder this time. "The power is limited to earth. Apollo made sure of that, so it couldn't be used against him or his kind. I don't see how it could now be used to save them."

"I've used it outside of earth."

"You are the child of Artemis, Lady; the acolytes are not."

"But we use the same power. I just access it better—for now. But if they get their hands on enough Tears . . ."

"Lady Phemonoe had full access to the Pythian power, and she was well skilled in its use," Rhea pointed out. "Yet she told me once that she did not dare go beyond the confines of earth. The power is chained here; it cannot leave this world."

"But that's what I'm telling you. It *did* leave. At least a few times—"

"Yet, if you think back," she said tentatively, "were you not in places close to earth on those occasions? Places accessible through portals or the ley line system?"

"Well, yeah. But that would be everywhere!"

"Not everywhere. You may be able to access your power through a portal, if you are close enough, or even through the ley lines, if our time line and that of the world to which you have traveled are somewhat aligned. But even then, it will not be reliable. The lines fluctuate, disrupting the flow; time lines go in and out of synch; and portals are notoriously—"

"Yes, I know. My power doesn't work well outside earth, but it *can* work—"

"Through a conduit. But the ouroboros is not a conduit, Lady; it is a wall. Your mother's spell was designed to keep things out, not to let them pass through. It is the opposite of a portal."

I started to say something, but then stopped, because she had a point. "So you're saying they couldn't do it."

"I am saying . . ." She licked her lips. "I am saying that I do not think they can. It seems to me, if such a thing were possible, Myra would have already done it for Apollo."

And, okay, I couldn't argue with that. Apollo had tried to bypass the barrier my mother put in place by overloading a ley line, and had ended up barbecued. I didn't think he'd have chosen that option if he could have just had his pet acolyte shift him here.

"So what do they want this for?" I held out the bloody bottle.

Rhea just stared at it. She still looked stunned, pale, and

more than a little freaked out. So much for an easy first assignment.

We don't get the easy jobs. . . .

I'd said it to Pritkin once, and it had never felt more true. The Pythia's position sounded so powerful, so invincible. What couldn't be fixed with the ability to manipulate time?

A lot of things, as it turned out.

But maybe one of them could be fixed another way.

I went back to the bedroom and started rummaging around under the bed for my sneakers.

"I need you to talk to Casanova," I told Rhea, when she followed me in. "Tell him I want rooms for the girls and I want them now. This place is too dangerous for kids."

"I—yes. Yes, of course."

"And make it a suite—or three. We don't need the littler ones figuring out how to turn a doorknob and wandering around the damned hotel."

"Yes, that sounds like a very good—"

"And get them some clothes; they haven't changed in days."

"I will, of course, but—"

"And make them normal ones. The less they look like initiates, the safer they'll be!"

"Of course. I mean, I will, that is, I would, but—"

"But what?"

"It's just that . . ."

"It's just that what?" I asked, coming up with two sneakers, but they were both for the left foot.

"It's just that there's a problem with the money," she admitted.

"What problem?"

"The . . . fact that we don't have any?"

I looked up at her, one arm still under the bed, trying to snare another shoe. "You're telling me the Pythian Court is *broke*?"

"No." She looked shocked. "The court has plenty of money; we just can't access it."

"Why not?"

"The Circle locked the accounts. I had to borrow money from your chief bodyguard for groceries—"

"From Marco?"

She nodded. "I didn't know what else to do. The accounts were accessible to the Pythia and her heir. But the Lady is dead, and Myra is—"

"Also dead."

"—and Mage Marsden, that is, the Lord Protector, said the accounts were frozen until a new Pythia was proclaimed—"

"Which I have been."

"—but he hasn't released the accounts yet."

"Why does he even have them?" I asked, finally coming up with matching shoes. "That's court business!"

"It's supposed to be," Rhea agreed. "But because of the unsettled state of affairs at the time of the Lady's death, she left him the pass codes to give to her successor—"

"And instead, he decided to use them as blackmail, to get the court back where he wants it."

"I—don't know," Rhea said, but she was frowning. Because yeah, that's the way it looked.

"So test a theory," I told her, jerking on the sneakers. "Ask him for them and see what he says." She nodded. "In the meantime, surely the court has some money? It's been running on something for the last three months!"

"Our main bills were automatically paid by an arrangement with the banks—electricity, water, that sort of thing—"

"And food?"

"We had accounts with local grocers—"

"And incidentals? There had to be some cash on hand!"

"Yes, there is. Was. Until it went up in—"

"Smoke, along with everything else."

She nodded.

I closed my eyes. I wasn't getting a headache so much as realizing that I already had one, a pounding, pulse-hammering explosion behind my eyes. "Then tell Casanova to give them rooms anyway. If he has a problem with that, he can take it up with me. Tell him he'll get his money as soon as we get ours."

"Yes, Lady."

"And call Jonas and explain what happened." She grabbed a pad and pencil off the nightstand and started scribbling. "Tell him what Elias said, and have him send us whatever Tears he may have on hand. We're best suited for guarding them."

"I—yes. We are. But he may not agree after—"

"No, because that would be too easy," I snarled.

Rhea was also looking a little overwhelmed and more than a little frazzled. Probably wondering how she was going to tick all the things off her list and also take care of all those kids. And it wasn't like she was going to be getting much help from me, or the bachelor brigade.

"You must have had help with the kids in Britain, right?" I asked.

She nodded. "A daytime staff—cooks, housekeepers, tutors—"

"Nannies?" I asked hopefully.

But Rhea shook her head. "The acolytes and the older initiates were expected to help with the younger girls, and assist with their training. But—"

"But you ended up doing the lion's share," I guessed.

She nodded.

But that wouldn't work here. I had only one acolyte, and I needed her for other things. Like training me.

"There's a woman named Tami," I told her. "Tamika Hodges. The front desk can put you in touch with her. She's staying here at the hotel with some kids. Give her a call, and ask her to help you."

"But . . . if she already has children of her own . . ."

I thought back to the brood Tami had when I first met her, which had numbered almost this many. Yet she'd still been out, scouring the bus stops and the soup kitchens, the parks and the homeless shelters, looking for magical runaways to take in.

She'd taken me in and calmed me down when I hadn't trusted anybody. When I'd been skittish and afraid and prone to jumping at my own shadow, she'd somehow made me part of her not-so-little family. You want to talk about magical? Tami was freaking magical.

"Call her. You'll be surprised."

Rhea nodded, looking hopeful.

"And if Jonas won't give us the Tears, tell him to lock them up. Somewhere secure. Somewhere even the acolytes can't get to them!"

"Yes, Lady!" Rhea scribbled fiercely.

"And arrange for Elias' body to be sent back to the Circle. Tell them he deserves a hero's funeral. He died in the line of duty, helping me."

"Yes, Lady."

"And call a guy named Augustine—he has a shop downstairs—and tell him I want clothes for the kids. He can pony up or stop calling himself couturier to the Pythia!"

"Yes, Lady. And—and what are you going to do?" she asked, looking worried, as I stood up and shoved the Tears back into my pocket.

"Get some insurance."

The great seat of the demon lords still looked like a municipal building, and a run-down one at that. There were boring benches framing a utilitarian lobby, ugly beige carpet fraying in spots, and a ficus-in-a-tub struggling not to die. Or at least, that's how it appeared to me. What it really looked like was anyone's guess, since the lords had their meeting place in the Shadowland, the demon realm closest to earth. It was near enough that my power worked, if only intermittently, but far enough away that nothing about it would have made sense to a human's mind. Or to anyone else's, apparently, which was why the beings who controlled this place had glamouried the city to make it appear blandly familiar.

A little too familiar.

I didn't look at the spot on the carpet where Pritkin had fallen. I could see it in my mind, like the whole thing had just happened, could see him hitting down and then lying there, so motionless. As pale and frozen as a statue.

Or a corpse.

But I didn't look, because it didn't matter. Any more than any of the other places he'd been injured did. He was coming back and this would all be over soon and it didn't *matter*.

I also didn't try to see behind the glamourie. It was boring, but considering the alternative, I was okay with boring. And it was my fault anyway. The spell pulled images from the viewer's own mind, because thousands of people came here from all over the demon realms, making "normal" subjective. Supposedly this was what I found nonthreatening.

Like the disguise worn by one of the two demons who entered a moment later, through the swinging doors in the back.

"What are you doing here?" Rosier demanded, striding

over and looking annoyed. Whether that was because I'd
showed up where humans weren't supposed to be, or because I hadn't waited for him at the hotel like a good little
girl, I didn't know. I also didn't care.

"I didn't come to see you," I told him, my eyes on his
companion.

Adra, short for Adramelech, was a being so old that he
figured in earth's earliest mythology. And he didn't figure
well. It was hard to know which of the horror stories told of
him were true, since I hadn't had time for more than a
quick Google search. But I'd read enough to doubt that he
actually looked like an elementary school teacher.

The current head of the demonic council was blond and
round-faced, with the deceptively bland features of someone using a glamourie as a courtesy, to keep people like me
from having nightmares, and not because he was actually
trying to fool anyone. His only concession to credibility, or
possibly vanity, was a cleft in his chin. It was deep and
round and made him look like somebody had poked the
Pillsbury Doughboy in the face instead of the tummy. And
it didn't even help, since it only highlighted how fake the
rest of the face was.

He smiled, and it was bland and unassuming, too. "Pythia."

"I have a problem," I told him abruptly.

"One that you have solved, it would seem." He was
looking at the pocket with the Tears, although there was no
way he could have known what was in there.

"I'm talking about my acolytes." I pulled out the bottle.
"I took this away from them while they were searching for
more."

"For what purpose?"

"What is that?" Rosier interrupted, eyes narrowing on
the little vial in my hand.

"That's the problem," I told Adra. "I don't know for
sure—"

"You don't *know*?" Rosier repeated. "Where did you
get it?"

"—but they might be trying to use it to bring back one
of the gods."

"How?" Adra asked mildly.

"Let me see," Rosier said, and snatched for the vial, before I yanked it back, glaring at him.

"I don't know that, either," I told Adra. "But they have to be dealt with, and there's five of them, and only one of me, and there's a chance that they're not all staying together—"

"They would be wiser not to."

I nodded. "One was already missing when I saw them, and after what happened, they might have scattered even farther. But I can't sense them, which probably means they're hiding out in faerie, like Myra. But their power doesn't work there, so they'll have to come back to earth to do anything—"

"You want us to find them for you," he guessed.

"We can't find them for her!" Rosier exploded, before I could answer. "My people have been searching all day, ever since you mentioned the damned things, and there's not a vial of Tears to be had for love or money anywhere. And I mean that literally!"

I ignored him, because that's the only way to get anywhere with Rosier. He loves the sound of his own voice so much he often forgets to listen to anybody else's, treating them like background noise. I decided to do the same with him.

"It would help," I told Adra. "I have to do this, but I can't let them run amok in my absence, and there's no one else who can deal with them—"

"I am not certain we can deal with them," he said quietly.

"But you're the demon council—"

"Something that is less than useful when dealing with the crooks of the merchant class!" Rosier spat.

"And they are channeling the power of one of the old gods," Adra pointed out, without so much as a glance at Rosier. He must have been used to him.

"But they're *not* gods," I reminded him. "They're human."

"A fact that does not make their power any easier to counter."

"Those bastards would sell their own mothers for what I've been offering," Rosier grumbled. "And probably throw in their daughters, too, yet not a single one has so much as seen the formula! It's of no use to anyone here—"

"It's a lot easier than it will be dealing with the real thing," I told Adra. "If they succeed in bringing him back—"

"If. They've had long enough to try. Your predecessor died more than three months ago."

"But Apollo didn't."

"Not that it stopped one of the crooks telling me he could find some, if I ponied up enough to pay off the right people," Rosier complained. "When everyone knows he's rich as Croesus! I told him, if I was desperate enough to hire mercenaries for a raid on the Circle's supply, I could do it myself without paying him an exorbitant fee as a go-between!"

Adra's eyes narrowed. "What does Apollo's death have to do with this?"

"The Tears only work on earth," I said, "or somewhere with a link to earth. Or a crack—"

"You think Apollo's transition through the barrier weakened it, making it possible to shift someone through?"

Damn, he was quick. "I don't know," I repeated, because I didn't. "But one of the acolytes mentioned that she'd been talking to Ares on a regular basis and she shouldn't be able to do that. She shouldn't be able to talk to him at all. Apollo could talk to Myra because the Pythian power was originally his, and he always maintained a link to it. But none of the other gods were ever able to get messages through before. Yet suddenly Ares is communicating with earth all the time? Something changed."

"What is all this?" Rosier asked, finally waking up to the fact that no one cared about his useless search. "What are you talking about? The gods aren't coming back."

"One of them already did."

"Yes, and fat lot of good that did him!"

"But he got through—"

"Only to be eaten by Rakshasas." He looked disgusted. "The mighty Apollo taken down by filthy scavengers—"

"But he got through," I ground out. "That's the point—"

"No, the point is that we need some of those so-called Tears. Now, do you have them or not?"

"Yes!"

Rosier blinked, as if surprised that I'd yell at him.

Adra's eyes narrowed slightly. "If the barrier is weak

enough for your acolytes to shift Ares through, why haven't they already done so?"

"Maybe they don't have enough strength yet. There's five of them, but their ability to access the power is limited—"

"Unless they find some Tears to boost it."

I nodded.

"We will find your acolytes," he told me abruptly. "If they remain within our reach."

I let out a breath I hadn't known I was holding. "Thank you."

"Don't thank me, Pythia. Just return from this errand of yours quickly. Unless I am much mistaken, we have a war to fight."

Chapter Fourteen

My epic journey fifteen hundred years back in time ended on something cool and wet, with stars spinning wildly overhead. For about a second, until I collapsed. And was treated to the sight of a dozen pissed-off faces circling me in a merry-go-round of annoyance.

Or maybe that was just one, because they all wore Rosier's sneer.

He really did look like Pritkin sometimes, I thought vaguely, and then I passed out.

I came around what I guessed was a while later, since the sun was now shining in my eyes. It was intermittent, though, like it was flirting with a bunch of clouds. I finally realized that it wasn't clouds but ancient demon ass, and I wasn't flirting with it so much as rhythmically smashing into it. It seemed that Rosier had decided to act like his son for once, too, and had thrown me over his shoulder.

I bounced along what did not appear to be a road so much as a rock-strewn hillside, and thought about throwing up. But breakfast had been a while ago, and it decided it liked things where it was. So it and I continued to jolt along, because the many things Rosier got others to do for him must have included hauling around half-unconscious women.

'Cause he sucked at it.

Fortunately, I was only awake occasionally over the

next few hours; either that or the head lothario of the incubus clan wasn't in nearly as good shape as his son. Because the next time I opened my eyes, he was struggling through some marshy field and cussing up a storm. And then later panting across some sort of hill. And then finally dropping me at the edge of a wooded area, with all the care of a guy hauling a bag of sand.

And then cursing some more, because he appeared to have lost a shoe.

It was dark again, so I watched the stars through my lashes and vaguely wondered what some ancient Celt would think, coming across a half-decomposed Ferragamo in a week or three.

I decided I didn't care.

The cursing finally slowed down, and I risked turning my head to the side. And was greeted by the unlikely sight of a usually elegant demon lord furiously rubbing two sticks together.

I blinked, but the image remained the same. And—bonus—it was mostly steady. I decided to try offering an observation.

"You could always just use magic."

My voice cracked alarmingly, but the idea got through. Because a malevolent green eye stared at me through a fall of sweaty blond hair. "Why didn't I think of that?"

The stick rubbing recommenced.

I watched it for a few minutes before clearing my throat and trying again. "Is there a reason you're doing that the hard way?"

"Yes! I forgot the matches!"

"And you need them because?"

"Because I don't have magic right now, as you know perfectly well!"

"But you have that." I nodded at the man purse he'd been dragging around, along with me, an overstuffed backpack, and an attitude from, well, you know.

"That is for emergencies!"

"And this isn't one?"

"No." He threw the sticks down, panting. "A little cold won't kill you—"

"Neither would some heat."

"—but other things might!"

He paused to stick his head in the massive backpack and root around. And I decided to see how propping myself up on one elbow went. It wasn't comfortable—Rosier had dumped me on the hard bit near the trees while keeping the nice soft grassy stuff for himself. But I didn't pass out again, so okay.

"Such as?" I asked as he emerged with a canteen.

"Such as that damned madwoman from Amsterdam," he grumbled, after taking a long swig.

And oh, *shit*. I suddenly remembered that I was supposed to ask Rhea how Cherries had found us. I'd forgotten, what with Jonas and the acolytes and the forty-seven other things I'd had to do.

"Oh, don't look so guilty," Rosier told me sardonically. "While you were lying around the suite, I took care of it."

I was about to respond to that the way it deserved, but then he passed the canteen over. And I drained half of it before I came up for air, then pulled it back protectively when he tried to snatch it again. Oh God, that was good.

"Took care of it how?" I gasped, after another drink.

"By knowing who to ask!" Rosier snatched it back, frowning at the weight. "Did you have to drink the whole thing?"

"I didn't, and took care of it *how*?"

This time I got an answer, maybe because it allowed him to show off.

"I discovered that witches—of whom the Pythia is one, despite current appearances—are drawn to magic," he told me, starting to saw away with the sticks again. "*Any* magic. And the more power that is expended, the brighter the signal."

"And the Pythian power—"

"Is about as bright as it gets. That's what tripped us up in London, and again in Amsterdam: we stayed too close to the entry point. We put a big spotlight on ourselves, and then stood right by it. No wonder they found us!"

"So this time, you hauled me away."

He nodded. "Far away. It seems that the Pythias are especially sensitive to the use of their own magic, as you might expect, although anything might be enough to put them on the scent—"

"Them?"

"—and the last thing we need is a posse of pissed-off Pythias—how's that for alliteration—"

"Posse? What posse?"

"—on our trail. But thanks to me, they now have to find us the old-fashioned way, don't they? And they may find that a bit more of a trick," he finished, looking amazingly smug.

Smug and clueless.

"Who is 'they'?" I asked carefully. "You mean the Pythia of this era?"

"Among others."

"What others?"

He looked up in order to roll his eyes at me. "The Pythias whose times we just violated the hell out of—what do you think?"

"What?"

He nodded. "All the Pythias. From all the times you just dragged me through—"

"No."

"Yes."

"No!"

"Yes. Did you really think you could expend that kind of power and no one would notice?"

I looked at him in horror. "But . . . but they couldn't . . . But we didn't . . . We only stopped *here*—"

"But it's like a freeway, isn't it?" Rosier asked, sawing away and looking insanely unconcerned. "You get on, you get off, but it's not as if you disappear in between. Not as if that part doesn't *count*. You can't tell the officer who pulls you over, *Yes, sir, I know I was speeding, but it doesn't matter since I'm just passing through*—"

He broke off, possibly because I had just reached out and grabbed him. And dragged him through his nicely arranged pile of twigs and moss, scattering it everywhere. And causing a couple stray sparks to flare and then abruptly go out, making him curse, but it didn't matter. None of it mattered, because we were about to be so very, very dead—

"What the hell is wrong with you?" he demanded.

"What is wrong with *me*? You! You are what is wrong with me! You and a dozen Pythias—"

"Be quiet!"

"Like hell I'll be quiet! I can't fight—"

"No, you can't! And right now, neither can I. And there could be brigands in these woods—"

"*Brigands?* Who cares about *brigands*? Did you hear me? *I can't fight a dozen Pyth—*"

A hand came down over my mouth. "Shut. Up."

"You shut up!" I tore away from him. "You didn't mention—you didn't say *anything* about—"

"Why should I have to?" he demanded. "You're the Pythia—"

I pointed a shaking finger at him. "And you know damned well—"

"That you know nothing? That you're the most ridiculous choice to hold that office in memory? To have the power of a goddess wielded by an incompetent child ..." He broke off at my expression. "Oh, what?" he demanded, throwing out his arms. "Have I dented the divine pride? Hurt the heavenly ego? Offended the omnipotent—"

"Shut up!"

"And if I don't? What are you going to do, little goddess? Kill me?"

If I'd had any strength, I don't know. I honestly don't know what would have happened. Fortunately for both of us, if there was something below empty, I was sitting on it.

Which, of course, meant we were going to be dead even faster than normal as soon as the posse caught up with us.

"I don't have to," I told him unsteadily. "There's a couple dozen women on the way to do that already."

Rosier looked at me for a moment, and then sat back on his heels. And craned his neck backward to look at the vast, glittering band of the Milky Way, high above, unobscured by our nonexistent fire. The darkness hid the differences in the face, the slightly more aquiline nose, the slightly less rugged jaw, the completely different expression that separated two men who usually looked less like father and son and more like identical twins.

At least, they had once. But now ... I'd never make that mistake now. Only I wouldn't have to worry about it, would I? Those other Pythias would never listen, not in time, not with me dragging Rosier so far back, with the possibility for us to screw up time multiplying exponentially every year. And it wasn't like I hadn't thought of that, too, wasn't like I didn't know how dangerous this was. But did it matter? Did it matter if I screwed up the world when Ares was about to come back and set it all ablaze and I couldn't stop him and Pritkin—

I made a sound in my throat, and Rosier looked down to stare at me. But I was too upset to care. If they caught up with us tonight, it was over. I just didn't have anything left.

"They won't find us," he told me, after a moment.

"How can you possibly know that?"

He made a broad gesture that took in the whole expanse around us. "Wales."

"That doesn't answer anything."

"On the contrary, it answers everything. Rome's legions vanquished empires, their governors made kings shudder in fear, and their sprawl swallowed a good portion of the known world. Yet they took thirty years to conquer Wales, and even then, they never held it easily. The legions found it too damned hard to fight in these mountains, and far too easy to die, with bolt-holes behind every rock and tree, and wild men constantly dropping out of—"

"The Pythias aren't Roman legions," I told him unsteadily.

"No, but they still can't fight what they can't find. And they can't find us. I laid enough false trails, did enough circling around, and hacked my way over enough mountaintops to see to that."

"But ... dozens ..." The very idea was overwhelming. Dozens of Pythias. How could anyone stand against that?

"*Potentially* dozens," he amended.

I looked at him. "What?"

"Well, that other one, what was her name? The one before you?"

"Agnes?"

"Yes. She didn't show up in Amsterdam, did she?"

"I—no. But—"

"She must have felt us pass through, so to speak, but she let the Pythia of the day handle it. We only faced two Pythias in Amsterdam due to London following us out of her own era. Now, there may be more Londons out there, but it seems to me that more will likely stay where they are and let the local girl take care of it. Whoever that may be." He glanced around.

"But . . . but you just said—"

"Yes, well, I was playing with you, girl."

"Playing—" I stared at him.

"And giving you the worst-case scenario," he said, a little defensively. "Technically, they *could* all end up here. However, I think it more likely that they will only show up if the current Pythia fails to find us. Which, with the amount of territory she has to cover, and if we refrain from putting a spotlight on us by using magic, should buy us a few—look!"

I jumped, my head whipping around, my heart in my throat. But the moon was barely a sliver above the trees, and I couldn't see anything. And the starlight only managed to make every little hill and rut in the ground into a lurking enemy.

"What?"

"A flame!" Rosier went to his knees, hands cupped protectively around something in a pile of moss. I almost passed out.

Playing, I thought dizzily, watching him hunch protectively over a flicker in the dark. His cheeks swelled up, and he started feeding it tiny puffs of oxygen. After a moment, a glimmer of light danced in his eyes, making him look even more diabolical than usual.

I *was* going to kill him, I decided unsteadily.

Just not right now.

I lay back down.

After a bit, I heard him move off, probably in search of more wood for the hungry little flame. I didn't bother opening my eyes to check. Everything hurt. Every. Thing. It felt like I'd managed to sprain my entire body and possibly my brain, too.

And on top of that, I was starving.

"Did you bring any food?" I asked when I heard him return.

"What? Oh yes."

Something hit me in the chest. I opened my eyes to find myself looking at one of those little packs of crackers and cheese. Not the good kind. The kind you get at gas stations when you're hungover at two a.m. and aren't that picky. The kind where the cheese is half-liquefied neon yellow goo.

I ate them anyway.

"Isn't there an inn or something?" I asked.

"What?"

"An. Inn. You know, a medieval Ramada?"

He snorted. "Are you in for a disappointment."

"Meaning what?"

"Meaning that if you're looking for the majestic, flag-topped fortresses of Camelot, you're going to be looking awhile." He chuckled to himself.

God, I *hated* that man.

"I didn't ask about fortresses. I asked about an inn. Somewhere inside," I said pointedly, as a raindrop hissed on Rosier's cheerful little blaze.

He looked skyward, scowling. But it appeared to have been a lone sentinel, because no more were forthcoming. So he turned the scowl on me.

"They didn't have inns, either."

"Then where did travelers sleep?"

"Most people didn't travel, and those who did stayed at monasteries, some of which would put you up for a night or two if you said nice things about whatever bit of saint they had tucked away." He waved a hand. "But in this period in Wales they're mostly down by the coast."

"So what does anybody do who ends up inland?"

"Find an accommodating farmhouse if no one's looking for them."

"And if someone is?"

"Camp."

I closed my eyes. Wonderful.

"You're luckier than you know," he told me. "Medieval inns, when you could find one, were universally terrible. Flea-ridden, lice-infested, and teeming with thugs who would as soon shiv you in the side as look at you. And don't get me started on the food! I think they deliberately tried to poison me on more than one occasion."

"Then why did you come here?"

"The same reason anyone comes to this miserable little world." He looked around malevolently. "Power."

He didn't seem interested in explaining that, which was fine with me. If I never talked to the man again, it would be fine with me. "Did you bring sleeping bags, at least?" I asked, trying in vain to find a comfortable spot.

"No."

"*No?* If you knew there weren't any inns, then why—"

"I didn't know you were going to land us in the middle of the damned wilderness, did I?"

I choked down a few dozen comments about him being lucky we'd made it here at all, and instead focused on the pack he'd smacked me in the face with every other step. "Then what's in that?"

"Clothes, mainly. Or did you plan to go to court dressed like that?"

I looked down at my shorts and T-shirt, and then what he'd said registered. "We're going to court?"

"Such as it is."

"You mean . . . *Arthur's* court? We're going to *Camelot*?"

Rosier looked like he was about to say something, and then clamped his lips shut. "Yes. We're going to Camelot. Happy?"

"No!"

"Why am I not surprised?"

"Why can't we wait for Pritkin somewhere less . . . public?"

"Because, my dear, unlike you, my son bothered to learn something about his magic. Magic I do not have, remember? Approaching him on the road would be a very bad idea."

"But he knows you. Oh, wait. I see what you mean."

"He doesn't know me yet," Rosier snapped. "All he would see is someone who had disguised themselves as him, who was also trying to hex him!"

"And he won't see the same thing at court?"

"No. You're going to go in and lure him out. I'll hide and render him unconscious while he's busy with you—"

"Yeah. 'Cause that worked so well in London."

"—and then use some human drugs to keep him that way. No magic, see?"

I just looked at him.

"Do you have a better idea?" he demanded.

"Anything is a better idea. Trying to coldcock someone with Pritkin's reflexes—"

"My own aren't that bad, either!"

"—and why do I have to lure him out? Why can't you just go inside and—"

"I'll never get inside; there's too much security. People are paranoid here, and for good reason. Place makes your Wild West look like Disneyland."

"Then how am I supposed to—"

"Damn it, girl! You're an attractive female! That's a pass into virtually anywhere, if you know how to work it."

I looked at him some more.

"And I will help you," he said heavily. I started to comment, but he held up a hand. "You're making this harder than it is. We go to court. We lure him out. We take him down. Getting here was the challenge; the rest is going to be easy."

Chapter Fifteen

Easy, I thought mockingly, slopping along some "road" the next morning in the "shoes" Rosier had provided to go with my "dress," all of which were ungodly ugly and didn't even fit. And that included the "road," which clung to the side of a mountain like it had been cut to go somewhere else.

Like somewhere that wasn't at a forty-five-degree angle and located next to a cliff.

"I thought . . . Wales was supposed to be . . . chilly," I panted, feeling sweat drip down my neck.

"Do you always whine this much?" Rosier demanded, slip-sliding his way through the mud. And barely managing to avoid a rapid descent into the valley below.

"I was making . . . an observation. And this damned wool doesn't help."

"It's what people wore in this era. Wool and flax—"

Rosier cut off when he abruptly went down on his ass, which was funny. And then started sliding toward the cliff, which was not. I grabbed him and jerked back, but forgot about the mud—and my lousy excuse for shoes with nonexistent traction. I ended up going down myself, and planting an elbow in his stomach, or possibly something slightly lower, as we thrashed away from the edge, rolling and cursing and covered in mud.

But we ended up over beside the cliff face, so I guessed that was something.

Furious green eyes met mine, out of a slimy brown mask.

"So couldn't . . . we have had . . . some more flax?" I asked him after a minute.

"Why has Emrys not killed you? Why has *everyone* not killed you?"

"They've tried."

"Not hard enough!"

"I thought you didn't believe me," he said when we stopped under a dripping tree to gulp down some water. How it could be simultaneously rainy and hot *in Britain*, I had no idea. But it was managing. And slowly steaming us inside our lovely wool.

"About what?"

"About your mother."

"I don't," I told him, wiping my mouth on my dress, because it wasn't as if anybody was going to notice. I'd slipped in the mud three times, the last one face-planting, and the garment was beyond filthy. And I had a rock in my "shoe." I sat on a really uncomfortable root and pulled it off, shaking the thing.

"Then what was that quip?" Rosier demanded.

"What quip?"

"About me using my son!"

I shrugged. "Just that you can't have it both ways. You can't react like Mom's the Antichrist for supposedly trying to use me, and then turn around and declare yourself lily white when you're doing the exact same—"

"I am not doing the same thing!"

"Oh no. Of course not." We'd somehow gotten onto the subject of Pritkin's mother, and Rosier had gotten defensive. And so, of course, he'd started to attack mine. But considering everything, I didn't think he had much cause to feel superior. "You just impregnated some woman *you knew was going to die*—"

"I did not know that!"

"Because the last fifty dying in childbirth after their half-incubus kids drained them dry was a *coincidence*?"

"It wasn't fifty, and women died from childbirth all the time in this era!" he said irritably. "Along with a thousand other things. At first, I thought I was merely unlucky."

"Unlucky?"

"I didn't have anyone to tell me otherwise. It's not as if anyone had tried this!"

No, I didn't suppose so. Incubi, like all demons as near as I could figure out, tried to improve their line by mating up the power chain. So demon/human crosses were actually pretty rare. It would have to be a pretty sad excuse for a demon to find a human a decent match.

Of course, this was Rosier we were talking about.

But he hadn't been after Pritkin's mother for her power, had he?

"But when you finally noticed, you didn't stop," I pointed out.

"No, I looked for a woman I thought would live!"

"Because of a tiny bit of fey blood?"

"It wasn't tiny, and why do you know about all this?"

"Pritkin told me." Rosier glared at me. "What? It's his story, too."

He looked away, and his jaw tightened. "He never talks to anyone. Not about this. He doesn't talk to *me* about this."

"Did you expect him to?"

"Yes! He makes assumptions, and always—*always*—I am the villain!"

"You could correct him—"

"That's not my place!"

"—unless, of course, those assumptions are right. . . ."

He started to say something, and then stopped, lips tight. And then decided to hell with it and said it anyway. "You have no idea what it's like at court," he spat. "None! The plotting, the scheming—it never ends. The only way out is to die, or to get enough power that no one risks challenging you. But I can't absorb enough on my own to build up that kind of surplus, not when I am constantly having to expend it to break up feuds and maintain order—"

"So you decided to give yourself a backup."

"I wasn't supposed to need one! I was never supposed to have this position so young. Until your mother decided otherwise!"

He trudged ahead, stabbing at the ground with the makeshift walking stick he'd crafted out of an old tree limb and not looking at me. Although that could have been because of the treacherous terrain. I scrambled to keep up.

It was hard to imagine someone who was probably older than the pyramids as "young," but I guess it was relative. And he wasn't wrong about my mother. Not entirely, anyway.

She'd been the last goddess left on earth because she'd kicked out all the others, and the gods, too. I'd known that for a while. What I'd only just found out was how.

She'd done it by hunting demons, the oldest, strongest, and most powerful—including the ones that the other demons called "ancient horrors" and shuddered when they mentioned them. And Rosier's father, who hadn't been one of the above, but who had had the bad luck to get in the way. Then she used what she stole from them, energy collected over countless millennia, to kick out her fellow gods and to slam the metaphysical door behind them.

No one knew for sure why she did this. The Circle viewed her as the savior of mankind, because the gods had been doing a pretty good job of destroying the new world they'd found prior to their abrupt departure. It was why the Silver Circle took that name, why it was still their symbol: a circle of light, like the full moon on a clear night, like the age-old symbol of the best known of mother's many names: Artemis, goddess of the moon, the great huntress . . .

Of course, as the son of one of those she'd hunted, Rosier had a slightly different take. Namely that she'd kicked out the other gods in order to rule supreme on her own. Only they had resisted more than she'd expected, leading to her expending most of her newly acquired strength in the battle. And that had left her vulnerable to payback from all those outraged demons—if they could have found her.

They never did.

But they did find me. And naturally assumed that some nefarious plot on my mother's part had led to my conception. Rosier especially was a big fan of that idea. Recent events had mitigated the council's view somewhat, but Rosier . . .

He was still in tinfoil hat land, and showed no sign of coming back.

"It was a different age then," he told me, looking off over the spread of mountains. "My father strode the gaps between worlds like a colossus, magnificent in his power, breathtaking in his influence. In his era, incubi were respected, admired, even coveted. Our people were considered ornaments to any court, valued councilors, trusted spies, functionaries, diplomats . . ." He trailed off.

"And then?" I prompted.

He shot me a glance. "And then came the dark times, and the world we knew shattered and broke. Everyone was set adrift as courts scattered and people fled and my father—we never recovered."

"So Pritkin was supposed to help you reclaim lost glory?"

"He was supposed to help me survive!" Rosier said, slashing at some gorse bushes that had grown over the "road." "That's all any of us have done ever since. And it was damned hard, girl. Our specialized abilities, honed to a fine sheen over countless centuries, were suddenly useless. Beauty, luxury, flattery—none of these things mean a damn when you're scratching and clawing for survival! When your very civilization is coming down around your ears!

"But survive we did, among them all, among creatures a thousand times more powerful. The ones everyone assumed would be among the first to go, the soft, the indulgent, the useless incubi, survived when countless stronger races fell."

He whirled on me suddenly, so much so that we both almost went sprawling. "*I* did that, do you understand? I kept the remnants of us together; I forged us into a functioning whole; I found us a refuge! All I ask is for Emrys to help me hold it. And he could—easily, pleasurably. With two of us to absorb power, and with our gifts . . . no coalition would ever be able to challenge us. It would mean absolute security—"

"For you," I pointed out.

"For all of us!"

"Not for Pritkin."

"He's incubus whether he likes it or not!"

"He's human, too, and for him that sort of life is more like slavery."

"It's nothing of the kind!"

"Like those people whose world you turned into your refuge?" I'd seen it recently, a vast, sprawling desert world that had been taken over by the incubi. It and its people.

"If we hadn't, they'd have been conquered by someone else. In those days—"

"But those days are over, aren't they? They've been over for a long time. But I haven't noticed any emancipation going—"

"Bah!" Rosier suddenly yelled in my face, causing me to jerk back. And stare at him. "I'm through talking to you!" he proclaimed, and strode off, his feet throwing up little clumps of mud.

"You need to stop panicking," I said very clearly, some hours later. We'd made our way out of the steamy valley and onto a frigid mountaintop, but our luck was about the same. As Rosier was busy demonstrating.

"You stop panicking!" he snarled. "They're not trying to eat you!"

"They're not trying to eat you, either." Well, I was pretty sure. "They just want what's in the bag. Give them what's in the bag."

Rosier glared at me from his perch atop a birch, where he'd landed after the rock fall but before the avalanche. I'd taken refuge in a sort of cave-like depression in the rocks, but he'd been forced to jump over the cliff or be crushed by hundred-pound boulders and a mountain of snow. The good news was, he ended up grabbing the top of a tree. The bad news was that a mass of wild pigs apparently lived under it.

And had no intention of letting him down.

"How is giving them food going to encourage them to *leave*?" Rosier demanded, staring at them, wild-eyed.

"Because you're going to throw it away from the tree," I said, exasperated. "No, no. Take off the cellophane first. They won't know what it is!"

"I can't take the cellophane off and hold on to the damned tree!"

"Use your legs."

"What?"

"Your legs!"

Rosier stared at me like I'd lost my mind. "I'm an incubus, not a contortionist!"

I took a breath and closed my eyes. That seemed to be

the only thing that helped with him, if I couldn't see his stupid face. "Use your *legs* to hold on to the tree. Use your *hands* to unwrap the food. Throw the food away from you. Then, when they go after it, get down and run in the other direction."

There was some grumbling I couldn't make out very well, and then some cellophane crinkling. And then a lot of agitated squealing.

I opened my eyes to see several pigs jumping up onto the trunk like they were trying to climb it, Rosier screeching and retreating even farther into the swaying, leafy treetop, and cheesy crackers raining down like manna from heaven. I sighed. "I said *away*. You have to throw them *away* from—"

"I am not Sandy Koufax!"

"Who?"

"Oh, for . . ." The treetop shook some more, and an outraged face appeared through the foliage. "Just do what I told you!"

"I am not using magic," I said, grasping his big bag o' tricks a little more tightly. Fortunately, he'd decided to lighten his own load by making me carry it earlier. Unfortunately, I couldn't use anything in it without bringing the Pythian posse of doom down on our heads.

"Then use the gun!"

"The—you brought a *gun*?" I opened the pack, and sure enough, toward the bottom was a shiny new Beretta. "Why did you bring a gun? We can't shoot anybody—"

"The hell we can't."

"We *can't*! It would change time! I told you—"

"And I told you to shoot the damned pigs! Or will that change time, too?"

I put the gun away before I was tempted to use it on Rosier.

More tempted.

"Shoot them!" he yelled.

"That mountain just tried to bury us," I reminded him, trying to speak calmly. "Do you *want* another avalanche?"

"We don't have a choice!"

"It's only been a few minutes. If you stop screeching—"

"I don't screech. I have never screeched!"

"—maybe they'll get bored and go away."

"Perhaps if I hadn't just thrown food at them! They'll never leave now!"

"You don't know that," I said, just as several more pigs started trunk jumping. "And can I remind you that it takes all of a second for a Pythia to pop in?" I added, over his renewed screeches. "Once they know where we are—"

"Shut up and get me down, you appalling woman! Get me down, get me down, get me down!"

"I can't talk to you when you're like this, you know; I really—"

"Aughhh!"

I would have put the infernal noise down to Rosier's tendency for hysterics, but then I heard something else. Something like the creak-crack-pop of splintering wood. And, okay, it was just barely possible that this tree wasn't in the greatest of shape.

Annnnnd now the pigs were ramming it.

I started rooting around in the bag. "What else do you have in here?"

"Use the yellow ones. The yellow ones!"

"The yellow *what*?" There were only about a thousand things in here. "Pills, potions, amulets—"

"Aughhh! Aughhh! Aughhh!"

I turned the bag upside down and scrabbled around in the snowy, muddy slush. And found a bunch of individually wrapped little yellow rubbery things falling out of a small bag. Great, now I had to get one open. And thanks to recent events, my nails were shot.

But I managed, and a moment later looked up. And saw Rosier's tree swaying back and forth madly, like it was trying to do the hula. Or, you know, like it was about to topple over into a herd of crazed wild boar.

I licked my lips. "Okay, now what?"

"Their throats!"

"What?"

"Their throats! Their throats! You have to get them down their—aughhh!"

I stared at him. Yeah, like that was happening.

But for once, Rosier's panic was justified. I didn't have to be a lumberjack to know that tree was on its last leg. Or limb. Or—

"Throw me the backpack!" I yelled.

"Oh yes. Yes, you'd like that, wouldn't you?" he said furiously. "So you can take off with the food and leave me here—"

"No! You stupid—I'm not planning to leave you!"

"Then why?"

"For the pigs, you stupid, stupid—"

A great leather thing hit me in the face, hard enough to knock me down.

But there really wasn't time to complain. My butt smacked down into an icy puddle, and the next second, I was throwing junk food everywhere. And this was not the moment to mess about with crap like strawberry roll-ups or turkey jerky. No, this called for the big guns.

I pulled out a little white box and went ballistic with the Twinkies.

A moment later, Rosier's tree gave up the ghost, and fell into some others with a great snap, creak, *crack*, as loud as a bullet echoing out over the forest. It normally would have had me flinching and panicking and fleeing in the opposite direction, before everybody and their dog came to find out what the hell. But right then, I was having a problem doing that.

Right then I was having a problem doing anything but standing and staring with my mouth hanging open.

I was still doing it when Rosier joined me a few moments later. His tree had ended up wedged against an outcropping of rock a little way down the path, instead of hitting the forest floor, allowing him to scramble back onto solid ground. And I guess the intervening time had given him a chance to get his shit together, although the usual smugness had yet to return.

Or maybe he was having a hard time finding the right words, too.

"You . . . didn't use the knockout pills, I take it?" he finally asked, staring out into the void.

I shook my head.

He sat down and we split the last Twinkie.

"You realize we just sent a herd of flying pigs soaring out over medieval Wales," I said, sometime later, when the last little oinking cloud had disappeared over the horizon.

"Hm."

"You don't look too concerned."

Rosier got to his feet and then actually extended a hand to help me up. "Maybe it will give the Pythias something else to do. And in any case . . ."

"In any case?"

"Well. The expression had to start somewhere, didn't it?"

Chapter Sixteen

"I thought you knew where this place was," I said as we passed a familiar-looking mossy stump for the third time.

"I do."

"So we're taking the scenic route, is that it?" It was half-way through the afternoon, we were drenched with sweat, and we'd been rained on twice. Even worse, we hadn't even managed to locate the court, much less Pritkin. At the rate we were going, we'd still be wandering around the wilderness when the cursed soul came and went and not even know it!

Rosier stopped abruptly. "Do you see that?" he demanded, pointing at something between the trees.

"No."

"It's a mill!"

I peered into the shade. "Okay."

"Stay there. Find a seat, sit on it, and wait for me. Do not wander off, do not get in trouble, and do not talk to anyone!"

I glowered at him. Our brief moment of camaraderie had faded in the dreary sludge of nonexistent roads, chilly mountaintops, and steamy valleys, and he'd been getting progressively more ill-tempered all afternoon. Not to mention slower, as the missing shoe took its toll despite being replaced by a spare length of gray wool. Well, gray-red now, Rosier's tender flesh having been lacerated by a couple thousand sharp-edged rocks.

"I can't talk to anyone when I don't speak the language," I pointed out. "And where are you going?"

"To find the right road!"

"Why can't I go with you?" I wasn't thrilled about the company, but I was even less happy about being left on my own in the Wild West of Wales.

"Because I can travel faster alone," Rosier said, his voice clipped as he tried to fish rock number 2,914 out of his makeshift shoe.

I scowled. "I've been matching strides with you all damned day, and even been ahead most of the last—"

"And if I have to endure your infernal chatter one more minute, I will murder you," he added, panting. "And while that would undoubtedly be to earth's great advantage, it would stick me here, without magic, for the next millennium and a half!"

He stomped off.

I stared after him, and scowled some more. Then I went to find this "mill." I did not have high hopes.

Of course, I could be wrong, I thought, breaking through the trees. And finding a tumbledown structure with a water wheel that might be mistaken for a mill if someone squinted. But I barely noticed.

Because there was a stream, and it looked like a small, gurgling slice of heaven.

I hacked and stumbled and then slid the rest of the way down the hill and sat on the bank, tugging at the "shoes" my sadistic bastard of a traveling partner had supplied me with. Because, apparently, if anyone caught a glimpse of my Keds, it might change all of history. He was probably just pissed that he hadn't thought to bring any hiking shoes himself.

Not that thin sneakers would have been all that great, either, since apparently Wales is a Celtic word meaning "muddy rock pit," but at least they had soles. The closest thing these had was a hardened piece of leather, and then a bunch of leather flaps with a drawstring loosely pulling them up to where they tied around the ankle. They weren't so much shoes as baggies for the feet, and they sucked, oh my God.

But I finally got the laces to release and plunged my blisters into the water and *oh*. It was *cold*. It was *perfect*.

I lay there awhile, gazing up at the tree canopy. A couple of determined feeder vines were blowing in the wind toward the branches on the other side. Dip and reach, dip and reach. I kept thinking they'd grab hold any minute, and start stitching up the remaining seam of the sky, but they never did. It was sort of hypnotic to watch, though. Especially with liquid pleasure coursing over my bruised heels and battered toes.

After a while, my feet started to feel better, but my legs began to point out that they could use some attention, too. They were all scratched up, thanks to the fact that the latest "road" had been more of a goat trail and we'd had to tramp our way through miles of prickly flora. I wiggled down a little lower, but that left me with hard little pebbles under my butt, and a sweaty, mud-splattered body crying out for a swim.

I glanced around.

The big wheel was lazily turning, but I didn't see anybody around the mill, which was half obscured by weeds anyway. Of course, that didn't mean it was abandoned; everything around here had weeds. But even if not, people didn't use mills all year, right? The harvest came in, you did your thing, carted off your flour or whatever, and that was it until next year.

At least I hoped so, because I really, really wanted a bath.

I sat there, chewing my cheek for a while and thinking it over. And scratching, because the damned dress was rubbing me raw. It was basically another sack, only with holes in it. Which would have been fine since my head and arms needed somewhere to go. Only these holes didn't make sense. Unless the thing had been designed for a hunchback with an arm growing out of her chest and a neck where her shoulder ought to be. So I wasn't wearing it so much as being imprisoned by it, and suddenly I couldn't take it anymore.

After another surreptitious glance around, I shucked it, and just that, just getting rid of twenty pounds of damp, scratchy wool, was the most amazing feeling I'd had in a while.

I sat there for another few minutes, with the scratchy mass in my lap like a dead Snuffleupagus. And waited for someone to call out something about a trespassing naked chick. But nobody did.

Nobody appeared at all, and there were no sounds, except for the occasional call of a bird, the gurgle of the stream, and the rhythmic *creak, creak, creak* of the distant wheel. A fish flipped into the air and did a happy little wriggle before disappearing again. A fat rabbit stuck its nose out of a bush, regarded me for a moment, and started chewing on some grass. A tiny breeze sent a ripple across the top of the water, breaking the late-afternoon sunlight into a scintillation of gold.

And I left the wool monster on the bank and eased into the stream.

And, okay, *that* was cold.

Just stay in, I told myself. Stay in, stay in, stay in, and it'll get better. And it did. In a minute, it got awesome.

I felt my whole bruised, scratched, and wool-tortured body relax into a feeling of quiet bliss. Oh God, I thought tearfully. I loved Wales.

I spent maybe ten minutes paddling around, mostly floating on my bruised butt, and watching my toes peek out of the water. It was a sweet little place. Very green. Of course, saying that about Wales was like saying that the desert was brown. Or that the sky was blue. Or that Rosier was a dick. Wales had to be the greenest place I'd ever seen in my life, almost startlingly so after Vegas.

Back at what I'd started secretly to think of as home, even places that should have been green often weren't. Like down near the waterline of Lake Mead or along the banks of the Colorado. If you were lucky, you might see a few scraggly bits of desert scruff here and there, stubbornly clinging to the rocky soil, or a mostly brown vine trailing up a cliff. But that was as good as it got, at least from nature.

Of course, it was Vegas, so everybody cheated. The casinos and shopping malls and golf courses all had greenery around them. The Bellagio had its own indoor garden. And Boulder City, a little town where the workers had been housed during the building of the Hoover Dam, had installed a lush carpet of grass in the new playground they'd built for their kids.

Only to come out the next day and find thirty or more hardy bighorn sheep munching on the free buffet.

Hey, it was Vegas.

The townspeople had eventually made peace with the sheep, who simply refused to budge, and in true Vegas style had even set up tours to the place. If you went at the right time of day, you could see the standoff between the visiting sheep and the local kids, each on their respective side of the playground, each ignoring the other. What you couldn't see was anything like this.

I looked around at the complete opposite of Vegas, where even things that *shouldn't* be green were anyway. Like the mill wheel, with its fine coating of bright green moss. Or the water, which was a dappled emerald thanks to the treetops that almost met over the stream. Or the sky, which was taking on an olive tinge in the east that foretold more rain in my future. Even the rocks under my feet were all rounded and mossy, having long ago given up any rough edges to the relentless flow of the soft, soft water.

It was heaven on my sore heels.

It was hell on my hundred or so scratches, but I decided I could live with it.

It was providing a bath for a future war mage.

"That's nice," I thought, drifting lazily over into a reed patch, where some little fishies started trying to nibble on my toes.

And then realization struck, and I almost drowned.

I came up, spluttering and coughing, and staring around—at a mass of black birds that had just taken off from the treetops. Their flapping and cawing covered the sounds I was making, like the weeds covered my body. Which was lucky. Because the river wasn't that wide and Pritkin was just down from me, dabbling a foot in the water on the opposite bank.

I grabbed a bunch of weeds in both hands, and stared.

He was dressed in some whacked-out ghillie suit, or considering where we were, possibly something a drunk Druid had devised: a tunic covered in branches and leaves and vines, a hood shaggy with more of the same, and a pair of brown boots barely visible under the drooping foliage. His face was painted like a commando's, too, all brown and green splotched, and his hair was midlength and shaggy instead of short and spiky.

But it was him. I knew him instantly, and almost yelled his name in sheer relief before I remembered. And clamped my teeth on my lower lip, hard enough to hurt.

Because this Pritkin didn't know me.

This Pritkin wouldn't even know the name I'd been about to shout, since he didn't go by it yet. This Pritkin was a dangerous mage in a dangerous time, and he probably wouldn't take it well if he knew he was being spied on. Fortunately, the reeds ensured that he didn't immediately see me.

Unfortunately, that didn't really help, since I had no idea what I was supposed to do now.

My thought processes, such as they were, went something like: urp.

Oh, shit, oh, shit, oh, shit, oh, shit!

Rosier. Scan hillside frantically. No Rosier.

Damn him!

What a time to disappear—and for me to let him go!

But it shouldn't have mattered. We hadn't seen a soul all day. We were out in the middle of nowhere and Pritkin was supposed to be at court and it shouldn't have *mattered*.

But he was here and it did and Rosier had only just left, maybe half an hour ago. It couldn't have been much longer than that, so who knew when he'd be back? And what was I supposed to do in the meantime?

What was I supposed to do when Pritkin decided to *leave*?

Only he wasn't.

He was getting naked instead.

For a moment, I just stared. I don't know why. Probably still in shock. But the great ghillie-what's-it went thump on the ground, leaving him standing there bare-chested in a pair of cut-off drawstring trousers and a decent tan.

I blinked. Pritkin didn't tan. Pritkin was British-tourist pale even in Vegas because of all the war mage paraphernalia he carted around. It required a full-length coat or, when jogging, a bulky hoodie, to hide the various lethal bulges, and neither left the sun a lot of opportunities.

But he wasn't a war mage yet, was he? And it looked

like he could tan, after all. Which was more than a little
disconcerting, because with the shaggy, sun-streaked hair
and the Celtic version of board shorts, he looked less like a
dangerous mage than a surfer from Malibu.

He looked like it in other ways, too. The man I knew
didn't have a choice but to work out. No chance to use his
incubus abilities anymore meant no chance to boost his
magic, and war mages were constant targets. But this guy
didn't have that problem. And while he was still nicely defined, he looked more like someone who liked to stay active than a bodybuilder.

Except when he stood up and turned away in order to
strip off the shorts. Leaving it impossible not to notice that
the legs were the same, thick and hard with muscle, probably due to the daily Wales workout. Like the thighs, which
were slightly paler than the calves and chest, as if they
didn't see the sun as often. And the still lighter mounds
higher up, which stretched and flexed when he moved, to
toss the last of his clothing on the heap.

And then to turn around and stretch on the riverbank
instead, giving me a chance to see that other things were
the same as I remembered, too.

Like the fact that he was injured.

Pritkin was sweaty and muddy, which didn't worry me
much because *Wales*, but one knee was scraped bloody.
And so was his right leg, where what looked like a livid
burn snaked down from midthigh to just above the shin.
And his hip ...

I bit back a sound as he turned this way, because it was
one huge bruise.

It looked like he'd recently been in a fight that, considering the shape he was in, I wasn't sure he'd won. But he
must have, I told myself, before my blood pressure went
through the roof. He was here and in one piece, and I
doubted he'd be stripping down in the presence of an enemy. Or leaving his stuff on the riverbank. Or diving into
the water unarmed—

And not coming up again.

I looked both ways after a minute, when he didn't reap-
pear, but there was nothing. Just the old wheel, leisurely
turning, a lot of slow-moving water, and no Pritkin. I waded
out of the reeds to get a better view, thinking that maybe

he'd swum under the surface somewhere I couldn't see, but still nothing.

And, suddenly, I lost it.

The combo of shock, vast relief, panic, and then more shock made the second mental shutdown more extreme than the first. All I could think about was him being hurt and passing out after he dove in. And drowning while I just stood there, stood there like an *idiot*.

Okay, that didn't make sense, I knew that, because he hadn't died in medieval Wales! But what if I'd somehow changed things? What if he'd caught a glimpse of me just as he dove and it threw him off course and then he hit his head on something? What if I'd come back to rescue him, only to kill him myself, and that might sound crazy to anyone else, but they didn't *know*, they didn't know my *life*, and—

And I dove, trying desperately to see something in water that was all dapples—swaying tree limbs above and darting fish below and shadows and sunlight and waving water plants—the whole place was moving! And I couldn't hear any better, not over the water rushing in my ears. Or feel anything but the current tugging at me, stronger now that I was completely under and fighting to go farther.

And fighting hard. But instead, I felt my feet leave the slick stones of the riverbed, and my body start to move back toward the surface. I thrashed and kicked, but it didn't do any good. In seconds I surfaced anyway, gasping and dizzy, because I'd been down longer than I thought. Which meant that Pritkin—

I dove again, or tried to, but this time, I didn't go anywhere at all. I pushed down, and the water pushed back. I was so confused by then, so terrified, and so close to crazed, that I didn't even stop to wonder why. I grabbed at it, tearing it like it was cloth, or dirt that I could dig my way through if only I tried hard enough. But it wasn't—it ran through my fingers and then re-formed into this suddenly impenetrable barrier that mocked me, mocked me until I slapped at it, yelling in fury and rage, and scaring a water bird half to death.

Which was nothing to how I felt when strong arms suddenly went around me from behind.

The bird erupted from the patch of reeds, its narrow

wings slicing through the air with a whistle. It dipped low
to the water, its long tail skimming the reflected sun, shattering it into a thousand gleaming pieces until the whole
river ran gold under the weight of the clouds. Except for a
dark silhouette in the middle of it all, solid and real in the
dance of light as I spun in his arms.

And saw the light of late afternoon reflected in a pair of
green eyes.

Chapter Seventeen

In the distance, the heavy clouds that had followed me all day broke open with a sigh, and rain fell like a veil across the horizon. More startled birds took off with ululating trills of complaint. And a feeling leapt up in my chest, so bright and full that it was almost pain, the lightning a dim echo, the sky too small to hold it.

And then Pritkin laughed, and the mood broke, leaving me blinking and shell-shocked.

And kneeling on a mat of rubbery water that steadfastly refused to accept me.

"You . . . you bastard!" I breathed, slipping and sliding and trying to cover up with what felt like a giant, over-stuffed water balloon that I had somehow ended up in the middle of. And being watched by a hairy-chested forest sprite who appeared to find the whole thing very funny. I glared at him, caught between relief and outrage, until the bubble burst as abruptly as it had formed and I plunged under again.

Warm hands grasped my waist, helping me back to the surface. And then hauled me close to an amused face, which promptly cracked into an even wider grin. And then into a full-on laugh, rich and loud and long, at whatever expression I'd managed to come up with.

Which was probably shock, since I'd never heard Pritkin laugh like that.

And because, weirdly, he looked even less familiar close up.

There were similarities to the man I knew: the stubbled chin, the let's-be-generous-and-call-it-a-Roman nose, the green, green eyes. But the differences were bigger, and they were everywhere. Like the mouth, which was fuller than it should have been, maybe because it was currently stretched into a smile. And the cheeks, which still had some of their baby fat, softening the hard lines I knew. And the eyes . . .

Which, other than for the color, I didn't know at all.

They lacked the suspicion, the cynicism, and the wariness I was used to. Instead, they were sparkling with wicked humor, and the delight I'd seen on rare occasions when he had just done something breathtakingly dangerous. Not to mention being mischievous and curious and more than a little flirty.

Which might explain the hands on my ass.

Pritkin said something while I stood there and gaped at him, but it was just gibberish to me. After a moment, he changed cadence and tried again, and I guess it was a different language because he looked expectant. Only to purse his lips in thought when I shook my head.

And then to glance to his left and narrow his eyes. I followed his gaze but didn't see anything particularly interesting. Just weeds and rocks and the gently turning water wheel.

And a very naked me on top of a very naked Pritkin.

I did a double take, and then one more for good measure, but the view didn't change. That was definitely a Pritkin clone who had just popped into being on the riverbank. And that was definitely me on top, back arching, thighs flexing, while we did some, uh, very naked things. . . .

And before I had a chance to assimilate *that*, another me and another him appeared a few yards off, only he was on top this time, and sliding steadily down to—

I abruptly looked away, but another couple blinked into existence on our right. And then more and more, on both sides of the river, each one with a slightly different specialty. Like some kind of crazy *menu* . . .

And that's exactly what it was, I realized. An incredible display of magic for no other reason than to bypass the pesky language barrier. And maybe to show off a little. Because this Pritkin had his full incubus abilities and power to burn, and none of the hang-ups of the man I knew.

Or, you know, *any*.

Because he *wasn't* the man I knew. He was a young incubus princeling who was injured and in pain, and had just spied a naked chick perving on him from the weeds. And who probably thought he'd found an easy way to heal. And who . . . and who . . .

And who was being pretty damned optimistic, I thought, staring at the closest couple. And yes, I knew it was an illusion, I *knew* that. But for some reason, it was still a shock to see the look on my—on her—on the woman's face as she—

And I guess maybe I'd stared a little too long. Because Pritkin—the real one—said something. And I looked up to find him smiling and nodding and appearing enthusiastic about my choice.

"No," I told him forcefully. "No, that was *surprise*. That was not a *selection*."

An eyebrow raised, but he didn't appear too put out. Maybe, I realized a second later, because I'd just taken the vanilla stuff off the table. I blinked as more couples popped into being, peppering both sides of the bank with carnal delights.

And damn, I thought, staring at a threesome just down a bit on this side of the river. And then tilting my head to the side, because I couldn't quite figure out what . . . Oh. Oh yes. Well, *that* wasn't happening—

Only, suddenly, it was.

"Oh, shit," I whispered as two more warm arms encircled me from behind.

And that was what I'd been looking at, wasn't it, I thought, as hard hands splayed on my lower belly, pulling me back against an equally hard torso. While Pritkin number one's hands framed my face, pulling it up as his head came down. For a moment, there was just warm breath against my lips, fingers caressing my cheekbones and hip bones simultaneously, and identical lines of thick, needy hardness pressing against me on both sides, silken soft and rigid strength and aching, seeking heat.

"Uh, look, I, see, uh," I said intelligently.

And then he kissed me. And it was nothing like Pritkin's kisses, and everything like them. It was less desperate, starving man at a banquet than I was used to, but just as demanding, just as possessive, just as borderline arrogant. With an added enthusiasm-makes-up-for-lack-of-technique technique that just really, really worked on some level I wasn't in a headspace to define just then.

He pulled back after a moment, although it didn't feel that way since the fake him was still plastered to my back, and his lips had started roaming around my neck. Like his hands around my torso. I was about to make a fuss, but real Pritkin took that moment to step back and execute a very formal and completely surreal bow, considering that his doppelganger currently had my tits in his hands.

"Myrddin," he told me, putting a hand on his chest, his laughing face looking up into mine.

"Um—I—what?"

"Myrd-din," he enunciated more slowly, straightening up and tapping his chest again. Because I guess even in medieval Wales it was considered polite to introduce yourself before—before—

"Oh, shit!" I squeaked, and began desperately scanning the riverbank. And the hill, and the area around the mill, and the opposite freaking bank—anything for Rosier. Because this would be a *really* good time for him to show back up.

"Ohshit," Pritkin repeated, rolling it around on his tongue thoughtfully.

"No," I told him distractedly, trying to see what was moving behind the trees. "No, that's not my—I didn't mean—I—oh, *shit*."

The latter was because someone had just broken through the tree line, all right, but it wasn't Rosier. It also wasn't the Pythian posse, which should have made me happy considering how much magic we were splashing around. But for some reason, I wasn't getting that vibe.

For a second, I just stood there, taking in the sight of three too-lithe bodies coming down the bank. They had weird black armor, long silver hair, and a fluid, alien way of moving that was less *Lord of the Rings* sexy than intensely creepy.

Fey, I thought blankly.

I wonder what they're doing here.

And then one of them pulled a spear out of some contraption on his back. And stood over one of the writhing couples on the riverbank. And brought it down in a savage move that skewered the two of them with a single thrust, like a human shish kebab.

"Oh*shit*!" Pritkin said, more confidently that time.

My thoughts exactly.

The diddling duo shattered and then evaporated into mist, and I started wading madly for shore. Which would have been easier if fake Pritkin hadn't decided to come, too, still trying to kiss my neck. And if this whole damned country wasn't covered in moss.

Real Pritkin murmured something seductively while trying to help me up off my ass. "No!" I said, with feeling.

"No?" he repeated, as if wondering what this new word was.

"No!" I grabbed his head and turned it toward the fey. Who had fanned out and were now systematically butchering illusions left and right.

"Oh*shit*," Pritkin breathed, as another brutal blow scattered a squirming duo to the winds.

"That should be our motto," I muttered, and scrambled for the bank.

At least I did until he grabbed my arm, saying something I couldn't understand. But it became a little clearer when he started pulling me farther into the water. Which made no sense, no damned sense at all, because I'd just spotted some fey on the other bank, too. At least four or five who were busily turning carnal into carnage, and we needed to *go*.

But Pritkin at twenty, or whatever the hell he was, was just as stubborn as the man I knew. And a second later I decided that maybe he had a point, and not just because he was about to pull my arm out of its socket. But because one of the fey on top of the ridge had spotted us.

And I guess we weren't looking sufficiently amorous anymore. Because he broke off from the rest and started heading down the bank straight for us. I had an instant to see my panicked expression in his shiny, shiny armor—

And then Pritkin threw himself at me, just as something flashed by us, blindingly bright, like the blaze of sunlight off a car window. And the patch of water where we'd been standing a second ago erupted into a geyser of steam. We both stopped to look at it, and then at the stuff around us, which had gone from straight-off-the-mountains chilly to lava. And then we leapt for the bank, because the threat of being boiled alive tends to end arguments pretty damned quick.

Not that things were looking a lot more survivable on land. The three fey I'd seen must have been a vanguard, because there were double that many now. And more were coming over the ridge every second, like they were sprouting out of the damned ground. And then another flash of something flew by, missing us despite the fact that the closest fey couldn't have been more than a dozen yards away.

But it didn't miss the bank we were trying to scale.

Half of it suddenly exploded out at us in an eruption of flying, stinging dirt. It felt like a mortar had hit right in front of us, ripping Pritkin's hand out of mine and catapulting me backward through the air onto my bruised butt. Leaving me half stunned from the landing and half blind from the dirt and almost completely suffocated from the amount of Wales I'd just inhaled.

And then it happened again, to my left. And then to my right. And all I could think, in the middle of what felt like a combo of mortar barrage and an earthquake, was that the fey didn't aim any better than I did.

Of course, I could be wrong, I thought, when I felt something whoosh by my head. But this time it wasn't weapons fire or spell fire or whatever kind of fire they were throwing around. It wasn't a weapon at all.

It was a boot.

Followed by another one.

Followed by a whole stampede of them, along with the guys in them, who *ran right by me* as if I weren't even there.

For a second, I just froze, confused and half blind, with my eyes full of grit and a dirt cloud hovering in the air. But twenty-twenty vision isn't necessary to see your own hand in front of your face. And I couldn't.

I couldn't see anything.

Only no, that wasn't quite true. I waggled my fingers and saw a vague ripple in the air, not a hand so much as a hand-shaped void where there was no dust. But that was really good enough, wasn't it, I thought, and slammed back down as some more fey ran my way.

This bunch should have seen me. Even glamouried or whatever Pritkin had done to hide us, because they were *right there*. Literally right on top of me in the case of one of them. Who didn't go by so much as over, leaping through the air above my head in a move an Olympic long-jumper would have envied.

And then kept right on going with the rest of them, in huge strides that looked more like a bouncy antelope should be making them than anything human. But then, they weren't human, were they? As they demonstrated by eating up the ground even weighed down by all that armor, tearing down the beach after—

Shit!

I'd flipped over as soon as they passed, scanning the ground for a ripple of nothingness that might be a disguised incubus-in-training. But I didn't find one. Maybe because instead of hiding, he was tear-assing down the embankment just ahead of the fey, a colorless, Pritkin-shaped void that was all too visible because he was moving, displacing the dust in a long streamer behind him. Which might as well have been a red flag to a bull, because the fey were—

"No!" I screamed, as what looked like a glowing spear tore through the space where Pritkin's body was outlined, erupting clear through the middle of the torso—

And then kept on going.

I stared in confusion as it exploded against a tree, sending it up like a Roman candle, while the Pritkin void it had just skewered simultaneously shattered, sending dust flying in all directions, like a sand-based firework.

But that was it. There was no body, visible or otherwise. One of the fey extended a booted foot to press into the pile of wet sand at their feet, but all it did was give further evidence that their prey wasn't there.

Because he was here.

A nearby lump of earth was suddenly thrown back like a rug, and Pritkin's full-color head stuck out. It was a little wild-eyed and a little sand-filled and more than a little red-faced, but very much alive. Like the rest of him, which emerged a second later and grabbed my hand, and then we were running in the opposite direction—

Right at an even bigger group of fey coming down the riverbank.

That would have been bad enough, even with a glamourie. But the one Pritkin had used to hide us had vanished. And then the fey caught sight of us, because of course they did—we were just standing there out in the open like a couple of crazy people!

A second later, those glowing spears were flashing into hands all around and my hand was tightening on Pritkin's, because screw this, I'd rather deal with Cherries!

Only I wasn't going to be.

Because my power didn't work.

I tried again, and then again. But the result was the same, because I was still too tapped out from the massive shift it had taken to get here. And it didn't look like Pritkin had another glamourie in him based on his expression, which was a little frantic and a little desperate and a lot scared.

And then amorous and passionate and naughty, in turns, as three more Pritkins suddenly ran past us, chasing three more Cassies. Followed quickly by maybe a dozen more. And then a second dozen, and maybe a third for all I could tell—I didn't have time to count them. But there were a lot.

Because Pritkin might not be able to make more glamouries right now, but he didn't need to, did he?

He had a whole crowd of them already.

A crowd we were now in the middle of.

Suddenly, instead of standing alone and exposed on the riverbank, we were surrounded by a large group of carnal clones. Half of whom were still trying to have sex with the other half, and the rest who were looking with lascivious intent at the fey. It was like Woodstock had come to Wales.

Until they broke, scattering in all directions, and we broke along with them. And I guess even fey eyesight had a problem telling one of those jiggling, bouncing, shrieking duos apart. Because they scattered, too, running after us, only that was the collective "us," leaving only a couple on the right trail.

But a couple was more than enough, so we ran, too, straight down the bank and into the carnage. On all sides, fey were systematically slaughtering every happy humper they came across, including the ones wearing my face. I had the surreal sight of my own severed head bouncing back down the incline before it popped like a balloon filled with steam.

And then we were into the trees and under cover.

Chapter Eighteen

Running through a forest naked is not fun. Running through it naked with homicidal crazies after you, throwing energy blasts that turn trees into stinging rain, is terrifying. Although it really helps you to ignore the whipping branches lashing your skin and the stones bruising your feet and the fact that bark hurts like a bitch when you run into it.

But we pelted full speed ahead anyway, trying to get as far as possible while the fey were preoccupied. And it looked like we just might make it, because the fakes didn't have adrenaline on their side, which slowed them down and made them easier targets. But that also meant they weren't going to last long.

Which was why I pulled back hard when Pritkin suddenly broke to the left.

"No, no—this way!" I told him, because I didn't know Wales, but I knew enough to run *away* from the fire.

But Pritkin wasn't listening to me, which would probably be true even if he could have understood, because "stubborn" wasn't the guy's middle name, it was his whole philosophy of *life*, and that was usually really irritating but was now about to get us *killed*.

Like when a tree burst apart nearby, sending fiery limbs and pieces of trunk everywhere. And would have sent them into us if we hadn't thrown ourselves behind an even bigger one. And then I stopped arguing and just ran, because anything was better than here!

We pelted behind the mill and then kept on going, splashing through the river, back toward where Pritkin had been when I first saw him. We were too close to the general mayhem for comfort, and the wind was blowing smoke the other way, making us a lot more visible suddenly. But at least most of the fey were on the other bank, since the ones on this side had waded across in an attempt to catch us.

And right now, if I never saw another fey, it would be too soon.

I finally figured out where we were going when we reached the ghillie suit and Pritkin's abandoned clothes. I was surprised that an incubus would be shy, but maybe finding a place to hide would be easier if we weren't flashing the natives. Only Pritkin wasn't getting dressed. Pritkin was searching around under the clothes and then throwing them aside, looking increasingly frantic. And then spotting something off to the side, something that was half buried by weeds, something that looked a lot like—

"A stick?" I stared at the ugly thing, which was a homelier version of Rosier's walking stick. Except it must have fallen into a fire at some point, because it was not only cracked and missing part of one end, but also charred almost black. Only Pritkin was gripping it like it was made of pure gold. "We came back for *that*?"

Pritkin saw my expression and shook his head. And said a bunch of rapid-fire stuff that I couldn't understand. And then thrust the thing at me, along with its coating of mud, which he was wiping away as his finger ran along its length, tracing a line of—

Well, I guess it was writing, only it wasn't anything I could read. It wasn't even in an alphabet I recognized, more rune-y, all hard, sharp angles and deep, angry lines. At least they looked angry to me, but maybe I was projecting.

"We could have been half a mile away by now!" I whispered furiously.

But Pritkin was shaking his head again. And gesturing at the opposite side of the river. And then back at the stick. And then back at the river.

Or no, I finally realized as light belatedly dawned.

Not at the river.

At the creatures on the other side of it.

"You . . . you stole their . . . you stole their *stick*?" I asked, incredulous.

But of course, Pritkin didn't understand.

So I gestured at them. And then at the stick. And then at him, and —

And he was nodding and smiling. *Smiling.*

"Are you crazy?"

Okay, less smiling now. And more of hand clenching on said useless piece of —

"Give it back!"

But Pritkin wasn't going to give it back. I didn't need to be fluent in whatever they spoke in sixth-century Wales to know that. It was in the line of his jaw, the glint in his eye . . . the way he suddenly took off running.

Goddamnit!

I ran after him, and actually managed to tackle him because he'd suddenly hit the dirt — why, I didn't know. Until I looked up. And saw a couple fey sauntering by the bank above, not rushing, almost casual. Like they were taking an afternoon stroll, enjoying the forest fire.

And coming within a couple yards of us.

God, I thought wildly, I'd never been so grateful for weeds in my *life*.

We waited, motionless, until they'd passed by, a minute lasting what felt like an hour. And then another minute, Pritkin tense and alert, fingers digging into my arm where he gripped me, breathing fast but quiet. Because yeah, this side wasn't so deserted, after all.

And then we ran up the bank and across the patchy undergrowth at the top, across a terrifying open space and then into another tree line on the far side. Where we stopped, breathing hard and listening. But there was nothing — nothing except the distant crackle of fire, the chirrup of a pissed-off bird, and the sigh of the wind through the treetops.

And the almost silent footfalls of another fey we hadn't seen, not until we ended up practically right on top of him.

Pritkin slammed us back against a tree, but it was too late. The fey had seen us, and the next moment, the canteen in his hand hit the dirt, and a glowing spear replaced it. And I tried to shift, tried hard, because it was now or never.

But it wasn't happening. I was too exhausted or too freaked out, or probably a combination of both, and did it matter when we were about to be roasted alive?

But then something changed in the air around us, something powerful. It felt like a rush of wind, but not like the kind that was tossing the treetops around. But hot, hot, almost searing, like something straight off a desert. Yet it managed to send a wash of goose bumps shivering up my body anyway, furling my nipples and wrenching a cry from my throat.

And I suddenly noticed something else weird.

The fact that the fey was just standing there.

It wasn't because he didn't see us. He was looking right at us, lit spear in hand, only he wasn't throwing it. He wasn't doing anything, in fact, except blinking. And then casting a quick glance over his shoulder.

But there was no one there. And when he turned his attention back on us, the spear abruptly faded out of sight. Because he thought we were a couple of happy, naked hippies, I realized, one of the fakes he'd been destroying for the last fifteen minutes along with his buddies.

Only his buddies weren't here now. And he was hot and probably tired. And suddenly seemed a lot less interested in continuing the wild-goose chase than in . . .

Than in watching the show, I realized, my heart beginning to pound.

Pritkin's hand abruptly clenched on my thigh.

His back was to the tree trunk; mine was to him. So I couldn't see his face. But I didn't need it.

I didn't need it to know that he was giving me the choice.

The body behind me was tense, the arms flexed, prepared for a contest if it came to it. And for all I knew, Pritkin could take a single fey. My Pritkin could have.

But this wasn't my Pritkin. And this one didn't have hundreds of years of fighting experience. Or weapons. And after everything, his magic had to be redlining if it wasn't already there.

And even if he managed it, even if he won, he might well lose, because this place was crawling with fey. If this one got off a single cry, we'd have another dozen down on us in a moment, and we couldn't handle that. We couldn't handle half of that.

I slowly reached up and put a hand behind Pritkin's neck.

The fey picked up his canteen and leaned against a tree.

And another rush of sensation flooded over my body like a warm tidal wave.

A callused hand found my breast, and the breeze blowing across the water became a warm, dragging caress. It smoothed down my stomach, and the dappled light sifting through the treetops hit my skin like golden coins, holding warmth and weight. It dipped between my thighs, and the light burst apart into a thousand individual suns.

My hair was all in my face; the fey couldn't have seen much of my expression. Which was just as well. Because I doubt stunned disbelief was the expected response when Pritkin began to explore, gently at first, questing, searching. And then becoming more assertive as he learned what made me shiver. And shudder. And arch back, a flood of goose bumps cascading up and down my body.

I cried out, and the forest shattered around us. Colors, already brilliant in the lead-up to sunset, exploded like strobes were behind them. They flooded into the air like mist; blues shimmered, greens were slick and wet, golds *hurt*. And they all sent spikes and waves of pleasure everywhere they touched, soaking into my skin, making the treetops whirl in a kaleidoscope of sensation and emotion and—

And it was too much. I cried out, writhing back against him, and would have fallen except for the hands on my body. Their grip tightened, holding me up when I would have drowned in sensation, drowned and not cared because God, and help, and please, and *God*.

And then a new hand gripped me, wrenching me away. Throwing me to the ground while my head was still spinning, my body was still shuddering, spell-induced euphoria making me laugh. Laugh even when I was kicked over onto my back, when my legs were pried apart, when a face I didn't know hovered over mine—

And was suddenly jerked back.

By the staff in Pritkin's hands, the one he'd slipped around the fey's throat.

But the man—the fey—wasn't trying to get away. He wasn't attempting to throw Pritkin off. He wasn't doing anything I'd have expected while his face reddened and his eyes popped and his tongue began to swell.

Because he was still coming for me.

And he continued to come, to reach, to claw, even as I sobered up, sobered up fast, and scrambled back out of reach, sweating and shivering and staring—

But not as much as when he suddenly blinked and stared around, disoriented, his hands coming up to grasp the stick. Which almost immediately began to move away from his neck because the fey were strong; they were so damned strong. And then I was back on my feet, breathing hard, unsure how to help, before scrambling for the fey's discarded pack, hoping for a knife—

Which I didn't get. Because another wave of incubus power hit, as Pritkin struggled to reestablish control. And this one was less like a fist than a freight train, sending me back to the ground, writhing under a wash of sensation too strong for pleasure, too euphoric for pain.

The next few seconds were a blur of contradictory images: The fey's lust-filled face hovering over mine, once more focused and determined. The grass licking my skin, like a thousand tiny tongues. The sound of the carnage across the river, cries and screams and shouted commands. The smell of wood smoke, rich and pungent.

The crunch of neck bones, soft and subtle, but as loud as a gunshot in my ears.

I wasn't sure—I was never sure—if Pritkin had done it. Or if the fey had done it himself by pushing against the restraint, still reaching out as he toppled over, the purple face still staring, the dead eyes still wide and fixed—

On me.

And even with the muffling effect of the spell, it was too much. I felt a scream building, felt it clawing its way up my throat, felt Pritkin pull me back against him, his hand over my mouth, his lips whispering something I couldn't hear and wouldn't have understood if I did, probably *don't scream, don't scream, don't scream* in whatever language they spoke here.

But I was doing it anyway, almost soundlessly against the pressure of his palm, screaming and screaming and screaming, even as he dragged me away, deeper into the forest.

Only that didn't work too well with the trees shaking all around me, like someone using a camcorder who doesn't know how. But you can steady a camcorder, and I couldn't seem to steady myself. Or to stop the sensory overload or whatever had me suddenly able to taste colors and smell sounds and touch light and shadow as if they were tangible things.

Pritkin pulled me through an Alice in Wonderland–type forest filled with familiar things that suddenly made no sense: trees recognizable only by their height, ground just a huge thing that tilted under my feet like a carnival ride, sky an expanse so immense I couldn't look at it, couldn't look, not without feeling like I might fall into it and go mad.

Only I was sort of feeling that way anyway.

And instead of better, the sensory distortion was getting worse, and getting worse fast, along with a gut-twisting craving I couldn't identify, but that had my hands shaking and my skin chilling one second and flushing hotly the next. I looked at my hand and thought I could see actual steam rising from it, an orange-red haze so bright, so bright against the darkened forest that I could only stare.

The branches that we pushed through lashed my body like a hundred little whips. They painted my skin with lines of fire, hot and peppery. Until the sound, the taste, the scent of them swirled up around me with every new stroke, leaving me writhing under their pain-filled touch in a different sort of ecstasy.

Pritkin stopped abruptly, and I ran into him. And discovered that I hadn't known ecstasy at all. My front connected with his back, and he felt so good, so good I couldn't believe it. All the other impressions faded, leaving just this: just smooth, warm, rigid, flexing under my hands. Salt under my tongue. Musk in my nose from the sweat I was still trying to lick off when somebody pulled me away, when somebody else wrapped me in a coat, when they separated us.

Pritkin was cursing. I couldn't understand the words, but the sounds spoke right to my brain, like the sounds of scuffling. He was fighting them; who was he fighting? I didn't know, couldn't tell. Just knew that I missed him, that I needed to get back to him, that I had to touch—

I found him again—I have no idea how. I was all but blind, my eyes working but not seeing, my senses so overwhelmed they had practically shorted out, my head reeling and steps faltering—

Until I touched him. And suddenly, everything made sense again. He was still trying to talk, to say something, whether to me or to them I didn't know, but it was a problem with my tongue down his throat. I didn't care. He tasted good; he tasted like life, and sanity and steadiness. Where my hands touched him, they felt almost normal, except for this weird sensation that they were sinking into his chest, merging with it. But that was fine, too. I wanted to merge with him, wanted to sink inside, wanted—

Hands wrenched me away, a physical pain. Harsh voices sounded in my ears, but I didn't understand. And then someone stopped in front of me, pulling my face up to the light, but I couldn't see anything; my eyes had gone crazy again. They kept trying to taste things, and that wasn't right . . . was it?

"See what happens when you play around with time, girl?" a terse voice asked. And then the hands were pulling me farther away, and I was starting to panic, and fight to get back, slipping out of the coat and out of their grip, and running—

For a second. Until they caught me, and wrestled me back, and someone said, "Enough of this!"

And then there was a light.

And then there was nothing.

Chapter Nineteen

I woke up in what I guessed was the Pythian Court, since I was pretty sure Gertie was the one who'd just snatched me out of Wales. Pretty sure, but not certain, because Pritkin's spell was still in full force. And right then, I couldn't be certain of anything.

But I came around on a chaise in a small, dark room. It had garnet curtains with pompom fringe, an open door with light spilling in, and people talking in heated but hushed voices outside. And some wallpaper, some terrible, terrible stripy wallpaper that I fell into before I could decipher what they were saying, and then couldn't get back out of again.

Every which way I turned there was another line, shooting up immensely high, into the sky. Like the tallest of trees in a strange forest. And for some reason that thought made me panic and run, and get even further entangled in the never-ending jungle of lines, like bars on a cage, like poles on a merry-go-round, like light posts flashing by in a long, steady line. . . .

The carriage stopped.

Which surprised me since I hadn't realized I'd been in one.

Someone pulled me out, onto the sidewalk by one of the light posts, and I stumbled into it. I couldn't catch myself because my hands were cuffed behind me. Someone else gripped my arm, steadying me, and tried to say something, but he was cut off by voices from several sides.

It didn't matter. I couldn't concentrate on the voices. I couldn't concentrate on anything.

Because whenever I did, it was terrifying.

A monster twisted its neck around to look at me, a horrible, elongated thing, like something out of a nightmare. Its massive curve filled half the street, along with a head full of flaring nostrils and enormous teeth. And rolling eyes that stared at me, before it gave an awful, whinnying roar, like it was laughing at my terror—

"Get her away from the horse!" someone said, and I was jerked back, screaming.

And was then marched down the sidewalk in the middle of a crowd of people I didn't look at, was afraid to look at. I just stared at the sidewalk instead, a boring stretch of brick that even my messed-up brain couldn't seem to do anything with. And at the feet of the guards or whoever they were, marching alongside me in their black, black boots.

The boots started to leave tarry footprints on the stones, like rubber on a hot day melting in the sun, even though it wasn't day. I knew that because we kept passing under streetlamps that threw circles of light onto the sticky footprints. And then onto pools of melted leather as the boots began to dissolve, first into puddles, then into holes that opened up in the perfectly uniform brick, deep and dark and—

The sidewalk swallowed a guard.

It just opened up and gobbled him down between one second and the next, I was sure of it. But no one else seemed to notice he was gone, no one else seemed to *notice*, and what if I was next? What if—

A surge of panic hit, and I tried to run, in a burst of speed that got me nowhere. Because the coat I was wearing again tripped me and arms caught me, and I was twisting and fighting and I must have hit someone, because a voice cursed. And someone else asked a question I didn't hear.

"Damned if I know!" the first voice said. "Just get her inside. Sooner she's put away, the better!"

And then I was thrown over someone's shoulder, and

carried down an alley and up some rickety wooden stairs, and into a hallway. It was dim, too, almost dark, with just a few patches of diffuse light from above giving any illumination at all. But even that was too much.

Because there were posters on the walls, most small, more like flyers, others as large as a newspaper page. But almost all of them contained faces, sneering, jeering, hateful faces that seemed to leap off the walls, yelling and threatening, or rattling the bars of the cells many of them seemed to be in, trying to get at me. And some weren't even human.

A large Were leapt out of a page and into the hall, snapping at me with huge, slavering jaws, causing me to shriek and twist away and end up on the floor when the man carrying me lost his grip.

I leapt to my feet, in a crouch, panting, looking for the threat—

Which was suddenly gone.

I stared around in panicked confusion, not sure where to go or what was real. Someone had hit one of the hanging lights, and the dim circle strobed the small corridor, making the gallery of horrors that much more terrifying. They all seemed to be coming for me now, a hundred ghostly hands stretching impossibly long, reaching, reaching, reaching—

Until one of them jerked back with a curse. "The bawd bit me!"

"What do you expect?" someone else asked. "She's off her chump."

"She isn't mad; she's bespelled!" a more familiar voice said, sounding furious. "I would expect a group of magic users to be able to recognize the diff—"

There was a sound of a fist hitting meat.

The voice cut off.

And then I was dragged into a room that branched off the corridor.

It was wood floored and walled, with old gas lights overhead and a large wooden piece of furniture in the middle, like a freestanding counter. There were no posters. But there were two boxes on the counter, black ones the size of shoe boxes that looked familiar, but that I didn't look at too long in case they turned into something else.

I looked back toward the door instead.

And found Rosier standing just behind me, bleeding from the lip.

"It'll wear off," he told me, low-voiced and hurried. "Until then, don't trust your senses. They've been compromised—"

"No shit," I told him thickly, and had the pleasure of seeing him stare.

And then one of the men on the other side of the desk slapped a baton down on it, with a crack that reverberated through my confused brain like a gunshot. "No talking!"

Okay, I thought, trying not to collapse in a heap.

And then someone was stripping the coat off me, but he'd forgotten about the cuffs. So the leather pooled at the ends of my arms and sent me to my knees when he jerked on it. He finally figured it out and released me, so I could sprawl naked on the dirty floor.

I looked up to see another leather coat coming toward me, with one of the boxes in his hand. And Rosier suddenly tried to fight, and then to run, and he seemed really dedicated to the idea. Because it took three of them to wrestle him to the floor as well.

I didn't run.

What was the point?

The sidewalk would just eat me.

And then the lights went out.

It was wonderful.

It was *wonderful*.

I didn't know where I was or how I got here. But suddenly, there was no light, no sound, no anything to provide stimulus for my overheated brain. Just a lot of warm, floaty nothingness, peaceful, calm, allowing me a chance to breathe.

Which made it pretty damned close to paradise.

After a while, I put out a hand but didn't touch anything. I felt around with a toe, but there didn't seem to be anything down there, either. And strain as much as I liked, I still couldn't hear a sound.

That was okay; it gave me time to think.

I thought about taking a nap.

It would be so easy here, to just drift away. . . .

But there was something I needed to do first. Something that scratched at the inside of my head like a persistent fingernail. It was annoying, like an insect I couldn't shoo, or like Rosier when he was talking and talking and —

Rosier.

I needed to find Rosier. And then we needed . . . we needed . . . we had to do something that I couldn't remember right now, and chasing down the memory that skittered around inside my skull sounded like way too much work. But it was important, and Rosier would know what it was.

I had to get to Rosier.

I wondered how.

And the next second, my butt hit a dusty, hardwood floor with a thump.

It was a loud thump, and it hurt like I'd fallen from a height. For a moment I just stayed there, dazed from the shock of the fall, waiting to be grabbed, to be jerked up, to be reimprisoned. But none of that happened.

Possibly because no one was there.

I took stock.

Dirty wooden floor, check. Big, hulking wood thing, check. Rosier — no Rosier. But I was back in what I guessed was the Victorian equivalent of war mage HQ, where I'd been a second ago. Or maybe not a second; I couldn't really tell. But it felt like longer, and my head felt a little clearer.

I realized I was holding a box.

It was black and shiny, the same one they'd imprisoned me in, at a guess. And I'd been right: I had seen ones like it before. The mages used them as magical traps, and as an alternative to coming up with cells for bad girls like me.

Or bad boys.

Slowly, I got into a crouch, and then even more slowly, I poked just my eyeballs over the edge of the wood thing.

There was another box.

It was just sitting there, all alone, out in the open, without even anyone to guard it. And I guess that made a sort of sense. Why worry about people in little boxes? People in little boxes didn't go anywhere.

Well, not usually.

But whether it had to do with mother's blood, or with being Pythia or what, I'd never had any problem opening the things. It had mostly gotten me into trouble before, when I'd let out stuff I wasn't supposed to. Like when I'd ended up rooming for a while with three old women, ancient demigoddesses the Senate had imprisoned and I'd accidentally released.

That had been fun.

I'd spent more than a few moments in those weeks cursing whatever Fate thought it was a laugh to constantly mess with me.

I was sort of okay with it now.

Now I just had to let out Rosier.

Which would have been a lot easier if another man hadn't just come in from the hall.

He was big and brown-haired and bearded, and dressed like a war mage. I'd just stood up when he banged the door open and I spun around and stared at him. For a moment, we just stayed like that, me with my back to the counter, my box hidden behind my leg, and him with his coat half off, water rolling off the waxed leather to puddle at his feet.

And then he blinked and finished taking off his coat.

"If this is Cavendish's idea of a birthday surprise, I approve," he told me, hanging the coat on a rack. And revealing a Victorian-era version of Pritkin's war mage getup of potion belts and holsters, guns and knives. But he didn't draw any of them, or even look particularly concerned.

Maybe he didn't find a blond naked chick all that intimidating.

His eyes went over me, and a slight smile broke out behind his beard. "It'll be hard to top this come November," he told me. "If I do the same for him, the poor gel'll freeze!"

I didn't say anything.

"What do you have behind your back, little one?" he asked, finally noticing my awkward stance.

I shook my head and still didn't speak.

"Oh, come now. You can show me." He came toward me, face cracking into a full-on grin. "You can show me anything you like."

So I did.

And then the room was empty again, and the box didn't even feel heavier.

I clutched it.

I really liked this box.

His coat was still dripping onto the floor where he'd left it. I went over and put it on. It was huge on me, even bigger than the last one, and it didn't have any weapons in it. But I still felt better.

I'd been a naked chick with a box.

Now I was a clothed chick with a box.

That's what you call progress.

I grabbed the second box off the counter and fled.

Back through the door into the hall, back through the gallery of monsters, who still tweaked and flinched a little as I passed, but no longer tried to leap out of their wanted posters to claw at me. Back through the door, which wasn't locked, because who locks the front door of a police station? Even a supernatural one? And then back into the narrow alleyway, which had turned into a narrow, brick-lined, water-filled canal, because it was bucketing down outside.

I stopped abruptly.

I might just as well have run straight into hell.

Rain pelted me in stinging silver lines that burst on my skin, hissing and fizzing like miniature comets. Lightning flashed like fireworks overhead, illuminating the street and making all the shadows grow and writhe. I stared around, seeing van Gogh's *Starry Night* come to life if you added a few Goya monsters in the corners, and I suddenly wondered if either of them had known an incubus.

And then thunder hit, practically on top of me, crashing like a nuclear blast inside my skull, until it was all I could do not to start screaming again.

I slammed back inside, put my back to the door, and then just stayed there, shuddering and shaking and breathing hard.

And realizing just how much of a mess I was in.

I couldn't go out. I couldn't stay here. I couldn't shift, might never be able to shift again, the way I felt, which meant they were going to find me. They were going to find me any minute and lock me up, because the trap might not work, but they'd find something that did. I knew war mages well enough to know that, and I didn't have that kind of time; I didn't have any—

I didn't have any.

Boots hit a wooden floor, coins jingled in a pocket, and the smell of a cigar, sweet and pungent, teased the air. And then a cry from inside the room I'd just left: "They're gone!"

And I was slamming back into the rain-drenched hell outside, leaping off the wooden landing, and scurrying under the stairs, just before three guys burst out of the door behind me, the rattling of boards over my head as they descended almost worse than the thunder.

But in a way, that was good. Because I was so preoccupied with the drum, drum, drumming in my head that I forgot to react. I don't think I so much as flinched when brilliant lights illuminated the outside of the building a second later, or when an alarm began blaring inside, muffled but still distinct this close, or when more thundering feet tore out of the door, calling instructions to each other.

Or when a man stopped, right over the top of my head.

And just stayed there.

I felt my heartbeat, which had already been pretty fast, edge into the danger zone. All he had to do was look down. The area under the stairs was dark, but light from above striped it like Gertie's damned wallpaper.

I could see the soles of his boots through the slats of wood, scuffed and worn but still solid. Like the bulk of him, heavy enough to make the boards groan when he shifted weight from foot to foot, although that could have been because of all the hardware he was wearing. Hardware I didn't have, because I didn't have anything, not anything, just a soaking-wet coat and a shivering body and a couple of—

My breathing, which had picked up speed to match my heart-attack-in-progress, suddenly caught in my throat.

And then slowly, so freaking slowly, my hand felt around the water-slick bricks beneath me. And pulled my box out from under my left leg, where it had somehow ended up. And began to raise it, trying to keep it out of the light, so that the shiny surface didn't reflect anything.

Like the flash that suddenly flared across my vision, like a small red sun.

It dropped, rattling against the boards overhead. And then fell through a crack between two of them. And splashed in the mud in front of me.

Because the guy had stopped to light a cigar and had just dropped his lighter.

I looked up, in heart-clenching panic, and met a pair of narrowed blue eyes looking down. For all of a second, before the man's face flushed and his mouth started to open. And I jammed a corner of the box against the underside of his shoe.

And then sat back against the building with my eyes closed, and just concentrated on breathing for a minute.

I could feel the mud squelching beneath me, and the rain coursing down the spaces between the bricks onto my back. But the coat was waterproof, and I wasn't standing in a lashing torrent, so my brain seemed to be able to handle it. Like the box in my hands, which was smooth and shiny and slick, but also solid and unchanging. Reassuring.

Like Rosier's presence would be right now, strange as that sounded.

He'd lived through this era; he'd know what to do.

Assuming I could find him.

I looked around, my heart back in my throat, where it should just stay and save me some effort, I thought viciously. And then I felt it, the other box, hidden under a fold of the coat, where I'd dropped it and then sat on it. I hugged it to my chest in dizzying relief.

And a second later, I was hugging the guy who popped out of it and onto the street beside me, which would have been great, which would have been awesome.

Except he wasn't Rosier.

Chapter Twenty

For a second, I looked at him and he looked at me, a small wiry guy with a patchy reddish beard and abundant acne. And then he took off, scrambling out from under the stairs and into the blaze of light in the alley, which seemed to confuse him. He stopped, dropped into a crouch, and looked around wildly, this way and that. And then abruptly took off again, running toward the street.

Only to stop after a few strides, because that way was blocked. War mages had clustered in the opening to the bigger road, leather-coated bulks of solidity that were fortunately facing the street, not us, at the moment. But that could change any second, as the guy seemed to realize. He swung back around, only to find himself facing the building that constituted the other end of the alley, with bricked-up windows and no convenient fire escape.

Well, that's why I'm still sitting here, I thought, as he joined me again.

"Wot's all this?" he asked, gesturing around.

"War mages looking for me."

"Why? Wot you do?"

"Nothing."

"Wot a coincidence," he told me. "I 'ave also been maliciously persecuted and unfairly detained."

"How about that."

He looked at the box I'd just let him out of, which I was

currently shaking. And turning upside down. And beating on the bottom of, like a stubborn ketchup bottle, only nothing else came out.

"Wot's that?"

"Nothing."

"Naw, now that's not right, is it?" he asked. "That's not nuffing. That's one of them traps the Circle uses on people. I oughter know!"

"Yes. Yes, it is," I said, frowning at it. And then beating on it some more, not that it seemed to help.

"Wot's in there, then?"

"Nothing," I said, looking up at him in frustration.

"You like that word, don't ya?" He tilted his head to the side. "But if there's nuffing in it, why are you bothering wi' it?"

"Because there's supposed to be something in it! Or someone."

"Like who?"

"Like a demon."

"A demon?" The man looked me over again, assessing. "Wot you doin' with one o' them?"

"Nothing right now!" I glared at the mages at the end of the street. "They switched boxes on me. He isn't in here!"

"Well, o' course he in't," Red told me. "They never put no demons in those."

I blinked. "What?"

"Naw, why would they? When they c'n just ring up the old demon council, tell 'em to come pick up their wayward boy?"

"The . . . council?"

He nodded. "The Corps patrols *humans*, which demons ain't. They got a treaty with the council. Says if one o' their kind gets out o' line, the Corps calls 'em up, and they come for 'em. Unless the demon makes 'em mad in the meantime, and he 'dies trying ter escape,' wot has been know ter—"

He broke off when my nails sank into his wrist. "Where would they keep him?"

"Wot?"

"The demon! Where would they keep him until the council comes for him?"

"In maximum security, most like. They don't like demons."

"And where is that?"

The guy looked upward. "Top floor, but you'll never get in."

"Why not?"

" 'Cause I'm going to have that coat, ain't I?" he asked, and I suddenly realized he was holding something out at me.

It was a knife. A small pocket variety, which he seemed to have pulled out of nowhere. "How did you get a knife in there?" I asked, looking from him to the box.

"The Circle don't know everyfing, does it? Now hand it over."

"What?"

"The coat!"

"Why?" I looked at him. "You've got a coat."

And he did. It was a pretty nice one for a thief, being thick wool and fairly new. In fact, it looked better than mine.

"It looks better than mine," I pointed out.

"It ain't the looks I care 'bout, is it?"

"What, then?"

"You never mind! You just give it—"

"Get your hands off me or I'll scream."

"You scream, 'n they'll be down on the both of us!"

"Which would be inconvenient for you, wouldn't it?"

He glared at me. But the hand on the front of my coat loosened. And then dropped away entirely, because he really didn't seem to want to deal with the war mages again.

I could sympathize.

"Tell me what you want it for, and maybe I'll give it to you," I offered.

He scowled. And then his eyes narrowed. "Maybe we could work together, at that."

"How?"

"That's a big coat. Too big for a little girl like you. Big enough for two maybe, if we work it right."

"Why would we want to do that?"

" 'Cause it gets us inside the wards, don't it?"

I looked up at the door, which was still slightly open from where the mage had left it. "There aren't any wards."

"Not on the door," he said impatiently. "The *inner* wards. The ones they got on the upper floors. The ones on all the 'spensive and dangerous things they steal from people like you 'n me."

I didn't know how I felt about being lumped in with the criminal element, but at the moment I couldn't really argue the point.

"The coat gets you through those?"

He nodded. "'Course, it don't usually matter. Too many war mages prowling around for it to matter. More a time-saving device for them than anythin' else." He looked over his shoulder. "But seems like you got 'em all riled up. Seems like you got most of 'em out combing the streets for you. Which means there's a skeleton crew in there, and that means—"

He jumped me. And the next thing I knew, my back was against his chest, and his knife was pressing against my throat. Hard enough that, if I screamed, I'd slice my own windpipe.

"—this is my main chance," he hissed in my ear.

"I thought we were going to work together," I said, very carefully.

"You know that old sayin' about honor 'tween thieves?"

I nodded.

"I ain't never had no truck with it."

I tapped him in the leg with the trap.

"Neither have I," I said.

And a second later I was up the stairs and back into HQ.

The place was *not* deserted. There were people everywhere. *Everywhere.* It looked like our little escape had put them on high alert, and that meant halls packed with every war mage in the place.

And that went double for the stairs.

They only ones I saw were at the far end of the entrance hall, almost lost in gloom. Of course, I thought, before dodging into a side room to avoid being seen. And then slowly starting down the hall, throwing up the hood on the coat and ducking into more rooms whenever anyone started my way, praying there was nobody in them.

There wasn't.

Maybe because they looked like the sort of administrative offices any police department needs, and which closed in time for everyone to get home for dinner. There was also a library, filled with musty old books but no readers, and the Victorian version of a break room, complete with a fireplace, a few scarred old tables, and some dented tea-making things. And a hand-lettered sign, in ornate Victorian script: PLEASE RETURN SOILED DISHES TO BASEMENT FOR WASHING UP.

I looked at it. And then I looked out the door at the stairs, which were momentarily empty. And then I ran for them, scurrying down the hall silently—bare feet are good for something, after all—and reached the landing without anyone screaming for my head. But I didn't go up, because I wouldn't have made it one flight.

I went down.

Like most basements, this one was dank and dark and ugly. And filled with things like a belching furnace, a bunch of old furniture, and a pyramid of barrels piled in a corner almost ceiling high. But it also had a small area reserved for a kitchen, which, judging by the part of the floor that was tiled, had originally been much larger.

It didn't surprise me. The place had a converted house feel to it, with the kind of small touches that a police force, even an unusual police force, wouldn't have bothered with. Like the mahogany paneling in the library. And the curlicues on the bannisters and stair railings. And the quality of the wood floors, which were scuffed and weathered now, especially in the main hall, but which had been inlaid with a delicate border design at some time in the past.

And if this had once been a gentleman's residence, it should have an item, one of the must-haves of the nineteenth century. One my old governess had often bewailed the lack of in the farmhouse where I grew up, because it meant she had to go down to the kitchen to make her evening tea. And sure enough, the remnants of the kitchen area had a sink, some shelves, a huge old iron stove it looked like nobody ever used . . .

And a dumbwaiter set into a wall.

A huge grin broke out on my face.

And then faded as soon as I realized two things; it was small, like really small, and it was hand-cranked.

Well, *crap.*

I thought about it for a second, biting my lip, but there was just no choice. There might be another way upstairs, but I didn't have time to find it. If the demon council reached Rosier before I did . . .

I didn't think it would be a good idea for them to reach him before I did.

So I let Red out.

"Ha!" he said, slashing at me with his little knife, making me jump back.

And smack him in the arm with the trap.

He winked out, and I leaned against the wall, kicking my heels against the water-stained plaster for a few minutes.

I let him out again.

"Ha!" he said, and lunged for me.

Back inside he went.

I tapped my toe, wishing I had shoes. The floor was like ice, and it was leeching my body heat. I started trading off feet, so at least one stayed warm, and waited another few minutes.

"Are we going to keep this up all night?" Red asked when I let him out again.

"That's up to you. I need your help. In return, I'll help you."

"How?" He crossed his skinny arms and sneered at me.

"I need to get upstairs, to get my partner back. But the stairs are full of mages. I'll never make it."

"Not as a twist," he agreed.

"What?"

"A twist and twirl."

"What?"

He rolled his eyes. "A *girl*. There's no women in the Corps. Everybody knows that."

"There have to be a few."

"I ain't never seen one. And I think I'd a' noticed." He leered at me.

"So, like I *said*, I can't get up the stairs—"

"But I bet I could," he said eagerly. "You give me the coat and I'll get yer man out—yer demon. You 'ave my word."

It was my turn to roll my eyes. "I have a better idea."

"Then get someone else to help you wi' it, 'cause I got better things ter—"

Back he went.

"Cut that out!" he told me when I released him again, a minute later.

"Then stop wasting my time! We do it my way or not at all, and you can go back in here for good for all I care."

He glared at me sullenly. But he didn't say anything or try to attack me again, so I guessed that was something. "Here's the plan," I told him quickly. "I get into this box—"

"Wot?"

"Don't interrupt me. And then you put it on the dumb-waiter—"

"Wot?"

"I said, no interruptions! And then you crank me up to the top level. The coat will bypass the wards, if they can even read me in here, which I doubt. And then—"

"And then you sit there, 'cause there's nobody ter let you out!"

"I can let myself out."

His eyes abruptly narrowed. "All right. Now I know yer telling me porkies."

"What?"

"Porky pies."

"Do you speak English?"

"Lies! Ain't nobody c'n do that!"

"I can," I said impatiently. "Or if not, I'm about to trap myself in a box in the most secure level of war mage HQ."

He thought about that for a minute. And then his eyes brightened. "Y'know, I know some people who would be real interested—"

"We can talk about that later. Right now, I need you to get me up there."

"And wot do I get?"

"The *coat.* As soon as I'm up, I'll drop it back down the shaft. I won't need it anymore. Then you can see if your run up the stairs works for you or not."

"And how do you get back out, wi' no coat?"

"My demon friend will get me out. He can shift us into the demon realm—"

"Then why ain't he already done it?"

"Because he won't leave me! That's why I have to get to him—he doesn't know I'm out!"

Red mulled this over.

"I'll also need your coat," I added.

His hand closed on the neck. "Fer wot?"

"It's cold."

He just looked at me some more. And then decided he didn't care. He shrugged out of the nice wool number, but caught my arm when I went to grab it. "If you do get out o' here, return it to the Bull and Bollocks. I'll see you don't lose by it."

"What?"

"It's . . ." He looked awkward. "It's just . . . me mum made it fer me, and she's . . . not here anymore, and . . ." He looked at me. "Y'tell anyone I said that, 'n I'll cut yer throat!"

"No, I . . . just never heard that name before," I told him.

"Wot name?"

"The pub name."

"Y' never heard o' the Bull?" He looked astounded.

I shook my head. "Is it any good?"

"Good?" The incredulousness grew. "It's where hope dies, and then sobers up and kicks you in the bollocks. But if yer itchin' fer a job or trying ter lay low, ain't no better place."

"I'll see what I can do," I told him.

He nodded and shrugged out of the coat. And I took a deep breath, wondering for the eighty-seventh time today if I was crazy. And for the eighty-eighth, I decided I really didn't want to know.

"Here goes nothing," I told him. And a second later, the kitchen winked out, and there was only darkness.

Chapter Twenty-one

The dark, dark world of nothingness inside the snare was a lot less comforting this time, maybe because I wasn't quite as punch-drunk. In fact, it was seriously creepy, a noiseless, frictionless, lightless cage that wasn't a cage, since I couldn't even feel any walls around me. I stared at the dark and tried not to imagine that it was staring back.

I assumed that the Circle knocked most people out before they put them in these things, unless they were planning on taking them out shortly for questioning. I stared around some more. And wondered if they ever forgot. And then I wondered if they ever "forgot."

It was more than a little disturbing that I wouldn't be willing to offer odds either way.

But there was nothing to do but wait. And worry, because there was no way to tell time in here. Or to tell if I would "rematerialize," or whatever it was I'd been doing, inside the tiny, tiny space of the dumbwaiter. Because that would be . . . bad. Really bad. Cassie-breaks-every-bone-in-her-body bad. But I hadn't materialized on the table before; I'd hit the ground in front of it, so presumably . . .

I really wished I'd thought of this before.

I really wished an LED clock would light up all this darkness.

I really wished I didn't have to pee.

Damn it!

Finally, I couldn't take it anymore. I scrunched up my eyes, even though there was nothing to see, and concentrated. And fell onto a desk covered with papers, stabby little pencils, and a porcelain vase that rocked back and forth and to and fro and no, no, no, I thought, grabbing it with both hands.

And then breathing a sigh of relief when it didn't fall off.

Well, that's a first, I thought, slightly shocked.

Until a glass paperweight hit the floor behind me, bounced across the boards loud as a cannonball, before smacking into the side of a glass-fronted cabinet.

And shattering it.

Damn it!

I grabbed the box, grabbed Red's coat, and took a flying leap off the desk. And then ran across the room, opened the window, and shoved the box out onto the sill. But it was still visible, so I shoved it onto a nearby stretch of roof instead and hopped out after it. And then dove back into the box, because footsteps were coming this way, and there was no chance they wouldn't see me otherwise.

I sat there, in the dark once again, chewing my nails—if I had nails in here, which I probably didn't, but it felt like I was chewing them.

And waited.

And waited.

And waited.

And damn it, Rosier was going to be dead or back in hell by the time I got to him, because Lara Croft I wasn't. What if I couldn't get back in the window? What if the wards were smarter than a two-bit crook gave them credit for? What if I got attacked by a bunch of crazy-ass birds as soon as I reappeared?

Because the latter actually happened.

There was a huge flock of them, which had decided to take refuge from the storm on the roof where an overhang gave some protection. To them. I had no protection at all, other than what was offered by the coat, which was damned little when I reappeared and startled them. And they rose up in a clawing, flapping, furious cloud all around me, and I suddenly understood why Hitchcock made that stupid movie, which wasn't sounding so stupid anymore.

I didn't scream, but mostly because I couldn't. There

were about a thousand beating wings in my face and feathers up my nose and sharp little bills pecking and sharp little claws digging and I couldn't see and I could barely breathe and any second now I was going to fall off the roof. And *screw* this!

A second later, there were no more birds. Just me and the blowing rain and, okay, one last fat pigeon that must have been out of the box's range and was perched on top of the eaves, staring at me. Before it abruptly flew off, I guess before whatever happened to the others happened to it.

I clutched the box.

And belatedly realized that I'd grabbed the wrong one, the one with the two mages in it. Which now also contained a crap ton of angry birds. But they probably wouldn't interact . . . right?

I peered back in the window. There were a couple of mages still in there picking up the mess but not appearing particularly alarmed. Maybe because it wasn't as bad as I'd thought. The desk was a wreck, but it kind of looked like it might have been anyway, and most of the papers had somehow stayed on top.

One of the guys bent over and grabbed the paperweight, and said something to the other that I couldn't hear because of the storm. But he must have been blaming the wind for the calamity. Because he walked over a second later, forcing me to quickly flatten myself against the side of the building.

Right before the window was firmly shut, leaving me out on a rain-slick roof all by myself in the middle of a thunderstorm.

And still needing to pee.

I looked skyward with my eyes closed, letting the rain hit me in the face for a minute, telling myself to calm down. I didn't want to be Lara Croft, I decided. Lara Croft sucked. I wanted to be home, in a soft bed, with a warm cup of something seriously alcoholic. Like Irish coffee. Yeah. Irish coffee would be really great right now.

But I didn't have an Irish coffee. What I did have, when I opened my eyes, was an empty room beside me, because the mages had left. And, okay, I'd take it.

I finally got the window up enough that I could get a

hand under it, and my body back through it, and my feet onto the slick wood floor. I tiptoed over to the dumb-waiter, because the mages had left the door to the hall slightly open, and was serenaded briefly by some very distinct curses that were starting to float up from far below. At least they were until I stripped off the coat and dropped it down.

The curses stopped. That left me with Red's wool number, which I hadn't needed except I was damned tired of being naked. I pulled it on.

And then I went in search of Rosier.

And this time, I found him.

He was in the middle of a large room, surrounded by a circle of war mages, who were busy doing what they probably called enhanced interrogation and I called torture. He had two eyes so black that it looked like he was wearing a mask, the rest of his face was either red or purple, his nose was seriously off to one side, and his lip was less split than pulverized. I felt my hand come up to my own neck; I didn't know why.

Maybe because I was having trouble breathing.

He had to be.

My other hand clenched on the box.

But there were too many of them and they were too spread out. I'd never manage to trap them all, not before one of them took me out. Or took Rosier out, although they looked like they were well on the way there already. And I didn't have any weapons, and even if I did, I couldn't fight them all. So what did that leave?

Before I could figure it out, Rosier went sprawling, hitting the ground with his hands over his head, trying to ward off the mass of steel-tipped boots that were slamming into him like the fists had been a moment ago. And I felt a wash of pure, cold rage hit me, because he hadn't done anything to them, couldn't have done anything in his current state. Nothing but die.

And that wasn't happening.

I took a half second to memorize his location, and then I pushed open the door. Not a lot, just a couple inches. Just enough to throw in an already opening box.

And this time, I didn't get the wrong one.

A second later, the room all but exploded in caws and screeches and whirling feathers and red demonic eyes. And damn, pigeons were scary up close, particularly when there were about a million of them. I darted into the fluttering mass and suddenly couldn't see—I defy anybody to have seen shit in there—but I knew where Rosier had been, and a second later I grabbed him.

Or I grabbed somebody, anyway. And God, I really hoped it was him. But I kind of thought it was, because instead of cursing me into oblivion, the guy was hitting and kicking and trying to bite. Or maybe that was the birds, because who could tell in here? But I was getting hammered anyway.

Because he couldn't see me.

"It's me! It's Cassie!" I yelled, right in his face—or what I hoped was his face—but it didn't help. Because he couldn't hear me, either.

Hell, *I* couldn't hear me, not in the middle of Birdgeddon. But there was no stopping. Not in a room full of war mages, who any second now were going to deploy some spell I'd never heard of and kill us both.

And they probably would have, except for one thing.

Or make that two things, because I hadn't just released the birds, had I?

And I guessed maybe some interaction had been going on, after all, because suddenly in the middle of the mass of birds was a mass of explosions, a virtual cyclone of curses flung by what I strongly suspected were two formerly trapped and now seriously pissed-off war mages, that caused birds to start dropping like rain.

But the other mages presumably couldn't see any better than I could, and they didn't know those were their buddies, or that they'd just been released from bird hell. They didn't know that the curses were being fired at the *birds*; they assumed they were being fired at *them*. And being war mages, they naturally didn't stop to find out why.

I hit the floor, jerking Rosier down with me, and started crawling through a hail of blood and feathers and sizzling spell fire back the way I'd come in. Because there was no other choice. This must have been a holding cell and had no other doors or windows.

Which meant that there was nowhere for the now seriously panicked flock to go but around and around in a frenzy of fury.

Although surprisingly, that wasn't the main problem, since it was mostly going on above our heads. The problem was the fist to my chin that had my head reeling, and the elbow to my stomach that knocked most of my wind out, and the crazed demon lord who at one point I think was gnawing on my arm.

Until I fished the other trap out of my pocket and smacked him upside the head with it.

And God, that felt good.

And so did being able to scurry ahead, burdened only by the trap that I shoved back into my pocket. A second later, I hit the wall, and a second after that, I found the door and grabbed the handle. And almost got trampled by a bunch of mages flooding in from the hall.

Damn it!

I jerked back against the wall, pulled up the hood on my borrowed coat, and waited for a break in the line. And then I bolted through a crowd of boots, staying low and keeping my head down, although I'd have had to do that anyway. Because I wasn't the only one trying to escape.

The momentarily empty door had provided somebody else a path to freedom—or should I say, somebodies. Because cawing chaos burst out of the room along with me, over my head and around my body, a flapping, screeching, furious storm that almost knocked me down. But that also filled the corridor to the point that one more dark-coated figure didn't attract any notice at all.

Pigeons, I thought fervently, racing for the stairs.

I loved pigeons.

And then somebody grabbed my arm.

"Here! Where d' you think you're going?"

I looked up wildly at a dark-haired mage I didn't recognize but who must have been more observant than his buddies. Because a second later a cuff clicked shut around my wrist. The one I needed to grab Rosier's trap and defend myself.

And then a second later, someone grabbed the other one.

"Go ahead, Sergeant, go ahead," a familiar voice said. "I've got 'er."

I looked around to see Red wearing my old leather coat. And a stern expression. And slicked-back hair, because he was doing a damned fine impersonation of a war mage. Except, you know, for the two feet of leather he was dragging, 'cause the guy wasn't much taller than me.

Aren't you a little short to be a storm trooper? I thought hysterically, and bit my lip.

"And who's got you?" the sergeant asked dryly, because he wasn't buying it, either.

"Good question," Red said, and hit him over the head with a heavy-looking vase.

It broke with a splintering crack nobody heard over the din, the sergeant took a nose dive, and I took another kind of dive for the stairs. Only to have Red catch me and drag me back into the office. "What are you doing?" I rounded on him. "This is our chance! We can get out while they're distracted!"

"Which would be a fine and admirable plan," he agreed, slamming the door behind us. "If not for one small inconvenience."

"What inconvenience?"

"They just locked down the building. Why d'you think I'm up here?"

"I don't know. Why *are* you here?"

"So your demon can get us both out! Did you get him?"

"I got him," I said, pulling out the trap.

And then Rosier fell out.

Onto his face.

What was left of it.

Red looked down at the motionless creature, and then up at me. "Now what?"

A minute later, Rosier was back in the box and we were out the window and onto the roof. Where it was still raining cats and dogs—and war mages, by the look of things, because a wave of them were prowling around the streets below in twos and threes. And even if I'd wanted to drop into the middle of that, there were no fire escapes, and the nearby buildings weren't anything like nearby enough. And they had steeply pitched roofs running with rivers of dirty water that were busy pouring off into the street six stories below.

I'd have had to have a death wish to try landing on one of them.

And I didn't.

I really, really didn't.

"Y'know, I'm not trying ter seem ungrateful," Red commented. "But I'm not seeing how this helps us."

Neither was I.

Until a cart pulled by a single, sway-backed old horse came trundling down the street. It looked to be full of trash. Smelly, smelly trash that the war mages were ignoring as utterly beneath them.

Fortunately, I didn't have such high standards.

I looked at Red. "Do you trust me?"

He blinked, like he wasn't used to being asked that question. "More 'n I trust them."

"Good," I said, and bopped him.

A moment later, I'd climbed around the window to the biggest, swiftest-moving waterfall I could reach, which was cascading down to the roofline and off the edge, into the street below. The street filled with war mages. The street that passed right by the front of war mage HQ.

The street the horse cart was going to be passing along in about a second.

And then I reentered what was becoming familiar darkness, praying that I wouldn't rematerialize in a gutter, or hanging off a building, or splattered on the ground below from an impact the box wasn't rated to withstand.

Or with a war mage's boot on my jugular.

But I didn't. A few minutes later, I materialized half buried in a pile of trash. Along with a wild-eyed fake war mage with an apple peel hanging off his head and an unconscious demon lord.

Who promptly face planted again, into a pile of something nasty.

But a second after that, Rosier was back in his little home, and Red and I were scrambling out of the back of the cart. And pelting through the rainy streets of Victorian London. And trying not to double over in hysterical laughter, which is hard when you're tripping balls and having to restrain yourself from mooning all the clueless mages milling around the streets behind you.

And then Red did it anyway, while I hugged a light post and laughed and laughed and laughed. Until I couldn't *breathe*. Until he looked at me and shook his head. "Yer about 'alf gone, arn'cha?"

"Way, way more than half," I gasped.

"Then yer orter fit right in."

"Fit right in where?"

He grinned.

Chapter Twenty-two

I made it back to the suite, hours later, sans Rosier. I'd had to leave him at the pub, in Red's tender care, because even after some food and rest I hadn't been able to shift two. I was kind of surprised I'd been able to shift one, which was why I was relieved to see nobody in the atrium when I returned. Except for Rico, leaning against the wall, smoking a cigarette.

"Is it late?" I asked hopefully. Because for once it would be really nice to be able to sneak back inside and change before anyone—read Marco—saw me.

"You mean, is he up yet?" Rico asked, letting out a smoky breath.

I sighed.

"The answer is yes," he told me. And then flashed a set of strong white teeth. "But he isn't here."

I felt my spine relax slightly, and then I felt bad. Marco had a shitty job, and he was only doing his best. I knew that.

"Can you deal with this?" I asked, sticking out my arm, where the mage's magical cuff still dangled. I could shift out of the regular kind, but these were a bitch.

Rico took a look at it, and then pulled a little case out from inside his leather jacket. And didn't even raise a brow at the request. Or at the massive amount of dirt I'd dragged in with me. Or at my naked feet protruding from the bottom of the grimy coat.

I watched him work and wondered, not for the first time, what it would take to ruffle Rico's perpetual cool. Unlike most of the other guys, I'd never seen him lose it. I'd also never seen him in a suit.

The other guards wore them religiously, probably something to do with keeping up the dignity of their house. Except for Marco, who preferred comfort to pride, and his beloved polos. But Rico preferred a combo of black tee, black jeans, and black leather jacket. It made him look like an updated, better-looking version of the Fonz, right down to the ability with all things mechanical.

An ability that held true again, when the cuff almost immediately sprang off my wrist.

"Where *is* Marco?" I asked, rubbing it gratefully, because he haunted the suite more than a certain ghost I knew.

"Shopping."

"Shopping?" Marco was a senior-level master. They didn't shop. They had people to do that for them. "For what?"

Rico's lip twitched. "Go in and see."

I looked from him to the large, ornate door of the suite. And suddenly wished I was back at the Bollocks with Rosier. And how sad was that? When a dirty, smelly, freezing pub was better than my life?

Get a grip, Cassie, I told myself. It's probably not a catastrophe this time. I mean, what were the odds, right?

But I just kept on standing there, my hand on the door latch, not pushing it. Because I couldn't deal with another thing tonight; I just couldn't. The trip back had taken everything I had, and even then I hadn't been sure I was going to make it. Yet, somehow, I had to come up with more Tears, and I had a court to take care of now, and then there was Jonas and my acolytes and freaking *Ares,* and I just couldn't deal with *one more thing*—

"Not all surprises are bad," Rico told me gently.

"You don't know my life," I told him back, trying not to sound as terrible as I felt. Although that probably would have worked better without the lip quiver. Or the swaying-on-my-feet thing. Or the tremor in my hand that juddered the handle just enough to make a mocking little sound until I let it go, feeling like a fool.

And probably looking like one, too, which wouldn't help. Vamps admired power, strength, stoicism. And I was exhibiting exactly none of the above.

But to my surprise, Rico's face relaxed, and not into a scowl. "Go on," he told me. "You look like you could use it."

I didn't even ask what he meant. What were my alternatives, sleeping out here? And tripping up Marco when he got back from whatever he was actually doing?

I shook my head. And then I grasped the door latch again. And actually turned it this time.

And found myself face-to-face with a giggling two-year-old.

That wouldn't have been so weird, except that no one was holding her.

She had black curls and big brown eyes, and a brand-new T-shirt in a bright, shocking pink. It had a bunch of balloons on the front in iridescent colors, with a signature below in an exaggerated curlicue that I knew all too well. Augustine, Dante's resident designer, had struck again.

The little girl giggled some more, completing a slow somersault in the air. And when Rico gave her a gentle push, she tumbled back into a room filled with more jumping, floating, levitating kids, bouncing off the sofa and pushing off the walls, and being watched by a bunch of usually stoical bodyguards who were grinning like I'd never seen them, because how could you not?

Rhea was sitting in the middle of the group, on a chair like a normal person, maybe because the charm wasn't strong enough to lift a grown woman. But it didn't seem to matter. She was still laughing delightedly. And so was the woman at her side, with her own set of curls, because Tami liked a good weave, yes she did.

And I felt an answering grin break out over my own face, one so broad it felt like it might crack open.

I'd never been so glad to see someone in my *life*.

She looked up and saw me at the same second, and the sharp dark eyes took in the same clues Rico had, but Tami wasn't big on silence.

"Damn it, girl! What happened to you?"

I couldn't help it; I burst out laughing. And then laughed

some more because of the look on her face. And then it sort of got out of hand, and I was leaning against the door, practically dying, because she'd never, *ever* believe me if I told her.

"Okay, yeah," she said, getting up and coming over. "Time for beddie bye."

"No, no, I'm fine," I protested. Because I was. Suddenly, I felt about a thousand times better. It was just so good having her here.

Everybody else looked like they felt the same. The girls, who had been pretty damned bedraggled when I left, were clean and had on new—if somewhat bizarre—clothing. They were also smiling and, for the first time since I'd met them, not looking especially traumatized.

I shouldn't have been surprised. Tami knew all about traumatized kids. Tami could write a freaking *book* on traumatized kids. And her attitude was that what most kids needed was affection, humor, and organization. And it looked like she'd organized the shit out of everything.

The overflowing ashtrays were gone, because of course there was no smoking allowed around the kids. The coats and ties and sometimes shoes that tended to get spread around were nowhere in sight, and the tape/blankets/covers on everything were missing. The carpet looked freshly vacuumed, there were flowers on the table in the lounge, and the pervasive smell of beer and sauerkraut from the foot-longs Marco dragged up from the lobby were conspicuously absent. Instead, the air had a distinct scent of—

"Cookies?" I asked, sounding almost tragically hopeful.

"After dinner," Tami told me automatically, and then she laughed. But she meant it. If I tried to snatch one early, she'd . . . well, I didn't know, but it would probably involve a lecture on setting a good example.

I was beginning to understand why Marco was "shopping."

And then I found myself surrounded by a bunch of small, human balloons that floated around me like the tide, an ocean of pink shirts and pink cheeks and bright eyes, like the ones on a little red-haired girl with a too-serious expression, who was staring down at the glittery, multicolored parts of her shirt in awe, her hand stroking them tentatively. Like she was more taken with them than with the sensation of flying.

But then, if I'd never been able to wear anything but boring white, maybe I would be, too. I suddenly thought I understood Cherries' crazy, colorful outfits a little better. And then I thought of something else.

My manicure kit was where I'd left it, in one of the sofa table drawers. And was still mostly full, because when the heck did I have time to do my nails? I grabbed it and turned to the girl, throwing back the top of the box and showing off a line of bottles of super sparkly polish in every color you could think of.

I didn't use bright purple or acid green or brilliant orange, but the kit had come with them and it had been on sale, so they were all in there. Along with my favorite pinks—four different shades—and a fiery red, a pearlescent white, a rich gold, a polished silver, and a luscious black. And every single one of them was loaded with glitter, 'cause that's how I like it.

And it looked like I wasn't the only one.

The little girl's eyes went huge.

"Pick a color," I told her, but she just stayed where she was, bobbing gently up and down, staring at them. So I picked one for her, the brightest of the pinks, because it matched her shirt. "Do you like pink?" I asked, but she just stared some more.

"It's okay," Rhea told her, coming up and lifting a small, chubby hand. "The Pythia uses them."

That seemed to make it all right, because the girl relaxed. And the others crowded around to watch me carefully paint the tiny nails. Like, intensely watch. You'd have thought I was teaching them some major life lesson or how to shift or something.

I finally finished. And a kid who had taken levitation in stride, who had probably seen magic in her short life that would blow my mind, stared at her hand in absolute disbelief. And then began flapping it around, trying to show all her friends at once, so excited she didn't know what to do.

"You've created a monster," Tami told me, as the other girls dove for colors and Rhea rushed for paper towels, to keep the glitter from decorating the whole suite.

"What's with the shirts?" I asked as I was shooed into the bedroom, probably because I was about to fall over.

"That damned Augustine," Tami said. "I told him we needed clothes for the girls, but since he wasn't getting paid—"

"He wasn't?"

"—he decided to give us the bargain-basement stuff. The balloons on those tees are supposed to float around, not whoever's wearing them!"

"Tami—"

"So they didn't sell, and we got stuck with 'em. Luckily, the girls are having a good time anyway. But Marco wasn't happy, said it was a slight on the court, and went down to have a talk with the man himself."

"Tami—"

"You know, he's not so bad—Marco, I mean. I think the girls are starting to warm up to him. Of course, it might be easier if he didn't look like a bad-tempered bear half the—"

"Tami!"

She looked around. "What?"

"Why don't we just pay Augustine?"

She blinked at me. "'Cause you're broke. Why you think?"

"What?"

"Broke. B-R-O-K-E," said the woman who could stretch a dollar until it shrieked and begged for mercy.

Only apparently we didn't have any to stretch.

"Jonas still hasn't released the accounts?" I asked, surprised in spite of everything. I thought he'd had a momentary freak-out yesterday, in response to some really bad news. But if he wasn't any better today . . .

I face-planted on the bed.

"Not a damned dime," Tami said, sitting down beside me. "Should I ask why you aren't wearing any shoes?"

"No. Tell me about Jonas."

"There's nothing to tell. Haven't heard a peep out of him, and when Rhea called him, he handed her off to some secretary type to set up an appointment." Tami made a disgusted sound. "You hear that? An *appointment*. For the *Pythia*." She shook her head. "Girl, you gotta kick some butt."

Yeah. That was what I felt like doing, I thought blearily. Butt kicking.

And I guess I looked it, because Tami grinned. "Well, maybe not right now."

"They say anything else?" I asked, rolling over.

God, my feet were *filthy*.

"No, just to call. But Rhea doesn't think that would be a good idea. She says—well, she can tell you," Tami said, as Rhea came in.

"I said that it is customary for the Pythia to be put through immediately," she told me quietly, looking concerned. Her eyes went over me and a worried frown appeared on her forehead. And I suddenly realized that she'd never seen me looking much better.

None of them had. It was entirely possible that my court was starting to think that I always went around with black feet and mud-splattered ankles, wearing a stolen war mage coat and reeking of cheap booze. Really cheap.

I shuddered at the memory of what passed for wine at the Bollocks, and put my head down on the bed.

"Hand me a phone?"

She obliged, biting her lip, but Tami wasn't so shy.

Tami didn't know what shy meant.

And Tami didn't think I ought to make that call. "You let them walk on you, they're gonna walk on you," she told me. "You know that. This is the Circle we're talking about."

And yeah, Tami had never been overly fond of the Circle. Or vice versa. Maybe because some of those kids she'd rescued hadn't been on the street. They'd been in the Circle's little reeducation camps; at least they had until she broke them out.

She'd started with her own son, and then some of his friends, and then it had become something of a habit, gaining her the nickname in the press of the "Vixen Vigilante." Because climbing into well-warded prison compounds does not mean one has to do it ill dressed. Unfortunately, the Circle hadn't been as fond of her as the press, and had slapped a sizeable bounty on her head. I'd managed to wrangle her a pardon, back when Jonas was playing nice, but he would probably not be happy to learn that I had his old enemy as my newest staff member.

Not that she knew she was on staff yet.

And not that he was happy anyway, so it didn't really matter, did it?

"I'm not calling Jonas," I told her.

"Who, then?"

I hit the button for the front desk. "Augustine," I told it, and there was some ringing and then there was some beeping and then there was the sound of an outraged genius who was yelling about something. I heard Marco's voice in the background a second later, which probably explained the yelling, only that didn't work on Augustine.

Fortunately, I had something that did.

"You know," I said, not waiting for a break in the conversation because there probably wouldn't be one, "I was thinking the other day that what I really need is a new design for the initiates' uniforms."

There was sudden silence on the other end of the phone.

"Or whatever they call their formal wear. Jeans and stuff are fine for every day, if nothing special is happening, but there are times when they're going to have to get dressed up. And then they're going to need something a bit better than the nightgowns they've been wearing. I mean, have you see them?"

"Yes, they're appalling," Augustine said. "Who designed them?"

"I think it was one of the Pythias, Gertrude something, back in the nineteenth century. And maybe they looked okay then, I don't know, but—"

"You can't have them running around like that," he agreed, sounding suddenly reasonable.

"Well, that's what I thought. And then, naturally, I thought of you."

"Naturally." He sighed, and it was long-suffering. Because he was so overworked and my request was such a burden—a burden he would shortly have plastered on every bit of ad space he could find.

Augustine found his association with the Pythia very lucrative.

He just didn't like paying for it.

I heard some pages flipping. "I suppose I could fit it in," he told me. "It will be difficult, mind you. I have the pre-fall show coming up on the twentieth, and then there's the—"

"And in the meantime," I said, because Augustine could

give Rosier a run for his money in the loving-the-sound-of-his-own-voice department, "I asked Marco to pick up some everyday stuff for the girls, to tide them over. You heard about what happened to their wardrobe?"

"If the rest was anything like that nightmare, they're well rid of it."

"But they have to wear something, until you're ready to show the world your masterpiece. Don't they?"

There was another pause.

"See what I can do," he told me curtly, and hung up.

I lay back on the bed.

"Okay, now do that with Jonas," Tami told me, bright-eyed.

I cracked a lid at her. "I thought you didn't want me to call him."

"Yeah, but that was good. Call him and do that."

Sure. Like it was that easy.

"Jonas isn't Augustine," I told her. "I don't have that kind of leverage with him."

"But you're *Pythia*—"

"And he's the head of the Circle. I piss Augustine off, and there's other designers. I piss Jonas off, and I've damaged a relationship with a close ally." And that would not be a great idea right now.

"And you don't think you pissed him off the other night?" Tami demanded. Apparently, news traveled fast.

"Probably. But he was seriously out of line then. I didn't have a choice."

"He's out of line now. Tell her." Tami looked at Rhea.

"She knows," Rhea said, watching me.

"I'm giving him a chance to cool off," I told Tami. "I'm not trying to show him up or make an enemy. This can't turn into some kind of . . . of pissing contest."

"It's already a pissing contest—"

"Not to me. And I'm going to give him some time, see if he comes around."

"And if he doesn't?"

I closed my eyes. "Let's hope he does."

"You're more of a . . . diplomat . . . than me," Tami said.

I wondered if that was some diplomacy on her part, to avoid saying "pushover." If it was, I couldn't blame her. I'd been acting like one, not intentionally, but in a we're-all-in-this-together kind of way, because we were. And because I had enough to worry about with my enemies; I didn't need problems with my allies, too.

But maybe they hadn't taken it that way.

Maybe they'd taken it Tami's way.

I sighed.

"What about housing?" I asked, keeping my eyes closed because it felt really good. "Do I need to call Casanova, too?"

"Good luck," she said dryly.

I opened my eyes. "What does that mean?"

"It means that at least Augustine answers his phone. Casanova has gone AWOL."

"AWOL?"

She nodded. "Like last month, when the damn electricity went haywire in my room. Looked like a horror movie in there—blink, blink, blink, about drove me nuts. But you think I could get anyone up to fix it? And when I called him to complain, and to point out that it was his hotel that was going to burn down if there was a short, you think he'd take my call?"

"He isn't taking anyone's," Rhea told her. "I tried yesterday, and again this morning. They say he's out."

"He's not out—he's hiding," Tami insisted, the light of battle in her eye. "But he can't hide forever."

"We'll try again tomorrow," I said, because I really did not feel like trying to track down an elusive vampire right now.

Tami nodded. "You look done in. Have a nap, Cassie."

"I'm not going to nap," I told her. "I have to take a bath. I can't possibly sleep like this."

"Mmhm," she said, and closed the bedroom door.

Chapter Twenty-three

Rhea didn't go with her, and a second after the door shut, a silence spell clicked into place.

I *had* to learn how to do that.

"The Tears?" I asked, even knowing that would be too easy.

She shook her head.

I put mine back down onto the bed.

"I'm sorry, Lady."

"It's okay. If he didn't send the money, I really didn't think he'd send those." I turned to the side and propped my head up on an elbow so I could see her better. "Does Jonas understand what the acolytes might want with them?"

"He was in a hurry when I spoke to him . . . and a temper," she added, grimacing slightly. "But I did explain—"

"And what did he say?"

"Only that they would not obtain any from him. But he did not say how he knew that, or . . . much of anything else. I can try again tomorrow—"

I sighed. Because yeah, she could. And so could I. But that raised its own problem, didn't it? "We can't give him the idea that we're too interested, or he'll use them as leverage to get control of the court."

"It isn't the court he wants," she said, quietly furious. "It's you."

"Then he'll use them to get leverage on me. Not that it'll do him any good."

"Not do him any good?" Rhea looked confused.

"Jonas has been telling himself porky pies," I told her, rolling off the bed.

"I . . . beg your pardon?"

"Lies," I translated and went into the bathroom.

And then changed my mind, because a bath sounded awesome, but it also sounded like a lot of work right now. And like I might just fall asleep halfway through. But I had to at least wash my feet. I really couldn't sleep like this.

I ran some hot water in the bottom of the tub, sat on the edge, and grabbed a sacrificial washcloth. God, Victorian London was *filthy*. My soles were black, I'd stubbed a toe on a higher-than-usual cobblestone, and I didn't even want to know what was wedged in between the other ones. I loaded up on the soap and went to town.

"Lady?"

"Hm?"

"What kind of lies?"

I looked over my shoulder to see Rhea standing in the doorway, watching me.

"What? Oh. The kind where everything is going to be fine, because Cassie is going to wave a hand and save the day. I think Jonas forgets sometimes that he's not dealing with Agnes."

"Why do you . . ." Rhea cut herself off.

"What?"

"Nothing."

She started picking up the bathroom, and soon had an armful of little soiled dresses. The formerly pristine white cotton was creased and sweat-stained, and, well, looked like it had been lived in for three days. But I guess it would have been hard to have them washed when the kids didn't have anything else to put on.

I thought of Agnes' perfect little court, so manicured and well behaved.

And then I thought of the giggling, glitter-streaked, slightly grimy one outside.

And, oh, look, I was having an effect already.

"Too bad we couldn't have rescued more of Agnes'

stuff," I said when Rhea noticed me watching her. "We could have outfitted the older girls, at least."

"Most of her things were too warm for Las Vegas . . . if the court is to remain here?"

"I haven't given it a lot of thought. Do you want to go back to London?"

"No." It was emphatic. "The weather," she added, grimacing.

"I can see that," I agreed, remembering Agnes' many coats. If I'd been her, I'd have moved the court somewhere sunny. The south of France maybe, or the coast of Spain.

Mmm, Spain. Paella and sangria and gorgeous guys . . .

Only Agnes' gorgeous guy had been in rainy old London, hadn't he? Well, her *guy*, anyway. I tried to imagine Jonas as a hot young stud and failed miserably. But he must have been once. Or at least she must have thought so. And they'd looked happy. . . .

I grinned, remembering the photo. The woman laughing and joking and kissing Jonas had had windblown hair and a top with half the buttons undone because it was being used as a beach cover-up. She'd had sunglasses on her head and what looked like a smear of that old white sun cream over her nose—to avoid more freckles, I guessed. She'd looked familiar in a way that her elegant rooms hadn't. More relatable. More real.

More like the woman who had once shot me in the butt.

I wondered again where all the other pictures were. She must have had some . . . right? I mean, people did, didn't they? Even before the era of the selfie.

But then, where were mine? If I died tomorrow and Rhea had to go through my stuff, what would she find? Some tacky old T-shirts? A few ratty tarot cards? A closet full of unsold ball gowns Augustine had foisted off on me so he could use my name in advertising, but that I'd never worn because I didn't have a social life?

I shook my head; I didn't know what was wrong with me. I was in the middle of a war. My lack of a social life didn't matter.

Only, it did, somehow. Maybe because it had started to feel, especially lately, like I just jumped from one crisis to another. The idea that, sooner or later, things would calm down and I'd have time to get to the personal stuff didn't seem to be happening. If anything, everything was speeding up, with even the thought of actually making it through to the other side getting harder to visualize.

And what if I didn't?

Agnes hadn't. She'd been something like eighty when she died, which might be a damn good run for a human, but not for a mage. For a mage, that was like dying at forty. And here I was at twenty-four, not at all sure I was going to make it to twenty-five, and—

And I suddenly wondered if that was how she'd felt. Like life was going by really fast, but nothing was *happening*. Not for her.

"In comparison to you?" Rhea asked suddenly.

I looked up. "What?"

"Yesterday you said something about Lady Phemonoe . . . in comparison to you?"

"Just that there isn't much of one," I said, grimacing.

But Rhea didn't look like she got the joke.

"She was a very good Pythia," she told me quietly.

"But?" I asked, because there had been one in there somewhere.

She bit her lip. But when she spoke, her voice was determined. "But she was too close to the Circle."

"She and Jonas were lovers," I pointed out. "Not that most people knew it."

"They knew. Maybe not the man on the street—they kept it out of the papers. But there were rumors. And the major players, they always have spies. . . ."

The Senate sure did. I thought briefly of Kit Marlowe's smiling face. The Senate's chief spy had always been kind to me, charming even. I liked him.

I wondered if I still would if I knew everything he had on me.

"Enough people knew that the other groups felt excluded," Rhea continued. "It didn't matter so much with individuals, someone wanting a judgment on a personal matter. But if it touched the Circle . . ."

"And what doesn't touch the Circle?" They weren't the only magical game in town, but they were the biggest and everybody knew it.

She nodded.

"So what did groups like the Senate do when they needed a judgment? How did they approach her?"

"Most didn't," Rhea said quietly. "Not about the big things. It bothered her—I could tell—when they would sort things out for themselves, only to find that the solution they'd come up with didn't work. She would have known, could have told them . . . but they hadn't asked her."

"You're telling me their relationship was *that* damaging? To the point that no one listened to her afterward?"

"It wasn't that no one listened. It was more that . . . it confirmed what everyone had always suspected. That the Circle and the Pythia worked in tandem."

"So it started before Agnes?"

"Oh yes." As usual, she looked slightly surprised at my ignorance. "It started with the Coven Wars."

Damn. That sounded like more of the kind of stuff I should know about but didn't. I sighed and womaned up. "The Coven Wars?"

"It's the reason the Circle and the covens don't get along. They had a huge war back in the sixteenth century over who was going to control Britain. The Circle won—barely—partly because the Pythia of the day prophesied that it would. The other groups took that as a sign that helping the covens would be a waste of time, and afterward, they couldn't get allies anywhere."

"A self-fulfilling prophecy."

She nodded. "That's what the covens said. They were furious, and many refused to allow any more of their children to go into the Pythian service. And those who did . . . didn't do well."

I remembered that Rhea had a cousin in the covens. It's why she'd run to them when she found out my acolytes were rotten, and why the coven leaders had been willing to help me. But it sounded like her connections hadn't made her too popular at court.

"The Pythias were unique in the ancient world, did you know?" she asked, sitting on the edge of the tub, hugging an armful of soiled cotton. "Every other seer, every other temple, was dominated by wealthy men or women whose families had put them in that position. Every single one. Except for Delphi. Some of the Pythias came from wealth, too, from time to time, but there were just as many who were farmers' daughters or shepherdesses or . . . or nobodies. Just nobodies. But these days . . ."

"These days?" I prompted when she trailed off.

"They say the power goes where it will. But it almost always goes to the one best able to use it. And that means the old Pythia's heir, the person who has received the most training."

I was starting to see where she was going with this. "But if you only allow some people to be trained—"

"Then you decide where the power goes—or where it doesn't go. It has become a monopoly among a few old magical families that have strong connections to the Circle's leadership. Lady Phemonoe was from one; her predecessor from another. And on and on, back beyond the wars."

"And the current acolytes?"

"Old families, every one. Lady Phemonoe's parents were unusual in not wanting their child selected. Most see it as a path to power, influence, and wealth, and push their daughters to get the position at all costs."

"And so they breed a bunch of ambitious little hellions like Myra."

But Rhea shook her head. "Not like Myra. She was selected for her ability, yes, but also for being quiet, unassuming, seemingly humble. The others . . . were not. They wanted the power terribly, and it showed. And I think the Lady must have seen something. . . . She told me once that none of them could ever be allowed to succeed her."

"But she didn't see anything about Myra, because Apollo was protecting his little puppet," I guessed.

Rhea nodded, looking troubled. "He must have been, at least enough that the Lady did not see Myra for what she was."

"So Myra got the job, and everyone else got bupkis."

Rhea nodded.

I started rinsing off. "Tell me about them."

"Victoria—the redhead—is from one of the founding families who first started the Circle, the Roupells. She's one of the Lord Protector's distant cousins, and everyone thought she would be the heir, until Myra was unexpectedly named. She was always the leader—even as a child—and still is, it seems."

"And the others?"

"Elizabeth—the blonde—likewise came from a founding family, but her grasp of the power isn't as good. She's more of a follower and . . . not as intelligent. I think she was named acolyte as a political move. The Warrenders—her family—were among the Lord Protector's chief supporters."

The Lord Protector seemed to have a lot to say about something that wasn't any of his business, I thought, and grabbed a towel.

"And the brunettes?"

"Amelie de Vielles—the one with longer hair—is the best with the power. In fact, she's the best I've ever seen. She clearly expected to be the heir, and was furious when it went to Myra. Jo—Johanna—Zirimis is the one who wasn't there. I don't know if she is acting with them or not. She was always difficult to read. Quiet, bookish, but a little . . . odd. She never seemed to really be *there* in some way."

"And the fifth?"

"Sara Darzi, the one with short dark hair. She's the one you . . ." Rhea abruptly cut off.

"Threw out a window?" I finished grimly.

"You're doing what you have to do," she said, seeing my expression. "A Pythia is responsible for her court as any coven leader is for her coven. And who else could possibly—"

"What about the covens?" I interrupted, because I didn't want to talk about this right now. Or ever, because what was there to say? She'd been trying to kill me; I hadn't had a choice. I already knew all that.

But it didn't make it any easier.

Those girls might be a disaster, but they hadn't gotten that way on their own. The Pythian position wasn't supposed to be some kind of prize to be won, some kind of trophy for the prominent families to fight over. It was a job, and a damned hard one. And it needed somebody who *got that*, not some political appointee drawn to the glamour.

I watched about an acre of Victorian mud slush down the drain.

Not that there was a lot of that these days.

"The covens?" Rhea repeated.

"If they don't send hardly anyone to court, they can't think they have much chance of getting a Pythia," I pointed out.

"They don't believe they have much of one anyway. They haven't had a Pythia in more than five hundred years, haven't had anyone who might take their side—until you."

"Except I'm not a coven witch, either, am I?" I wrung out my filthy washcloth, and decided I'd been right—it was beyond saving. I chucked it into the trash. "And I was raised by vampires." Which never seemed to make anybody happy.

Except the vamps, of course.

But Rhea was shaking her head. "The leaders were hesitant to come to you at first. There was a huge debate on it after I asked. I think they only agreed because they were curious. They didn't know what to expect from you, this Pythia from a vampire's court. But then they met you and . . ."

"I can imagine."

"They were impressed," Rhea said, watching me.

I snorted. "At what? My ability to play pool?" Because that's what we'd spent half the night doing. And the rest . . . well, I hadn't exactly been much help there. Shifting five people back in time, even a short distance, had all but wiped me out. If the witches hadn't taken up the slack, we wouldn't have made it out of there.

I was kind of surprised that we had anyway.

"No," Rhea said. "At the fact that you passed the Gauntlet."

I just looked at her, hoping for more information. I did not want to have to admit to yet another thing I didn't know. But I guess the idea got through, because her eyes went round.

"The *Gauntlet*!" For the first time, she looked genuinely shocked at my ignorance.

I sighed. She might as well get used to it. "I'm afraid I don't know what that is, either."

"Of course!" She suddenly looked angry. "The Circle doesn't make teaching Coven lore a priority!"

"Maybe not, but they didn't oversee my education; a vampire did. And his only priority was making himself money."

"Maybe it's just as well," she said bitterly. "When the Circle does teach something about the covens, it's usually not . . . complimentary."

"But this Gauntlet thing is important?"

"It's not just important: It's what gives a Coven leader her legitimacy. It varies from coven to coven, but the basic premise is the same: a prospective leader must pass a test, a physically and emotionally grueling, possibly deadly test, if she wants to prove herself fit to lead. If she doesn't have the courage to go through with it, she won't be selected, no matter how good she may be otherwise."

"That sounds a little . . . barbaric," I admitted, not wanting to offend her. But damn.

But she didn't look surprised that time; I guessed she got that a lot. "It isn't!" she insisted.

"Okay. I understand people have different traditions. . . ."

"It's not just about tradition! A leader has to prove herself. Why should anyone lend her their power if they don't know what she'll do with it? If they don't know that she'll fight for them, die for them, if she must? You fought for us. You fought for us when Jonas wouldn't. To the covens, that means you *earned* your court; someone didn't give it to you—you bought it with blood and pain. To them, you have a legitimacy the other Pythias didn't have—that they've never had! And then you defied him. . . ."

She broke off, but I kind of got the idea. "And Jonas . . . knows about all this?"

She nodded.

Well, that explained a few things. Like why he went ballistic the other night. I'd thought it was because I'd broken a rule to save my court.

But maybe it had more to do with who I'd broken it with.

Typical. I managed to stumble over one of the Circle's biggest hot-button issues without even knowing it. I needed a crash course in Magical History 101, like, now. But I wasn't going to get it now.

Because I'd just realized that, for the first time since taking this job, I finally had someone to ask about things—a lot of things. And who sounded like she might actually know what she was talking about. And I had a question, oh yes, I did.

Chapter Twenty-four

"Rhea." She looked up. "You seem to know a lot about the Pythias."

She smiled. "I like to read the histories."

"Good. I could use some information."

She hugged her armful of soiled cotton and nodded. "Yes, Lady?"

"About . . . changing time."

"You were right to rescue your court," she told me quickly. "The Lord Protector should not have—"

"No, not about that." That had been all of a fifteen-minute jump, to rescue kids who hadn't been doing anything but sleeping before I showed up. I didn't think I could have screwed things up too badly there. "Not about that," I repeated.

She nodded.

"But say a Pythia did something . . . or caused something to happen . . . or helped something to happen . . . that changed time. How . . . bad is it?"

"That is difficult to say," Rhea told me, looking a lot calmer than I'd expected. Like maybe that wasn't as unthinkable a question as I'd believed. "It would depend on the circumstance."

"Say it was something . . . kind of big."

She still wasn't looking freaked out. "I was always trained that time is malleable," she told me. "And can heal itself to a large degree. An invention or discovery not made by one person can be made by another; a chance meeting, if missed, may happen at another time—"

"Yes, but say we're not talking about chance meetings," I broke in, because she still wasn't getting this. "Say we're talking about something serious. Something . . . like a death. That's got to change things, right?"

"There are certainly things that can be done that the time line cannot compensate for," she agreed serenely. "But your power should warn you of those instances, Lady."

"But what if it doesn't?" I asked, getting worried. "Because I haven't heard anything. I never hear anything!"

For the first time, Rhea frowned. "You never hear—"

"And I should, shouldn't I?" I cut her off, because I wasn't feeling serene. I wasn't feeling serene at all. "If I'm supposed to get a warning when I change something, then my power should be going off like a fire alarm right now! Because there *was* a death. A . . . a man . . . died who wasn't supposed to, and it was my fault. But not a peep!"

Rhea thought for a moment. "The acolytes—the real ones—would be able to answer your question better—"

"You *are* a real acolyte. You're my acolyte."

She smiled suddenly, a small expression, but it lit her whole face. "Thank you, Lady. But the fact remains that they received training that I did not. However, I am certain I was told that a Pythia will know if the time stream is being disturbed. That she will receive an unmistakable warning. If you received none . . . then perhaps you did not change anything, after all."

"But a man is *dead*—"

"He might have died soon afterward in any case."

"Of what? A heart attack?" Because I didn't think—no, I *knew*—that Pritkin wouldn't have been fighting those fey if I hadn't been there. He'd have probably gone into hiding as soon as they showed up and, based on what I'd seen, done a damned good job of it.

But with me in the picture, he'd have had to hide two, which didn't seem like it would be a big deal. But then, people thought the same thing about shifting. Like, what's one extra person when you're already going somewhere anyway?

But it made a big difference—just huge—and maybe

making someone else invisible wasn't any easier. Not and keep it up for however long the fey might stick around, anyway. So he'd grabbed his stick and he'd grabbed me and he'd started booking it for the nearest highway—or, since it was medieval Wales, the nearest sheep trail—out of there.

But he hadn't made it.

And now a fey was dead who shouldn't have been.

But Rhea didn't seem to agree.

"If you were given no warning, this man could not have survived," she insisted. "By whatever means, he must have been fated to expire before he could do anything for which the time line could not compensate."

Unless I was too out of it to notice the warning, I thought grimly. Or unless I didn't know what a warning was supposed to sound like. Or unless whatever he was supposed to do, he did back in faerie, where my power didn't work, so who knew what I'd just screwed up?

God, it was supposed to be so easy! Find Pritkin, have Rosier say a few words, done. But we'd missed him three times now, and I didn't even have a way to get back for a fourth, and even if I found one—

"Lady," Rhea said, and it brought my head up, because it sounded unusually stern.

I blinked at her.

Gray eyes searched my face, and the frown on her forehead grew. "You are tired," she told me. "And have been working far too hard. You have had too many people depending on you and too little support. You are, if I may say so, badly in need of rest."

"I know. I can't shift again if I don't get some sleep. But first I need to—"

But Rhea was shaking her head. "Not sleep. *Rest.* You need some time free from stress and worry. You need to relax. You need a—"

I burst out in half-hysterical laughter before she could say it.

"I'm sorry," I told her after a minute. And I meant it, because she didn't deserve to be laughed at. But a vacation was *not* in my near future.

Probably not in my far one, either.

"Then some kind of stress reliever," she said determinedly. "I could make you . . . a drink?"

I shook my head. I could still taste the wine from the Bollocks. Which meant I might never taste anything ever again.

"It's okay," I told her.

"Then let me run you a bath."

I thought about it. And suddenly, all the aches and pains of a very long few days, of sleeping on a tree root in Wales, of climbing up and down, up and down, more hills than I could count, of being so sure we had him . . . only to have him slip through our fingers again, hit me.

"A bath sounds good," I told her fervently, and got out of the tub.

I went to get some nightclothes, and by the time I got back, a bath pillow had been put in place, the dirt had been washed away from around the drain, and hot, frothy bubbles were taking its place. Rhea bustled out, and I eased my aching body into the hot, hot, almost-too-hot water, wincing because it caused every scratch and bruise to stand out in sharp relief. But it felt good, too, soothing away the pain almost as fast as it caused it. And in a minute, Rhea was back with that drink I hadn't wanted but suddenly did.

Because it was milk and there was a plate of still-warm chocolate chip cookies to go with it.

A bubble bath and chocolate chips, I thought, slightly in awe. I might have just died and failed to notice. I dug in, and they were as good as ever, soft and melty and perfect. Tami always had been the best cook, and most of her stuff was homemade, because it was cheaper.

And better, I thought, looking up halfway through.

And caught Rhea watching me with a strange expression.

"Did you want some?" I asked indistinctly, because I had a cheek full of happiness.

"No," she whispered. She sat on the vanity stool.

For a while, she just watched me eat cookies.

"You said your power doesn't communicate with you?" she finally asked.

I nodded.

"At all?"

I thought back to my early days in this job, before I had completed the ritual to get the top spot, and was just another heir in competition with Myra. My power had jerked me around all over the place, like some kind of wild, time-traveling puppet, trying to stop whatever she was about to mess up. I'd really resented it at the time. Now ... well, it wasn't like I *wanted* to meet my acolytes again, but I preferred it to meeting Ares. But I wasn't meeting them, because my power wasn't taking me anywhere. Or telling me anything.

I swallowed milk. "No. Agnes told me once that I didn't have to worry about learning how to be Pythia, that my power would train me. Like it did for the early Pythias who had to figure things out for themselves. But it hasn't."

She frowned. "It ignores you?"

"Well, it does what I want ... if I'm not too tired. So I don't think you can say 'ignore.'"

"But when you talk to it, it doesn't answer back?"

"What?"

"When you ask it a question. You don't get an answer?"

"Ask it ... a question?"

It was her turn to look at me.

And then to keep on doing it, longer than was comfortable.

"You ... have never ... asked your power ... *anything*?" she finally said, in a tone that could only be described as "appalled."

Poor Rhea. I kept freaking her out and I wasn't even trying.

I sighed. "Asked it how?"

"I ..." She stopped. And then just sat there some more, blinking. "I'm ... not sure."

"That would make two of us."

"But you *can* do it," she insisted. "Lady Phemonoe said many times that she had to ask the power about this or that. And you are her heir, and a Pythia of great ability—"

I choked back a laugh.

"You are! You have done more already than some ever did! And you have done it alone!"

"Not alone," I corrected. "I've had help—"

"I have yet to see any!"

Rhea seemed to be getting a little upset, for some reason.

"I *have* had help," I repeated, because it was true. "It's just that, right now, people are a little freaked out about the war. Like I am about this."

She shook her head. "But you shouldn't be. The power is your partner, your helper, your . . ." She threw her hands up. "I do not understand how you have done so well without it. I truly do not!"

"Well, that's what I'm saying. Today *didn't* go so well. And I really need to know if I screwed something up." And how badly, and if I was supposed to fix it, and God, I hoped I wasn't supposed to fix it!

"I cannot help you," Rhea said, looking upset. "The lady . . . she never said . . . merely that she had to ask."

"Like you would a person?" I asked. "Because Apollo's dead—"

"But the power isn't Apollo. It came from him, long ago, but since coming to us, it . . . ." She stopped, and thought for a minute. And then started speaking slowly, as if trying to remember some long ago conversation. "The Lady said that we don't know what it is, exactly, or what it's become since Apollo released it. But we know what it isn't. It isn't human and doesn't think like a human. But it isn't a mindless energy source, either. Those who try to exploit it find that it actively works against them."

I nodded, thinking of Myra. Every time she'd shown up to cause trouble, the power had thrown me at her, ruining her day. It might not have been able to stop her from using it to travel around, but it could make sure she regretted the trip. "So . . . I work for it, basically?"

But Rhea shook her head. "No. Some people have thought that the Pythias are merely the power's avatar, a body for it to inhabit. But that's not the case. Nor are you subject to it. You are partners."

Which was great, but that didn't do me a lot of good if we couldn't communicate.

"Partners how?" I persisted, because any information was more than I had.

"The power uses your clairvoyant abilities to look into the past, into the future, and provide you with information," she told me. "And options. The Pythias have to do the actual work, and make the final decisions. But the power gives you information that no one else could have. It is why all Pythias have to be powerful seers."

I blinked as something finally made sense. "So you're

saying I almost never have visions anymore ... because my power is using up all the bandwidth?"

Rhea nodded. "The more you use it, the fewer visions you will have, as it needs your abilities to see where to take you in the past. That is one reason for the court—our clairvoyance compensates in the times when yours is ... busy."

"Like when you saw Ares' return," I said, and immediately wished I hadn't. Rhea blanched, whatever details she was remembering haunting her eyes. I wasn't sure whether that had been her first vision, but since she'd said the power didn't come to her, it was a possibility. And what a way to start!

But a moment later she swallowed and recovered. "Yes. The power may have tried to show you as well—I am sure it did—but the amount that you have been using your gifts ... and for so long ... and it couldn't risk exhausting your abilities when you might need them again at any time ..."

"And it couldn't give a heads-up to the acolytes, since they'd have just thrown a party," I said sourly.

She nodded again. And then frowned. "Are you *sure* it has not been helping you, Lady?"

I thought about it while I washed off more Victorian-era grime. Maybe it had been, in some ways. Like maybe Rosier and I hadn't ended up in the middle of the Welsh countryside by accident. Maybe we'd gone there because I hadn't been thinking about a particular place when I shifted; I'd been thinking about Pritkin. And he hadn't been at court.

It was possible, now that I thought about it, that we'd originally landed somewhere pretty close by. But I'd been unconscious and Rosier had been trying to get away from the entry point as fast as possible, and we'd missed him. Only to meet up again later, because we were still in the same general area.

My power had known where he was, even though I hadn't, and it had taken me to him.

That sounded like help to me.

But, on the other hand, if my power *was* trying to help me, it had seriously bad timing! It had taken me to a Pritkin in the middle of a crisis. He must have thought he'd lost his pursuers—he wouldn't have been stopping for a swim otherwise—but he hadn't. And I hadn't been with him for more than a few minutes when they showed up. So why take me back *then*?

I mean, honestly, wouldn't a week earlier or later have been a whole lot better? Some day when his biggest problem was deciding what to have for dinner? Or that he spent washing his socks? Or was sick in bed with a head cold and didn't do *anything*? Basically any day when I wouldn't be at risk of changing time, because absolutely nothing danger-ous was happening?

I'd thought my biggest challenge would be getting to Wales. Once I had that potion, and we actually got all the way back to the *sixth freaking century*, I'd thought my job was done. And the damned thing is, it should have been. Pritkin should be back, this should be over, and I should be able to concentrate on other things.

So why wasn't I?

"Maybe," I said slowly. "But . . . I wouldn't give any odds. You said Agnes asked it questions?"

She nodded again. "I've heard her say so many times."

Hello, I thought, feeling slightly ridiculous.

Nothing.

"Hello?" I said, out loud, because what the hell.

More nothing.

I sighed again.

"I should know this. I should be able to help you!" Rhea said, looking about as frustrated and upset as I felt. Which wasn't fair.

"You have helped me," I told her. "You got the power's warning to me when I was too tired to see it for myself. And you told me something tonight that I didn't know, something important." I smiled. "And it's kind of hard to get answers when you don't even know the questions. So thank you."

She nodded, biting her lip. But she still looked misera-ble. "Here. Have a cookie," I told her, passing over the plate. There was exactly one left. She looked at it and then at me. And then she ate it.

And finally smiled back, because there was nothing Ta-mi's cooking couldn't fix.

Chapter Twenty-five

The riverbank was fuzzy, indistinct, like daylight seen through fog. It matched the sky above me and the river beneath me, but not the man in front of me. He was all too real as he squatted down or went to his knees or did something that caused most of his body to disappear underwater.

Except for the golden head, which ended up on a level with my gently floating body.

And the warm hands that slid, water slick, between my thighs.

I could feel his twin at my back, slipping an identical pair of hands beneath my hips, lifting and supporting them at the same time. Although the river was already doing that, so I didn't see why he needed—

A pink tongue flickered out, tasting the beads of water on my inner thigh.

Oh.

That was why.

A question I didn't need a translation for appeared in a pair of green eyes. And stayed there as more water was slowly licked away with each drag of his tongue. Lower calf became upper, became knee, became behind the knee, and I should stop him, I thought; I should stop him now.

But I didn't want to stop him now. He'd started to feel like a mirage, there one minute and gone the next, or like a ghost, only less real because ghosts came back. But he was here now, warm and alive and catching my gaze again, his own burning hot even with his lips curved in a grin, like he was laughing and asking and daring me, all at the same time.

This was what Rosier took away from him, I thought. The chance to be this carefree—he never would be again. The chance to explore who he was, what he was, instead of being told. The chance to develop free of the creature who was never around when he was younger and needed him, but was the first to show up when he started giving evidence that he might be useful.

Twenty-four years. He'd had twenty-four years. And then fighting and running and ... God, I knew exactly what that felt like!

Only no, I didn't. Because I'd never even had that. I'd been brought up in a place where walking on eggshells was everyday life; where a madman ruled over a personal fiefdom and could have people killed at any moment; where there was no choice about anything, from what I wore to what I ate to how I used my gift, and no freedom, no freedom at all.

Until I took it, or thought I did, and ran away. But to what? Years of paranoia, of living with the idea that that madman would find me again, any minute. Of watching everything I said and everything I did and still jumping at shadows, because he might be in them.

I hadn't even been able to dance at the club where I worked part-time, because I had to keep an eye on the door. Tons of people my age came every night to laugh and talk and enjoy themselves. And to let loose, just for a little while ... but not me. Never me. What if I let loose and it was the night one of Tony's boys showed up? What if I got too carried away and didn't see him? What if he saw me first? What if, what if, what if?

I'd been young, but I couldn't act like it; I'd been free but only in name.

God, I really had been the perfect Pythian candidate, hadn't I?

Warm breath ghosted over me, heating me in ways breath had no right to. Stop him, some still slightly rational part of my brain was demanding. Stop him now!

But then Agnes' apartment flashed across my mind, so perfect, so pristine. Of course it was. There'd been no hus-

*band there to come home and kick off his shoes, had there?
To throw his jacket and whatever all over the sofa. No children to scatter mess around, and leave toys in the middle of
the floor for everybody to trip over. Not even a dog. Just a
perfectly kept apartment full of exactly no one, not even
quiet-voiced initiates half the time.*

Where were the others? Where was her life?

*But then, Pythias didn't get a life, did they? Pythias got
responsibilities and protocol and politics and the job. And I
suddenly didn't know if I could live like that, not again, not
forever.*

Of course, I didn't really have a choice, did I?

Only, suddenly, I did.

And I didn't want him to stop.

*And for some reason, that little revelation shocked me to
my core. Or no—I guess that had been surprise. Shock was
when a mouth suddenly closed over me.*

*Not a mouth, some small voice corrected. His mouth.
Warm and wet and echoed by an identical one at my breast.
And so very different from that other time, the one I'd tried
really hard to forget. That desperate, life-or-death time when
he'd been so careful, deliberately holding himself back.*

He wasn't being careful now.

*He wasn't being careful at all, I thought, arching up. And
why would he be? None of the stuff that had messed him up
had happened yet. Hell, maybe he didn't even know what he
was doing, didn't know what he was. Probably just thought it
felt good and gave his power a boost, and it wasn't like I was
screaming and running up the riverbank—*

*Okay, I wasn't running up the riverbank, I corrected, and
sank my teeth into my lower lip to stop the noises I'd been
making.*

*But he didn't seem to like that. Or maybe he took it as a
challenge. He growled against my skin, against me, and a rush
of sensation flooded over my body, another of those warm
tidal waves. A tongue swept around me, hands clenched beneath me, and the prick of fangs scraped across—*

Fangs?

*I looked down the length of my body, blinking, and dark,
dark eyes lifted to meet mine.*

"You have an interesting fantasy life, dulceață."

I stared back for a heart-stopping second, and then a

surge of panic hit me, like a bucket of ice water. The cocooning warmth receded into cold, stark terror, the languor became agitated thrashing, and a moment later I almost drowned in the tub I guess I'd fallen asleep in. Because I surfaced gasping and panting and making weird squeaky noises at Roy and the group of vamps that burst in through the door a second later.

And who didn't get an explanation before I threw the loofah at them and yelled, "Shut the door!"

Okay, it took me a little longer to calm down that time. I'd managed to rinse off, to wash the bubbles out of my hair, and to drain the tub before I was calm enough to think. And to tell myself that I was being ridiculous, that it was just a dream. A mish-mash of that scene in Wales, fear of ending up like Agnes, and incubus-induced horniness that, yeah, was about the last thing I needed right now.

It all made sense, as much as dreams ever did.

Wide, worried blue eyes stared back at me out of the brand-new bathroom mirror. They didn't look like they believed me. They kind of looked spooked, which was ironic considering that I was a clairvoyant and dealt with ghosts all the time.

"It was a *dream*," I told my reflection out loud, and started rubbing cold cream onto my face. Those hadn't been Mircea's eyes at the end, hadn't been his voice, hadn't been anything except my overactive imagination. Just my brain playing tricks on me. Although why that particular trick, I didn't know.

Mircea wasn't worried about Pritkin. Why should he be? When Pritkin wasn't getting dragged off to hell or back through time, he was my bodyguard. And self-appointed drill sergeant. And official nag. He yelled at me about what I ate, how much I exercised, and anytime I ended up in danger, even if it wasn't my fault. He frequently gave Marco a run for his money in the let's-pile-on-Cassie department; he sure as hell wasn't whispering sweet nothings into my ear.

I wasn't even sure the man I knew remembered how. In fact, most of the incubi I'd met had badly needed a dose of charm school—why they didn't all starve was beyond me. And, of course, Pritkin *did*; he didn't have a choice, thanks to his father's prohibition.

But that was before he was dragged off to hell, a sly inner voice corrected. His father was able to snatch him back *because* he broke their deal. And had demon sex with you.

It wasn't sex, I thought irritably. It wasn't anything like sex. It was nothing more than he'd done in Amsterdam—giving me energy when I was all but out. It was his bastard of a father who had decided to count it as something more.

Because it was something more, wasn't it? In the demon world—

We weren't in the demon world! And I counted it as what it was—an energy donation. Like I'd done for him a couple of—

You're not helping your case.

Damn it! I set the cold cream jar down harder than necessary. There were only so many ways to save an incubus' life, and I hadn't been about to let Pritkin die on me! Not when most of the time he ended up half dead *because* of me. So I'd donated energy a few times to help him heal. It was no different from feeding a vampire, and I did that all the time!

You *used to* do that all the time, my inner critic corrected. You don't do it now. Because feeding had a sexual undertone in the vampire world, too, and Mircea prohibited anyone else from biting you. How would he react if he knew—

He didn't know! There was nothing *to* know. Pritkin never so much as touched me if he could help it. It was like being trained by a freaking ninja monk—

Was until recently, my little voice said. But wasn't he different when you found him in hell?

I picked up the comb and started attacking the bird's nest on my head. No, I thought angrily. He hadn't been. He hadn't even been glad to see me. He'd been . . . Pritkin. Just like on that damned hillside that night.

I'd been dying, injured in a fight I'd expected to lose but had somehow won, if winning meant that I was going to die later than the other guy. But Pritkin had reached me just in time and basically did the same thing he'd done in Amsterdam. And gave me some of his energy, thereby saving my life—and losing his own in the process.

At least the meaningful parts of it. Because Rosier had a damned loose definition of what constituted sex, and by the impossible standards he'd imposed on Pritkin, a mutual feeding was close enough. Pritkin had broken the taboo, and been abruptly snatched away to hell, and I'd been left screaming on a hillside with only one thought in mind: go get him.

And I had. I'd had no idea how to get into hell, or what to do once I got there. And my power didn't work well outside of earth, if at all. But I'd gone anyway. And then, when I finally found him, when I tracked him down across entire *worlds*, what had he done?

Yelled at me and threw me off a balcony!

And that was after reading me the riot act for daring to come after him in the first place. I'd ruined his selfless gesture, and he'd been *pissed*, although not half as much as I had been. Damned infernal mage. Didn't know why I bothered sometimes—

But after that, my little voice reminded me. After you two escaped Rosier's court and ended up in front of the demon council. After all the drama was over and you were awaiting the verdict that would either free him or condemn him, hadn't he acted differently? Hadn't he acted like he wanted *to say something*?

I scowled. He'd been under a massive amount of stress. He knew the council better than I did, knew the odds. He'd tried to tell me, but I hadn't listened. I'd been so sure they'd see reason. Didn't they know we were fighting the same enemies? Didn't they see that I *needed* him?

But no. They'd spent centuries with their heads so far up their own asses that they couldn't see anything. They'd killed him. They'd killed him right there in front of me, and then acted like it was no big deal, like I should have expected it. But I hadn't expected it, and if Adra hadn't decided he might need me, and given me that counterspell—

Yes, yes, that's very nice. Very scary, my inner voice mocked. I'm sure you'd have taken on the big, bad demon council all by your little self. But that isn't the point, is it? Pritkin wanted to tell you something, and it had almost sounded like—

He hadn't wanted to tell me shit! He'd known there was a better-than-average chance they were going to kill him. He hadn't known what he was saying!

Or maybe he hadn't cared, my little voice insisted slyly.

Maybe he'd decided it didn't matter anymore. That if he was going to be killed anyway, he might as well—

Goddamnit! There was nothing going on between us!

And yet you dreamed about him tonight.

I glared at my reflection, and it glared back. Defiantly. Even a little smug. Like it thought it had made some kind of irrefutable point, and honestly, sometimes I thought this job was driving me crazy.

I put down the comb before I ended up bald.

So what if I dreamed about him? I couldn't be held responsible for what I dreamed. And anyway, Mircea didn't know. And even if he did—

If he did? My inner voice prompted. Because my inner voice doesn't know when to call it a freaking *night*.

My fingers dropped to the two small bumps on my neck, vestiges of the evening that had started with a spell gone wrong and ended with a half-crazed master vampire. Who did what half-crazed vamps tend to do and bit me. Only it hadn't been a normal bite.

I swallowed, and felt the tiny bumps move under my fingertips. They weren't the blood-dripping gashes of the movies. They might easily have been mistaken for pimples by a human, if anybody noticed them at all. Which was unlikely since they weren't even red anymore. Just two bits of raised skin, hardly anything . . .

Unless you were a vampire.

To a vampire, they were a flashing neon sign that said *hold up, back off, take a moment and rethink your life*. Because this one is taken, and by a senator, no less. Who will destroy you and everything you love if you so much as look at her too long.

Or, at least, that's what I'd been told they meant. I had a hard time visualizing it, because I didn't see that side of him. Yes, I knew Senate members didn't get the job of supervising a society of "blood-sucking fiends," as Rosier had called them, by being nice. But that wasn't my Mircea. My Mircea was laughing eyes and silky hair and knowing hands and quick wits. . . .

Which probably explained why I'd had a crush on him since I was a kid, when he'd paid a visit to the court of the vampire who raised me.

Tony had taken in my parents, who were on the run

from the Spartoi, some nasty types Ares had left to hunt my mother, in exchange for Dad doing a few spells for him. Vampires weren't able to do magic like humans, so most employed mages to create wards and such. And for a while, things seemed to have gone along fine.

Until Tony had figured out that his mage's young daughter was a true seer, a rare and potentially profit-making commodity in the supernatural world. And tried to take me. My parents objected, Tony insisted, and in the end, the issue was settled by a deadly car bomb. Which had killed a weakened goddess masquerading as a human. And left her four-year-old daughter an orphan and Tony's new house seer.

At least it had until his master found out about me.

Because unlike his servant, Mircea did his homework. And he'd discovered that the mage Tony had taken in wasn't some down-on-his-luck hack, like most of the freelance types, but Roger Palmer, a former member of the infamous Black Circle. Who was best known for eloping with Elizabeth O'Donnell, the Pythia's designated heir, and for somehow keeping her hidden for years from all attempts to retrieve her.

Mircea had found that very interesting, since the missing heir also just happened to be my mother.

Agnes had been getting old and everyone knew that the power would soon pass to a successor. Which was supposed to be a carefully groomed acolyte as usual. But it was the Pythian power itself that chose a host, not the former Pythia, so technically it could go anywhere.

And Mircea had bet that it would go to me.

The long shot had paid off, but another gamble hadn't. He knew the Circle had never stopped looking for my mother, and would take me as soon as they found out who I was. They had jurisdiction over magic users, not the Senate, who only governed the vamps. And I couldn't be changed into a vamp, because that sort of thing ruined magical skill, including the ability to channel the Pythian power.

So he'd left me at Tony's, which, unlike his own glittering court, was about as far out of the limelight as it was possible to get. Before he went crazy and joined the other side in the war, Tony had dealt mainly in human vices, so wasn't of great interest to the Circle. And anyway, I was already there. No one had any reason to question the origins of the little orphan girl Tony had taken in out of the goodness of his cold, clammy heart.

And so we had waited. For me to grow up. For Mircea to see what would happen. And in the meantime, he'd had a mage put a spell on me to ensure my safety at the court of a guy who made the human mafia look like sweethearts.

He'd thought of everything—except the possibility that the damned thing would backfire.

Like most strong magic, the spell he'd used had a reputation for being unpredictable, and a few time-travel shenanigans after Mircea and I met again as adults had resulted in a real mess. And in an obsessive, lust-fueled relationship that had been sorted out only when the spell was finally broken. But by then, his bite had ensured that, according to vampire law at least, I was now his wife.

And divorce isn't a thing in the vamp world.

Not that I had asked for one. No, I'd asked for something almost as strange. I had asked to date.

The idea had been to find out if all that spell-induced attraction had something else behind it. Or if I was just wearing rose-colored glasses left over from a childhood in which Mircea had seemed like the only port in a constant storm. Tony had been scary. His master, on the other hand, had been kind and caring and handsome and thoughtful. . . .

And maybe I really was stupid. Or chronically naive. But I didn't believe that all of that had been a lie.

Did Mircea want to profit from me? Of course he did. He was a *vampire*. But that didn't mean he didn't care about me, too.

It also didn't mean that he did, my little voice commented, before I squashed it and leaned across the counter to grab my toothbrush.

And felt a hand slide down my naked ass.

Chapter Twenty-six

For a second, I froze, staring at nothing. Except for the toothbrush hanging out of my open mouth. And then I spun, my heart hammering—

And still saw nothing.

Except for swirls of steam that looked faintly ghostlike even under the bright, cheery bathroom light.

And maybe there was a reason for that, I thought hopefully. "Billy?"

My ghost companion didn't answer.

I licked my lips.

That didn't mean he wasn't there. Billy Joe liked to play games, a relic of a life spent as a professional gambler on the Mississippi. Not a good gambler, mind you. It was why he'd ended his twenties with a tour of the river bottom, courtesy of a croaker sack, a lot of rope, and a couple pissed-off cowboys who he'd been trying to cheat.

I assumed his body was still there. His soul, on the other hand, was hanging out in Vegas these days, courtesy of an ugly old necklace he'd won a few weeks before his untimely demise and hadn't had time to pawn. That had turned out to be his one bit of good luck, because the necklace was a talisman, a relic that collected the natural energy of the world and used it to support the owner's magic.

Or in this case, the owner's ghost. Billy now haunted it like other ghosts did graveyards and creepy old houses.

And ever since I'd bought it, intending it as a birthday gift for my old governess, he had haunted me.

Only I didn't think he was haunting me now.

There was no flash of red ruffled shirt or smug smirk to be seen. There was no ghostly Stetson falling over laughing hazel eyes. There was no anything, which probably meant that I was imagining things again.

I grabbed another towel and started scrubbing my dripping hair.

One of these days, I was going to have to consider the concept of just avoiding bathrooms altogether. Weird shit happened to me in bathrooms. Maybe I needed to come up with another way to get clean. Maybe I needed to find a room with a Jacuzzi. Maybe I needed some long-term therapy, although I wasn't sure even a Pythia had that much ti—

There was a tinkling crash on the other side of the bathroom door.

I froze again, hands on my head, peering out from under a yard of Turkish cotton. And stared at the door. It stared back. But nothing else did, because it was closed.

"Roy?" I called softly, because a vampire's ears didn't need a shout. And because I felt more than a little absurd.

A feeling that melted into something else when nobody answered.

Damn it, get a grip, I told myself harshly, and grabbed the doorknob. There's nothing scary on the other side. It's just a freaking bedroom!

And it was.

It just wasn't mine.

I stumbled into a room with high ceilings, beautiful molding, and tall windows looking out over the night. And then spun around in panic, and almost broke my nose on a stretch of old-world paneling. Because there was suddenly no door there anymore.

I staggered back, confused and pained, and landed on my butt beside an overturned teapot. It was on the floor underneath a small table, leaking onto the remains of a porcelain cup and saucer. And sending a rivulet of fragrant liquid running across some highly polished wooden floorboards.

It did not help with the confusion.

Neither did the large, unfamiliar bed containing rumpled bedclothes. Or the towel and robe that had been tossed over a pillow. Or the window I wasn't close enough to see out of, but which was allowing moonlight to filter over expensive rugs and a Jackson Pollock–like painting on the far wall.

I didn't know this place.

I didn't know any of it.

But the vampire who walked through the door a moment later was another story.

I scrambled back to my feet, but he didn't appear to see me. Which was the first thing that had made any sense. Because his name was Horatiu and he couldn't see anybody.

He was Mircea's old tutor—very old. He'd been middle-aged or more when he'd been trying to drum some Latin through his charge's young skull. But that meant Mircea hadn't reached master status—the level needed to make new vamps—until Horatiu was on his deathbed. And that sort of thing tends to mess with the formula. The end result was a doddering, half-blind, mostly deaf vampire who nonetheless insisted on earning his keep. As a butler, since I guess that was the safest job Mircea had been able to come up with.

Well, sort of safe, I thought, as the white-haired old vamp set a tray down precariously on the edge of a chair instead of on the adjacent table. A chair just above the overturned teapot, which I was starting to understand better now. But Horatiu didn't seem to notice it, either.

Maybe because he was busy gathering the clothes off the bed and throwing them out the window beside a laundry chute. And watering a silk potted plant. And starting to do something to a bookshelf adjacent to the fireplace right before another vamp came in.

"Goddamnit!" The vamp was Kit Marlowe, the Senate's curly-haired, goateed, impossible-to-ruffle chief spy. Well, make that normally impossible because he was looking a little ruffled now.

Maybe because the bookshelf had just caught on fire.

"Lord Marlowe," Horatiu said, in his quavering old man's voice. "Did you wish to join the master for breakfast?"

"No!" Marlowe said, rushing past the stooped figure to the adjoining bathroom.

"There's plenty of kippers," Horatiu called after him. "But not enough toast. I wish the master had said something—"

"Damn it, I don't want breakfast!" Marlowe said, running back in with a wastebasket full of water. Which he proceeded to use to save the bedroom and destroy a bunch of probably expensive old volumes.

"I can make more, of course," Horatiu offered querulously. "But I do believe we're out of rye."

He tottered out, doubtless off to find more trouble to get into, and left a fuming, damp, and cursing Marlowe behind him. Who hadn't seemed to notice the chick in the towel yet. I opened my mouth to ask what the hell, only to shut it again abruptly when Marlowe strode out through the room's only other door.

And right through the middle of me.

There was this weird sense of disorientation as our bodies merged, the same kind I got when Billy stepped inside my skin for an energy draw. Only there was no missing energy here. Just the skin-tingling sensation of someone occupying the same space as me for a split second, before he was gone.

I spun around, clutching my towel and breathing hard, because vamps don't leave ghosts. And even if they did, I doubted one would be able to argue with Horatiu. Or to put out a fire quite so effortlessly.

But it sure as hell had felt like he'd been a ghost.

Or . . . or that I was, I realized, with growing horror.

I stood there for a second, wondering if one of the many attempts on my life had somehow made good, and if so, why I hadn't heard the blast or seen the shooter or felt the pain before I ended up here.

But I couldn't be a ghost—I *couldn't* be. My guards would have sensed an assassin. So something else was going on, and vampire senses were the most likely to help me figure out what. As long as I didn't lose him.

Only it seemed like I already had, because Marlowe had disappeared through the door on the other side of a sitting room. One that started to close even as I ran after him. And when I flung myself through the narrow opening, barely making it before the door clicked shut, I saw—

An empty room.

It looked like an atrium, or one of those weird cubby-holes where several hallways meet and then branch off. There was another nice rug on the floor, a potted plant in a tub, and a fireplace with a mantel but no chairs in front of it because this wasn't a room you hung out in. It was a room designed to do nothing and be nothing, besides a way to get from one place to another.

Except in this case, because there weren't any other doors.

It would have freaked me out, but I'd seen this before. It was a popular security feature in vampire residences, meant to slow down intruders by forcing them to play find the exit. But I didn't look for one.

Because I'd already found something else.

Something that cast a bright splash of color against the old-world paneling on the opposite wall. Something that made me momentarily forget about Marlowe and Horatiu and even my own predicament. Something that drew me forward like a magnet.

Something beautiful.

I couldn't see it as well as I wanted, because the only illumination was a couple of recessed lights set on low up in the ceiling. And a candle burning on the mantel for some reason. So I grabbed it. And illuminated a painting.

A large one, judging by the way the light only reached the bottom half of a gown. I lifted the candlestick higher, and the golden haze gleamed off a surface cracked from age, but still vibrant with jewel-like colors: rich cream, salmon pink, dusky coral, and pale aquamarine. They formed a sumptuous gown in satin, a hand wearing a huge pearl ring, a gold-and-pearl snood over a bun of sleek dark hair, and . . .

And a face I'd seen before.

Not in painted form but in photographs, a whole book of them that I'd found by accident in another of Mircea's many residences. I hadn't known who it was then; still didn't, because Mircea didn't like to talk about his past, much less the women who populated it. Whenever I brought the subject up, he went into evasion mode.

And nobody evaded like Mircea.

I wasn't completely naive. I knew he'd had other lovers; how could he not in five hundred years? But I hadn't found photograph books stuffed to the brim with them. Hadn't stumbled across a painting that must have cost a fortune of any of them. Hadn't seen evidence that any of them were more than a passing fling.

I stared at the high cheekbones, the full red lips, the sparkling dark eyes. And felt my hand clench on the candlestick. Because this woman didn't look like a fling to me.

The photos I'd seen had been modern, but the dress was Renaissance-era Italian; at least it was if you had pots of money. I'd seen ones like it occasionally, in some of the paintings that Rafe, Tony's resident artist, had scattered around. It had a low-cut bodice over a delicate chemise, a high waist, and long, fitted sleeves that tied onto the shoulders with little bows. The cross draped around the wearer's slender neck was heavy gold, and the fat, lustrous pearls that dangled from her ears might have come from a sultan's treasure.

And it wasn't just her clothes that were costly.

I held the light closer, because I wanted to be sure. And yes. Her jewelry glinted dull gold by candlelight because it *was* gold, made with applied gold leaf. Likewise, the red on her lips and cheeks wasn't ochre but outrageously expensive vermilion. And the sea gleaming behind her . . . well, that wasn't indigo.

That pure, intense color could only be ultramarine. Imported all the way from mines in Afghanistan, it was extracted through a very laborious process from genuine lapis lazuli. Rafe had told me about it while he mixed up some for his own use one day. How it might not be especially dear in modern times, but had once been the most expensive pigment in all Renaissance art. Literally worth more than its weight in gold.

Yet it was splashed around everywhere here, from the sky to the sea to the bright blue in the embroidery on the woman's gown. A gown that must have cost a fortune yet wasn't half as lovely as the woman wearing it. A woman who occupied not only an album full of photographs, but a canvas that took up an *entire freaking wall*—

Only no. Not a wall, I realized a moment later, when I reached out to touch the shiny surface. And fell through that doorway I hadn't been looking for instead. And into a vortex of light and sound and oh-holy-shit that ended abruptly with me on my hands and knees in another room with another fireplace and another master vampire.

But this one wasn't Marlowe.

Mircea sat in a big leather chair behind a bigger mahogany desk. It looked a little incongruous, because he was wearing only a pair of deep plum sleep pants. His chest and feet were bare, and his dark, shoulder-length hair, which was almost always pulled back in a clip, was loose.

He looked like he'd just gotten up, but then decided to nap in his . . . office?

It looked like one, if a somewhat generic version. The rest of the house had been an eclectic mix of old-world charm and expensive modern chic—kind of like its owner. But in here, that had given way to upscale hotel bland in beiges and browns, if hotels were regularly lit by candles: a highly polished desk, a Kerman rug on the floor, and a wall of expensive-looking books. It said upmarket accountant or big shot lawyer. It did not say Mircea.

Except for a broken Chinese figurine, a happy potbellied guy with a tambourine who was serving as a pen cup.

And, of course, the man himself, seated behind the desk, slowly caressing the chair arms.

He really liked that chair, didn't he? I thought blankly. For a moment. Until I felt another not-so-surreptitious stroke down my naked backside. A stroke that matched the movement of Mircea's hand on the slick leather.

Exactly matched, I realized, as he smoothed down to the end of the arm, and then swept back up, completing the circuit. And a simultaneous caress swirled around my left butt cheek. It was one of his favorite moves, and it normally would have gotten me all hot and bothered.

Except that I was already hot, and not in a good way.

And then Marlowe walked through me again.

"You might want to check in before we leave," he said as I choked and flailed and fell back. "Horatiu is trying to burn the house down."

"He doesn't have to try," Mircea murmured, without opening his eyes. "It comes naturally."

"He needs a keeper!"

"We tried that. But he noticed their presence." Mircea's

mouth quirked. "And complained that he was too old to be training all the new arrivals."

"Better that than a raging inferno!"

"We've all become rather good at discerning the smell of smoke."

Marlowe snorted. "No doubt. And why aren't you dressed?"

The chief spy was, if you could call it that, in a rumpled burgundy suit and a shirt Mircea wouldn't have used to shine his shoes. Not that he shined his own shoes. And not that Marlowe was known for sartorial splendor. Or for giving a damn about impressing anyone.

That was Mircea's job.

"It isn't even dark yet," Mircea commented mildly. "And the portal to the city is virtually instantaneous. What purpose would it serve to get there hours before everyone else?"

"So what do you intend to do? *Nap?*"

"No. But it would appear that you could use one."

Kit glared at him. And then flung himself into a green club chair in front of the desk. And sat there, pretending to relax, while practically quivering with repressed energy.

I'd have been more curious as to why, if I'd been slightly less furious.

Because Mircea *kept doing it.* The phantom touches kept gliding over my skin, and I kept getting steamier and steamier. Because he was playing with me while killing time and chatting to his buddy, and because he was in my *head*.

He had to be, to do this, whatever the hell this was. Some new vampire power, something I'd never heard of, something that went a lot further than just picking up a stray surface thought once in a while like some masters could do. Something he hadn't told me about because this wasn't surface, this wasn't passive, this was *in my freaking head*.

Son of a *bitch*.

And then he goosed me.

I saw it before it landed, a quick contraction of his fingertips on the chair arm. A subtle pinch of the smooth leather. Only it didn't feel subtle. It felt hard, a sharp sting that, okay, under the right circumstances might have been welcome, but these were not those. These weren't even *close* to those, and—

And then he did it again.

I looked up to see a small smile curving the perfect lips, just a little smirk, which would have been enough on its own. But it wasn't on its own. It was hanging out with a couple of whiskey-dark eyes that were sharp and amused — and open.

And fixed on mine.

And steamy abruptly went nuclear.

Chapter Twenty-seven

"You're too damned calm," Kit said, getting up to pour himself a drink. "It's annoying at the best of times, but right now it's verging on the obscene."

"You would prefer me to panic?" Mircea asked, his eyes on me as I slowly got up off the floor.

"I'd prefer you to act human—"

"That would be difficult."

"You know what I mean," Kit snapped, sloshing something into a glass. "Show a nerve for once!"

"You needn't be concerned," Mircea said, watching me walk toward him. "We've put together an excellent team."

"It's not the team I'm worried about. It's the damned fey!" Kit swept out a hand. Which went right through me, like I wasn't even there.

Because I wasn't. Not for him. I was in Mircea's head, or he was in mine; I didn't know which.

But I knew one thing.

Two could play this game.

"If any fey are injured tonight, it will be on their own heads," Mircea said, one eyebrow going up as I rounded the desk. "They are acting illegally, in violation of treaty—"

"Yes, and the treaty matters so much to them!" Kit said bitterly. "They've never followed it, never had any intention of doing so. The Green still farm us for slaves, the Dark are constantly trying to slip past the border, and the so-called Blue Elves—"

"They prefer 'fey,'" Mircea murmured as I stopped in front of him. "'Elf' is considered pejorative."

"Like I give a damn what they prefer!"

Mircea didn't comment. He also didn't move. He just sat there, looking up at me, eyes glinting wickedly.

Because he thought I was bluffing.

No, I thought grimly; he *knew* I was. He played these games with me all the time. Like in those dreams I'd been having lately, which I was now sure had been him. Like all those times he'd evaded questions, ignored hints, dodged open-ended comments. And he always got away with it. Because how do you tie down a master vampire? How do you get his attention? How do you make him *listen*?

I decided I might have just figured it out.

I watched his eyes widen slightly as I dropped the towel and straddled him.

"At least the Green are up front about it," Kit said, glaring at a map on the wall. I assumed it was of faerie, since that's what he was talking about, but I didn't more than glimpse it. Because Mircea had already recovered.

Strong arms pulled me abruptly against him, the height difference assuring that, even with me kneeling on the chair, we were face-to-face.

"They look down those long noses of theirs and tell us to mind our own business," Kit said. "But the damned Blue Fey, oh, they're our good friends, our staunch allies—and they smuggle more than the rest combined!"

"It's unfortunate," Mircea murmured, dark eyes gleaming into mine. "But some friendships outlive their usefulness, and have to be discarded."

"You don't get to choose my friends," I told him. "Any more than you get to play around in my head!"

"I'm not playing."

"Neither am I!"

"Well, I'd like to know what you call it, then," Marlowe grumbled. "You know we can't drop the Blarestri. We have to have allies, particularly now."

"Indeed?" Mircea asked me. "Then what are we doing here?"

"Wasting our time!" Kit snapped. "I've said it all along."

"You tell me," I gritted out as Mircea suddenly leaned back, taking the chair to a steep recline. And pulling me over him, onto the sweet spot where slim hips met thickly muscled thighs. And where the heavy weight of his sex was barely concealed by a thin layer of silk. It was more an enticement than a barrier, a soft, seductive caress as I fought to find purchase on the slick material.

"Some people specialize in trouble," Mircea said, as warm hands curved around my hips, steadying me. And then pulled me up until his lips rested against my stomach.

Marlowe was still glaring at the map, his back to us, and Mircea took full advantage. Those wicked lips began to move, slowly, draggingly, openmouthed against my lower belly. Followed by a hint of tongue, sliding across my skin, tasting me. Making me shiver.

And who was supposed to be teaching who a lesson here? I thought dizzily.

"Some even seem to prefer it," Mircea told me, sounding amused.

And then he made another sound as I shifted position slightly, deliberately dragging over him.

And suddenly, things weren't so soft anymore.

"Like those triple damned Svarestri," Marlowe agreed, freshening his drink. "They don't mingle with us lesser beings, oh no. Except when that bastard Geminus offered them carte blanche, even bringing them in through the official portals, since who would suspect a senator of smuggling?" He made a disgusted sound. "Me, for one! I knew he was up to something, but I thought it was those illegal fights he'd been running for decades. Should have known he'd branch out sooner or later, with that many contacts. . . ."

I stopped listening.

Mircea's hands had tightened, holding me in place. But my hands found his shoulders anyway, because the support wasn't enough. I didn't know why; he was nowhere near an erogenous zone. Except that suddenly everything was, and my knees kept trying to buckle.

I had a moment of disconnect, of utter, mind-numbing disbelief. I wasn't kneeling here, naked and dripping, in Mircea's office. And he was definitely not licking the drops of water from my skin.

Only I was and he was, and I couldn't seem to move, could barely breathe as the strokes became longer, slower, wider. Or when he followed the swell of a breast, the warmth of his breath only tightening my body more as he stopped short of the nipple, even though a drop of water trembled on the tightly furled tip. It shone in the lamplight, reflecting the room for a few seconds. And probably a tiny version of my increasingly desperate face.

Until gravity had enough and it finally dropped onto his lips.

He held my eyes as he licked it away, as he laved the skin around it, as he—

My head went back, staring at the wall behind his head because I couldn't watch him anymore. But it didn't matter. I could still see his shadow mingled with mine, moving together softly. Could still feel every stroke of the warm roughness dragging over me. Could still hear the sound he made, low in his throat, as he started to pull.

My back arched, my fingers in his hair tightened to fists, needing something, anything to ground me.

And trying to hold that damned head still before I went crazy.

But, of course, that did nothing about his hands, and they were busy. Smoothing down my back, over the curve of my butt and down my thighs, to the sensitive skin at the back of my knees. Only to retract their course in reverse a moment later. And every trip pushed me against that not-so-soft bulge, simulating something that wasn't going to be simulation much longer, because I was going to rip those damned trousers off him and—

"Explain. Now," I gritted out.

"That might be difficult," he said, shooting Marlowe a look.

"'Difficult' isn't the word I'd use," Marlowe groused, returning to his chair with what looked like a triple. "Trying to plug up a city leaking like a sieve with damned portals everywhere. Even if we succeed, what have we done? Stopped some smuggling, maybe made things a little less convenient for the other side. But we aren't going to win this playing defensive, and we both know it!"

"And the alternative would be?"

"You know damned well. Our enemies are in faerie, not here. We either go after them where they're holed up, or — this isn't going to go well, Mircea."

Actually, I thought it was going perfectly. Mircea's technique, formidable as it was, was also limited with his friend sitting right across the desk. But mine wasn't. Kit couldn't see me, couldn't hear me.

Which left all kinds of possibilities, didn't it?

I smiled and saw Mircea's expression change. But he didn't get up, and he could have. Because that would mean admitting there was something he couldn't handle, wouldn't it?

And we both knew that would never happen.

I smiled again and bent to lick up the water I'd been thoughtlessly shedding onto his chest.

"Close enough portals and it will start to matter," Mircea said, ignoring me. "Kill off enough of the dark mages they're working with, and it will hurt even more. The fey don't know this world, can't walk in it easily — "

"Some can."

"Not enough. And even those who can, don't like to try it. Their magic is weak here; it leaves them vulnerable."

His voice changed slightly on that last word, maybe because he was feeling a little vulnerable himself suddenly. Because I'd just reached his neck. A human male would have been more affected if I'd gone in the other direction, but Mircea wasn't human. And I'd recently discovered an Achilles' heel I should have suspected before.

But it was always nice to learn something new, I thought, scraping the edge of my teeth over the strong cords in his throat.

"Then why do I feel like we're sitting ducks?" Kit groused.

Mircea didn't answer him that time, maybe because his throat was already busy, working under my lips. Like his pulse was pounding, pounding, pounding beneath my tongue. I was right above the jugular now, right above the source of a vampire's life and power, his virility and strength. Right above his most vulnerable area, even for a master.

I wouldn't take his blood, of course; didn't want it, couldn't use it. But it was still heady, having him like this. That big, hard body spread out under mine, the hands

clenching on the chair arms because they couldn't on me,
the heartbeat under my mouth jumping when I closed my
lips over the pulse point.

And began to suck.

And felt more than one thing leap against me.

"Mircea?" Kit prompted.

"Perhaps you need a drink," Mircea told him, sounding
a little strangled.

Marlowe looked down in confusion at his glass, which
was still almost full. "I have a drink. What I don't have is
information—especially about the so-called light fey!"

Kit jumped up again and began to pace, but I barely noticed.

My god, it was good, the salty-sweet taste of his skin, the
little shivers of his body beneath mine, the way he reacted
to every draw of my lips. I squirmed on top of him, knowing I was playing with fire, but I couldn't help it, didn't care.
Even when I pulled back enough to see his eyes, filled with
heat and fire and the promise that I would pay—and pay
dearly—for this, just as soon as Kit left.

But he hadn't yet, had he?

He was pacing, still running on about the fey, gesturing
and bitching—

And not paying any attention to the man behind the
desk.

Who watched me as I slowly sat up, raising the stakes.
Mircea could have asked his friend to leave, could have left
himself, could have done a hundred things he wasn't doing
because he still didn't believe it. He didn't think I'd do it.

And why should he? I'd let him get away with a ton of
crap these last months, things I wouldn't have put up with
from anybody else. I'd backed down every time he challenged me because he was Mircea and I loved him and he
was *Mircea*.

But I'd just reached tilt.

He didn't get to wander around *inside my head*. He
didn't get to decide who my friends were. He didn't get to
keep me in the dark even more than Jonas did, and tell me
not to bother my pretty little head about it because the big,
strong men would protect me. Because the big, strong men
didn't understand what we were facing any more than I did.

We were all stumbling around in the dark, even Kit,

even the Senate's chief spy-who-knew-everything—except about the fey, apparently. And the demons. And the crazy creatures from another world we'd been fighting, who called themselves gods and thought about humans the same way we thought about bugs. And killed us just as easily.

If we were going to survive, we needed to at least start stumbling around together. But we weren't, because Jonas didn't trust me, Mircea didn't respect me, and nobody believed in me. And as long as I kept backing down, they were never going to.

I sat up slightly, pulled down those damned sleep pants, grasped him gently.

And then sat back down, taking him inside me.

"The dark fey aren't as much of a problem," Kit said, oblivious. "We've had so many refugees from them, especially lately, that my people have managed to build up at least a basic image of their power structure and main players. But the light worries me."

I knew how he felt. Because Mircea's eyes had just changed, tiny pinpoints of amber swirling up out of the velvety darkness, a signal that maybe, just maybe, I should have thought about this a little more. That maybe I was in over my head.

Way over.

And I didn't care.

Not enough to stop me from squirming about, getting comfortable, while watching him get less so. Not enough to keep me from groaning when he abruptly hardened inside me, even more than he'd already been, filling me fully, deliciously. Not enough to keep me from beginning to move.

Kit was still droning on, but I barely heard him anymore. And God, if I'd thought the other was heady, it was nothing to this. Watching that powerful body squirm, feeling him moving inside me, hearing his breath speed up as I did, as I undulated on top of him, as I set the pace for once. It was glorious.

Until he suddenly sat up, shifting the weight of him, making me gasp. And grasped the back of my neck, jerking me within a hair's breadth of his face. And abruptly let his fangs descend.

My heart was beating out of my chest, my breath was

caught in my throat, my body was tightening around him enough to make us both gasp.

And I still didn't care.

"What are you going to do?" I asked breathlessly. "Bite me?"

And, just like that, his eyes flashed gold, the brown of the man completely eclipsed by the power of the vampire.

"What was it Churchill said about Russia?" Kit asked, almost surreally at this point. "A riddle, wrapped in a mystery, inside an enigma—"

"Why don't you go look it up?" Mircea growled.

"What?"

"Go!" he snarled, and simultaneously swept all the items off the center of the desk, sending books, papers, and the smirking, potbellied pen cup flying.

I'd have liked to have seen the expression on Kit's face just then. Liked to have known how a first-level master took to being ordered about, especially so abruptly. But I didn't.

Because I was busy.

Hitting the polished surface of the desk even before I heard the door click shut, feeling smooth hardness as my hands spread out, trying to find purchase that wasn't there, discovering I didn't need it when a furious master vampire grasped my hips, pulled me to the edge of the desk, and thrust back into me hard enough to make me gasp.

And then to laugh, like the crazy person I was really starting to believe I was, because I'd won. For once, he'd been the one to back down first. For once, I'd actually made the great Mircea Basarab cry uncle.

And then I was the one crying. And thrashing. And screaming as he took me harder than he ever had, harder than he'd ever dared, because human bodies break so easily.

But my body wasn't here, was it? I was nothing more than a figment, a dream, an illusion. And illusions don't break.

But they do feel, and this was raw and savage and everything, everything I'd wanted since that damned dream left me hot and aching and desperately unfulfilled.

Which wasn't really a problem now, I thought deliriously. And then I didn't think anything else. I just wrapped my arms around him and hung on as power slammed through me, into me, over me, a golden haze sinking into my skin that exactly matched the color of a pair of golden eyes.

"Well," I said breathlessly, some moments later.

"Well?" Mircea replied, the voice muffled since his face was currently buried in my hair.

"Well . . . I hope . . . that taught you . . . a lesson," I said, vaguely concerned that there was a flaw in my logic somewhere but too limp to care.

Mircea's head raised. And I saw with some real satisfaction that he was almost as flushed and sweaty as I was. And his throat was working and his eyes were a little crazed. But he wasn't out of breath, because he was a vampire and they didn't technically need to do that.

"I told you, *dulceață*," he said grimly. "I am not in your head."

"Really? Then what would you call—"

"Any more than I was in your room tonight, or in the shower last week."

"The shower?" I began, confused.

And then I stopped. Suddenly, vividly, recalling a certain incident in the shower that, yes, had been fairly memorable. And which I probably should have thought about more, if I hadn't already had too much to think about.

But it was coming back to me now. Along with the explanation I'd discovered later. Which, come to think of it, didn't really have anything to do with Mircea at all, and—

And uh-oh.

"I think," Mircea told me evilly, "that it is time we had a talk."

Chapter Twenty-eight

"Cedar? You are sure that is how it's spelled?" Mircea demanded, as he hustled me along a crowded corridor.

"I—I'm not even sure that's how it's pronounced," I told him, feeling more than a little flustered. I'd just been dragged off the desk, barely in time to snatch up my crumpled bath towel, and then towed through a door I hadn't noticed on the other side of the room. And then through a fireplace, of all things, and into a cramped little hallway with no windows and almost no light. And then through another fireplace and a room I didn't have time to see before we exited into a wide, brightly lit hallway that didn't feel all that wide at the moment because it was stuffed with vampires.

Masters, by the feel of them. Make that senior masters, I thought, as I stumbled through a body, which was almost impossible to avoid in a press this tight. They deferentially made way for Mircea, but closed up again right behind him, leaving me struggling through a sea of vampires. Or more like a sea of flashing colors and sounds and half thoughts:

"—so the masters can gut you with it?"

"I don't care. I want my damned sword—"

"A gun has better range."

"And a sword doesn't run out of bullets!"

"Botas malditos están demasiado ajustadas—"

The vamps didn't seem to like the situation any more than I did. Some seemed pretty oblivious, but others jumped and flinched and stared around as I passed through them. As if they knew something was happening.

And it was; I just didn't know what.

"What's going on?" I asked Mircea, trying to stay as close behind him as possible, to avoid freaking out any more vamps.

"We've been having a problem with some illegal portals that our enemies have been using to bring in weapons," he told me.

"Portals from faerie?"

He nodded. "Even our allies don't seem to care who they sell to, and it's becoming a problem."

"So you're going to shut them down."

"We're going to try."

"And if they don't like that?" I asked, dodging one swiftly moving form, only to hit another slam on.

"They'll learn," he told me, and pulled me out the other side of the wildly staring vamp.

And then into a knot of several more going in the same direction as us.

The corridor was so small, and they were grouped so tightly that it was like being swamped by a wave at the beach. An unexpected deluge of color and noise and over-whelming sensory assault. And minds and limbs and the electric buzz of a master vampire times five.

"Have you seen the dhampir? Wonder where they're keeping her—"

"It. And who cares?"

"I care. I've never seen one—"

"Which would explain why you're still here."

"Speak for yourself. I could take her—"

"It. And feel free to try."

"Sure. And then have to deal with Daddy? I don't think—"

"So the rumors are true?"

"What rumors?"

"The ones that say she's not just any dhampir. That she's actually—"

"Cassie! In here."

That last was Mircea's voice, and a second later, I found

myself being pulled through a door into a tiny room. With nothing in it. And that included master vampires, thank God, because I'd been about to drown out there.

But this . . . this was nice. Or calm, at least. We were in what I guessed was some kind of reception room, although it wasn't very welcoming, without so much as a picture on the wall or a single chair, and then we were through a door on the far side and into—

"Don't step on the rugs," Mircea told me. "Just in case."

"Just in case what?"

I didn't get an answer. Because the room's only occupant had just looked up from a small desk to scowl at us. Or at Mircea, I supposed, since his eyes passed right over me to fix on his colleague.

"Are you through with your little fit?" Marlowe asked acidly.

"No. Cedar. What do you know about it?"

"The *tree*?"

"No. The spell. We think that's how it's pronounced."

"'We'?"

Mircea looked at me. "I only heard it once," I said awkwardly.

"But if you had to guess?"

"Say-duh? Say-drr? SAY-der? I'm not real sure. I was kind of—"

"Who are you talking to?" Kit demanded, getting up. His eyes swept over me again but didn't stop. I pulled my bath towel a little higher anyway.

Mircea repeated my variations on a theme. "Some type of ancient magic," he told Kit. "I need everything you have on it."

"You realize we're leaving in less than an hour?"

"Then you'll need to hurry, won't you?"

Kit scowled harder, but then he got that constipated look a lot of vamps used when they were communicating mentally.

Mircea threaded his way expertly through the carpets. I followed, a little gingerly, because the floor was slick, highly polished marble tile, and the slippery little rugs were everywhere. They were odd-looking, partly because none of them matched, partly because most weren't more than a couple of feet wide, but mostly because they were the only attempt at décor.

Mircea's office had lacked the stamp of his character, but at least it had been fairly attractive. This . . . was not. It didn't have a plant or a picture or a pillow. It didn't have a single chair other than the one Marlowe was sitting in. It didn't have much of anything, despite being a fairly large room, just the small rolltop desk, a hell of a lot of carpets, and—

And a couple utilitarian cabinets along the far wall.

A record scratched in my head.

I was still staring at them a moment later, when a fat little vamp with a bad black toupee came bustling in through the door carrying an incongruously modern-looking electronic pad. "Type of magic?" he asked without preamble.

Kit looked at Mircea. Mircea looked at me. Kit scowled again.

"Mircea. Is there something you want to tell me?" he demanded.

"Um," I said, trying not to look at the cabinets, "that depends. What kind of magic did the gods use?"

"What?" Mircea asked sharply.

Kit scowled harder. "I *said*—"

"Not you," Mircea told him brusquely.

And caused the curly-haired vampire to flush almost as red as his coat. "Mircea—"

"Well, what did you think it was?" I asked, a little defensively. Because Mircea wasn't looking happy.

"An extension of your power, some new facet you were exploring. But you're telling me the gods are involved?"

"The *gods*?" Kit asked, his voice going up. "Mircea, what the *hell*—"

"It—it was mostly demons," I said, hoping to defuse the situation.

Annnnnnd made it worse.

"Demons?" Mircea repeated, frowning.

"Um—"

"What kind of demons?"

"Well, sort of . . . a little of all kinds. It was the demon council—"

"The *council*?"

Kit started to say something, but Mircea shushed him with a gesture. Kit did not look happy about that. Mircea looked even less so. But it wasn't like he was going to be able to help me if he didn't know the truth.

"My mother wanted to talk to the council," I explained. "And she used this seiðr spell to do it—"

"Your mother is *dead*."

"Yes, well, that's why she needed a spell," I said awkwardly.

In fact, she'd needed it to address the council on behalf of Pritkin. Not that she'd done much of that. In fact, she'd barely mentioned him. She'd mostly talked about the war, and how we needed to ally if we had any chance of winning this. Which was true, but not helpful, since nobody else seemed to agree.

"But the spell is on *you*," Mircea pointed out. Because Mircea is not stupid.

"Yes, well, I was sort of . . . channeling . . . for her," I explained, as little as possible.

He just looked at me.

I looked steadily back. Because, sure, Mircea, I was going to talk first. I'd lived with vampires for most of my life; give me credit for *something*.

"We don't know the type. Possibly used by the gods," Mircea told them, his eyes still on me.

"Ah yes," the little vamp said, a smart pen going to town on the small screen, almost too fast to follow. "That does simplify . . . ah. Here it is. '*Seiðr*,' meaning 'a cord, string, or snare,' a form of old Norse magic and shamanism concerned with making visionary journeys."

"Is it dangerous?" Mircea demanded.

"To which party?"

"To either party!"

The fat little vamp blinked. He did not appear to be used to hearing that tone from the Senate's senior diplomat. "One moment," he said, and started stabbing about with the pen again.

I risked another glance at the cabinets.

They were ugly old things, steel gray and slightly beat up along the bottom where too many feet had closed them too hard. They were the sort of catchall pieces that could be found in any office—well, any office that didn't care about impressing clients. Hell, they could have been found in plenty of garages, holding old paint cans and half-used bottles of motor oil.

But that wasn't what they were holding at the moment.

I knew that because I'd raided them once.

At least, I was pretty sure I had. They looked the same, but the old ones had been at the Senate's former headquarters. Which was currently little more than a scorch mark on the desert due to having been an early casualty of the war. And considering how that had gone down, I hadn't expected anybody to have waited around to rescue some old metal cabinets.

But then, they hadn't had to wait, had they? They hadn't had to empty and then repack them like a human, because they weren't human. All a vamp had to do was snatch one onto his shoulder and walk off with it, which made packing in a hurry a whole lot easier, didn't it?

And left me with a dilemma.

Because, if they were the same ones, they contained stuff the Senate had been squirrelling away for centuries. Like potent weapons they'd confiscated from other people so they could use them themselves. And ancient relics with powers they thought might come in useful someday. And old enemies trapped in magical snares . . .

And a potion called the Tears of Apollo.

"Hm, it's all very vague," the little vamp was saying. "A good deal about altering the course of fate . . . traveling in spirit form throughout the Nine Worlds . . . seems to have originated with the Vanir, the old Norse fertility gods. They taught it to the Æsir, the gods of battle, who eventually communicated it to the Scandinavian covens . . ."

"Can it be removed?" Mircea asked.

"Oh, certainly. The caster would merely have to—"

"Not by the caster. By one of the other people involved in the spell."

"Oh, well, then. No."

"I beg your pardon?" Mircea said mildly, but the vamp flushed.

"I simply meant—that is to say—well, you did ask about dangers earlier—"

"And?"

"And, well, that is the main one. In fact, it is the only

one, at least that I can find so far. I can check the Edda, and of course I will, although frankly it's not likely to be very useful in this case. The Vanir weren't well liked, you know, by the Christian scholars who wrote most of the accounts, long after the fact, of the old Norse religion. The Æsir were the strong, manly, warlike types that the scholars' own culture valued. But the Vanir . . . well, their association with fertility was considered a bit . . . effeminate . . . and therefore their magic—of which seiðr was a prominent part—is not well documented. It was considered somewhat beyond the pale, if you follow me."

"No."

The vamp blinked. "No?"

"No."

"I—well, that is to say, I thought I was being rather plain—"

"You were mistaken."

"I—I merely meant—that is to say—"

"For Christ's sake, man!" Marlowe exploded. "Stop saying 'that is to say' and just say it!"

"Well, I'm trying to!" The little guy had more backbone than I'd expected. "I am trying to point out that *seiðr* wasn't named after a snare for nothing! It is said that the gods would establish a link with someone they didn't like, and then . . . hang up the phone. So to speak. And leave that person forever in a dream world, all alone, to eventually wither away from starvation, thirst, or madness . . ." He trailed off.

"The gods were a lot of fun," I said.

Mircea ignored that, but his lips tightened. "But that is not the case here," he pointed out. "No one has 'hung up' anything. That is the problem."

"It is?" I asked.

"It is?" the man repeated, without knowing it.

"Yes!" Mircea told him.

"Why is it?" I demanded.

"Why is that?" the man asked.

Mircea closed his eyes.

"You don't like me being in your head, do you?" I asked, light dawning. I'd been so freaked out about the opposite, it hadn't occurred to me that he might feel the same. And now that it did . . . "Why don't you?"

"You didn't seem pleased when the shoe was on the other foot," he pointed out.

"This is getting surreal," Marlowe murmured. "Even for this place."

"Cassie is here—mentally," Mircea told him.

"I'd gathered that."

"She seems to find it difficult to understand why I do not wish to have her in my head, unannounced, at any time she pleases—"

Marlowe gave a bark of a laugh. "Oh, this should be fun."

"It isn't fun!" I said, looking at Mircea. "And I wasn't happy because I thought you were doing it on *purpose*. I didn't do it on purpose. I didn't know I was doing it at all!"

"Yet here we are."

I felt my brows draw together, which was stupid because I didn't have brows right now. But it felt like I did, and it felt like they had just knitted. "You're blaming me for this?"

"No. I am merely pointing out that it is a security risk—"

"How? I thought we were on the same side."

"We *are* on the same side—"

"Then how is it a risk for me to be in your head?"

"It's a privacy issue—"

"A minute ago it was a security issue."

"It is possible for it to be both!" he snapped.

I blinked.

"I'm starting to wish I had popcorn," Marlowe murmured.

"You can leave," Mircea informed him.

A dark eyebrow raised. "This is *my* office. You already threw me out of yours."

"This really has you freaked out, doesn't it?" I stared at Mircea in amazement. I'd been pissed, sure, when I thought he was tiptoeing through my head. But he didn't look pissed. He looked almost . . . "What are you afraid of?" I asked, hardly believing I was saying the words.

"I am not afraid. I simply think—"

"Yes, you are. I've seen you fight a whole squadron of dark mages, and look like you were enjoying yourself. I saw you be *electrocuted* and not lose your cool. And now you're freaking out because—"

"I am not 'freaking out'!"

"Well, what would you call it?"

"I—I should go," the small vamp whispered, edging toward the door. But Mircea grabbed him by the front of his natty brown vest.

"You. Tell me how to remove this!"

"But—but I already—that is to say—"

"If you utter that phrase one more time—"

"God does exist, and he loves me," Marlowe said, bright-eyed.

"Tell me how!" Mircea roared.

"Mircea!" I said, appalled.

He shot me an exasperated look. "I am not threatening him, Cassie! He is a second-level master and under the protection of a senator. And he is expected to know his business—"

"I do know my business!" the man said, brushing himself down huffily when Mircea released him. "But as I explained—in some detail, I might add—no one knows much about seiðr. It isn't used anymore. It's too expensive, magically speaking. The gods found it useful to communicate with one another, even across different worlds. But for humans—well, a phone call is rather easier!"

"A phone call is also voluntary," Mircea pointed out.

He really did not look happy.

And I suddenly felt stupidly hurt. Or maybe not so stupidly. I wasn't sure. This was my first big romance—my first romance period, really, unless you counted one night with a friend to complete a spell and keep from dying, and I somehow didn't think you were supposed to count that. But this . . . this was supposed to count.

I felt my face crumple.

And Mircea suddenly sighed and ran a hand over his own face.

"You manage to make me forget all my training," he told me ruefully.

"You're not supposed to need training with me," I whispered. And I wasn't crying, damn it. I wasn't!

Mircea came over and pulled me against his chest, a strong hand in my hair. "I'm not good at relationships," I told him, sounding muffled.

"I hate to tell you, but it doesn't get any easier," he told me back.

"Well, it was fun while it lasted," Marlowe said, sighing, and headed for the door, taking the wide-eyed little vamp along with him.

"I'll—I'll look for a solution," the vamp threw over his shoulder as he was hustled out.

"Do that," Mircea said dryly.

"Don't step on the rugs," Marlowe said, and then they were gone.

Chapter Twenty-nine

"What happens if we step on the rugs?" I asked.

"Probably nothing." Mircea sat in Marlowe's vacated chair and pulled me onto his lap, maybe because there weren't any others. "It's a running joke."

"What is? That his rugs will kill you?"

"That everything in here will kill you. Kit has a reputation for having truly vicious wards, to the point that anything new that appears in his office is automatically suspect. He began to notice that people avoided even stepping on his rugs. And he . . . found it amusing."

"So he bought more of them?"

Mircea nodded. "I think he enjoys seeing everyone have to wind their way through them."

"But . . . you still don't step on them," I pointed out.

"With Kit, it is always best to err on the side of caution." Great.

I let my head rest on his shoulder.

We just stayed like that for a while.

I had a ton of questions, and he probably did, too. And there were so many things we needed to talk about that I'd lost count. But I didn't want to do that right now. I didn't want to do anything. Except sit here like this, just like this, because how often did we get downtime anymore? How often did we get a chance to be just us, just Mircea and Cassie, instead of senator and Pythia? How often did we get a chance to be together at all?

I realized that I'd missed him this last week, or whatever it had been. With time travel, I never knew exactly how much time had passed anymore. But I knew I'd missed the sound of his voice, the feel of his hands, the way he had of immediately making things seem easy, simple, right. The feeling of comfort and security that enveloped me like a warm blanket whenever we were together. I'd missed this, I thought, as he kissed my neck.

And then bent me backward over the chair arm to kiss my breast instead.

Sharp fangs scraped across the nipple, not enough to hurt, just enough to let me know he could. It furled tight, tight under his tongue, and a shiver of anticipation ran through me. He bit down, hard enough to draw blood this time, and I felt the room revolve around me. Like I was already light-headed from blood loss when I wasn't, when I couldn't be, when I wasn't even here.

But it felt real anyway, like when he tugged the towel away and bent me over the desk, because there was no room on top. And entered me thickly, sweetly, less urgently than before but just as good. Oh God, so good.

He was big, intimidatingly so if I was watching him. It was easier this way, the sweet burn of him overriding everything else. I shivered and he kissed my back, tracing the spinal cord with his lips, and only caused me to tremble harder.

"I've dreamed of taking you like this," he whispered, breath warm in my ear, like the body draped over top of me.

"Does Kit know?"

Mircea laughed, and it echoed down into me, making me gasp and squirm. "His office didn't actually factor into it," he clarified.

"And what will he say when he finds out what we used it for?"

"Nothing, if he knows what's good for him."

It was my turn to laugh, until he shifted position, sliding fully into me. And then pulled me suddenly back against him, claiming a final half inch I hadn't even known I had. And before I could recover from *that*, his lips found the marks on my neck, the ones he'd left there, but he didn't puncture the skin.

He didn't have to.

The old wound, long since closed, to the point that there was hardly even a trace anymore, opened for him like it had been waiting for his return, his own private orifice. His fangs slid in, clean, painless, easy, and my blood welled up, his for the taking. Like my body, like everything.

He began to feed, something he hadn't done in a long time, and my whole body stiffened in surprise. And then contracted, beginning to pulse in time to the suction of his mouth, to the throb of his length inside me, to the feel of his hand between my legs, clenching. He wasn't *doing* anything yet, wasn't even moving.

And yet I was shivering and shaking, on the brink of orgasm with barely a touch.

"I dreamed about bending you over a table," he growled into my ear. "A chair, a desk—anything you please. And taking you until you couldn't breathe, couldn't walk, couldn't remember your *name*."

Halfway there, I thought, slightly hysterically.

"Careful," I gasped. "You know what happens in our dreams lately."

I'd been thinking, okay, fantasizing, a few nights ago about Mircea, and suddenly, there he'd been. Or there I'd been, because it had sort of felt like I was suddenly in his shower on the opposite side of the country. But I hadn't tried to go there, much less to put a spell on him. And I still didn't know how I had.

"That wasn't a dream," he murmured, warm tongue licking the blood from my neck. "I was pleasuring myself, thinking of you, and there you were. I thought I was going mad for a moment, in the best possible way."

"But you didn't say anything," I said, trying to concentrate and mostly failing.

Full-body shivers will do that to you.

"No more did you," he pointed out.

"I wasn't . . . sure . . . I hadn't imagined it," I said, trying not to squirm. Because he *still wasn't moving*. If there was any doubt that vampires were superhuman, this ought to cinch it. No human man could just stand there like that. Could be buried in my body, to the point that I could feel his heartbeat echo my own, deep inside my flesh. And then *just stay there*.

He was going to freaking kill me one of these days.

"I was," he told me. "But I didn't know what we were dealing with. I still don't."

"That's what had you so upset?" I asked. "That someone could tap into your brain through mine?"

"Not just mine. I am in mental communication with the Senate on a regular basis. If my mind was compromised . . ."

"That's really what you thought?" I'd noticed that Mircea had been avoiding me lately, but I'd just assumed he was busy. And once or twice I'd wondered if he was having the same trouble defining our relationship that I was. But I should have known better. Mircea was a master vampire and a Senate member. And despite what he'd said, they didn't have problems with relationships.

They took what they wanted.

Like when he finally, finally started to thrust.

And I suddenly forgot how to breathe.

"We are at war, Cassie," he murmured against my skin. "And our enemies have proven . . . resourceful. They tapped into the power of your office through the ward you used to wear, did they not? Used it to help them bring a god through the barrier?"

"But I . . . I don't wear that anymore."

"No, but you now wear a spell, one invented by the same people we are fighting."

"But laid by my mother."

"Yes. To allow her to talk with the council. Can they still access your mind?"

"I . . . don't think so," I told him, because yeah, time for twenty questions, Mircea!

"But they could at one time," he pointed out, his breathing still even, although mine was becoming ragged. "They must have been able to, if your mother could use you as a conduit."

"Yes, but they shut that down. Or . . . or they said they did."

"And the word of a demon is to be trusted," he said sardonically.

"Maybe not," I said breathlessly. "But they're on our side in this—"

"The demons are on their own side."

"But that happens to be ours right now, doesn't it?"

"Does it?" He shifted position slightly, and the gentle undulation he'd been doing picked up speed.

And strength.

Oh God.

"How do we know?"

"We know . . . because they hated . . . the gods," I told him stubbornly. Refusing to let him have the last word just because he was pounding me into the desktop. "They . . . fed off them, like the demons feed off us. They slaughtered . . . thousands of them. My mother did in particular. It was demon energy she used to build her wall—"

"Something you did not bother to mention."

"We haven't exactly . . . had much time . . . to talk!"

"Something I will have to remedy," he told me, sounding faintly ominous. "Yet you do not think they would spy on the daughter of their old enemy?"

"Yes . . . but I also think . . . they could be . . . good allies. They don't want the gods back . . . any more than we do."

"Allies bring something to the table."

"They . . . bring something to the table," I said, trying to look at him over my shoulder. And finding it hard, since I needed both hands just to hold on.

Damn; I knew I'd pay for that little tease in the office, sooner or later.

"They killed . . . Apollo," I managed to say.

"Your mother's spell killed Apollo, for all intents and purposes."

"But they finished him off."

"Yes, that is what they do. Scavengers, vultures, leeches—"

"Some people . . . would say the same thing . . . about vamps."

"Then those people are fools. We live on earth. Contribute to it in many ways. It is our home. The demons use it as a hunting ground, nothing more."

I didn't entirely agree with that, but I was having a hard time thinking clearly with him shuddering to completion. "But . . . but they still wouldn't . . . want the competition . . . would they?" I asked. "The gods . . . controlled earth when they were here. When the demons came, they . . . fed off them. If the gods come back, the demons lose their favorite snack bar. And maybe become snacks themselves!"

"The fact that you are still able to reason at this point worries me," Mircea said, and sat down, taking me with him, his body still inside mine. And God, I need a chair like this, I thought dizzily, groaning from the abrupt change in position. And then groaning again as he began pleasuring me with his fingers, teasing, expert, maddening. And had me writhing on his lap in seconds.

And, okay, that was better than talking, which I hadn't wanted to do anyway. But that was back when I thought we'd be discussing us, which I didn't know how to do. But this . . . yeah, we needed to talk about this.

But we weren't. Because I was too busy thrashing and wriggling and squealing and coming. And then lying back against him, exhausted and happy, with what was probably a totally goofy smile on my face. Which, fortunately, he couldn't see, because God knew he didn't need the ego boost.

"That doesn't . . . refute . . . my point," I said, when I could talk.

And felt the sweaty chest behind me shake slightly.

Mircea had always had what many people viewed as an unfortunate sense of humor. I viewed it as a plus, and one of the most human things about him. He couldn't help but see the absurdity in things, like us trying to talk politics now of all times.

But when else was I likely to get the chance? And he needed to understand this. Only Mircea didn't seem to think so.

"Whether the demons are 'on our side' or not, they are useless to us," he told me.

"But they're powerful—"

"In their own realm, yes. But in faerie?" He shook his head. "Their magic doesn't work there."

"Are you sure?" I knew mine didn't, at least not well. Different worlds had different time streams, and my power seemed to be tied to this one. But the demons didn't have that problem, so maybe—

But Mircea crushed that idea. "Quite sure. Their strength remains intact, for those who have a body, but their magic falters outside their own realm."

"But they could be helpful here, couldn't they? On earth?" I asked, because, as strange as it seemed, earth *was* their realm. Or, to be more precise, it was one of the hell dimensions. The hells, which weren't a single world but thousands, were all on the same metaphysical plane, so the same magical laws worked across all of them.

That didn't mean there weren't issues. The main one being that human mages, and I guess demons and fey and whatever, manufactured some of their own magic. They were magical creatures, which meant that their bodies acted sort of like talismans, soaking it up from the world they were born in and then generating usable power, like a regular human's body making vitamin D if they sat in the sun.

But outside their home world, magical beings didn't absorb as much, meaning their store of power ran low really fast. It would be like trying to make vitamin D while in northern Alaska during winter, when there's all of a couple hours of sun a day. Possible but not easy.

But it looked easy compared to trying the same thing in faerie.

Because faerie wasn't a hell, it was a heaven, hard as that was to believe after having been there briefly. And having barely surviving the trip. But, technically, it was in one of the heavenly dimensions, and therefore had magic that worked on totally different rules.

That basically meant zero absorption from the natural world while you were there. You would have what magic you went in with, for as long as it lasted you, and then that was it. Instead of Alaska, it would be like being in a dark room and being told to make vitamin D—not happening.

But, of course, the same was true of the fey when they came here. They had what they had when they arrived, and that was all they had, magically speaking. And that didn't last long, because it was harder to cast your spells on an alien world. It was like it was trying to reject them or something.

It was why there'd never been a war between the two realms and probably never would be. What were people going to fight it with? Clubs?

But that didn't mean the demons couldn't be useful on earth, which was their own backyard. "They could help us with Black Circle," I pointed out, talking about the corrupt mages that were a perpetual pain in the ass to Jonas' organization. "And free up some of our own mages for the war."

But Mircea was shaking his head. "The Black Circle is a nuisance, nothing more. Like the smugglers we're taking out at the moment. Destroying them is helpful, and we will do it where and when the opportunity arises, but we will not win the war that way. Kit was right; our enemies are in faerie, not here. And they are not likely to come here."

I would have twisted around to look at him, but I was too tired. And it would have meant pulling myself off him, and I didn't want to do that yet. Didn't want to let him go. "You're planning to invade."

It wasn't a question because it wasn't really news; the idea had been batted about for a while. Not to start a war, but as a commando raid. Go in, grab Tony and his bunch of assholes, who were the ringleaders in the campaign to bring back the gods, and then make a run for the border. The trick was, how?

"We cannot win a war by remaining forever on the defensive," Mircea agreed.

"So you take the offensive through what? Your fey allies?"

He made a sound partway between humor and disgust. "The fey have nothing but contempt for humans—or for us that used to be so. Our 'allies,' if they deserve the name, tell us little and act as if we're fit for servants and nothing else."

I took a moment to absorb that. It was kind of hard. Vampires had always been the elite in my world, godlike, immortal creatures—well, until they pissed off a stronger vamp, anyway—who had abilities and knowledge and centuries' worth of experience I lacked. It was a bit of a mental adjustment to imagine someone else viewing them as inferior. But it did explain a few things.

"That's why you still don't know where Tony is."

Mircea nodded. I could feel it against my back, as he started combing his fingers through my wet hair. "He and the leaders of the coalition against us are in hiding in faerie, meaning they must have allies among the fey. But fey politics are . . . To call them Byzantine is to miss the mark considerably. There are only three main factions of light fey, but hundreds of family, clan, and alliance groups among them, none of which see any reason to discuss their affairs with humans. Nor to assist us with an invasion of their world. They are deliberately keeping us in the dark to ensure that we have no choice but to leave it in their hands."

"And yet they're not doing anything."

"Not that they have bothered to communicate to us. And this cannot continue."

"But what's the alternative? If you can't invade—"

"I did not say that, *dulceață*."

I leaned my head back at that, so I could see his face, but he looked serious. Which didn't make a lot of sense. "How? The Circle—"

"Is useless. Their magic is weak in faerie; they wouldn't make it five miles from whatever portal they used to enter. And it wouldn't matter if they did; the fey would wipe the floor with them in any battle. The same would be true for your demons."

"So how do you invade?"

Mircea smiled down at me, dark eyes glinting. "Well. Since you asked."

Chapter Thirty

Mircea took my hand and we threaded our way back through the rugs. But this time, we went through another door, set into the opposite wall from the one where we'd come in, and then down a tiny corridor. It had rooms branching off on both sides, including a small bedroom near the end.

Where a tousled-headed guy named Jules was sitting on a bed with his legs drawn up and a bunch of magazines spread out around him, none of which he was looking at. In fact, he didn't appear to be looking at anything. He didn't even raise his head when we came in, which was unprecedented in the presence of his master.

Only . . . Mircea wasn't Jules' master anymore, was he?

That was such a weird thought that I didn't know quite what to do with it. Vampires didn't simply stop being vampires. They just didn't.

Except for Jules.

He had been one of my bodyguards until he'd blundered into a terrible spell, a war spell, by mistake. It had still been in the experimental stages but was nonetheless powerful enough to turn him into little more than a human ball of flesh. Rendering him unable to talk, or move, or even see, once his own skin finished stretching over him like a shroud.

It would have been deadly to a human, but Jules wasn't

one. And vampires are a hardy breed. But no one—including the spell's inventor—had known how to reverse it, so I'd decided to try something a little crazy.

I'd tried to de-age him, to take him back in time to before the spell was laid, hoping that would deactivate it. It had seemed like a long shot, but nobody else had known what to do, and Jules had been . . . God. He'd begged me to help him or kill him, since I was the only one he could talk to. The spell had screwed him up so badly that even the usual vampire mental communication hadn't worked anymore.

But seiðr had. And after Mom put the spell on me and then forgot to mention it, I'd made a couple of random connections. One to Mircea, during that little episode in the shower, and one when I sat next to Jules, horrified and speechless and not knowing how to help him.

Until he told me.

On the plus side, de-aging him had gotten rid of the malicious spell, so that was something. But on the other . . . it had gotten rid of everything else, too. All the other spells, that was. Including the one that made him a vampire.

The guy who slowly raised his head, belatedly registering our existence, was still young, blond, and attractive.

But he was also very, very human.

Which I guess is why he flushed bright red as soon as his eyes fell on me. Well, that and the seiðr link that let him see me at all. I grabbed for my towel, thinking maybe it had come loose, but no. For once, I was actually decent.

And then I looked up—

Only to be tackled by a human dynamo who literally knocked me off my feet.

"Cassie!"

"Ow," I said, because my back had just hit the wall, and despite the fact I wasn't actually here, it had hurt. And so did the fingers sinking into my arms. And the rapid-fire shaking that commenced immediately thereafter until Mircea pulled him off.

"Cassie!" Jules said again, staring at me out of huge eyes and a flushed face and a weird-looking mouth that, well, frankly I didn't know what that expression was, because he could love me or hate me right now, and both would be perfectly fair.

And then he burst into tears and grabbed for me again, and, okay, maybe he wasn't mad? I still couldn't tell. But I went into his arms anyway, 'cause if ever anybody looked like he needed a hug . . .

"They wouldn't tell me—I asked and asked, and they wouldn't tell me anything!" he said, drawing back. And grinning. And then crying some more, even while still grinning, and can you blame me for being confused?

"Are . . . you okay?" I eventually said, because I still wasn't sure.

"I don't know!" he told me. And laughed.

I looked at Mircea.

"We've been keeping him sedated," Mircea said wryly. "But that sort of thing is hard on a human's physiology."

"Hear that? Hard on a *human's*," Jules repeated, his face filled with a strange mix of things, which kept making his mouth go all weird. Wonder and fear and elation and sorrow and joy and confusion—I finally realized that I didn't know what he felt because *he* didn't.

Which, yeah.

"So . . . you're all right?" I repeated. "More or less?"

"More or less!" he said, shaking his head.

I decided that he really didn't know, and that maybe I should find another question.

A vamp appeared in the doorway, one who actually looked like the stereotype: tall and gaunt, with creepy red eyes. And then just stood there until Mircea deigned to acknowledge his existence. "Yes, Lawrence?"

"Louis-Cesare has arrived, my lord. He wishes a word."

"Excuse me for a moment," Mircea told me.

They went off somewhere, and I sat down on the bed. I needed to go, too, to check out those cabinets and see if they held what I hoped they did, to finagle some Tears out of Mircea if so, and to get some sleep. But it was really hard with Jules' shining face staring at me like that.

"When are we leaving?" he asked, grabbing a duffel from the end of the bed.

"What?"

"You're taking me back with you. That's why you came, isn't it?"

"Um."

"That isn't why you came?"

"Not . . . exactly."

"But you will, won't you?" He squatted down in front of me, but because Jules was over six feet tall that still left us almost on a level. "You can ask," he told me urgently. "They'll let me go if you ask!"

"Let you go? But you're a human. They don't control you anymore."

"Tell them that!"

"You mean they're keeping you here? Like some kind of prisoner?"

"They're . . . I don't know. They say I can leave eventually, but they won't tell me when. And in the meantime I've been here, right here, since just after you changed me. They were afraid of people seeing me at the hotel, so they brought me here—"

"Where is 'here'?"

"I don't know. The consul's place, I think. I just know I went to sleep and woke up here and haven't been out of here since! I asked to go outside, just to see the sunrise, but they wouldn't let me. Said somebody might see me, and—and you've got to get me out, Cassie. Promise me you'll get me out!"

"I will," I said, trying to calm him down. Because he'd finally settled on an emotion and it was panic.

And I didn't get that. I glanced around the room, but it didn't seem so bad to me. No windows, of course, but presumably this was a vampire residence, so no big shock there. And everything else seemed comfortable enough. There was even a small TV.

And he'd been here only a couple of days.

Of course, Jules wasn't exactly the most stoic of guys. Jules tended to freak out over a hangnail. But still.

"What's so terrible?" I asked, honestly puzzled.

"Everything!" He lowered his voice; why, I don't know. It wasn't like Mircea couldn't have heard him half a mile away. "Nothing. I don't know." His eyes darted around. "It's creepy!"

"Creepy?"

"This place is crawling with vampires!"

"Jules. You used to *be* a vampire."

"Yes, but I'm not one *now*. And they don't look at me

the same way anymore. All of a sudden, I'm not a person. I'm ... lunch. Or a lab rat or—I don't know. But they're planning something, I know they are, and I need to get out of here before they figure out what!"

"A lab rat? Why a lab rat?"

He looked at me incredulously. "Cassie. Don't you get it? Don't you know what you *did*?"

"Made history," Mircea said from the door.

I looked up and oh, goody, Kit had come, too. He looked even more rumpled than before, because he'd found an overcoat that had apparently been at the bottom of a laundry hamper somewhere. Or possibly been towed behind a van. With his wrinkled clothes and messy curls and sharp, dark eyes, he looked like a slightly better-looking Columbo. Or maybe more than slightly better, if he hadn't been standing next to a shirtless Adonis.

And frowning at me.

"Mircea ..." I said, starting to get creeped out, because I wasn't imagining it. Kit's dark eyes were boring a hole into mine.

"I let him into my mind," Mircea explained. "Not into the spell," he added, at my look of alarm. Because the last thing I needed was the Senate's chief spy probing around my cranium. "I don't control that; you do."

"My mother did," I corrected.

But Mircea shook his head. "She may have laid the spell, but she wasn't powering it. You were. And unless this magic runs counter to every other kind we know, the one who powers a spell controls it."

"But I haven't been controlling it. I don't know how to control it." I'd fallen down the rabbit hole and didn't even know how to get home.

"Yet you have been placing it on other people. On me, and on Jules."

"By accident."

"And that matters why?" Marlowe said sharply. Because vampires didn't get concepts like extenuating circumstances. At least, their law code didn't. If you did something, you were responsible for it, no matter why it happened.

So, as far as Marlowe was concerned, the loss of a master vampire was one hundred percent down to me. But

Jules hadn't been his vampire, so I didn't see what his beef was. Jules had belonged to Mircea, and he seemed to be taking it in stride.

Seemed to be taking it suspiciously in stride.

It was one of the reasons it had taken me a while to notice that he'd been avoiding me lately, because I'd kind of been doing it right back. I'd expected him to have a few things to say about Jules, along with some other stuff that had happened recently. But he was looking awfully good-humored for someone who had just been deprived of the vamp equivalent of a winning Powerball ticket.

I started to get a bad feeling about this.

"These things happen," Mircea said easily, causing my alarm meter to tick up another few notches. "However, your new ability may be the solution we've been looking for."

"What solution?" I asked, looking back and forth from him to Kit. But, strangely for a guy who prided himself on knowing everything, it didn't look like Kit knew this. He had transferred his frown to Mircea, and it was growing.

"What were we just discussing?" Mircea asked me.

It took me a moment, because I didn't see what the two had to do with each other. "The . . . invasion of faerie?"

Mircea smiled.

Marlowe didn't. But his eyes narrowed. And shifted from Mircea back to me, with a new expression in them.

It wasn't one I liked.

"What?" I asked him bluntly.

But it was Mircea who answered. "As we just discussed, the only option for ending this war is to ferret out the ones responsible for it. And we must do that soon, before they manage to bring another of the gods back to fight it for them. Yet that has seemed impossible. They are hiding in faerie, and no one goes into faerie in force. It has never been done. We have therefore been stymied, waiting for our fey allies to aid us or at least to tell us where our enemies are to be found. They have done neither."

"And they don't intend to," Marlowe said. "They won't even help us stop the damned smugglers; how can we expect them to do something that requires actual risk?"

"We can't," Mircea said, still looking at me. "The onus is on us. We alone among the supernatural community are unaffected by faerie. A vampire is a vampire, wherever he is. We do not acquire our magic in the same way as the other groups, and therefore do not feel the effects of a strange world as they do."

"You do when it's time to feed," I pointed out, wondering where he was going with this.

"But a master does not need to feed often—"

"He does if he's injured."

"—and he can draw strength from his family in the case of injury, feeding through his connection to them. We alone have a link to this world, to our family, to our source of magic, that remains the same regardless of where we are."

"*If* you're a master," I pointed out, because all vamps had links to their families, but masters were the only ones who could pull the kind of power Mircea was talking about. "And most aren't."

"No," he agreed. "Most aren't."

There was a pregnant pause.

Which stayed that way, because I still wasn't getting this.

"I don't get how you expect to do this alone," I said. "Or why you want to. The vampires aren't the only ones in danger, so why does it all fall to—"

"Think about it, Cassie," Mircea said, sitting on the bed beside me. "The mages are all but useless in faerie; the demons likewise. The Weres might be somewhat of a help, but they are too few in number and too unreliable to be counted on. Who does that leave?"

"The covens, for one," I said, talking about the groups of magic users who had never come under the Circle's control. "And they use a form of fey magic—"

"But one designed for use on earth. And they have the same organizational problem as the Weres, only more so. They are leaderless, fractured, unreliable. To avoid being subsumed by the Circle, they withdrew from it. But in doing so, they ceded much of their power in the community the Circle now governs. You would be wise not to put too much faith in them. They may need you, but they cannot be an asset to you."

Which, in vamp terms, made them irrelevant.

"But the vamps *can't* invade on their own," I said, feeling like I was taking crazy pills. "You barely have enough masters to run everything now."

Masters were the backbone of the vamp world. They were the administrators, the ambassadors, the rulers, and the police. Not to mention the font of all new vamps, since no one below a master could make any, and the reason the whole vampire world hadn't been wiped out by the mages centuries ago.

Back in the day, vampirism had been viewed like the plague, and the mages who hunted them thought of themselves as doctors trying to eradicate it. And they'd done it easily, killing the rank-and-file vamps they came across by the hundreds and then by the thousands. Until they met with a bunch of masters who had banded together to fuck some shit up.

And they had. And it led to centuries of conflict thereafter, with each side renewing the war anytime one of them got what they thought would be an advantage. I'd been taught it as a child mostly from the vampire perspective, but the vamps had caused just as much damage, viewing a world without mages as a paradise where they could live and feed and spread at will.

But that didn't happen because the two groups mostly stayed at equilibrium with each other, and so served as a kind of unofficial checks-and-balances system. They'd signed a treaty years ago professing "friendship and cooperation," but no way would that last if there was suddenly some big advantage to one side or the other.

Like most of the world's masters being wiped out in faerie, for instance.

"You don't have that many vamps to spare, or to risk," I pointed out. "Even with all six Senates, you don't—"

I stopped, the clue bat having just smacked me sharply between the eyes.

I looked at Jules, who was now sitting on the far side of the bed, since Mircea had taken his space. He looked back at me, blue eyes wide and oblivious. Marlowe, on the other hand, was practically vibrating.

No, I thought.

No, I'm imagining things.

But one look at Mircea's face told me I wasn't.

He was watching me, a small smile on his lips, the kind that said he'd already done all the math and was just waiting for me to catch up. But I wasn't catching up, because there were diseases and then there were cures, and some of the cures were just as bad as the illness.

"What happens after the war?" I asked abruptly, and had the tiny satisfaction of seeing him blink.

Not because he hadn't thought of it, too, but because he hadn't thought I would.

"We have to win it first," he pointed out.

"Yes, we do. But not this way." I started to get up.

He caught my arm. "Then what way? What would you have us do?"

"I don't know. But there has to be another—"

"Do you think we haven't looked for one? Do you think we haven't had every expert we possess working on the problem? For *months*? Where faerie is concerned, there simply aren't many options."

"Then look some more! This is crazy!"

"Why crazy?" Mircea asked, still sounding oh so reasonable. "If you can unmake a vampire, you can do the reverse."

"No, I can't! I can age him, but I can't give him power—"

"But his master can."

I stopped. I'd been about to point out that this whole discussion was a waste of time, since what I could do would result in nothing but an older baby vamp, like an eighty-year-old toddler, which wouldn't help anybody. Which meant we didn't have anything to discuss, did we?

But then Mircea's words sank in. "Meaning what?"

"That there has long been a way to speed up the process, for the right candidate." He glanced at Kit, who scowled ferociously.

"Now I know why I was invited into this little conversation," he said sourly.

"Tell her."

Kit looked like there were a few things he'd like to tell both of us, especially Mircea. But he didn't. His expression didn't get any happier, though.

"It's called the Push," he said tersely, and Jules gasped. Like the clue bat had just found another victim. Marlowe ignored him. "It's a method used to make a master in a few days instead of a few centuries. It originated in wartime, when too many masters had been killed and replacements were needed immediately to avoid disaster. I was made this way, and almost died as a result. Most who attempt it do, which is why it is used only in extremis."

He didn't look like he wanted to talk about it, so I didn't ask. Except for the obvious. "And this has what to do with me?"

"You know how vampires are made," Mircea said.

"Of course."

"The bite infects the body, but the strength to rise again, to live as a new creature, that comes from the master," he said, telling me anyway. "But with the Push, the new Child is not given merely the basic energy needed to rise, but much, much more. For most, it is too much, too soon. They can't absorb it, and never rise, dying not from the power but from having *too little time* to properly absorb it."

"You want me to age them up while their master feeds them power," I said. I didn't bother to make it a question.

"Yes."

"And risk killing them if it doesn't work?"

"There are many who would gladly take that chance. Many who have given up hope of such a thing, of a status they were never destined to earn."

"And there's a reason for that, isn't there?" I demanded. Masters were the powerhouses of the vampire world, but they were also dangerous. Extremely dangerous. And hard to control.

Mostly, it didn't matter, because there weren't that many masters and the Senate ruled them with an iron first. And because the hundreds of years of time it usually took to make one gave even the most crazed specimen, even someone like Jack, the Senate's happy-go-lucky chief torturer, time to gain a measure of self-control. Jack liked his work, but he didn't go running around making extra for himself these days, as he'd done in life. When he'd had the cute little nickname of The Ripper.

But what if he'd gotten master status early—real early? What if he'd never had that time? What if he had the same power but none of the control?

I shuddered in horror, and that was *one man*. And if they were planning an invasion . . .

"How many?"

"Cassie—"

"How many?" I said tightly, hugging myself. The towel had felt okay before, but it was suddenly clammy. Like my skin.

"I don't have the exact figure—"

"Then ballpark it!"

"No more than necessary—"

"The fact that you don't want to tell me is really worrying me right now."

Mircea frowned, like he honestly hadn't expected this to be difficult. Like, sure, I'll make you an army of master vampires to lay waste to faerie, no problem. And then pretend it's not my fault when they turn around and do the same thing to earth!

"We will be careful about the selection," Mircea said, watching me.

"You won't have to worry about that."

"Cassie—"

But before he could reconfigure his plan of attack, the same vamp who had called him out last time came back.

"Showtime," Marlowe said grimly.

"We'll talk later," Mircea promised me.

"No, damn it! We'll talk—"

And just like that, I was back at Dante's. Sprawled on the floor of my half-flooded bath, because I hadn't turned off the sink before I was abruptly snatched away.

"—now," I finished furiously.

Son of a bitch!

Chapter Thirty-one

I spent the next twenty minutes mopping up. I must have knocked the liquid hand soap when I toppled over, and it was the frothy kind. So I'd woken up in a sea of bubbles, with a loofah bumping me in the nose, and a sink cascading over everything like a miniature Niagara.

And an imminent flood, because I'd had my butt on the drain.

I got up, turned off the water, and started shooing the tide toward the exit. But that was only somewhat helpful, since it left me with soap scale all along the walls, like a high water mark. It took every towel I had to scrub it off and to soak up the rest of the overflow. Except for the one I appropriated for me, because my old one was as drenched as everything else in here.

The boys would have told me to leave it for housekeeping, but we gave them enough trouble as it was. And cleaning gave me a chance to work off some energy. And right now, I had a lot of it.

Because I was *pissed*.

Which was both infuriating and seriously confusing, because I didn't know why.

I mean, I knew *why*. The obvious why, anyway. Mircea was running scared, just like Jonas. But when master vamps were scared, they didn't circle the wagons and go on the defensive. They ran *toward* whatever was scaring them,

weapons out and fangs bared. They became more dangerous when afraid, not less so, their every instinct telling
them to go for blood. And Mircea, being smarter than
most—about some things, I thought, scrubbing fiercely—
had found a nifty new way to do that.

"We'll be careful about the selection."

Yeah, I bet. But say they were. And say the Senate could
keep all those giddy-with-their-shiny-new-power masters
under control. Which was debatable because the ones they
already had caused them enough trouble sometimes. But
just for the sake of argument, say they could do it. That still
left some big damned questions, didn't it?

Like whose vamps would they be?

After the war was over, who would they fight for? Because there was an alliance between the vampire Senates
right now, but it was shaky at best since they all pretty
much hated one another. They just happened to hate the
gods more. So right now, the world's vampires were one
big, unhappy, seriously dysfunctional family, but normally,
there were six separate Senates. And there would be again
about a nanosecond after the war ended.

So I had to wonder. When all the dust settled, assuming
we won, because otherwise it didn't really matter, did it,
who would they fight for? Or, more important, who would
they fight against? Other Senates? The Circle? *Humans?*

Because they could. With an army of master vamps, the
Senate so very, very could do any damned thing they
pleased. And old or not, mature or not, responsible or not,
you didn't give a vamp unlimited power like that. You just
didn't. Because they would use it. Sooner or later, somehow or other, and what would be the point of all this then?
Save the world from Ares just so we could rip it apart ourselves? Yeah, that would be an improvement!

And I wasn't stupid enough to think they'd just have me
reverse the process after the war. Take all those shiny new
masters and turn them back into regular old Joe vamps?
Sure.

The vamps themselves wouldn't stand for it, would run
for the hills, would do whatever they had to do to avoid
becoming little more than slaves again. And the senior
masters over their families would probably back them, because any masters you had in your stable fed into your

power base way more than a regular vamp. So you'd be cutting your own throat to let them be turned back.

And that was if I could even do it, which I doubted, because I wasn't to be the source of the power, was I? I was just supposed to make the process more tolerable. The spoonful of sugar that helped all that power go down without burning the vamps in question to cinders.

So no. Once they were here, they'd stay here. And that so wasn't happening!

But as fantastically bad as the whole idea was, that wasn't what had me angry. And I *was* angry, I realized—not just pissed or peeved or irritated. I was hot, something it had taken me a while to realize because it wasn't an emotion I felt very often. You couldn't afford emotions around Tony's. Emotions made you visible, emotions got you noticed, and getting noticed was usually a very bad thing.

I threw my toothbrush, which I'd found on an epic voyage to the tub, into the trash, wrapped up the towels in the soggy pelt of a bath mat, and tossed the whole mess in a corner. It wasn't a perfect job, but at least we wouldn't flood out the guys in the room underneath.

Which was just as well since they were part of my guards, too, and no way was anybody else fitting into this suite!

Then I got back in the shower, because I was soapy and sweaty, and because I needed to cool off.

And to figure out why I was pissed, because I still didn't know.

I wasn't angry because of what Mircea had asked, I decided. I might not know much about being Pythia, but I knew vamps. And no vamp in the world would have passed up a chance like that.

And, anyway, he might have thought of it first, because Jules was his so he'd heard about it first, but somebody else would have come up with the same idea sooner or later. Marlowe or the consul herself or *somebody*. Vamps didn't overlook stuff likely to increase their power base, even by a small amount.

And this wasn't small.

So no, I wasn't mad at him for trying.

But if it wasn't about the question, what was I so livid about? Because I was. I so very, very was.

And I didn't really know what to do with that.

Fear, I knew, and panic—we were practically best buddies. And annoyance and irritation and happiness and relief and a lot of other emotions, because all of those were ones I'd been allowed to have growing up. Encouraged to have in the case of the first, to keep me in line.

But at Tony's, only one person had been allowed to be angry, and it hadn't been me.

Anger was an emotion for the guy in charge. Anger was something masters felt, a vivid, red-hot emotion they used like a lash to keep their households in line. At least, they did if they were Tony. I knew all about anger from being on the receiving end of it often enough, but the reverse . . .

I used to think it must be wonderful to be able to carry on like that. To just let go of all those bottled-up emotions and yell and stomp around like he did, to slash at the air and throw things and . . . and just get it all out. I used to think, when I had to stand there in court, blank faced and careful, with everything tightly bottled up inside, how wonderful it would be, just once, to get angry.

But it wasn't feeling so wonderful now.

Now it was making me nauseous and shaky and faintly ill.

I didn't like being angry at Mircea.

I liked being held by Mircea.

And I really *had* missed him this last week. I hadn't realized how much until I saw him again. And even that first glance, when I'd been seriously annoyed, had been so nice . . .

Until he had to go and spoil it.

And finally, light dawned.

I wasn't mad at Mircea as much for *what* he said but for *when* he said it. Because we had a deal. A deal he had come up with, so that what we did as Pythia and senator stayed away from what we did as Cassie and Mircea, and didn't trash our personal life. Work was work and personal was personal, and they were supposed to stay nice and separate.

It was a nice theory.

I'd liked the theory.

I'd even thought it might work.

But not if he kept doing stuff like this. Because tonight hadn't been a date, hadn't been a *Hey, I've missed you; let's hang out*, or even an *I haven't seen you for a while, so how about we get together and explore the hornier possibilities of this new power of yours?* No. If it had, then he should have left it at that and said, *Good night, Cassie*, at the end. But instead, where had I ended up? In Jules' room, getting propositioned in a whole new way that wasn't nearly as much fun, and—

And damn it! I'd forgotten about Jules. And the Tears, which were a little more pressing right now, because Jules wasn't about to die. But no way was Mircea going to give them to me, assuming he had any. He might trade me, oh yes, that he might damned well do. But give? When I had something the vamps wanted and I wasn't giving in return?

Uh-uh.

Horse trading in the vamp world didn't work like that.

And especially not when the item in question was something like this.

Mircea hadn't put a crap ton of vamp bodyguards on me because he wanted me running around. Mircea wanted me to stay put in my nice penthouse. Mircea wanted me to get my hair and nails done and maybe see a show once in a while—heavily guarded, of course. Mircea wanted me to act like those other women he'd had, the ones I kept hearing hints about but that no one would give me specifics on, women who were beautiful and elegant and stayed where they were damned well put.

Like that woman in the painting.

I bet she never gave him any trouble, I thought enviously. I bet she never slouched home looking like a war victim. I bet she was perfect and beautiful and sweet and gentle and—

I realized I was scrubbing until I was about to take skin off. I put the remaining loofah down, nice and slow. And started rinsing instead.

So, no, bringing up the Tears with Mircea wasn't going to go well. I knew that without even asking. I'd have a better chance getting some out of the Circle, although Jonas would probably also want an explanation, and I doubted I'd get any until I told him something he'd like.

And that was maddening. It was *my* potion. It was brewed specifically for the Pythia, to use when needed. Since when did he get to tell her when that was?

Since the Pythia was me, apparently.

I bet he wouldn't have demanded an explanation from Agnes. And Mircea, if she'd gone to him for some crazy reason, probably wouldn't have, either. The Senate had wanted a Pythia for so long—they'd have jumped at the chance to help her, to have her owe them a favor.

But not me.

And, abruptly, the final puzzle piece fell into place.

Because I *would* be expected to tell everyone why I needed it, wouldn't I? And to have it be something they approved of to have any chance at getting it at all. And while that was infuriating with Jonas, it was worse with Mircea.

Vampires respected power and strength, and that was pretty much all they respected. I'd shown that I had power recently, by somehow managing to kill a Spartoi, one of the demigod sons of Ares, in a duel that many of the vamp leadership had happened to see. They'd liked that. They'd liked it so much that they'd signed the treaty of alliance shortly thereafter, doing what nobody had ever expected and putting themselves under the leadership of the North American consul.

That was a huge deal. That had never happened before. And it had only happened now because they were dealing with a power they didn't know how to counter and they needed somebody on their side who did.

I'd shown them power, power they didn't have, and it had helped.

But I hadn't shown them strength.

Because strength in the vamp world didn't mean the ability to bend steel. The smallest vamp girl could do that. No, strength was something else.

Strength was the consul calmly saying to five other Senate leaders, each of them hundreds of years old and staggeringly powerful, *I will lead this alliance*, and making it stick. Strength was one master vamp bowing to another and giving way for him, not because he might not be just as strong, but because he wasn't willing to find out. Strength was why Senate seats were still determined by duels, as archaic as that seemed these days. Because being a leader in the vampire world didn't require just being powerful, it required being able to say to another first-level master, *this seat is mine and I will take it.*

So yes, I'd shown power, but so far, from a vamp per-spective, I hadn't shown strength. And now I was paying for it. Mircea might love me, but he didn't respect me. He wouldn't have pulled that stunt tonight if he respected me.

And that, ladies and gentlemen, is why I was angry. Not because he'd asked, but because of when and how. Because of the assumption that I would just do this, without ques-tion, without thought. That he could just tell me what he wanted and that would be it.

Or point me at a problem like a gun, because guns didn't act on their own, did they? Guns didn't have ideas and opinions. Guns were pulled out when needed and left in the drawer the rest of the time.

Or in a hotel suite in Vegas.

Chapter Thirty-two

Something jolted me out of a dead sleep the next morning, and I rolled over to see the clock. Barely seven a.m. But I didn't go back to sleep. Because I had a job to do and because I needed to find something to stop the pounding in my head.

Which I belatedly realized wasn't coming from my head.

It was coming from the door.

I stared at it blearily and wondered if I cared. And then the door burst open, and a wild-eyed, dark-haired woman came in, yelling my name even after being tackled by Marco in a flying leap.

Which turned into a trip in the opposite direction when she deflected him with a gesture, sending him slamming back through the air and then through the wall.

I sat up.

I guess I cared.

It took me a second to figure out who I was looking at, because I hadn't seen her too often. And when I had, she'd been a little more indistinct. Incubi—or succubi, I guess, in this case—don't normally have bodies, because it takes a huge amount of power to manifest them.

But then, this particular succubus had been on earth something like four hundred years and had power to burn.

"Rian?" I said blearily, and held up a hand so that nobody decided to shoot her.

Including Marco, who had just rushed back in, weapon drawn.

"It's okay," I told him. "She's . . . she used to be Casanova's girlfriend."

"I am still his girlfriend!" Rian looked at me wildly, dark hair everywhere. I guessed real hair was harder to handle than the spirit kind she'd had until recently. Because it was a little scary.

Then again, that might have been because she kept pulling on it.

"Okay, you're still his girlfriend," I said, because this seemed to be important for some reason. "I'm sure he'll be happy to hear that."

"He won't be happy! He won't be happy at all!"

"And why is that?" Marco demanded, looking like he'd like to introduce her to the nearest window. The kind without a balcony.

But Rian didn't look like she cared. "Because he's about to be killed!" she shrieked, and grabbed my hand.

And the next thing I knew, we materialized in a roar of noise, like a wave crashing onto a beach. Make that a thousand waves onto a thousand beaches, I thought, momentarily deafened. And staring around at a bunch of backs, because we'd landed in the middle of a crowd.

I never shifted into crowds for fear of ending up inside another person, but Rian must have had better control. Possibly because she didn't exactly shift, but instead could transition between the human and the demon worlds. Which is where it looked like we were, in the middle of a crowd on what appeared to be some old wooden bleachers.

I thought there might be an arena down there that the bleachers were surrounding, but it was hard to tell since almost everyone was taller than I was. And many of them were holding containers of beer and popcorn in the way. Along with the usual bad-for-you stadium snacks like nachos and chili dogs and huge squirming black insects on a stick, still trying to claw and bite despite being drilled through.

Rian dragged me past, still staring, and the scene rippled at the edges. Other holes appeared here and there, maybe because there were just too many people for any glamourie to compensate for. Or maybe because there *was* no substitute for some of them, nothing except shuddering horror.

I jerked back from something I'd seen once before, a giant clear slug of a man, with an evil-eyed demonic thing crouched inside his overlarge belly, black and red-eyed and visible through the layers of translucent, glistening fat. Which was horrible enough, even before the red eyes swiveled to mine. And I started backing up the other way because no, no, no—

And ran into something else.

Something that looked like some kind of centaur, if instead of the back half of a horse you substituted a horse-sized scorpion, complete with curling barbed tail, and way too many legs and pincers in the place of hands. I shied back from him—it—as well, looking this way and that, but seeing no way out. Just a crowd of monsters who had just seen me, too, and were closing in on all sides, popcorn or whatever the hell it actually was forgotten in the headlong rush for a real meal.

I screamed and shifted, with nowhere in mind, just "away."

And away is where I went, only it wasn't an improvement. I looked up from the panicked crouch I'd landed in, and found myself in the middle of a huge open space, surrounded by towering stands full of monsters. And, yeah, it was an arena, all right, filled with what must have been ten thousand screaming fans, like a major league football game. Only I didn't see a football.

I did see the giant pincer that plowed into the ground a second later, though, throwing up a great welt of sand. And Casanova, the usual suave and impeccably dressed casino manager, running past wearing a loincloth and an expression that went beyond panic, left fear in the dust, and was well into full-on heart attack territory. Only he was a vampire, and his heart didn't attack.

But something else did. I had a half second to see a massive carapace coming my way, black and oily and shining under the lights, before it blocked out most of them. Along with the stands and the crowd and the sky, because the thing was big as a bus. And that wasn't counting the hairy legs large as tree trunks that caged me in on all sides, before some protrusion as big as a sword flashed down—

And missed, because I'd just shifted to Casanova. Who was halfway across the sandy soil of the arena, and moving fast. At least he was until he ran into me and we boiled over in a rolling, cussing, screaming ball, and I shifted—

Back into my atrium at Dante's.

I hit the marble floor, scattering sand everywhere, and Marco grabbed for me with a snarl—why, I wasn't sure.

Until I realized—Casanova hadn't come with me, despite the fact that I'd been clinging to him with both arms and a leg when I shifted.

But something else had.

Something else that I didn't even get a good grip on before it jumped from my back to Marco's face, like a prop out of freaking *Alien*. Long, black, king-crab-sized legs wrapped around his head, extending from a beetle-like body, a miniature of the one I'd just fled from. And which I felt like fleeing from again but instead I was screaming, "Get it off him! Get it off him!" while a dozen vamps tried to do just that.

Fred burst out of the suite with a kitchen knife and plunged it into the space on the creature where hideous body met ugly head. And jerked back, I guess trying to peel off the horrible shell. And ended up with only a broken knife for his trouble.

So he tried using his hand instead, before jumping back. "Shit! Shit!"

"What is it?" I said, afraid he was going to say "poison."

"The damned shell is razor-edged. It almost cut my hand off!"

"Here!" One of the boys threw him a jacket, which he wrapped around his bleeding digits before trying again.

And this time, he actually managed to peel off the shell, with a horrible squelching sound that I thought I might hear in my nightmares from now on. And then Rico was there, blocking the entry to the main part of the suite with an expression that said a platoon wasn't getting past him, and Marco was grabbing the knife. And throwing himself onto the creature, which had just rebounded off the wall and onto the floor and *was still moving*.

And biting and fighting and scurrying around the atrium, leaving a trail of slime behind that wasn't eating through the floor but was tripping hell out of the vamps trying to catch it. And then the creature lunged for me again, only to get caught in midair by Marco's knife, before slamming into the wall over my left shoulder.

We both looked at it for a second, the knife quivering out of the still-moving body, the splatter of black ooze that had smeared the plaster and left flecks all over my shorty pink nightgown, and the chittering, squealing thing.

That suddenly burst off of the wall *and came at me again*.

"The *fuck*!" Marco said, grabbing and stabbing it over and over, and then Rian was back and we were suddenly somewhere else, somewhere with a cheering crowd and dazzling lights and a groaning buffet table.

I stared at the latter for a second, unable to keep up. And then I noticed: the crowd was still audible, but muffled. And the dazzling lights were outside a large viewing window, like a skybox at a stadium. And the well-dressed group around the buffet was looking at me with polite surprise, but no more. The most I received for standing there covered in black blood and panting at them was a slightly raised eyebrow.

And that was from Adra, the head of the demon council, who was looking as blandly agreeable as always.

"Is there a problem?" he asked pleasantly, right before Marco bellowed and went for him, because he'd somehow come along, too.

I tried to stop him, but a master vampire moves like lightning, and I didn't even get my mouth open before he passed me in a blur of motion.

And then froze, midleap, held in place by nothing I could see, because Adra hadn't so much as moved.

For a moment, everything stopped. There was no sound, other than the ocean crash of the crowd, no movement except for the thing that two master vamps had been trying to kill for the last minute wriggling off the end of Marco's knife and scurrying away, no anything but a vampire suddenly realizing he wasn't in Kansas anymore and rolling shocked dark eyes over at me.

I licked my lips.

And then Rian burst in from a door I hadn't noticed, wild-eyed and frantic, her long dark hair tangled about her beautiful face. "They're killing him!" she told me, grabbing my hand.

And we ran.

The sound of the crowd slapped me in the face when we burst out of the main room onto a balcony, a wide, plush thing like the suite behind us, and unlike the rest of the run-down stadium. But when I crossed the expanse and hung over the railing, I saw the same thing I had before, only from a better vantage point: Casanova in the middle of a sea of sand, being chased by half a dozen different kinds of creatures, and naked, bleeding, and defenseless—or as much as a master vampire ever is.

Which was looking pretty damned defenseless right now.

Rian stared down at him, her hand clenched, her face frantic and furious and terrified, as he narrowly avoided being skewered by what looked like a giant beetle. It was the same one that had almost steamrollered me, and I'd been wrong about the size. The legs were as big as cranes, the shell was the size of a house, and it must have been diamond hard, because the next second Casanova vaulted over the top of it and brought down two joined fists with a master's strength behind them.

And didn't even dent it.

The creature had better luck, flinging him off with a twisting motion. And the legs, which might have been huge but were really freaking fast nonetheless, started slamming down, here, there, everywhere, which was pretty easy considering that the thing had six. And Casanova was doing what looked like interpretive dance but was more like fleeing for his life while the creature's movements threw up huge spouts of sand, half hiding him from view.

And then they did hide him, as the thing stopped trying to skewer him and started trying to bury him instead, crashing down against the soil and flinging up great gobs of sand on top of its shell with every leg it had.

Until I shifted it to the other end of the arena, in a move that sent me to my knees, whether because of the thing's size or because we weren't on earth anymore, I wasn't sure.

"Cassie—Cassie!" somebody was yelling, I think it was Rian. Possibly because my blurry vision showed me that I'd just expended a lot of power for very little result. I stared through railings as Casanova clawed his way out of the sand, his usual Spanish good looks dirt-streaked and wild-eyed, although the latter might have had something to do with the fact that the massive beetle thing was already on its way back toward him.

So I flipped it, and oh God, *not good, not good, not good*, I thought as a wave of crippling nausea hit like a sledge-hammer, hard enough to drop me the rest of the way to the floor. But I had to get it together, because something was happening. And I doubted it was anything good, because when was it ever? And because the crowd seemed to like it.

The upswell of sound from below was almost deafening even this high up, adding to the confusion in my head and the pounding in my ears and the sickening queasiness in my gut when I grabbed Rian's hand, trying to get back to my feet.

And discovered that it was Adra's hand instead.

"Impressive," he told me, hauling me up as easily as if I weighed nothing.

He looked like a pudgy banker today, in a nicely pressed gray suit that I was seriously considering hurling all over.

But I didn't. Because I could see the arena over his shoulder, and . . . and it hadn't been so bad, after all. I let go of his hand to grab the railing, in time to see a bunch of the little bug things attack the big bug thing. Along with some other things, half of which made my brain hurt to look at them, because I guess the glamourie couldn't do anything with them, either. But they suddenly surged forward, hav-ing been hugging the sidelines, waiting for scraps, but were now seeing an opportunity for a feast instead.

Because the big beetle was still on its back, rocking side to side, trying to get back up but not having much luck. Maybe because it was being chowed down on by what had to be a hundred other creatures. And I guess the belly wasn't as hard as the shell, because they were chowing fast.

I looked away, relieved and sickened in about equal measure. Until I caught sight of Casanova running back this way, looking up at us and yelling something I couldn't hear over the crowd. But I guess Adra did, because he glanced over as well, and shook his head.

"Denied."

And I guess Casanova heard that, because he started waving his arms furiously and screaming something I still couldn't hear but didn't have to.

"What—what's denied?" I asked as Rian stared at Adra with open hate on her face.

"He killed it," she spat. "You said he could go if—"

"He killed nothing," Adra told her, smoothing down the small moustache he'd acquired since I last saw him, I guess trying new ways of dressing up the pudding face. It was as blond as his hair, though, so didn't make much of a difference. "He was saved by the Pythia, if only momentarily."

"Momentarily?" I asked, looking back and forth between them. "Wh-why momentarily?"

"But it's dead!" Rian shouted. "That's what you wanted, entertainment for your creatures—"

"This isn't about entertainment," Adra said.

"—and you've had it! Now let him go!"

"When he has defeated an opponent on his own. He broke the law, invaded a sovereign state—"

"What state?" I asked, suddenly seriously afraid that I knew.

The almost invisible brow went up again. "You were there."

"Rosier's."

I received a slight nod that I didn't need, because getting Pritkin out of his father's court had required getting into said court in the first place. And that had required Rian, who, as one of Rosier's succubi, knew it like the back of her hand. But, unfortunately, the reverse was also true.

She was known by sight to too many people, who might have guessed what we were up to if they'd glimpsed her. So she'd needed to travel inside her host's body, said host being the unfortunate Casanova, where she was all but invisible. And she'd said she could protect him, that he wouldn't be in any danger, and we'd both believed it—

And now we'd just gotten him killed.

No. *I* had gotten him killed. I had put the damned mission in place; I had convinced Rian to help; I had ordered Caleb, a war mage friend of Pritkin's, to drag Casanova literally to hell and back, kicking and screaming and protesting the whole way. And now he was paying for it.

"He did it on my orders," I said, trying to keep the tremor out of my voice. Because I doubted demons liked weakness any better than vamps.

"Yes!" Rian said, latching on to the comment. "Yes! The

Pythia gave the order, and she just defeated your creature! This is over!"

"This is not over," Adra said mildly.

"You're supposed to be helping me find my acolytes," I pointed out, trying to keep my voice level. "Not depriving me of an ally."

"A poor ally."

"He managed to raid one of your courts."

"Yes." Adra glanced over the balcony. "I am sure he was a huge help."

I didn't look to see what Casanova was doing. I probably didn't want to know. "Then why punish him?"

Adra shrugged. "Process of elimination. The prince was punished already. You are a needed ally, and in any case, your power makes any such contest . . . unequal. Rian informed her master of your intent, and thereby won a pardon. And the war mage you used—" He snapped his fingers.

"Caleb Carter."

"Yes. He is protected by a treaty we have with the Silver Circle. And even were he not, the case could be made that he was functioning as your bodyguard and was therefore under your control."

"And Casanova? Why can't he be considered a bodyguard?"

Gray eyes looked behind me. I turned to see Casanova fleeing from a group of tiny bug things, none bigger than the size of my hand, that were hopping along the dust cloud behind him, nipping at his heels.

I turned back to Adra and tried another tactic. "Why punish anyone? No harm was done. Rosier isn't even—"

"I beg to differ. Harm has been done. Our borders are inviolable; have been so since the Sufferings following your mother's time, when vast armies held them at great cost. The armies are no more, long since disbanded. But the idea remains. To allow anyone, even you—especially you—to violate their sovereignty with impunity would be to challenge that idea, and could lead to untold misfortune."

"You're going to make an example out of him," I said, because of course they were.

I felt a lead weight drop into my stomach.

"We're allies." I tried again. "New ones. As a gesture of friendship—"

"But I am already making such a gesture, am I not? And it is not only I who have a say. The council will be hard-pressed to find a reason to return to you the one with whom you breached our borders."

I swallowed.

Yeah.

That could be tricky.

"Cassie, please!" Rian said. And then whirled on Adra. "How can you—"

But he held up a hand. And focused somewhere behind my head. "Ahh," he murmured.

I would have turned around, but I didn't really want to know what the head of the demon council thought worthy of that sound. And because I was trying to scan the arena, to see if there was anything Casanova could possibly use as a weapon. But I guess those weren't allowed. Because all I saw was the huge oval, terribly pitted now, and filled with scattered scurrying things. And a massive gate of iron-banded wood at the far end, which was currently closed but which several lumbering creatures were plodding toward from either side.

I didn't want to know what was behind that door.

I really didn't.

Even more, I didn't want to fight it. Adra could probably keep this up all day, but I couldn't, and neither could Casanova. We needed another solution. We needed one now.

What we got instead was more trouble.

A slender wrist draped over the balcony railing, right beside mine. It was honey-colored and elegant, with emerald green nails, and had a viper curled around it like a bracelet. The snake flicked a slender black tongue out at me.

I closed my eyes.

"I don't need this," I whispered.

"And may I ask," a familiar, sibilant voice asked, "what 'this' is?"

Chapter Thirty-three

I turned around and saw what looked like the whole damned Senate milling about the balcony, looking a lot less blasé than usual. Including Mircea, darkly handsome in a navy business suit, and standing behind the queen with the snake fetish. He looked slightly surprised, which was the vamp equivalent of gob-smacked, but right then I didn't care.

Because why didn't I think he'd gotten here through a portal?

"Wrong number?" I asked sharply.

"Right number, wrong address," he murmured, all but confirming it. They must have planned to drag me into some kind of metaphysical teleconference via the link in Mircea's brain, but got dragged somewhere themselves instead.

Good, I thought viciously. Maybe it would teach them something. Although judging by her highness's expression, I doubted it.

The Senate's leader must have been on casual mode today, because she'd swapped the robe of writhing serpents she usually wore to freak out the humans for a flowing caftan in bright green silk. It set off her dark, sloe-eyed good looks, and would have made her look almost normal except for the twin living bands wrapped around her like a belt.

She usually looked bizarre.

She usually looked terrifying.

Right now, right here, she looked pedestrian, ordinary, almost dull.

Except for the eyes, which were sparkling and open and lacking the usual baleful ennui she reserved for most of life, but especially for me. Right now they were animated, and curious, and swiftly taking in the scene. Like a child on Christmas morning, which somehow managed to be even more creepy than usual.

I suppressed a shudder and tried to move away, but a bejeweled hand reached out and grabbed my wrist, swift as a snake.

Wonder where I got that analogy, I thought, as another of her little pets hissed at me.

I didn't hiss back, but it was close. It was damned close, especially when those green talons started eating into my skin. I was suddenly glad that I was almost tapped out, because if I'd had the power to spare, I swear to God—

"Where are we?" she asked, slightly less politely.

"Where does it *look* like?" I snarled, which I was probably going to pay for later, but damn it, I didn't need this right now!

"Cassie!" Rian said urgently.

"I'm thinking!" I told her. And I was. But mostly what I was thinking was that we'd just gotten Casanova killed.

And then I knew we had, when the crowd went crazy, the wash of noise like a physical blow. And the huge doors at the end of the arena opened with a sound like tearing metal, cutting through even the cacophony going on below. I gripped the railing, praying for something doable, something easy, something, anything, that Casanova might actually be able to handle.

Annnnnd that was not it.

"The *fuck*?" I said in disbelief.

"No," Rian whispered, her hand gripping the rail tight enough to bend it.

"How wonderful," the consul said, leaning over the balcony like a girl at a parade, trying to see better.

I seriously considered shoving her in.

But then Casanova was running back this way, no longer trailed by anything, because everything else in the arena had just dove for cover, a hundred little creatures burrowing under the sand all at once, melting away like they had never existed. Leaving him alone in the huge space except for the gigantic thing that had just crushed one of the guards under a massive claw, with a crunch that echoed off the stands and through my head. And then I was grabbing Adra by the front of his natty gray jacket.

"Why don't you just kill him? You may as well!"

"Cassie." It was Mircea's voice in my ear, and his hand on my shoulder, but right then I didn't care.

"The contest rules are clear," Adra told me.

"This isn't a contest, it's slaughter!"

"And the selection is random—"

"It's *bullshit*! Give him something else! Give him a *chance*—"

Soft gray eyes looked down into mine, but they weren't angry. They were watchful, curious, intent. As if he couldn't quite figure me out.

And then Rian pushed between the two of us, her beautiful face distorted by pain and fear and the same impotent rage I felt. "Let me go to him!"

Adra looked at her. "You have been pardoned."

"I renounce it!"

"We can *do* that?" I asked, my hands clenching on Adra's lapels.

Like Mircea's on my shoulder. "No!"

"Can we?" I asked urgently, staring up into bemused gray eyes. Because I might be able to—

And then I was being jerked away, hard enough to almost send me to the floor, but for the arms caging me.

"Mircea," the consul said.

"She isn't facing that thing!"

"That's not your call!" I told him, furious. "I got him into this—"

"And now you'll stay out of it!"

"I don't answer to you!"

"You are tired," Adra said, watching me. "And your power is weak here. You have defeated one challenger, but I assure you, this one will not be so easy. Do you truly believe you can take it?"

"I know damned well Casanova can't!"

"And you would risk yourself for him?"

"Yes!"

"He is not your kind; not your responsibility."

"I'm making him mine!"

"Why? We were surprised that you would risk yourself to save your court, but they are yours: your power base, your coven. They give you strength as well as prestige. Allowing them to die would cut at both—"

"Is that honestly all you can see? All you can understand?"

"It is all most people understand. Why risk yourself for someone who is not yours? Why not sacrifice him and save yourself?"

"He's a friend—"

"You lie. You don't even like him."

"How do you—"

"We know much. We understand much. We do not understand you."

"What is so damn *hard*?" I said, looking down at Casanova—right down at him. Because he wasn't running anymore. He wasn't fighting. He was just standing there, below the balcony, staring up at us. Because he knew this was the only chance he had.

And it was, but I didn't know these people, didn't know what might work on them even if I'd been able to think straight. "Mircea—" I said, because he was the one with the golden tongue, the one who could talk his way out of anything.

Anything except this.

"The council will ransom him back from you," Mircea told Adra tightly, his hand clenching on my shoulder, because Casanova was his, too.

"We will?" the consul asked archly.

"Then I will ransom him!" He looked at Adra. "Name your price!"

"There is no coin you have that we want," Adra murmured, his eyes on mine. "Explain it to me," he told me.

"I . . . don't know what you want to hear."

"The truth."

"Would you believe it?"

"Try me."

I spread my hands, desperate, terrified. Because that

thing was coming this way, shaking the ground as it walked, and I didn't have the words, not ones someone like Adra was likely to understand. How I'd had so few people in my life I could rely on for anything, so few who didn't use me or stab me in the back or betray me. How the few I did have were so precious, so very precious: Mircea and Pritkin, Tami and Billy, Marco, and, yes, even Casanova, surprised though he'd probably be to hear it.

"He's my friend," I said. "He helped me. I don't know what your criteria for 'friend' are, but I don't have to always like all of mine! He stood by me—grudgingly, but he did—and saved me when he didn't have to, and . . . and *helped* me. And now I'm supposed to turn my back on him? I'm supposed to stand here and let him *die*?"

Gray eyes scanned mine for a long moment, and then looked away. "No."

"No? Then I can—"

"Not you." Adra made a small motion with his head, toward the arena. "Rian."

And that was all she needed.

Before I totally understood what had happened, Rian had shed her human form and dissolved into a cloud of sparkling mist. And flown over the balcony, diving straight into the tiny form of her lover, so far below. And disappeared.

"What can she do?" the consul asked, leaning farther over the balcony.

"Watch and see," Adra said, right before we all had to fall back, when a scaly head came tearing through the balcony opening, ripping off chunks of stone, bending metal girders like aluminum foil, and sending a wash of dust and a blast of fiery-hot breath at us.

But not fire. Casanova wasn't facing a dragon, because dragons were fey, not demon. And because he wasn't that lucky.

And then Adra, who alone hadn't bothered to move, made a slight motion, and the thing pulled back, rejoining the mass of squirming, snakelike heads on the dinosaur-like body below.

At least, I assumed that it did, but since Mircea had dragged me almost to the door to the room inside, I couldn't see much.

"What is it?" I asked him, trying to see.

"Hydra."

"How do you kill it?"

"I don't know." His jaw was tight. Mircea wasn't used to being a bystander. Wasn't used to having to watch someone else fight while he stood helpless on the sidelines. Wasn't used to being the one without power in any situation.

Welcome to my world, I thought, and then Marlowe was beckoning us over.

He had rejoined the consul, who had returned to her former position as soon as the thing was gone. And appeared to be having the time of her life, kneeling on the edge of the precipice, because the railing was now mostly gone, too. There were just a few bits of curled metal and broken glass here and there, and a lot of open air with wind blowing her long dark hair around.

"It *can* be done," Marlowe said, looking up as we tried to find a clear spot.

"How?" I asked, staring down at that thing. And searching for Casanova, who I didn't see at all.

"Hercules did it—at least according to myth."

"Casanova is not Hercules," Mircea said grimly.

"Hercules was an idiot," the consul said. "Don't go for the heads."

"What else do you go for?" Marlowe asked as Mircea kicked some glass out of the way to make us a spot.

"The *heart.* It only has one of those."

"According to myth, the body would live as long as a single head remained."

"Have you ever known anything that can live without a heart?" she demanded. "Including us?"

"No, but . . ." Marlowe looked around. He was still in the rumpled reddish suit from yesterday, only it was more rumpled now. Like his windblown curls, which were flying everywhere. And those dark eyes, which seemed to be having trouble deciding what to focus on. "I'm beginning to think my expertise . . . may need an upgrade," he finally said.

"You really think that'll work?" I asked the consul, my heart in my throat.

She looked up, and for once, for maybe the first time

ever, she was smiling. No, she was *grinning*. "Tell him to carve it out and we'll see."

Sounded like a plan to me.

If we could find him. But it was like he'd simply vanished. The creature seemed to think so, too, prowling around the arena, the many heads stretching in all directions. Including into the stands in a few cases, lunging at demons who spilled back out of the way, causing what looked like tidal flows in the crowd.

But there was no Casanova.

"Can she make him invisible?" I asked, wondering what kind of trick Rian was pulling.

"No," Mircea told me. "Or, if she can, she has never chosen to do so in four hundred years."

"What can she do?" I asked, because I didn't think normal incubus powers were likely to help here. In fact, I didn't know what would, minus an army. Which Rian didn't have.

"What can *he* do?" Adra asked, coming over. And dropping down between the consul and me, to swing his legs over the opening.

"What?"

"What abilities does he have?"

"What difference does that make?" Nothing he had was going to help him now.

But Adra didn't seem to agree.

"It makes all the difference. That is what possession does. Occasionally, yes, it can give you powers you wouldn't normally have. But far more often, it simply increases the ones you do have."

"Increases by how much?" Marlowe asked sharply.

Adra smiled at him and kicked his legs some more.

The consul wasn't the only one having a good time, I thought.

"That would depend on the demon," Adra said. "But while incubi are not among the more powerful of our kind, Rian has been on earth for a rather ... extended stay. She has acquired a great deal of power, and therefore has more to lend."

"But what can she do?" I repeated.

Adra shrugged. "What can your vampire do?" he asked again. "Possession for humans will not increase their power greatly since, you'll forgive me, they have little to enhance. But a vampire . . . well. Strength, speed, all the senses, and any master's powers the vampire may have would be greatly augmented."

"You know about master's powers?" the consul asked.

Adra looked at her. "My dear."

"How greatly?" Marlowe repeated.

Adra shrugged. "See for yourself."

And, suddenly, we were. Casanova stepped out from behind the giant, hollowed-out shell, which by now was all that remained of his former opponent. He looked impossibly tiny from what had to be a couple of football fields away. Unlike his opponent, which saw him at almost the same moment we did, and went boiling down the length of the arena toward him.

"Mircea—" I said, gripping his hand.

"I've told him what we know. It will be enough or it will not."

He sounded calm, but his hand was almost squeezing mine in two.

But I hardly noticed, because the hydra had already crossed one football field's worth and was tearing up the second, and Casanova still just stood there. Not flinching, not moving, not panicking. Not doing anything—until the creature was almost on top of him. And then he moved, so fast I couldn't even track him with my eyes.

But I could track the results.

The giant beetle shell suddenly popped up out of the ground and went sailing through the air, cutting a dark swath across the arena like a massive Frisbee. A massive Frisbee with a knifelike edge and enough force behind it to have bisected a mountain—or a dozen thick, snakelike necks, snipping them off like tender flower stems.

Heads rolled everywhere, rivers of blood spurted, and a tiny figure of a man leapt for the thrashing body before it could regrow anything it had lost. I didn't see what he used for a knife—maybe another piece of shell. But whatever it was, it worked, piercing deep and sending the thing rolling onto its back, writhing in a spreading stain while the crowd went wild and Casanova stabbed it, over and over like a madman, until he was coated with as much black gore as the sand.

And the consul was yelling—yes, yelling—dignity forgotten, hair in her face, as jubilant as the crowd. Marlowe was staring, from Casanova to her to Adra and back again, his face blank but his eyes burning. And Mircea's arm was tightening, dragging me back into the other room.

Chapter Thirty-four

Immediately, the deafening sounds from the arena dimmed, leaving me with ringing ears and pulsing vision as my eyes tried to adjust to the darker interior. "What are you doing?" I asked as Mircea kept on going, past the buffet table and almost to the elevator doors on the other side of the room.

"Strange, I was about to ask the same of you!"

"You saw—"

"Yes, I saw!" He whirled on me, dark eyes glittering. "I saw you risk your life—again—needlessly, foolishly! I am beginning to believe—"

"It was necessary!"

"—that you have some sort of death wish! What were you *thinking*?"

"I was thinking that he needed help! I was thinking that someone asked me—"

"Then you tell them no!"

"He was my *responsibility*—"

"Your responsibility is there!" It was vicious and punctuated by a slash of his arm in the general direction of the buffet.

Where I belatedly noticed Jules standing awkwardly, holding a champagne glass and trying to look like he wasn't there. It was a little difficult, because he and a no-longer-suspended Marco were the only ones left in the room.

Everybody else had cleared out, all the finely dressed men and women now picking their way through the debris outside to clap politely for the victor.

While in here, another battle was brewing, and it wasn't one I was prepared for.

I had just woken up. I was still in the pink cotton nightie I'd slept in, my hair was everywhere, and my stomach was growling, demanding breakfast. I did not want to do this.

But Mircea obviously did, and he was standing there, visibly angry, which for a master vamp usually meant he was close to wrecking the *room*. I didn't even want to know what it meant for the Senate's chief negotiator, who usually kept his cool even when everyone else was on meltdown. I didn't want to know.

But I was about to, because I wasn't going to give him what he wanted.

"I can't change Jules back," I began.

"And why not?" It was clipped. "I explained the procedure. All you have to do is age him. I will handle the rest."

"Okay, 'can't' might not have been the best choice of word—"

"Then do it. We are running out of time."

"Out of time for what?" I glanced over, but Jules was apparently finding his champagne glass to be fascinating. "Is Jules going somewhere?"

"Our army is going somewhere—into faerie!"

I frowned. "I'm not making you an army, Mircea. I told you that last night."

"And you have now had time to reconsider."

"I'm not going to reconsider."

"Damn it, Cassie!" The explosion made me jump, because Mircea didn't speak like that. Not to anyone, and especially not to me. But then, he didn't usually look like that, either. The playful, daring, humorous lover was nowhere to be seen. Instead, I was facing a man who was visibly stressed and angry, like he'd had too little sleep and too much pressure, way too much, maybe over a long period of time. And what the hell had happened last night?

"This is for your good as much as ours," he told me tightly. "How many times have our enemies tried to kill you? How many assassins have they sent? How many times do you think you are going to get lucky—"

"Why is it," I cut in, getting a little angry myself, "that when someone else dodges a bullet, it's down to skill, but whenever I do it, I'm 'lucky'? I killed a Spartoi; I don't get credit for that? I just took on that . . . that thing . . . out there and what? It was just its time to *go*?"

"You have power, yes, something that can help us greatly in this war if it is properly utilized—"

"By you, you mean. Funny, Jonas seems to think the same thing."

"—but that is useless if misdirected—"

"Misdirected?"

"—and no matter how great the weapon, it must be—"

"I'm not a weapon, Mircea!"

"I am well aware of that—"

"Are you? Because I'm starting to feel like everyone thinks I'm just a gun for them to fire. But I'm not. My power is not. It came to me because I'm best able to use it—or to decide when not to," I said pointedly, looking at Jules.

"Jules wants this."

"Last night he didn't know what he wanted."

"He does now!"

"Do you?" I asked Jules, because some input here would be nice.

Annnnd now he was perusing the prosciutto stand, and trying to tease a paper-thin slice off with a little fork.

"Jules!" I said, and saw him jump.

"I—didn't have lunch," he said awkwardly.

"Have you decided?" I asked again. "Because Mircea seems to think you have."

"I . . . well . . . that is . . ." He looked at Mircea.

"Don't look at him! This is about your life."

"My life." Jules gave a burst of laughter, and then quickly shut it down.

"You can laugh if you want to," I told him. "You can do whatever you want. You don't have a master anymore—"

"I know!" He flung out a hand, and an arc of champagne went with it. And then he looked down at his empty glass and grimaced. "I *know*, all right?"

"Then what do you want to do?" I asked again. And got a half-angry, half-helpless stare in return. "Jules, you were a master. You've been able to make up your own mind about things for a long time—"

"Yes, but this isn't about *things*, is it?" he asked. "This is about *everything*. My whole future. My whole—I thought things were set. I thought—" He looked helplessly at Mircea. "It's not ... I appreciate, so much, all you've—I'd be dead without—I was going to do it, I was going to jump, and you saved me—"

"And I will again," Mircea told him.

"Yes, but ..." That helpless look was back, screwing up his face and fluttering the hand not holding on to his glass. Jules had always had such expressive hands, an actor's hands. And now this one was all over the place, painting stories in the air I couldn't read, but I guess he could, because his eyes were suddenly distant. "I never figured it out, you know," he finally said. "Life. I just ... never had the knack. Other people seemed to get it—they married, had kids, seemed to understand, to *fit*, in ways I never did. . . ." He trailed off.

"But then you became a vampire," I prompted, because I wanted him to get to the point already.

And it seemed to help, because he nodded vigorously. "That's just it. I was a lousy human. I wasn't even that great of an actor, to be honest, and that was the closest ... I thought it would be different, after. I thought, maybe this is it, maybe the reason I didn't fit in as a human was because I was never supposed to be one. Maybe this is what I was meant for. . . . But I wasn't. I was a lousy vampire, too!"

"You were a *master*," Mircea said. "You know how few—"

"Yes, I know!" Jules said, cutting him off. And then looked stricken because you didn't interrupt your master in the vamp world. You just didn't. "You see?" he said, voice almost a whisper. "That's me, right there. That's why you sent me to Cassie. That's why you sent me away."

"I didn't send you away," Mircea said heavily. "I sent you where you could be best utilized. You are—were—powerful but not subtle. But Cassie needs defenders, not diplomats—"

"But I didn't defend her, did I?" Jules interrupted again, unconsciously, and I bit back a smile. He really was almost completely tactless, which must have really sucked in a household renowned for its charm and diplomacy. "I tried, I really did, but she ended up having to defend me!"

He looked at me. "You asked what I want. How am I supposed to know? Maybe I'd be better off as a human again. Maybe a childhood not knowing when you're going to eat next, or if you are, of being traded to whoever has a few dollars to rent your pretty face for a night, of being told you're good for nothing when it was your work supporting the whole damned lot of them—" He broke off, lips tight.

"Jules . . . I'm sorry," I said.

Suddenly, I didn't feel like laughing anymore.

"It was a long time ago," he told me. "But I always wondered if maybe the start I had in life was what screwed it up for me. If maybe I'd had a different family, one who gave a damn . . . But you really can't go back, can you? You can make me younger, but you can't erase what happened—"

"I can," Mircea said. "If that is what you want—"

"No, you can erase the *memory* of it. But then who would I be? From a screw-up to . . . a blank?"

Mircea made a frustrated sound, which was another measure of how not-himself he was today. "It is difficult to help you when you don't seem to know what you want—"

"Yes!" Jules nodded. "Yes, *exactly*. Before I became a master, back when I was a baby vamp, I was told who I was supposed to be. I was given the right clothes to wear, the words to say, the jobs to do. And after, I was still expected to be that person, just . . . *better* at it somehow. It was like being in a play—put on the costume, say the words, try to stay in character . . . and I did. I did that. But I've been a character for so long now, I don't know who I am when I'm out of it." He looked at me and spread those expressive hands. "Cassie, you didn't mean to, but you stripped off the costume, took it clean away. And now you want to know what I want? *How the hell should I know?*"

I looked at him, and I thought maybe I did finally get it. I got something else, too. "We may not know what you want, but we know what you don't want." I looked at Mircea. "He doesn't want to make this choice today."

"And I did not wish to lose eleven masters tonight!"

"What?"

"The raid. The one you saw us preparing for?"

I nodded.

"Twelve operatives went out; only one returned. And they had power, every single one. And skill. And centuries of experience you don't have. *And they died nonetheless.*"

"But . . . what can kill twelve masters?" I asked in disbelief. Because the answer should have been nothing. Sending a senior master—a first- or second-level vampire—after a problem was to suddenly have no more problem. It was like sending a whole battalion. Losing eleven . . .

Nobody lost eleven.

"We don't know," he told me, running a hand through his hair. "As of right now, we have no idea. But it was a carefully coordinated attack that required intimate knowledge of us. There are very few people with that sort of information, very few who could have stage-managed a series of ambushes dangerous enough to kill first-level masters."

"You think Tony and his group were behind it."

"That is the current assumption. They certainly have the most cause. But whether it turns out to be accurate or not, until we root them out, they will keep coming. They've proven that much, at least. And Antonio—"

"Is a threat," I agreed. "And you know I want him more than anyone. But I'm a little more worried about Ares right now—"

"Ares may never return if his supporters are taken out!"

"But Rhea didn't see Tony returning to kill us all, did she?" I asked. "She saw Ares—"

"And you believe her? A girl you barely know?"

" —and so did my mother, and so did Jonas' prophecies—"

"Prophecies, visions—give me tangible enemies to fight. I can't fight air!"

And that was it, wasn't it? Mircea really *didn't* like feeling helpless, didn't like being on the sidelines, didn't like leaving his fate in someone else's hands. But a god at full strength was too much, just too much for any of us, and he knew he couldn't fight him.

So he was trying to take on those he could.

I understood that. But I also understood something else. That if I gave in to him on this, I'd be giving in on everything. Because how do you step back after giving someone an army? How do you turn him down when he knows you'll cave, even on the big things, even on the huge things, because you already did?

If I gave Mircea what he wanted, it might help now, but it would hurt later. And it would hurt a lot. Not just because of all the extra master vampires suddenly running around, but because I would have just confirmed that I was nothing more than a weapon for him to fire, whenever he chose, at whatever he chose, and I couldn't be that. I couldn't *do* that.

Not and have any legitimacy left.

"I understand—" I began.

"Do you? Then *give me an army*."

And, okay, I was getting pissed again, probably because that had sounded a lot like an order.

"I am not your servant, Mircea."

"I am not treating you as one. I am pointing out the best course of action under the current—"

"You are treating me exactly like one. You aren't asking me; you're telling me—"

"I am telling you what we need to do to survive!"

"And I'm telling you that taking out Tony won't solve the problem! Ares has other supporters—Agnes' old acolytes, for example. I think they may be after the Tears of Apollo to shift him across the barrier—"

"The barrier that has stood for thousands of years? Your acolytes are likely after the Tears to avoid capture by you."

I shook my head. "One of the Corpsmen overheard them talking. He said they are planning to bring back a god—"

"And what did Mage Marsden have to say to this, when you told him?"

"I didn't tell him. Rhea did—"

"Then what was his response to her?"

"He didn't appear too concerned."

"And did this tell you anything?"

"Yes! It told me he doesn't take me seriously. I had hoped for better from you!"

"I do take you seriously—"

"No, you take my *power* seriously. It's not the same thing! If you respect me at all, give me—"

I stopped, because Mircea had just crossed his arms

over his chest, an implacable piece of body language that he never used. His normal style was approachable, open, relaxed. There was a reason that, despite his being a powerful first-level master and a senator, people *talked* to Mircea, in ways they just didn't to others of the same rank.

Only it didn't look like he was too interested in talking right now.

"So that you can get killed with them?" he demanded.

"So I can do my job!"

"Your job is *here*, finding your acolytes and helping your allies. How exactly is the war effort to be served by running about time after a single war mage?"

"This isn't just about him—"

"On the contrary, this is wholly about him. Don't you see what they are doing? What Marsden is doing? He was the last Pythia's lover—oh yes, we knew—and is now trying to exert the same measure of power over you. But he is too old to use his own charm these days; therefore he uses another—"

"Pritkin?" I stared at Mircea incredulously.

"Ironic that it should be the man who began his association with you by trying to kill you," Mircea said grimly. "But you have come to rely on him—too much. And this has not gone unremarked, by us or by the Circle."

"Pritkin has never tried to influence me—"

"Has not tried to influence you yet. But it will come, if you keep him in your service. Perhaps whatever calamity he finds himself in is for the best, before he becomes even more of a problem than he already—"

"Pritkin is not a problem! And this is not about him. This is me making a formal request of an ally—"

"As I just did?" A dark eyebrow raised. "You know how our world works, Cassie; you have always known—"

"I knew how it worked for others. I thought we were different."

"We *are* different. But we have two relationships—"

"Until you decide otherwise!"

"Cassie—"

"Give me the Tears, Mircea!"

And I knew it, saw it in his eyes before he even got the words out. *"Give me an army."*

"God*damnit!*" I said, and shifted.

Chapter Thirty-five

"You're calling him?" Tami followed me from the lounge, where she'd been putting a puzzle together with some of the kids, into the kitchen.

"Yep."

"But I thought you were gonna give him more time."

"He's had time," I said, and grabbed the house phone.

She grinned and slid some cornflakes in front of me while we waited for the connection to go through. It didn't take long, which wasn't surprising considering that it was a little after eight a.m. here, meaning it was afternoon in Britain. And considering that it didn't go through to the right guy, even though this was his direct line.

"Lord Protector's office," a brisk-sounding functionary told me. "How may I help?"

"By putting me through to Jonas."

"And whom shall I say is calling?"

"Cassandra Palmer."

There was a small silence on the other end. "I . . . shall inquire."

"What's he doing?" Tami asked, leaning on the counter, eyes bright, while I listened to Elton John sing about tiny dancers.

"Inquiring."

"What is there to inquire about? You're the Pythia. They put you through."

"No, they put Agnes through."

Tami scowled.

"He ... the Lord Protector ... is in a meeting," the secretary informed me after a minute. "I was instructed to arrange ... an appointment?"

Jonas needed to get some new help, I decided.

Even his secretary sounded like he knew that was bullshit.

"Okay," I said. "I just wanted to check with him before anything was finalized."

"Finalized?"

"Yes, you know. About my court?"

"I ... The Pythian Court?"

"Do I have another one I don't know about?"

"I ... no. That is to say—"

"Please don't. Just tell him I called, so he doesn't say I didn't consult him—"

"Consult—"

"—before deciding to make the court's permanent residence Las Vegas—"

Tami laughed.

"—instead of whatever other possibilities we might have dis—"

"Be right back," the man said, and the Muzak cut back in abruptly.

"What's happening now?" Tami asked eagerly.

"I'm on hold again."

"At least it's Queen this time," Roy said, not even trying to pretend that he wasn't listening in.

I didn't care. If I cared, I'd have done this in the bedroom, under a silence spell. But I was getting tired of having to creep around my own suite, of having to keep secrets from the people who were supposed to be my allies, of trying to do my job with no support and with active opposition half the time.

And it wasn't like it mattered.

Mircea wasn't going to give me that damned potion anyway.

Of course, Jonas probably wasn't, either. I'd told Tami the truth last night: I didn't have a lot of cards to play with him. In fact, I'd had exactly one, which I'd just used to try to get him on the phone.

It was the same problem I had with Mircea. *I am Pythia, hear me roar* might sound good in theory, but in practice it was a lot more problematic. Because what were my options? Fight Ares on my own? Run the Pythian Court like some kind of island in the supernatural stream? Never talk to them again? I was pretty sure that wasn't in the job description. I was pretty sure that was the exact opposite of the job description, that the Pythia was supposed to be a bridge between the various groups, bringing them closer together.

Although it kind of sounded like Agnes hadn't been doing that.

It almost felt like sacrilege to question her, but I was beginning to think that maybe her relationship with Jonas had given the Circle delusions of grandeur. Like they didn't need anybody else, because they had the Pythia. And as for the vamps—

Well, they hadn't trusted the office at all.

Until I came along.

And now I was Agnes 2.0, only with a vamp lover instead of a mage one. Who obviously expected the same privileges he thought Jonas had been getting. And maybe that would have worked in peacetime; maybe I could have done the same thing Agnes apparently had, and let the powers that be believe what they wanted while I did whatever I damned well liked. Hell, I'd mostly been doing that anyway, because I hadn't had a choice. But it wasn't going to work forever.

Because I wasn't a peacetime Pythia. I was a wartime Pythia, and I *needed* them. I needed both of them to work *with* me instead of dictating *to* me, but they weren't. And I didn't know how to make them and I was running out of time and Jonas wasn't going to give me shit, I *knew* it, assuming he even deigned to speak with me at all, and—

And then he was on the line. "Cassandra."

"*Lady* Cassandra," Rian snapped, because she had come into the kitchen in time to overhear.

If he heard her back, he didn't react. Or probably care. I cleared my throat and grabbed an apple out of the bowl, because I needed something to concentrate on.

"I'm not calling about my court," I told him.

"I gathered that." It was dry.

"Or about the money."

And, okay, that got a slight pause. And a frown from Tami, who is more practical than me, and probably had a list of all the stuff the girls needed. But they weren't going to die if they didn't get it.

Someone else was.

"I'm calling about the Tears of Apollo," I told him evenly. "Rhea said she asked you for them."

"She did."

"She also said she told you why. My acolytes—"

"Will not obtain any from us."

I concentrated on the apple, which might have darkened a shade, although that could have been my imagination. And told myself to keep my voice steady. Because that had sounded a lot like "and neither will you."

"You can't know that," I pointed out. "They can shift in anywhere. Agnes trained them herself, and they seem to have paid attention."

"A fact of which you would be unaware had you not sought them out."

"They're my responsibility—"

"A great many things are your responsibility, and those girls are the least of it!"

"Not if they obtain the Tears," I said, staying calm, because I had to. I had to do this right. "At best, it will leave me dealing with multiple Myras, and at worst—"

"There will be no worst, as they shan't obtain any."

And, okay, that staying calm thing was getting a little harder. The apple definitely blushed darker, which probably matched my face as I struggled to keep the irritation out of my voice. "Jonas, they were looking for the Tears when I met up with them. They killed Elias for them—"

"For which they will be brought to account, I assure you." He sounded grim. "But that can be left to us. You need to concentrate on other things—"

"I can't concentrate on other things until I'm sure about the Tears! Send them to me, whatever stock you have, and then we can—"

"I can't do that."

"Damn it, Jonas! We're supposed to be allies!" I said, and belatedly noticed that the apple was now slimy apple mush, and seriously gross.

Tami handed me a paper towel.

"A fact you seem to be forgetting of late." It was acid. "But at any rate, I couldn't send them to you if I wished to."

"And why not?"

"For the same reason I know the acolytes will not obtain any from us. The last batch was sent to court a week before Agnes passed—"

"A week?"

"—and in her absence, naturally no more have been—"

Jonas was still talking, but I was having trouble hearing him over the sudden roaring in my ears.

How much is a batch? I mouthed to Rhea.

Three.

Three?

"—and in any case, it requires six months to—Cassie? *Cassie?*"

"Whoa," Tami said, grabbing my arm, and looking a little woozy. "You do this all the time?"

"Feels like it," I told her, glancing around Agnes' living room.

It was dark and quiet and empty, just like last time. Which wasn't surprising since this *was* last time, or at least the same night Rhea and I had visited before. I'd just brought us back to several hours earlier. The acolytes were probably still off at my inauguration, and with Rhea along, the wards were ignoring us.

Or maybe there was another reason for that.

Because Tami wasn't just awesome with kids and a great cook. She was also a magical null. One of the rare witches who couldn't do magic herself, but who could make sure nobody else did any, either. Or anything.

At least, I really hoped so, because safecracking was not in my skill set.

"It's behind the painting," I told Tami, who had gotten over the disorientation of a time shift and was staring around in apparent fascination.

"This is where the Pythias lived?" she asked, taking it in.

"Until it was blown up."

"Damn," she told me. "Your place needs an upgrade."

"I wouldn't feel comfortable somewhere like this," I said, pulling the painting open.

"You sure? 'Cause I could get used to it. I could get used to it real fast," she said, checking out the crystal on the bar.

"You don't like the suite?"

She rolled her eyes at me. "Honey, that's not a suite. That's a halfway house. You know you can't keep that up, right?"

"It's only been a couple days—"

"A couple days too long. You got to think of your image."

I glanced at Rhea, who hadn't said anything, but whose silence was kind of telling. "It's a penthouse suite," I pointed out.

Tami laughed. "It's a penthouse suite with bullet holes in the walls, cots all over the floor, and no privacy for those girls or for you. I don't know why you've put up with it this long!"

"Other things seemed more important."

"Yeah, but you have your court now," she said, joining me. And putting out a hand, ten inches or so away from the surface of the safe. "You've gotta think of the girls. Know how long I had to wait for the bathroom this morning? I should have gone down to the lobby—it would've been faster!"

"Casanova should be back to work soon. I'll ask him—"

"Why? Why ask him anything? You don't have to stay there. You could live anywhere. You could live *here*." She glanced around appreciatively.

"Did you miss the whole blowing-up thing?"

"Okay, maybe not *here* here, but you know what I mean. Somewhere like this."

I frowned. "What's wrong with Vegas?"

"It's *Vegas*?"

"I thought you liked it there."

"For a vacation, sure. But it don't exactly say serene and otherworldly, does it?"

"I'm not serene and otherworldly—"

"And you're not gonna be living there."

I frowned some more. "It's convenient. MAGIC used to be there," I said, talking about the supernatural version of the UN. Which had recently suffered a small setback in the form of an angry god. "They're talking about building it back. And even if they don't, a lot of groups still have reps in the area—"

"Those yard-long beers, always a draw."

"—and Dante's currently has the best wards anywhere!" The Senate had moved in temporarily while they sorted out long-term accommodations, and they'd upgraded the security almost immediately. "It makes sense to stay there."

"You just like it there," Tami accused.

I didn't deny it. Despite the glitter and the glamour, Vegas had started to feel like home. And what were my alternatives? Going back to Philly? Because I didn't have such great memories there. Or Atlanta? Where, yes, things had been better, if by better you mean living in constant fear of getting caught by my crazy old vamp master and then almost dying. I'd met some nice people in Atlanta, but it's hard to make friends when you know you're basically endangering them all. So, okay, but nothing I missed.

I thought I might miss Vegas.

There were places I'd been with people I did call friends. Memories I'd made, even whacked-out ones, that were important to me. And people . . .

Lots of people I cared about, even if some of them were currently acting like asses.

I glanced around. Someplace like this, I'd forever feel out of place, inadequate, like a little girl dressing up in mommy's clothes, pretending to be someone I wasn't. While in Vegas . . . you could be anybody you wanted to be. I'd often thought that was the real allure of the place. Not the cheap beer or the chance to get rich—which, on the Strip, at least, was basically zero—or the clubs or the shows. But a chance to try on a new skin for a while, to do something different, to *be* someone different.

A banker could be a biker.

A secretary could be a seductress.

And a palm reader could be Pythia.

Plus, London might be more posh, but it was also more structured. Everybody who'd been with the old court was here. If I came back, I'd be expected to do things their way, the old way. But in Vegas . . . it would be *my* court. And maybe it wouldn't be as serene or as perfect, but . . .

But it might be more fun.

"I think we'll stay there for a while, see how it goes," I told her nonchalantly.

Tami shot me a look. "Well, wherever you stay, you need

a bigger place—a lot bigger. You need some impressive areas for receiving guests. You need somewhere you can talk, with some damned privacy—"

"I need in that safe," I reminded her. "Are you almost there?"

"Give it a minute," Tami said, unconcerned. Because I guess after you break into a couple dozen Circle-run establishments, one little safe doesn't seem like a big deal. "And a decorator," she added. "The last thing you need is to let whoever designed that damned hellscape of a hotel anywhere near—"

"You could do it," I blurted out, before I thought.

And damn it! I'd planned to wait a bit to say anything, like until I had some money. But too late now.

"You could help with . . . a lot of things," I finished awkwardly, because she was looking at me.

"You offering me a job?"

"A . . . sort of job."

"What's a sort of job?" Ms. Practical asked.

"A . . . job with a delayed paycheck," I said, wincing. "But just until I can pry the money out of Jonas," I added quickly.

"You gave us a place to stay when the kids and I would have been out on the street. You got me a pardon from Marsden, to keep him from locking me up. I think I can forgo the salary for a while," she said dryly.

"Then you're on board?"

"On board as what? Chief babysitter? 'Cause I can do that, but—"

"No. I was thinking more like chief . . . coordinator. You can hire the babysitters and the tutors and whatever else we need. You can help me find a place for the court. You can help, well . . . coordinate things."

I couldn't be any more specific than that, since I didn't even know what we needed. I hadn't ever really thought about a court, not of my own. The one here in London had always been Agnes' in my head, and somehow, the fact that it was mine now just hadn't registered. Probably because the idea scared me to death.

But it scared me a little less with Tami around.

She glanced at Rhea. "You okay with that? I wouldn't be stepping on any toes?"

Rhea shook her head. "No toes. Or . . . or anything else. That actually sounds . . ." She took a deep breath, and I could almost see some of the weight falling off her shoulders. "That sounds wonderful," she said honestly.

"Well, I guess I could give it a shot," Tami told me, but distractedly. Like she was already making a mental to-do list.

"And the safe?" I asked, because it looked the same to me, with the pale, almost invisible barrier still glowing faintly in front of the door.

"No." Tami turned her attention to it. "Doesn't feel like I've drained it at all."

"Drained it?" Rhea said. "Is that what you're trying to do?"

I nodded. "Tami's a magical null. If she's not actively repressing her abilities, wards come down when she walks in a room."

"It was how I used to raid the Circle's damned internment camps," she told Rhea. "Hard to keep out somebody who can just walk in through the front door."

"Yet this one *is* keeping you out," I said, starting to get worried. I'd seen Tami drain bigger wards faster plenty of times.

She sighed. "Yeah, we may have a problem."

"What sort of problem?"

"You know how a null works, right?" she asked.

I nodded, but Rhea shook her head.

"Our magic is inverted," Tami told her. "Instead of projecting out, it pulls in. Specifically, it pulls in other magic in an area and destroys it. It's like we have a big, black hole somewhere inside, just sucking all the magic in. But unlike a black hole, we do have a limit—we do get full."

Rhea nodded.

I wondered where Tami was going with this.

"So, most of the time, it's not a problem," she said, looking balefully at the safe. "For a strong null, the limit is really, really high. A talisman, like the ones they use to power most wards, can usually be drained in a couple of minutes."

"But you've already been at it that long," I pointed out.

She nodded. "Yeah. And if I'm right, I could stay here all day, till I was full and running over, and it wouldn't matter. That thing's not coming down."

"Why not? It's just a ward—"

"A ward hooked into the ley line system."

"What?"

Tami nodded. "And the ley lines aren't some supernatural battery, like a talisman. They're more like . . . a direct link to the world's electrical system. To big rivers of metaphysical energy that just keep coming and coming and coming. I can't absorb that. No one can."

I stared at the little safe. "But . . . but if people can hook a ward directly into a ley line, why use talismans *at all*?"

She shrugged. " 'Cause the lines don't run everywhere. Plus it's expensive. Cutting into a line is dangerous work, and it don't come cheap. Someone must've paid a fortune for all the wards around this place. But if you really, really want to make sure that nothing and nobody gets in, that's how you do it."

"Then I can't age through the wards, either?" I asked, because that had been option number two.

"Sorry."

And that probably meant Marlowe's were done the same way. Not to mention whatever snares and traps he'd laid out for unsuspecting burglars, all of which were probably lethal. No wonder the damned acolytes hadn't found any Tears yet!

Of course, neither had I.

"Damn it! There must be a way!"

"If you have the pass code to the wards," Tami agreed. "Otherwise, you need a way to bring them down, and then a safecracker to get you in. Or you're going to be here a very long time."

Chapter Thirty-six

I found Rico in the kitchen when we got back, doing the breakfast dishes. He had his jacket off and his sleeves rolled up, showing off muscular forearms. His dark brown hair was disheveled, the neck of his shirt was open, showing a V of taut bronze skin, and a smear of soap suds decorated his cheek. He looked like every woman's dream, and I caught Rhea staring.

Rico did, too, and dropped her a wink.

Rhea did not appear to know what to do with that. Maybe because the only men at the Pythian Court had been about eighty. And because the initiates did not appear to have learned normal social skills. Like they'd been trained to be stoic and serene, but not how to interact with regular guys.

Or not-so-regular ones.

Rhea finally solved the problem by awkwardly winking back, which caused Rico to burst out laughing.

"I need a favor," I told him, and nodded at her. The silence spell clicked shut around us.

"My dream come true," Rico told me, still grinning at an increasingly flustered Rhea.

"I need a safe cracked. Do you know someone who can do it?"

Those liquid eyes slid to me. "What kind of safe?"

And some days, I loved vamps. No question about what

was inside; no debates about possible legality. Just *what kind is it?*

I pulled my cell phone out of my jeans and showed him a photo. "That kind."

A request to commit a felony didn't even rate a blink. "Does it have to be operational after?" he asked, taking the phone from me.

"I don't care if you rip it out of the damned wall."

An eyebrow went up. "What about wards?"

I glanced at Rhea. "The wards . . . aren't going to be a problem," she said, a little breathlessly.

"Not a problem? Then this is a human's safe?"

She looked at me.

I sighed and came out with it. "No, but the house it's in is about to blow up, so the wards will be offline."

A second eyebrow joined the first. "Sounds intriguing."

"It will be okay," Rhea said, as if she was trying to convince herself as much as him. "No one should be in the room at the time—"

"If the house is about to blow up, that would seem prudent," he said gently.

"—but to be on the safe side—"

"Was that a pun?" he teased.

Rhea looked confused some more.

"Rico," I said impatiently. "Do you know anyone who can do it?"

"Yes, me."

I hesitated. "You did get the part about safecracking in Armageddon, right?"

He just looked at me.

Okay. His call. "There is one other thing."

His look turned politely curious.

I bit my lip, trying to figure out how to phrase this without saying *you're a weird vampire.*

But he was. He did dishes, which master vampires definitely Did. Not. Do. He liked guns, which a lot of vamps disdained as being unnecessary and too human. And he had given me the impression in the short time I'd known him that he didn't care much for rules, even vampire sorts of rules.

Which was good, because I was about to ask him to break one—a big one.

"I'd just as soon Mircea didn't know about this," I finally said.

Rico frowned.

"You know, not right away," I added quickly, because of course he'd tell the boss sooner or later. I just preferred it to be later.

A lot later.

Like after I had Pritkin back and had time to be yelled at.

Not that Mircea would yell; it wasn't his style. But he would certainly make his displeasure known. Which was okay; I could deal with that. What I couldn't deal with was his trying to stop me, because he was damned sneaky and he might well succeed and I didn't have time for this!

Rico frowned some more. "We're not his men," he told me. "We're your men. He sent us to help you."

"And to report on me."

"He hasn't asked me to do that."

"He doesn't need to. There's plenty of others—"

"—and I wouldn't even if he did."

I blinked. "Excuse me?"

He leaned one elbow on the counter, going into a graceful slouch. "I am a senior master, Cassie. I do as I like."

"That's not how the vamp world works."

"Isn't it? I am emancipated. The blood bond no longer holds me."

"Then why are you here?"

"I like it here."

"No one likes it here." The guys called this place Australia. As in, they'd been exiled from the main court in Washington State and sent to a land down under, full of heat and craziness and frequent danger. It wasn't anyone's favorite posting.

But Rico didn't seem to see it like that. "I do. I found court life to be very pleasant and very pretty. And very dull. Everything is too perfect there, too controlled." He smiled. "I like things messy."

"Then you came to the right place."

He nodded. "The day I arrived, I was attacked by mages, almost blown up, and came very close to being eaten alive by a dragon."

"And you *liked* that?"

"I wasn't bored."

Okaaay.

"And Mircea?"

"I find I like the idea of knowing something the master does not."

"Me, too." I looked around to see Fred's head poking in through the shutters that separated the kitchen from the lounge, eating an apple. He must have been kneeling on one of the bar stools so he could spy on us. I scowled at him.

"Where did you come from?"

"My mother always said I came from heaven—"

"Fred!"

"—although others have occasionally expressed a different point of view."

"How did you do that?"

"Do what?" He munched at me. "Oh, the silence thing?" He shrugged. "It's a muffling spell, not a shield. And I get curious when the splashy splashy suddenly stops."

"Get less curious!"

"I won't have to be, 'cause I'll be along."

"You're *not* going."

"Of course I am."

"And why should I let you?"

"'Cause you're smart? You're gonna need someone to watch your back, and Rico can't do that and crack the safe at the same time."

"Who says I can't?" Rico looked offended.

"I do. Anyway, you'll need an alibi. I'll tell everyone we're going shopping."

I frowned at him. "I never go shopping."

"Well, you ought to. Your closet is full of ball gowns and ratty old T-shirts. You need normal clothes."

"I need my head examined."

"Don't we all? So, when are we leaving?"

I staggered a little and went down to one knee. But said knee hit polished marble instead of kitchen tile, so I was pretty sure we'd made it. I breathed a sigh of relief.

And then I threw up.

"Cassie!" Fred grabbed me, which didn't help, because I was already down. But then Rhea held my hair back, which did. And Rico took up a position in front of us, gun out, looking grim, giving me time to get it together.

Damn, I knew I shouldn't have tried shifting four. Four *sucked*. But all four were needed: Rico to crack the safe, Fred to watch his back while he did it, me in my usual role as taxi-through-time, and Rhea . . .

Rhea to give me a boost so I could get us all back, because I was bottomed out.

I wiped the arm of my shirt across my lips and looked up.

We were in a dark corner of the ballroom of the palatial house in London that until recently had housed the Pythian Court. It still housed them, actually, because I'd brought us back to just before everything went kablooie. Not because I was a glutton for punishment, but because the asshole acolytes who were about to blow this place sky high had thoughtfully turned off the wards first.

But since the reason the wards were down was the three or four dozen dark mages on the premises, I didn't think crawling around in the open was a great idea.

"Come on," I told them, and staggered to my feet.

We hurried across the open floor, past the French doors that had been replaced after Mircea and I helped obliterate them sometime back in the eighties. We stayed out of line of sight to the main hall, where another me was about to flash in with a trio of badass witches. And ended up beside the wall where Agnes had once been frozen by a goddess in disguise.

For a moment, all I saw was gothic wood paneling, the kind that looked like it belonged in a country gentleman's library rather than a ballroom. But it was there for a reason. Because when Rhea turned a wooden rosette, a narrow section of wall slid back, revealing a slender hidden staircase.

"Mages on the second floor," I reminded them softly as we left the first behind.

"So why aren't we on the third?" Fred whispered. "Or better yet, *inside the room*? Why are we taking the scenic route?"

"Because I don't want to materialize in a room full of dark mages?"

"Why would they be there? Why would *anyone* be there? This place is about to go up like a firework!"

"Because that's the way my life works," I hissed, as Rico cautiously pushed open the paneling on Agnes' hall.

And just as quickly pulled back in.

"What?" I asked, moving to the front so I could see. *"Crap."*

"What is it?" Fred demanded.

"Some of those mages who aren't supposed to be here."

"What?" He poked his head under my arm, so he could get an eye to the crack in the door. And saw the same thing I did—two guys lounging around, smoking. Like this whole place wasn't about to be.

"What in the hell are they doing there?"

"Having a smoke."

"Having—that's just stupid."

"Not if the acolytes failed to mention that this place was about to go up in flames," Rico whispered.

"They wouldn't do that," Fred said, sounding shocked. "Would they?"

"You don't know them." That was Rhea, her usually gentle face suffused by something that looked like hate. "The adepts, they're . . . They didn't care. Two dozen children, and they didn't *care*."

"It's safe to say they didn't care how many mages made it out of here, either," I told Fred.

"No offense," he whispered. "But your acolytes are *dicks*."

No argument there. But they weren't the problem right now, their stooges were, and how to get around them. And we didn't have a lot of time.

And then we had less.

A familiar sound came from below. A sound like a door opening in some paneling. And then boot heels started hitting stairs, a lot of them. Like maybe someone had seen us come in and got a few buddies together to check it out.

"Damn," Fred said.

Yeah, that about summed it up. I looked back the other way, but it was worse than before, since the smokers had been joined by a guy dragging a sheet made into a bag. A bag that clanked with what, at a guess, was every valuable he could find.

"They're plundering her," Rhea whispered, quivering because she was so furious.

"I can take them," Rico told me, dark eyes level.

And yeah, he probably could. But I didn't know for certain that these men didn't make it out of here. And while I wouldn't waste any tears on a bunch of child killers, I was risking the time line enough as it was.

"I could shift us inside," I said reluctantly, as the approaching boots hit the second floor.

"You sure?"

No. Furniture could have changed position, more of their friends could still be in there, a thousand things could go wrong. Like me not having the power to shift us back out, which wouldn't be fun.

But then, neither was this.

And then it got worse.

"Hey!" came from the stairs behind us. "Hey, up—"

"Here" went unsaid, because Rico's knife was buried in the speaker's throat.

Shit!

"Check it out," a voice growled from below, and the stairs started to shake under multiple boot heels.

And then we were stumbling out into the hallway, because the odds were better here, although the mages hadn't moved. And they still didn't, even to look up, when four strangers emerged from a wall just down the hall. The panel slid shut behind us, and then I noticed Fred, staring intently at the men bent over their bags.

"Got it?" Rico whispered.

"Think so," Fred muttered.

"Be sure."

"You be sure," Fred snarled in a whisper. "Three's damned hard!"

"Not if they're distracted," Rico pointed out. And a second later, one of the mages turned around and slugged the guy next to him.

"What the hell?" His buddy looked up, a silver candelabra in one hand and his bulging cheek in the other.

"That's mine!" the first mage said, grabbing the candlestick.

"Get your own. I found this!"

"And I want it."

"What you want is a fat lip to match that head," the second guy said. "And you're going to get it if you don't let go."

"Fuck you" was the elegant reply.

Which is why mage number one had his nose bashed in a second later.

"Hurry, before they start flinging spells," Rico said, and started pulling us toward the scrabbling duo.

"They're going to see us!" Rhea said, pulling back.

"They won't see anything."

She looked at me, and I nodded. I didn't know exactly what was going on, but I could guess. All vamps could do suggestions, but based on recent experiences, I was assuming Mircea's bunch were better than most. Which meant that Fred could probably make them swear the sky was red if he wanted to.

At least for a while. But it looked like maybe that kind of thing was hard, because he was already sweating. And considering that vamps don't, that wasn't a great sign.

"Let's go," I told her, and we started down the hall, just as someone began scrabbling at the paneling behind us.

"Don't. Run," Fred said tightly, pulling Rhea back as she darted ahead.

"Why not?" She looked around, eyes huge.

"Because people notice you when you run."

"And they won't notice if we *walk right by them*?"

"No."

And they didn't, being too focused on each other to pay us any attention.

Unfortunately, that wasn't true of the ones who burst out of the hidden stairwell behind us a moment later. "There!" somebody said, and a spell shot over our heads, missing us only because Rico jerked us down at the same second.

He didn't have to jerk Fred, who had already hit the ground, still staring at the mages ahead of us. Until the wall beside his face burst into flames when the spell hit, making him curse and draw back. And lose his grip on the little group of thieves.

Luckily, they were too busy fighting with each other to notice. And with the guys behind us, who they assumed had just attacked them. And it didn't look like the Black Circle was any better at talking out differences than the Silver.

So much for not altering the time line, I thought grimly. And for once, hoped my murderous acolytes actually were, and that none of these men had been fated to get out of here anyway. But there was no time to worry about it now, no time for anything except scrabbling forward on hands and knees as the battle raged above us and we made for the door.

Which we somehow hit before anything hit us, maybe because Rhea was shielding for all she was worth.

At least, I assumed that was why a spell deflected off the air maybe a foot above our heads, hit some other mage's shield, and then went ping-ponging around, striking shield after shield before finally finding a target in the ceiling.

And blowing a hole in it.

Plaster rained down, dust billowed out in a choking cloud, and the door we'd finally reached was thrown open. And a bunch more mages ran out, drawn by the crazy. But thanks to the camouflage we'd just unleashed, they didn't see us.

Until they fell over us.

Rhea's shield had given up the ghost at some point, so I felt every bit of the boot to the ribs I took when one of the mages tripped over me. And then Rico jerked the remainder, who were trying to draw back into the room, out into the fray. Boots stomped, coats were slung in my face, and the yelling, cursing, and spell slinging suddenly intensified. But I didn't care. I had my eye on the open door, and I dove for it, the others sliding, crawling, and, in the case of Fred, rolling through along with me.

And then someone slammed the door.

"Like that's going to *help*?" Fred said, his voice a little high.

"No, but this will!" Rhea snarled, and smashed her hand down on a small button on the wall.

I'd taken it for a dimmer, but I guess not. Because a shield shimmered into place right in front of my face a second later, almost close enough to cut off my nose. But it didn't matter, because we were in!

Chapter Thirty-seven

"Oh," Rhea said softly, her anger evaporating into shock as she stared around.

And, yeah. The place looked a little different now. The coffee table was cracked, the many sofa cushions were slashed, and the bar had been emptied of its crystal and most of the booze. A few half-empty bottles were lying on their sides, above stained and dirty carpeting, leaking onto the imprints of dozens of muddy boots. It looked like we'd arrived at the tail end of the pillage.

Which made it strange that the safe was still there and still intact, despite the van Gogh having gone.

A moment later, I understood why.

"Shit!" Rico jerked back his hand.

"What is it?" I hurried over.

"Wards."

"But they're supposed to be down. That's the whole point of this!"

"The safe was probably set up to be independent of the house grid. Either that or—"

He looked at the door.

But Rhea was already shaking her head. "It's a perimeter ward only. It shouldn't affect anything else."

And too bad if it did, because we couldn't exactly lower it, could we?

"How long will it hold?" Rico asked her.

"I— Ten minutes? Perhaps a little more? It was meant as an extra level of protection for the Pythia in times of distress."

"Well, I think this qualifies," Fred muttered from behind the sofa. He was doing something, but I couldn't tell what. But if it was cowering, I didn't intend to say anything.

Bet he didn't volunteer next time.

"I am no mage," Rico told us. "But I know a few tricks. As long as we have time, I will use it."

"We don't have much time," Rhea said, biting her lip.

"Then I will be quick." He shot her a devastating grin over his shoulder. "Although that's not my usual style."

She looked at him blankly. He grinned wider. I went over to see what Fred was doing.

He was behind the sectional of many pillows, but he wasn't cowering. He was peering myopically at something ugly. I assumed he'd pulled it out of the largish sack on the ground next to him, which one of the thieves must have dropped on the way out the door.

Although why any thief had wanted that thing was beyond me.

"Have you seen this?" he asked, looking up.

"Yes." And I didn't want to see it again.

"It's a hell of a thing," he told me.

"It's a bezoar."

"That's what I mean." He held it out to me. "Someone rescued that from *a goat's stomach*, prettied it up, and made it into a *cup*."

"I know," I said, trying not to shy back, but the thing was nasty. And that was despite the nice little framework of enameled gold someone had added in a seriously misguided attempt to add some class. Although what else they could have done I didn't know, since it was basically a dung-colored, hairy softball.

That now looked like a dung-colored, hairy Fabergé egg.

"Why would anyone *do* that?" Fred demanded.

"Lady Phemonoe collected poison remedies," Rhea told him, glancing at the empty shelving. Which, until recently, had held the world's creepiest cup collection. Which seemed to now be residing in the sack Fred was looking through.

"All of them?" Fred asked, clearly fascinated. "Even the horn?"

"Horn drinking vessels were believed to vibrate on contact with poison," she told him. "Vintners used to wear a piece of horn around their necks when they tested their wine, to make sure it hadn't gone off."

"Seriously?"

"Rock crystal was similar," she added as he pulled out another cup. "When exposed to poison, it was supposed to lose its transparency and turn cloudy. This one is set with amethyst, as it was believed to change brightness when near poisoned items."

"And the one with the shark teeth?"

"Fred," I said, interrupting. "Can you do me a favor and try to find any potion bottles that Rhea and I might have missed? Your nose may be able to pick up on something we didn't."

"Well, yeah," he agreed. "That's why I came over here. These things *reek.*"

"Of potion?" I asked sharply.

He nodded.

I suddenly got a lot more interested in the weird collection.

"There's probably residue on most of them," Rhea said, looking at me apologetically. "These weren't just for show. She used them. She wouldn't drink from anything else."

Fred whistled through his teeth. "Wow, paranoid much?"

"It wasn't paranoia," Rhea said. "It had been prophesied that she would die from poison if she wasn't vigilant."

"But she was *Pythia*. Wouldn't she know if someone was trying to slip her something?"

"How would she know?"

"I just thought she'd get a vision or something."

"We don't see visions about ourselves."

"Oh." Fred looked like he hadn't known that. "Well, looks like she took it seriously. Sharks' teeth?"

I glanced at Rico, who had just jerked his hand back again, cursing softly. But I couldn't help him. So I found a spot on the ruined sofa and sat down, and a moment later, Rhea joined me. Like we were having a polite chat instead of plundering a dead woman while thieves battered at the door and a bomb ticked away its last minutes.

"A cure rather than a preventative," she told Fred. "Sharks' teeth set in an agate cup—both said to render poison harmless. Like the bezoar."

"And these?" Fred pulled a miscellany of items out of the bottom of the sack. A small gold cup set with rubies. A handful of precious stones, some the size of a marble, others large as hens' eggs. A tangle of amulets. Some odd charred bones.

"For an extra precaution, you could add a bezoar or an amulet to the cup," Rhea explained. "Lady Phemonoe usually used several."

"But that's . . . just superstition. She had to know that, right? It doesn't work."

"It worked," I said. "Just not the way it was intended."

"Come again?"

"It's what killed her."

Fred looked down at the cup in his hands and dropped it like it was hot.

"They're not going to hurt you," I told him. "It was an amulet that did it. It contained arsenic—"

"Arsenic?"

"—because of an old belief that poison attracted poison and would draw it out of whatever it was dunked in."

"That . . . seems like a really bad idea."

"It wasn't supposed to be able to get out."

"But it did," he pointed out.

"It had help."

"Help?" That was Rhea. She'd been looking back and forth between the two of us, but now her eyes focused on me.

And I remembered: not too many people knew for certain how Agnes had died. There had been rumors, of course. But the reputable—read Circle-controlled—papers had done a pretty good job of hushing them up.

I guess they didn't want to give people ideas.

But Rhea had been part of Agnes' court; she deserved to know.

"It was Myra," I said, talking about Agnes' former heir, who had been a little too impatient to inherit. "She poked a pinhole in one of the amulets—"

"She did what?"

I suddenly wished I'd kept my big mouth shut. Because Rhea had just turned white as a sheet. But it was too late now.

"It, uh, it enabled the poison to leak out a little at a time, whenever it was used," I told her. "Agnes, well, she did the rest herself, every time she had a drink."

"Why . . . why weren't we told this?"

"I thought you had been."

"No. No." She looked stricken.

Way to put your foot in it, Cassie, I thought darkly.

"Did the Lord Protector know?" Rhea asked, using Jonas' official title. And then didn't give me time to answer. "Of course he did. Of course he did!"

"Well, yes," I said, because clearly.

"Why would he do that?" she demanded, her expression caught between tears and rage. "Why would he deprive her of her right?"

"What right?" Fred asked. "She's dead."

I shot him a look.

"The right to avenge herself on her attacker!"

"But . . . she's *dead*," Fred reiterated, as if maybe Rhea had missed that part.

"But her soul is not!" she snapped.

"Yes, well, I'm sure it's, uh, in a better place," Fred said awkwardly.

Rhea shook her head. "You don't understand. A Pythia devotes her life to her purpose, and is rewarded by being allowed to merge with another at death."

"Merge?"

"Her soul migrates to another body, a host body."

"Just . . . anybody's?" Fred asked, suddenly looking alarmed. And glancing at me out of the corner of his eye.

"Anyone willing," I clarified.

"Oh, good. Because I'm not. Willing. In case you were wondering."

"I wasn't."

"Good 'cause . . . I'm really, really not."

"Okay."

"I mean, not even a little—"

"Fred!"

"We have to find her," Rhea broke in. "We have to give her that chance!"

"Myra is already dead," I said, trying to think of a way to change the subject.

"Yes, but the others are not! They had to know! They were thick as thieves, all of them! There's no way they didn't—"

"Rhea."

"We can find her! She can help—"

She stopped suddenly, probably at the look on my face. And it was times like these that I wished I had a tenth of Mircea's diplomatic ability. Or even some of that weasel-out-of-questions-you-don't-want-to-answer ability. Because this answer wasn't anything she wanted to hear.

"Rhea," I told her gently. "Let it go."

"You know something."

The pallor from before had morphed into two high red circles on her cheeks. It made her look like a kid who'd gotten into her mother's cosmetics and gone crazy with the rouge. But it didn't look funny to me. It didn't look funny at all.

"Rhea, please."

"I want to know."

"Rhea—"

"It's my right to know!"

And I wasn't going to get out of this, was I?

But I really didn't want to tell her. If she looked this bad, just getting confirmation that Agnes was murdered, how would she feel about the rest of the story? How would she like knowing that her beloved Pythia had died on her last shift back in time, had thereafter hitched a ride in the body of a young girl kidnapped by the fey, and had waited out the centuries in faerie, where time runs differently. Just so she and the girl could make their escape back here at the perfect time for Agnes to merge with a new host—her old acolyte, Myra. And to slit her throat from ear to ear, releasing both their souls at the same time.

Not for revenge, but as her last act as Pythia. She had been determined to free the world from the horror she'd unwittingly unleashed. And to deny Myra the chance to come back in a new body, in the only way she could.

By dragging her soul away with her into the afterlife.

I could close my eyes and still see it, the red, red blood spilling down Myra's snowy white gown, the two souls entwined, fighting to the last, the small body slowly slinking to the floor, almost gracefully. I'd seen it in nightmares a few times since. I didn't want to pass them on.

But Rhea was right; as a member of the court, she ought to know.

"It's a long story," I finally told her. "And I don't know

most of it. If you want to hear everything, when we get back to Dante's, talk to a witch named Françoise. She works at Augustine's," I added. "She can tell you more than me."

To my relief, she seemed to accept that.

"May—may I be excused," she asked, "for a moment?"

I nodded, and she abruptly ran off. I watched her go, feeling crappy. And reminding myself to be careful what I said in front of the court from now on.

"Sorry," Fred told me. "I didn't mean . . ."

"It's not your fault."

"I didn't know she was going to take it like that."

That made two of us.

Fred retrieved his terrible toy and sat on the sofa, and I put my feet up on the coffee table, because it didn't matter anymore. And for a moment there was silence, except for the scritch, scratch, scritch of Fred petting his hairy cup. And damn, that was disturbing.

"Stop that," I told him.

"Stop what?"

"Touching that thing."

"It feels nice," he told me. "Like a fuzzy pet rock. Do you want to—"

"No!"

He looked down at it fondly. "It does seem weird, though, doesn't it?"

" 'Weird' is not the word I'd use."

"Not the cup. Myra."

"What about her?"

"That she left so much to chance. Killing someone like that . . . you know, when she didn't have to."

"She did have to. If an acolyte kills a Pythia directly, the power will refuse to go to her. It's something to do with the conditions laid on the power when Apollo gave it."

"Apollo," Fred said, frowning. "You really believe that stuff you told Jonas the other night, about us fighting gods?"

For a moment, it threw me. Maybe because, for the last three months, I'd been living in a crazy world of gods and demons, myths and monsters, and Fred hadn't. Well, okay, he'd been there for that last one, the demigod sons of Ares called the Spartoi, who could shift into dragon form at will.

And damn, you'd think something like that would have woken him up.

But there were dragons in faerie, and for all I knew, maybe he'd seen one. He hadn't seen a god. He hadn't been there when Apollo died, hadn't seen him glowing bright as a star fallen to earth, a boiling mass of power. And that was after he'd been seriously drained getting past the barrier. Yet I'd hardly been able to look at him. . . .

"Cassie?"

"Not gods," I told him tersely. "Just beings powerful enough to make ancient people think they were."

I started sorting through the stuff on the coffee table to give myself something to do. Maybe the girls would like some mementos of Agnes, if I could find a couple dozen that weren't too horrifying. Which wasn't looking like it was going to be easy.

"But why so powerful?" Fred asked, sitting forward.

"What?"

"The gods. Why were they so powerful here?"

"I don't know. They come from another world—"

"The fey come from another world. And their magic doesn't work here."

"It works. They use Elemental magic, same as the covens."

"Not the same," he argued. "The same idea maybe, but the fey can't feed from our world at all. The covens can 'cause they're from here, but the fey aren't. Their bodies generate some magic, and they bring talismans and shit with them to extend it. But when their power starts to run low, they hightail it back to faerie. They have to, or become sitting ducks!"

I blinked at him, because that had sounded . . . kind of vicious.

He saw my expression and grimaced. "We've been having some problems with the fey lately. It's one of the things the master's doing in New York."

I nodded.

"But none of this explains why the 'gods' were so damned powerful here," he persisted. "Shouldn't they have run dry eventually, like the fey?"

"They're not fey."

"But they're magical beings and all magic gives out eventually; why didn't theirs?"

I shrugged. "They cycled out, went home sometimes. That's why the old legends say they lived in places like Asgard or Olympus, not earth."

"But the legends also say that they fought wars *here*," Fred persisted. "Including some with each other. So, what did they do when their power ran low? Say time out and go home?"

"No," I said, and tossed a ruby on the pile. "They fed on demons."

"Demons?"

"That's what they wanted with earth in the first place: as a staging ground for their hunt. Humans don't have enough energy to bother with, but the demons had more, sometimes millennia of accumulated power, and it . . . fattened the gods back up."

"Ah. I didn't know that."

"It's why the demons hate them. The gods were using us as bait to lure them in. The demons came to feed off us, and then the gods fed off them." Like lions hanging out at the watering hole, as Pritkin had phrased it.

Hungry lions.

Fred frowned. It didn't look like he enjoyed learning that he was low man on the food chain. "Are the gods like us in other ways? Can they pull from family? Share power?"

"Not that I know of." I kind of got the impression that the gods didn't share much of anything.

"But then, how did they fight? Each other, I mean?"

"I told you. Maybe they fed off any demons that happened to be around, if they got low."

"Maybe." He didn't look convinced.

"Vamps do that," I pointed out. "Tony's boys did, in a scuffle. They used to drain their opponents to heal themselves."

"A scuffle is not a war," he argued. "And while that's technically possible, it takes concentration. And losing concentration, even for a split second, with one of us . . ."

I nodded. The best way to survive a vamp fight was not to get in one. Sort of like with the gods, I thought grimly.

"Here, put these in your pockets," I told him, scooping up the jewels. I'd decided against the amulets. The creep factor was high, and I didn't need anyone else poisoned. But some of the raw stones might be pretty all polished up. Maybe the girls could get rings made or something.

"You can tell me, you know," he said as I was stuffing his jacket pockets.

"Tell you what?"

"Why you've been running around like a headless chicken for two weeks—"

"I have not."

"You have. You stumble back in, dirty and beat up and wearing seriously weird clothes. You throw back some dinner, grab some sleep, and then you're off again. Everybody's curious."

"Then tell them to be less curious."

"Some of the guys think Mage Pritkin has gone and got himself in trouble, and that you're trying to help him—"

"They can think whatever they want."

"—but I told 'em that you were probably doing something about the war. Trying to find us some advantage maybe."

"Uh-huh."

"So which is it?" he persisted. "War or war mage? I got a bet riding on it."

"Can't it be both?" I asked, distracted by the sight of one of the cups, which had ended up under the coffee table. I picked it up. They were really beautiful, some of them. This one had been carved entirely out of amethyst, like a single great jewel.

But it hadn't saved her. None of them had. I was beginning to think that those sorts of precautions never did. Hunker down, play it safe, take precautions . . . and die anyway.

Because Mircea was right about one thing: how did you win a war playing defense? The answer was you didn't. Not usually, anyway, and not this one.

But what other choice did we have?

What did we have that could kill a god?

"Cassie?"

I looked up to find Fred leaning back on the couch, watching me. And maybe it was a trick of the light, or my overactive imagination. But for a second, the too-round face was grim, and the big gray eyes were narrowed and shrewd.

And then he smiled again, and he was just Fred.

"Both?"

And shit.

I was just putting my foot in my mouth every time I opened it tonight, wasn't I?

But this time I got a reprieve when Rico decided to rejoin us.

He was closing the little leather fold of tools he'd brought with him, and putting it back inside his jacket. The jacket was another leather one, which went with his bad-boy image better than the suits I'd never seen him wear. It also went with his somewhat checkered past as a "trouble-shooter" for the family, which must have included a little safe breaking since he'd volunteered.

Only a glance at the safe showed that he hadn't broken this one.

"No?" I said, because of course not. When was anything ever that easy?

"I can break it open or rip it out of the wall for you," he confirmed. "But I can't do it while those wards are up. We need a mage."

"And where are we supposed to find one?" Fred asked. "We can't just call up the Circle and ask 'em to send one over, or it'll change time. And we can't go back to our own time and snag one, because she's already exhausted. And all the ones around here are—"

He cut off when the door suddenly hit the floor, sliding halfway across the room, while the opening erupted into one giant fireball.

"Dark," I finished for him, as all hell broke loose.

Chapter Thirty-eight

The mages weren't the problem.

I threw a time freeze at them at almost the second they cleared the door. It wasn't quite strong enough to do the job, because I was tired and they were scattered, forcing me to spread the spell over a bigger area than I'd planned. But that actually ended up being okay. Because instead of stopping them in place, it encased them in a large blob of slow time, which left fire spells boiling out ahead of them and coats wafting out behind them and the mages themselves on what looked like might be a ten-minute journey to the other side of the room.

No, they weren't the problem.

The acolytes were.

"Shit!" I heard someone say, and a spell tore through the room at the same time that I tried to shift my group out of it. But shifting without being able to touch someone is a new skill for me, and exponentially harder. And that's without having to throw two spells within seconds of each other.

Fred winked out of existence, still clutching his hideous souvenir, but Rico knocked me back, trying to shield me. And in the process put himself out of reach. And Rhea wasn't even back yet, and shifting people without even being able to *see* them wasn't happening.

Especially not when you're already shifting yourself.

I never knew exactly what happened. But either the acolyte's spell or Rico's elbow must have thrown me off, because instead of the suite, I ended back at the top of the hidden staircase. That was good, since I hadn't wanted to leave with two of my people stuck here anyway. That was bad, because whatever had hit me hadn't just frozen my power, it had frozen *me*.

Annnnd now I was falling.

I tottered against the wall, which wasn't so bad. And then bounced off and hit the stairs, sliding all the way back down to the secret panel, which was worse. And which obligingly opened, spilling me halfway out into the room, because of course it did.

God*damn* it.

The awkward way I'd fallen had left my feet sticking out into the ballroom and my head inside the passage. And the pitch-dark stairs behind me and the wall of paneling in front of me ensured that I couldn't see shit. I could hear, though, and a few seconds later my ears were being treated to the sound of boot heels hitting marble.

My breath froze as still as the rest of me as I stared at the dim outline of the gothic arch. The room outside was lit only by a little moonlight, but it looked bright as day compared to the gloom of the stairs. And my jean-covered legs and the gaping maw of the staircase were going to be hard for anyone to miss.

If the boots were coming this way, that is.

They echoed loudly on all that marble, making it hard to tell, but it sort of sounded like it.

Of course, I thought desperately, and stuck out my tongue.

It was the only thing I could currently move, along with my lips slightly. It wasn't much, not even enough to keep me from drooling. More like the feeling a couple hours after visiting the dentist, when the Novocain begins to wear off and you start looking for your pain pills.

I didn't have pain pills. But I did have a pain. In the form of a guy who crashed in my necklace when he wasn't off ogling the casino's hoochie-coochie dancers. Which with my luck was where he was tonight, because he was *never* around when I—

There.

My tongue finally managed to find something other than the fuzzies off my shirt. Namely the chain of the necklace I wore, which had slid onto my shoulder next to my chin when I fell. I grabbed it with my lips and tongue and started trying to pull the main cluster of ugly, consisting of a ruby red stone surrounded by a lot of tacky gold filigree, toward me.

But the damned thing kept sliding on its chain, and the footsteps were definitely coming closer, and when I tried to shift a little farther back into the stairwell, nothing happened.

Except that Bootheels finally came into view.

He was a war mage, all right, in black commando gear paired with steel-toed boots, and an incongruous floor-length cape. Like a soldier of fortune crossed with a medieval monk. The boots were familiar from Pritkin's workaday wardrobe. Something else he had was familiar, too.

The elegant ballroom with its crystal chandeliers, velvet curtains, and highly polished marble floor was an incongruous backdrop for the crude creature standing beside the mage. Naked, taller than a man, and made out of dull orange earth, it looked like a piece of bad claymation that an artist needed to spend a little more time on.

It wasn't.

When I first met him, Pritkin had had one of the creatures called golems by the medieval rabbis, who had been the first to make them. And who hadn't bothered overmuch with looks, because that wasn't the point. The point was to create a mobile prison for the malevolent creature inside it, one of the nastier demon species that were trapped by the crazier mages to be used as servants.

Pritkin had used his mainly as a decoy and an added layer of shielding. The clay body absorbed spells and bullets equally well, keeping them from landing on him, and was also useful as a pack mule for carrying extra hardware. But they could attack, too, with a liquid speed that I'd rarely seen outside of a vamp.

And they were virtually unstoppable, since, unlike us flesh-and-blood types, they didn't feel pain.

I was so screwed.

Master and slave had their backs to me at the moment, staring out of the French windows. Because the only thing supposed to be over here was wall. But they'd see me as soon as they turned around, which meant that I didn't have—

Any time.

A faint sound, like that of a door panel sliding back, drifted down to my ears from the top of the stairs. And then heavy, measured footsteps started coming this way. I couldn't see who it was, but it didn't matter since a determined five-year-old could kill me in my current state and—

And then a flashlight beam hit me in the face.

"What the hell?"

The voice came from behind, but the mage in front of me heard it and spun. Leaving me sandwiched between two dark magic workers with the only question being which one would curse me first. And I guess it was Flashlight, because Bootheels' hand didn't even twitch before the area erupted in light.

But not in the shape of a spell.

Not unless the mages had crafted one that looked a lot like a genie rising from a lamp, if the lamp was an ugly ruby necklace and the genie was a pissed-off, transparent cowboy whose evening slumber had just been ruined by two thoughtless mages. Who were now no longer staring at me, I realized. But at my ghost buddy Billy Joe, who was glowing like the Aurora Borealis, with the sickly, neon green ghost light few humans ever get a chance to see.

And then with a whiter, brighter sheen, as the long, jeans-and-ruffled-shirt-clad body collapsed into a ball of pulsing ghost energy, throwing crazy shadows on the walls. And letting off a sound that felt like a knife in the brain.

If they ever wanted a sound effect for a scary movie, I had one for them, I thought, wishing that my hands worked so I could cover my ears. Or shut my eyes, which were starting to seriously dry out, but not so much that I couldn't see Billy Joe swoop up the stairs, with a psychic scream that sounded like a thousand nails on a thousand chalkboards and sent horrible shivers running over my skin.

The mage didn't seem fond of it, either, because he cursed and stumbled back, falling into the stairwell.

But it didn't stop him from drawing a weapon, and when Billy swooped around him and came barreling back down the stairs, a hail of bullets followed.

That would have been very bad, except for the fact that

I was lying down. So they flew over my head and hit the other mage, who had been standing there with his mouth hanging open. And his shields down, judging by the fact that he shuddered and fell over just as the other mage tore down the stairs.

And straight into Bootheels' last spell.

It looked like the dying mage had had a split second to get off a final curse, which caught his counterpart halfway down the short flight and sent him tumbling the rest of the way. Until he kicked me in the head, tripped, and sprawled out on the shiny ballroom floor, lying still. Leaving me with two dead mages, and a golem that suddenly lost interest in the attack in favor of nudging his old master with a clay-like toe.

And a ball of pissed-off energy that stopped just above my drooling face, resolving itself into a disembodied head wearing a Stetson and a scowl.

"You rang?" Billy demanded dryly.

"Nngghnh," I said, which was the best I could do with frozen vocal cords and a lolling tongue.

"Would you mind repeating that?"

"Nngghnh, nngghnh!"

"Very funny," Billy said.

"NNGGHNH!"

"Oh, for God's sake!" he said, disgusted, and merged with me so we could actually have a conversation. "Now, you want to tell me why you can't move?"

"I got hit with a spell."

"And why those guys wanted to kill you?"

"It's Thursday."

"And what the hell 'nngghnh' means?"

"It means we're running out of time!" I said, and cursed. Because nothing worked. And damn the acolytes! And damn the dark mages! And damn everybody who had magic but me! I was supposed to have more magic than everyone else, to be able to do things other people couldn't, not to get caught in a—

My thoughts screeched to a halt as my eyes fell on the golem. Which had just collapsed, probably because spells don't outlive the caster, including containment spells, and the mage had just departed for the other side. I hadn't been paying much attention to it before, but I was now.

And maybe I did have some magic that would work, after all.

"This isn't going to work," Billy told me a couple minutes later.

"It *is* working," I said, twitching a finger.

It was fat and orange, without a nail or a hair or the freckles common to a human. It looked more like an uncooked hot dog than a finger, but it was moving. Which was more than I could say for my broken doll of a body still sprawled in the stairway.

Billy remained in house, so to speak, because my body would die without a soul in residence. Which is why I was currently getting a death glare out of my own blue eyes. He could blink them now, and had managed to mostly pull my tongue back where it belonged, although my voice slurred like an old drunk's.

But it was an improvement. And hopefully an indication that the mage's spell was weakening. But not fast enough.

"I wish you could help me up," I told Billy.

"I wish you'd stop using that voice," he told me back. "It's ... disturbing."

"Sorry."

I kind of liked it. Deep and powerful and scary, it matched the body—and the body's former occupant, whom I could still smell as a pervasive stench. As if evil had permeated the very pores this thing didn't have.

Or maybe ancient demons just didn't wear deodorant.

"Isn't that freaking you out?" Billy demanded as I settled more comfortably into my temporary skin.

"Yes," I said, but it didn't sound convincing even to me.

But I *was* freaking out; of course I was. I was a disembodied soul trying to wear the shed skin of an evil demon, which I was controlling through the very illegal magic known as necromancy. Or was trying to, I amended, as I started to get up.

And had a ghostly-looking girl leg poke awkwardly out of the golem's massive shin.

"Told you," Billy said as I frowned at it.

I drew it back in, but when I tried to move the leg again, the same thing happened. I moved mine, instead. Or, you know, what would have been mine, if I'd still had one, and damn it!

Okay. Okay. This wasn't my first time at the possession rodeo. I should be able to figure this out.

Technically, my father had been the necromancer in the family, although he hadn't made zombies. He'd made something like this. Not golems; he wasn't a warlock. He couldn't summon a demon if his life had depended on it, which was just as well because it would have kicked his ass. So he certainly couldn't trap one.

But then, he didn't have to. Because he already had plenty of spirits around. Dad, it turned out, had been a ghost magnet.

It was something he'd passed on to me, along with his blond hair and blue eyes and tendency to fall over his own two feet. I'd grown up with the ability to see and talk to ghosts, which I'd assumed was just a clairvoyant thing. But apparently not.

Because ghosts didn't just like to talk to me, they hung around. And I guessed they liked to hang around Dad, too, because he'd amassed his own little group. Which he'd eventually realized would be more useful if they had bodies like the golems some of his warlock buddies made.

Crazy, right?

But then, so was Dad, or he gave a good impression of it sometimes. Like in this case, because nobody dealt with ghosts. Necromancers made zombies because they did as they were told. Ghosts would give you the finger before mugging you for energy and going off to the strip club. At least, they would if they were Billy Joe. Ghosts did what they damned well pleased.

But Dad had preferred them anyway, and so he'd decided to make prosthetic bodies for his ghosts. And yes, he was a weirdo, but that didn't mean he was wrong, because it had worked. Unfortunately, I didn't know the spell he'd used.

He'd told me that he'd managed to infuse the spell for making golems with his own necromancy, but he hadn't mentioned how. At the time, it hadn't seemed important. It was kind of feeling important now.

"Cass—"

"In a minute."

The whole point of it had been to mesh a spirit with a body. That was what necromancy did—use a little of the necromancer's soul to animate a body that wasn't his. It was why they could only make a handful of zombies at a time; there was only so much soul energy one person could spare.

So Dad had taken some of his soul, merged it with a ghost's, and then just . . . stuffed the resulting combo into a premade body. And Dad's bit o' soul had acted like glue to keep it there.

But if that was the case, then why did I need a spell?

I didn't need to bind another soul. I *was* the soul. And, according to Dad anyway, I was also the necromancer.

So why wasn't this thing working?

"Cass—"

"I said give me a minute."

"I don't think we have a minute," Billy said, rolling my eyes toward the door, where a couple more mages had just come in.

Damn.

I started thrashing around, trying to force the issue, and managed only to flip myself over. And apparently this thing was heavier on the front or something, because I couldn't seem to get upright. Which left me crabbing about on the floor, half crushing my own prone body and vulnerable as hell.

"Cass—"

"I'm trying!"

"Cass!"

"Damn it, Billy!"

And then something abruptly snapped.

Namely, my left leg into the same leg of the golem. And then my right arm into its arm. And then the rest of my body, which a minute ago had been trying its best to float up out of this thing, was now comfy cozy. And what the hell?

The only difference I could see was that my necklace had become partly imbedded in the clay thanks to my gyrations on the floor. Only it wasn't just a necklace, was it? It was a *talisman.* Like the control crystals the golems had but mine hadn't, because it had shattered and broken when the demon left.

I was so proud of myself for figuring this out that I forgot there were two dark mages headed my way, until I saw the utter panic on my own half-frozen face.

Shit.

I grabbed the necklace off my body and shoved it harder into the clay. And then tried to draw my wayward left leg, which was still trying to do its own thing, back inside my smelly suit. And felt it click back into place.

And this time, it moved under my command, although my coordination left something to be desired. But I managed to get my new big feet under me anyway, and stood up. And found the body to be amazingly light, no heavier feeling than mine, maybe even less so.

Maybe clay was a decent choice, after all.

"What happened?" one of the mages demanded, advancing with his hand on a holster.

"Nothing," I said as my leg tried to poke out the side again. "Don't—don't come any closer."

"Why not?"

"Uh, it's a trap," I said, feeling around inside the golem's leg with my wayward one, which didn't seem to fit. Maybe because the golem was something like seven feet tall and I wasn't. But no, no, no, you're a *soul*, I reminded myself. You don't have a size anymore.

But my brain didn't believe it, and my brain kept insisting that I didn't fit. And the second mage had now joined the first. And both were looking at me suspiciously as I juddered around, doing the golem equivalent of the hokey pokey.

"What kind of trap?" the second mage demanded, from beside his buddy.

"That kind," I said, and knocked their heads together.

It felt like I'd barely touched them, but their skulls sounded like melons hitting pavement, and they went down in a heap. I swallowed, feeling sick, but then my head jerked up at the sound of fighting coming from the main hall.

And damn it, Armageddon had just broken out, and I had to *go*.

There was no doubt at all that another me and a trio of dangerous witches were now in the house, and would soon be thundering through the second-floor hallway somewhere over our heads. And a moment after that, they would be gone, when the girls escaped and the past version of me disappeared. And a moment after *that*, the house was set to blow up.

I grabbed Billy and ran.

Chapter Thirty-nine

I stumbled into the stairwell and over the mage's body, up the stairs and around a bend. And damn, this thing didn't corner well! But it was fast, like, faster than I was, if you didn't mind hitting the wall a couple dozen times on the way. And right now, I didn't, despite the fact that my lolling body was starting to look a little worse for the wear by the time we burst out into the hall.

And straight into a bunch of mages tearing out of Agnes' old rooms, weapons at the ready.

Because, of course—they'd heard the commotion, too, hadn't they?

For a second, everything stopped. I looked at them and they looked at me, and nobody said anything. I would have swallowed, but I couldn't currently do that, or frozen in fear, but that hadn't been working so well lately, either. So after a moment, I just straightened my massive shoulders.

And walked right through the middle of them.

Because we were on the same side now, weren't we?

It might not have worked under other conditions. But with the chaos from downstairs as a backdrop, they didn't stop to question me. They took off again, flooding by on either side, heading for the fight. Forcing me to wade through a leather tide to reach the door of the suite again, only to stop and stare.

At the last thing I'd have ever expected.

My time spell was gone, along with maybe half the mages. The rest were clustered over by the safe, where one of their number was hard at work on the wards. Rico was by the sofa, frozen, with a hand raised and a snarl on his features. Fred was still missing.

And Rhea, little Miss Meek Voice, little Miss Whatever-You-Say-Lady, little Miss We-Wear-Grandma's-Nightgown-and-We-Like-It, was standing in the middle of the room, wand out and leveled on the redhead. And *screaming*, "Did you *know*?"

"Oh, look," the acolyte said. "The coven witch is going to curse us."

"Did. You. Know?"

"About dear, departed Agnes? Of course we knew. The power ages Pythias fast, but not fast enough. If we hadn't acted, she might have lived another twenty years or—oh," she said, smiling gently. "You *are* going to curse me, aren't you? Well, go ahead. Show us the power of the covens, witch. If you can break through *my* shields, I deserve to—"

She may have kept talking; I couldn't tell. Because the French windows behind Rhea abruptly slammed open, and a gust of rain and wind swirled in, powerful enough to rip one of the curtains down. A lamp teetered on a table, one of the last standing, and then fell, shattering into a thousand pieces against the floor. And a great flash of lightning flew through the open doors and hit the raised wand, splitting into a triple strand that targeted all three acolytes at once.

And blew the redhead off her feet and back through the damned *wall*.

I just stood there for a second, smelling ozone and seeing afterimages. And then three things happened at once: the mages targeted Rhea, I jumped in front of her with my broad orange back, and the brunette acolyte snarled and jumped back to her feet.

And was backhanded by a suddenly animated Rico.

Because nobody plays dead—or frozen—like a vampire.

"Get the safe!" I told him, in my scary demon voice. Which did not have the intended effect, because he turned his attention from the acolyte to me, probably because I was clutching my own apparently lifeless body.

But then I got help from an unexpected source.

"The golem," the blonde screamed. "She's in the golem!"

She hadn't even gotten all the words out when what felt like a dozen spells slammed into me, all at once. They didn't hurt, and they didn't seem to work as intended, I guess being designed for flesh and bone instead of enchanted clay. But they rocked me and slowed me, and when I tried to move again, a big crack appeared in the huge expanse of my thigh.

"The safe! Get the *safe*—" I shouted as Rhea threw another spell from behind me, blasting several mages off their feet and causing several more to abruptly shield, because nobody was laughing at coven magic now.

But several more got off spells that caused my damned left leg to go dead, and sent me lurching into Rhea. And caused her last spell to go askew and hit the chandelier, exploding it into a thousand glittering shards. And then kept going, running around the room, popping recessed lights, and raining down glass and electric sparks. Followed by a veil of darkness that didn't bother my golem eyes much but seemed to seriously freak out the mages.

Because, suddenly, spells were flying everywhere.

"The safe! The safe!" I kept repeating, I don't know why. Probably because I was a little freaked-out, too, having the unique experience of being taken apart piece by piece while Rhea threw spell after spell and Billy cursed and Rico—

I didn't know what the hell Rico was doing.

I was facing the other way, trying to shield my body and Rhea's, too, and couldn't see him. Until my big orange head got blown off my big orange shoulders and went rolling, and the eyes ended up facing the metal box that was still in the wall, although not for long. Because the next second, Rico threw aside the mage who was still working on the safe and plunged his arm *through the ward*. And through the front of the thick metal door.

And then jerked the safe out of the damned wall.

"*Go!*" he yelled, lurching toward us, but I was already going. Surging back into my own form, I got hit with the disorientation of a body swap, a rush of pain from a dozen new bumps and bruises, and blindness from the almost utter dark that my human eyes couldn't handle. And a body that still wasn't enthusiastic about following my commands.

But that was too bad, because we were out of time—in more ways than one.

"Go! Go! Go!" the blonde was yelling, while clutching the redhead's unconscious form. "Get out of here!"

"What?" the brunette staggered up, looking a little disoriented.

I assumed she'd had a shield up, or she'd have been looking a little dead, because Rico hadn't pulled his punch. But the fog seemed to clear up pretty well when the blonde screamed, "It's time!" and disappeared.

"Time for what?" one of the mages asked as the brunette winked out.

I kind of thought I knew. I grabbed Rhea and Rico, ripped Billy's necklace out of the golem's chest, and pulled my power around me. It didn't want to come; it really, really didn't. But if that damned brunette could shift while still half unconscious, so could I. So could I if it *killed me*, because it was going to kill me if I didn't—

Like right now.

I had a half second to feel something massive shake the house, to hear an explosion that deafened me the rest of the way, to see light flashes going off in front of my eyes.

And then something grabbed me. Not the gentle, familiar lift and swoop, but like a fist closing around my body, around all our bodies. And not shifting so much as *flinging* us out of space and into time.

And we were gone.

"Rico," I breathed.

"It's nothing."

"It's not nothing." I stared at his arm, or what had been an arm. It was now . . . God, I didn't even know. I'd gone to the first aid cabinet as soon as we got back, intending to dress it for him, but he hadn't wanted to let me. He hadn't even wanted to let me *see* it. And now I knew why. It looked like nothing more than a piece of charcoal from above his elbow to . . . to what had been his hand. His beautiful, perfect, long-fingered—

The other hand tilted up my chin, and his face swam in front of my eyes. "It will heal."

I shook my head. I couldn't speak.

"It will heal within a day," he told me quietly. "Two at the most. It is no different from you getting a paper cut."

And, okay, that stopped the waterworks, because that was *bullshit*. Just because someone healed faster didn't mean they didn't feel the pain to begin with. Didn't mean they couldn't be hurt. Didn't mean—

I looked back down at the arm, which he'd just covered with the sleeve of his leather jacket. He was hurt; he was hurt because of me. Because I hadn't been fast enough, hadn't planned well enough. And I *hated* it.

Suddenly, I didn't want to go anywhere, ever again. I wanted to do what everyone was always telling me: stay home, study up on my powers, stay safe. And make sure everyone around me stayed the same damn way.

I wanted to lock all the guys in the suite and never let them out. Because I'd once thought that nothing could hurt a master vampire, that they were like fleshy tanks, indestructible and immortal. And I'd liked that thought. I'd lost too many people in my life to ever want it to happen again, and surrounding myself with indestructible people had felt very reassuring.

It was less so now.

Because they weren't indestructible. They could be hurt; they could even die. And suddenly, nothing felt safe anymore.

"I shouldn't have taken you with me," I whispered. "I shouldn't have taken anyone with me."

"Then you did not believe what you said to Marco?"

"What?"

"That we are all in this together. That 'vampire,' or 'mage,' or 'Pythia' are not words that matter anymore."

"Of course I meant it—"

"Then you believe you are the only one with the right to risk, to fight?"

"No, but—"

"And that the rest of us should be content to just sit about, waiting for those *putanas* to bring back a god? I, for one, would rather go down fighting—or to take them down instead." He grinned suddenly. "And I wouldn't have missed you slamming into the room as an eight-foot golem for anything."

"Seven-foot."

"It was at least eight, possibly nine. When you started barking orders in that demon voice, I think a few of the mages wet themselves."

"They did not!"

"Well, that is the story I am going to tell," Rico informed me. "Are you going to contradict me?"

I let my head rest against his chest for a moment, because it was warm and solid and alive, and I hadn't managed to get him killed. My fist clenched in his jacket. "No."

"Good. My drinks should be covered for at least a month."

I didn't answer. I also didn't move. I couldn't without letting him see my face, and I didn't want him to see my face. I didn't know what was wrong with me. I used to be able to hide my feelings better than this. I used to not *have* so many feelings, not nearly so many, or maybe I just hadn't had so many people to have them about. And it had been better that way. It had been . . .

I made a sound and tried to pull away, but a hard hand caught me. "You are Pythia," Rico told me, dark eyes liquid. "Someday, people will die for you."

"I don't want people to die for me!"

"And that is why they will do it."

I stared up at him, wondering if all Mircea's masters were mind readers. And not even caring right now. Because everything I felt was probably on my face anyway.

"Okay, this is getting heavy," Fred said, sticking his head in the kitchen, and looking back and forth between the two of us. "Come on out if you want to see the big reveal."

They had put the safe in the lounge, on a big cleared spot on the floor near the pool table. Or what *had been* a big cleared spot, since it was now almost covered with people. Everybody was in there: the kids, the vamps, and Marco . . .

Who gave me an inscrutable look as we came in.

I found a spot on the carpet and settled down, because this might be a while.

It would have been easier if we didn't have to worry about the integrity of a small glass object, or if the mechanism hadn't gotten screwed up when Rico punched a fist through it, or if the safe hadn't been quite so high-end. But it was what it was, so I waited. And chewed my lower lip. And watched as a blond vampire nicknamed Teddy, " 'cause I'm so cuddly," worked on the safe.

I wished to God he'd speed up, and then a second later I was wishing he'd slow down. Because right now, it was like Schrödinger's potion bottle, both there and not there. But once that safe was opened . . .

I felt my palms start to sweat.

"It's like a whacked-out Christmas morning," Billy said, oblivious.

Several of the girls nodded, apparently agreeing with him, and a little one even reached out to touch him, giggling.

"What's so funny?" he asked her.

"Hat," she told him, looking at his Stetson.

"This hat?" He took it off and put it on her head. It didn't exactly fit, floating a few inches above her dark curls. But she seemed happy.

"I'm gonna want that back," he warned her.

She laughed.

"Hey, that's like giving away your right knee when you're a ghost! It's all me."

She laughed some more.

"This is going to take some getting used to," he informed me, staring around. And apparently being weirded out by the fact that half the eyes he met were staring back. "Make that a *lot* of getting used to."

Yeah, I thought, scanning the crowd of little faces. And suddenly feeling panicked. Because they were my responsibility now, too, all of them.

And how the hell did *that* happen?

"Remember that Geraldo thing?" Fred asked me suddenly. "With Al Capone's safe?"

"No."

"Oh, that's right, you're too young. Well, back in the . . . eighties, maybe? Geraldo did this big special where he was gonna open one of Capone's safes live on TV."

I wiped sweaty palms on my jeans. "And did he?"

"Oh yeah. In a big way, too. I mean, they promoted that thing for *weeks*." He beamed at me.

"So?"

"So . . . what?"

"So what was in the safe?"

"Oh, well, that's the thing. It was, like, this forty-hour special or something—at least it felt that way. It just went on and on and on. I mean, I think they interviewed anybody who had ever even looked at a *picture* of Capone. And they did all these reenactments. And they had all these talking heads come on to speculate about what kind of stuff might be in the safe. I guess they were just stretching it out for more commercial time, but I thought I was going to go crazy."

"I can relate."

"Yeah, and then, after hours and hours and *hours*, like I'm surprised they didn't have his *manicurist* on there or some—"

"Fred."

"So, anyway, I got bored and went out to eat with the guys. Then I stopped off at a place and had a couple drinks. And later decided to shoot some pool. And when I came back, they were *still working on the safe*. I mean—"

"Fred!"

"Okay, okay. So, anyway—"

"No! No 'anyways'! No 'and thens.' No nothing! *What was in the safe?*"

"Nothing."

"What?"

He nodded. "That was the real kicker. Bastard had pranked us all. There wasn't anything in there."

I stared at him. "And you're telling me this why?"

He blinked. "It's the only story I know about a safe?"

I shut my eyes.

And then opened them again a second later, when Teddy said, "Got it."

"Got what?" I asked, leaning forward, terribly afraid I was going to see a big old lot of nothing.

But there was definitely something in there.

A lot of something.

"Looks like this was where she kept all her personal stuff," he told me, pulling out jewel case after jewel case, along with envelopes of what looked like official documents, a passport, a bunch of different kinds of currency from a wide span of time—which, yeah, would be a smart thing to have around, wouldn't it? And photo albums. Lots and lots of photo albums.

Some looked relatively new; others had to be fifty or more years old, worn and scratched and crumbly around the edges. The photos, the ones leaking out the sides because clusters of them had just been stacked in there, were similar. Some were old enough to have the little crinkly edges they used to put on them; others had that weird, seventies-era color. A few were even Polaroids. But as interesting as they were, I didn't look at them. Because what I wanted . . .

Wasn't there.

"No," I said, searching through the papers on the floor. And then through the envelopes. And then through the thick spines on the albums, in case the little bottle had somehow gotten wedged down in there.

But it hadn't.

It wasn't there.

Chapter Forty

"You're going to eat something," Tami told me. It was not a question.

She put a tray on the bedside table and left, shutting the door. But somebody slipped in before she did. Somebody huge, but so quick and so quiet, I doubt she even noticed him. Vamps move like shadows when they want to, and Marco was no exception. Of course, he usually didn't bother, preferring to bellow and bluster and make the puny masses tremble in fear.

But that didn't mean he couldn't.

I'd grown up with vamps, learned to sense them in all their moods, even the quiet ones. Especially the quiet ones. That was when you were supposed to watch them the closest, because you never knew what they were up to. But I didn't watch him now. I stayed where I was, sitting beside the bed.

The curtains were closed, like they usually were in daytime. Masters could handle daylight, but why suffer the power drain when you didn't have to? But someone had been careless, or maybe one of the girls had been peeking out at the Strip, far below, and left a blackout curtain slightly ajar. Only it wasn't sunlight that was spilling in.

A spear of bloody light rippled over the bed and onto the floor like a crimson stream, the overflow from the big neon Dante's sign not far away. It normally added a barely discernable tinge to the day, a sultry haze on Vegas' already dust-reddened landscape. But the darkness of the room and the peculiar angle of the slant left only neon penetrating the gloom.

It glinted off the jewels spread out on the carpet in front of me, making them look like they'd been dipped in blood. I'd had a vague idea about mementos for the girls, some slightly less creepy than the ones from Agnes' apartment. I hadn't made much progress, though.

I couldn't seem to concentrate.

I picked up a necklace made of gold, with tiny seed pearls forming interlocking daisies. A lot of the sets were kind of heavy for young girls, but this one might work. It looked a little antiquated, like something out of the Victorian period, with little emerald-chip leaves and tiny diamond dew drops. Something Gertie might have worn as a girl. It was pretty. . . .

But I didn't want it. It was nice, but I didn't need it. I liked it, but I could give it away, because I didn't get attached to things.

It was one reason I'd never minded living in a hotel room in Vegas, where few of the things surrounding me were actually mine. I suppose it would have bothered most people. It didn't bother me.

I'd found out early on that if I liked something, Tony would find out and take it away if I displeased him. And I displeased him a lot. After a while, it was easier just to stay detached. That way, he didn't know what was important and what wasn't. And eventually, nothing was. I hadn't had a problem running away and leaving everything behind because I didn't get attached to things.

I didn't get attached to people, either. Because they left, too. My parents, who died when I was four, my governess, who Tony had killed—my fault; I'd gotten too fond of her—virtually everyone I'd ever known before the last four months.

Pritkin . . .

Pritkin.

Pritkin.

No.

I was stuck. My head was stuck and it just . . . wouldn't go there. I should be able to deal with this. I should be able to accept it. I should be able to add him to that list, the same list everybody went on, the same list I'd always known he'd end up on, too, because everybody did, everybody left. The reasons might vary, but that never did. *Everybody* left. . . .

No.

It was the problem I'd been having for more than a week, the problem I'd avoided even looking at, because I couldn't deal with it. So I'd handled it the way I did everything I couldn't deal with, and just ignored it. I'd find him; I'd get him back. It wouldn't come to this.

And now that it had, I didn't know what to do.

"She had some nice stuff."

The massive shadow crouched on its haunches in front of me, each thigh bigger around than my body. He blocked out most of the light. I was oddly grateful for that.

"Yeah. I thought the girls might like . . . something."

"What about you?" The big head tilted. "You don't like jewelry?"

"For a long time, I couldn't afford it, and then . . ." I touched Billy's necklace. "Not much matches this."

"No. Don't suppose so." A massive finger sorted through the expensive rubble. "Well, you've got plenty to choose from now."

I laid my head on the side of the bed.

Marco observed me for a moment, and then joined me on the floor, settling back against the mattress and taking out one of his awful cigars. For a while, there was just the crinkle of cellophane as he rolled it between his hands, loosening the leaves. Marco liked to savor the whole experience, from the rolling to the unwrapping to the trimming to, finally, the drawing of deep, sweet-smelling smoke into a body that would never have to pay for it.

But he wasn't smoking this one yet.

He was talking.

"Back when I was in the ring," he said, talking about his time as a gladiator, "I knew this guy. Short. Scrawny. Even kind of clumsy. You'd look at him and think, yeah, hope I get matched with that one. That one's a gimme. I'll beat him in two minutes, then go drink wine and watch somebody else bleed."

I adjusted my position to mirror his, and stared at the ceiling. "And did you?"

"No. Never got paired with him. Went out of my way to make sure I didn't, after a couple of times watching him fight."

I rolled my head over to look at him. "So he was good, after all?"

Marco snorted. "No, he was terrible. Terrible form, terrible reflexes, terrible everything. He was just as bad as he looked and then some. But he never gave up. Didn't seem to understand that he was supposed to. Some other guy, you get him on the sand, he figures it's over. You can see it in his eyes. He just starts to let go, you know?"

No. I didn't, actually, and was glad of it. But I nodded anyway.

"But not this crazy bastard," Marco said, shaking his head. "He'd throw sand in your face, he'd claw at your eyes, he'd bite your nose—bit one guy's clean off. He'd scratch and gouge and spit. He'd scream in your face to try to throw you off. He'd knee you in the *nuts*. He'd do all of them at the same time if he got half a chance, to the point that it was like pinning a mad wolverine. None of the guys wanted to fight him 'cause they all thought he was crazy. Me...I just thought he wanted to live."

"Did he?"

"Far as I know. He was still at it when my master got out of the game, anyway. You know, it's funny. You don't think of someone for a thousand years, and then suddenly you see him, clear as day. I saw him today, in you."

I let my head drop onto my knees. In Marco's mind, I'd somehow gone from weak woman who needed protecting to a bantamweight gladiator with possible brain damage. I wanted to laugh, because it was funny. I wanted to cry, because it was true.

"Yeah, I guess so," I finally settled for. The tone was noncommittal, but there was a catch in my voice I hadn't intended.

Marco grabbed my arm. "I was talking about his determination. His refusal to let others win, despite the odds being against him. I don't know where they picked him up, but he wasn't a fighter in his old life, I can tell you that. The rest of us were ex-soldiers, bodyguards, thugs. We grew up knowing our way around a sword—he barely knew how to hold one. But he *won*."

"Then he was nothing like me," I said, and this time there was something in my voice, something bitter. Because I hadn't won this time. Mircea had been right and I'd been wrong. I'd been lucky, or maybe I'd just had really good people around helping me, so I'd beaten the odds. But my luck had just run out, and so had Pritkin's, and I didn't—I couldn't— I needed to think, to figure something out, but all I could see was his face—

I started to get up, but the hand-on-my-arm thing didn't change. Except to give me a gentle shake, which had my head wobbling around almost enough for whiplash. Marco's gentle and everyone else's gentle were two different things.

"Listen to me," he said, and there was something in his voice that stopped me, even better than his grip. "I look at you and I see this . . . squashy little thing. This scrap of flesh with a mop of curls and big blue eyes and a stubborn tilt to her chin that scares the fucking life out of me, because anybody, anybody at all, could just snap her like a twig. When Mircea gave me this assignment, I didn't give two shits for my chances. Thought, "I'm gonna have to sit on her to have any hope that she'll survive the week." Figured this was the master's way of getting rid of me—give me an impossible job, and watch me fail."

I blinked at him in confusion, not understanding his point. 'Why would he want to get rid of you?"

He shrugged. "We butt heads. I have with every master I've ever had. Never had the power to go it on my own, but always resented the hell out of anybody giving me orders. My last master was ready to throw in the towel and stake my ass, until Mircea came along. You'd think I'd be grateful."

"I'm sure he respects you," I said, still confused. "He wouldn't have given you this job if he didn't."

"Yeah, maybe. I never know what he's thinking. Guess that's why he's the diplomat." Marco looked at me frankly. "I'm not. They did their best, dressed me up in all those fine suits, cut my hair—even got me a damned manicure!" He laughed suddenly. "First one in my life. It didn't help. I was what I was, not what I looked like. Just like Jules today. And just like you." He pressed something into my hand.

I looked down at it, and for some crazy reason, expected

a cigar. It wouldn't have been the weirdest thing that had happened to me today, and nothing was making sense anyway. But it wasn't a cigar.

Instead I was clutching something cool and hard and oddly heavy. Something vaguely triangular, with an uneven, pitted surface. Something—

"Where did you get this?" I whispered, staring at the little bottle in my hand. And then up at Marco, in utter disbelief. "I checked *everything*—"

"Not everything." He picked up something from the darkness beside him and handed it to me. A large, round, hairy something in a fine gold filigree setting that looked even worse in the low light. Like a balding severed head.

Fred's horrible souvenir.

"But . . . why would she put it *there*?"

"Way we figure it, this was the cup she used to take it in. Probably mixed it with something to cut the taste. And after, she just . . . forgot."

"Forgot."

"Or you can be romantic about it. She *was* Pythia. Maybe she knew you'd need it."

My hand closed over it, and I looked up, half blind. "Why are you giving this to me?"

"Couple reasons. The way I see it, you may not know what you're doing, but at least you know you don't. Everybody else thinks they got things all figured out. Jonas and his prophecies, the master and his army . . ." Marco shook his head. "They're not gonna find a way to fight Ares if they're not looking for one. You might."

"And the second reason?"

He finally unwrapped the cigar he'd been mangling. "That old Pythia—Agnes?"

I nodded.

"Seems to me that she was fighting this war, too, only nobody knew it. So she was fighting alone. And look how that turned out." He grimaced. "Thought it was time someone helped you." Dark eyes met mine. "Just don't make me regret this, all right?"

I nodded, biting my lip, and stared at the crimson glints in the almost full bottle in my hand. "You'll be in trouble when Mircea finds out you gave this to me."

"Probably."

I looked up. "And?"

Marco stuck the cigar between his teeth and grinned at me. And then mussed my hair. "I've been in trouble before."

"Well, what are you waiting for?" Rosier asked when I just stood there, looking at the bottle in my hand.

"I'm trying to figure out how much to take." It was the one thing Rhea couldn't answer for me. I assumed the acolytes could, but she'd never been around when Agnes was using the potion. And nobody had been nice enough to put a recommended daily dose on the label.

"Well, how much did you take last time?"

"Maybe an eighth of a bottle, because that's all there was. But it wasn't enough. I think that's why I was out for so long—I had to supplement it with my own power, and almost blew a fuse. But if I'm unconscious this time—"

"Then double the dose."

"I was out for almost a *day*," I reminded him. "If I double it, and I'm out half a day, does that help us?"

"Then take all of it. Be certain."

I stared at it, biting my lip.

I wasn't certain.

I wasn't certain at all.

"This is the last."

"What?"

I looked up at him. "The last bottle. There isn't any more."

"What do you mean?" He looked annoyed. "It's a potion, not a finite resource—"

"A potion that takes six months to make."

"What?"

I nodded. "Jonas said Agnes had to put in a request for it six months in advance, because of the brewing time, and that the last batch was delivered a week before she died—"

"Then get it from her court. If she just received a shipment, she can't have used it all!"

"I *did*. That's what this is. And your people checked with all the potion makers, and if the Senate has any, they're not giving it to me."

Rosier looked at the bottle in my hand and scowled. "You're telling me this is the last *anywhere*?"

"Yes. And I can't go into the past and retrieve any, because the Pythias only used it in emergencies, and that would screw up time in a way I might not be able to fix. So . . . this is it."

We both looked at the little bottle for a moment, the demon lord who ruled a world and the Pythia who controlled time, and neither of us had anything useful to say.

Until Rosier's voice cut through the pub, a harsh, discordant note. "Take all of it."

I looked at him, and my fist clenched around the glass.

"Damn it, girl! If those Pythias find us, they'll take whatever's left. Better it be in you, where it might do us some good!"

He was right; I knew he was. But for a minute, I just stood there anyway, feeling old, pitted glass slide under my fingers and cottony fear crowd my throat. I had to do this, and I had to get it right this time. And yet I just stood there.

And then I threw it back, a bitter, oily dose that moved horribly on my tongue.

"Feel anything?" Rosier asked.

"Nauseous," I gasped, staring at the bottle, afraid that maybe I'd gotten a bad batch.

Until my hand spasmed, and I watched it fall to the floor as if in slow motion, while every cell in my body exploded with light and warmth and power, so much power that I thought for a minute it was going to rip me apart.

And then I was sure it was. Reality warped, time telescoped, and the chair beside me duplicated itself into a thousand chairs that receded into the distance, like funhouse mirrors placed face-to-face. Like the rest of the pub, like the hand Rosier put on my shoulder, like the world around us . . .

Until everything slammed back together again, wrenching me off my feet and into a maelstrom of light and shadow, sound and silence, and wind that I couldn't feel but could hear in my ears, echoing in my head, screaming past us as we fell down, down, down, into nothingness so absolute that I wasn't sure anymore if the wind was screaming or if I was.

And, okay, I thought.

I guess it was good after all.

And then I passed out.

Chapter Forty-one

"Cassie! Cassie! Damn you, wake up!" Someone was shaking me. And cursing. And glaring down at me out of evil red eyes.

And then slapping me hard across the face.

And then looking surprised when I slapped him back.

I blinked and realized that the face was Rosier's, and that the weird eyes were reflecting the sky behind him. Which was red and dark and boiling with gray-green clouds. His hair was limned in red, too, and a whipping wind had it ruffling and sticking up in a good impression of his son's. To complete the scene, somewhere nearby, something was burning.

"Are we in hell?" I croaked, confused.

"Close enough," Rosier snarled. And then he snatched me up, supporting me as we stumbled for the scant cover offered by a nearby copse of trees.

They were on fire up in the tops, probably a result of the embers that were blowing about everywhere. But it didn't matter because everything else was burning, too. The trees all along the riverbank, the bushes, the *weeds*. It even looked like the river itself was on fire, the surface reflecting the flames and the wind gusts sending little gold-tipped ripples everywhere. Pretty much the only thing that wasn't alight—yet—was the old mill, but the dark hulk was visible because the moon had come out since we'd left, big and pale and floating serenely over the chaos below.

It was not illuminating Pritkin. Or if it was, I couldn't tell with all the leaping shadows everywhere. And with my eyes watering and my head spinning. And with the explosions, I added mentally, as another tree went up with a crack and a burst of flame, the wind whipping the burning bits at our heads.

"What are they *doing*?" I asked as we ducked for cover, both from the fire and the too-pale figures that had started it.

"Trying to flush out my son!" Rosier said, furious. "They obviously can't find him—"

"*We* can't find him! How are we supposed to spot him in *this*?"

It looked like the fey we'd run from earlier had given up on subtlety and were just destroying everything in their path. Which was soon going to be Pritkin—and us—if we didn't find him quick. And we weren't going to. I was choking just trying to breathe, the smoke from the ring of fire obscuring the areas under the trees like low-hanging clouds.

This wasn't going to work.

And, for once, Rosier seemed to agree.

"You aren't," he said, looking grim. "I am."

And then he was on his feet and moving fast.

I grabbed for his arm, but missed because my reflexes hadn't recovered yet. So I grabbed his leg instead. "*I'm* supposed to find him. You're supposed to—"

"I know what I'm supposed to do! But I can sense when he's near, girl; you can't! So I will get him out."

"But you're supposed to distract the Pythias!"

"There's been a change of plan," he said, shaking me off like a bothersome puppy. "*You* distract them, then meet me in town."

And with that he was gone, striding off before I could point out that I didn't know where "town" was. And that I wasn't in any shape to distract anybody right now. And that I didn't even have a weapon, because, unlike him, I actually cared about the—

My brain skidded to a stop on an image of Rosier's handgun. Which, no, might not help me much itself, since using it here could trash the hell out of the time line. But which was sitting in a pack of magic that might.

A pack I'd dropped on the shore before going skinny-dipping.

A pack that might still be there, concealed by the weeds.

I glanced around again, dropped to the ground, and started crawling.

The riverbank was oddly undisturbed, except for the stretch where chunks had been carved out of it by the fey barrage. It looked worse than I remembered, an ugly, bare scar in an otherwise pristine stretch of sand, but it did help me to orient myself. Between that and the mill, I managed to find my former patch of weeds, and soon after that my discarded clothes.

And the pack!

I hugged it to me, almost disbelieving, because let's face it, I don't get luck like that every day. And then I pulled the "dress" over my head. Because ugly and lumpish and hot it might be, but it was also darker than my white tank top. I ditched the Keds, too—also white—but couldn't make myself put my old "shoes" back on.

Until I thought of how extra crispy my soles were going to be, running through a fiery forest, if I didn't, and reconsidered.

I was trying to find a missing lace, which, being leather and brown and stringy was doing a good job of imitating one of the squashed down reeds, when another explosion burst across my vision. I looked up, because that one had been a little close for comfort, and scanned the riverbank. But I didn't see anyone.

Because they weren't on the bank.

I had a second to stare at the sight of Pritkin, not walking on water, but *running* on it, full out, his bare feet kicking up little waves behind him in the firelit stream. He'd reacquired the board shorts, but not the Ghillie top, I guess because it wouldn't be much use as camouflage unless it was on fire. And his precious walking stick was thrown over his back, in some kind of leather carrying device that didn't stop it from smacking into his legs with every stride, because it hadn't been made for a human's use.

It had been made for the things chasing him.

And they were chasing hard. Right behind him were a

bunch of fey, slipping and sliding and falling and half
drowning, because they were wearing armor, not thin flax,
and because they didn't seem to find the water as accommodating as he did. But others were converging on the
bank—a lot of others, a whole freaking lot of others, barreling this way like an otherworldly freight train—

And then Pritkin reached me. And snatched me up.
And the next thing I knew, I was doing it, too, leaving little spongy footprints on the surface of a river less solid
than land, but more than any stretch of liquid had any
right to be.

For a minute, anyway. And then it was like the strange
water balloon surface in front of us ran out, and we dove.
Or, rather, Pritkin dove, and I fell off the edge, cursing and
flailing and sinking, because he was pulling me down, I
didn't know why.

Until a flash of light missed me by a hair's breadth, boiling through the water just above my face, scalding my flesh
even through the chilly stream.

And, okay, I figured it out.

And we shot down like a bullet.

In a minute, my lungs were burning—it felt like bands of
my skin had been seared off, and yet still we dove. Into
blessedly cold water that was going to kill us anyway, because no way could we swim farther than the fey. There
were too many of them and this wasn't going to work and I
was about to try to shift us out even if it sprained a magic
muscle or brought every Pythia in five miles down on our
heads, because at least we'd *have* heads—

And then I saw it: something glowing blue at the bottom
of the river.

It was hazy and seemed to fluctuate with the current, so
I couldn't see it clearly. Or much of anything else, because
we were too deep now. But a second later I felt it, like a
drain pulling us in, pulling us down. And before I could try
to shift again, before it even fully registered, we *were* in,
vacuumed up and sucked down a vortex of swirling light
and color and sound, until it stopped abruptly.

Really abruptly.

Bug-on-a-windshield abruptly.

And I realized that I'd just fetched up against some kind
of stretchy membrane that covered the opening to a cave.

The cave appeared to be full of rocks and dark and wet, although not as much of the latter as you'd expect with a gaping hole in the wall. It was also full of Pritkin, because the membrane hadn't stopped him. He had passed through just fine and landed in a crouch on a wet stretch of rock on the other side. And was now arguing with some waist-high shaggy thing that appeared to be mostly nose and hair and attitude.

An attitude that got noticeably worse when I started thrashing against the barrier, distorting it into the cave in fist- and foot-shaped protrusions, because a ton of water was pressing down on me and shifting wasn't working and I was about to be drowning and—

And Pritkin grabbed the thing's spear and threw it straight at me.

I would have screamed, if I weren't suffocating. Or moved out of the way if I weren't being crushed by all that water. Which was suddenly falling all around me, as the membrane dissolved in a burst of light.

And I exploded into the room, along with a few thousand gallons that tsunamied through all around me. And around Pritkin. And around the hairy little nugget, who was now an angry little nugget, appearing here and there through all the churning water to stab at us with a couple of knives.

That would have been more of a problem if we hadn't been simultaneously rushing headlong down a rock-strewn corridor on the torrent of water gushing through the wall. And doing it with only intermittent light, because the roof of this cave was not in great repair. Big gaps flashed by overhead, showing not the hellscape we'd just left, but instead pieces of a discordantly beautiful day, with bright blue skies, fluffy clouds, and riotous vines waving cheerful tendrils at us.

And a bunch more angry nuggets peering down through the greenery.

I was more worried about drowning than about the locals, so when a wave tossed me at a huge stalagmite, hard enough to knock what little air I'd managed to suck in right back out, I held on for dear life.

And struggled to breathe with what seemed like an ocean's worth of water crashing by on both sides. It looked like waves breaking against a cliff, to the point that I couldn't even see the floor anymore, just a swirling mass of roaring water that wasn't just rushing by and foaming off the walls, but was also flaring up in miniature water spouts that I didn't understand until I looked up again.

And saw the hairy nuggets raining bowling-ball-sized boulders down through a gap in the roof.

"What the—what are they *doing*?" I yelled, before remembering that Pritkin didn't understand me.

"Saying hello!" he yelled back from a perch by the wall. "We're not armed!" he added, shouting upward.

The only answer was a bunch more rocks, peppering down like gray hail. But I barely noticed. Maybe because I was too busy staring at Pritkin. "What the—how did—did you just—"

"Translation spell!" he told me over the roar of the water.

"Transla—*Then why didn't you do that before?*"

"I didn't do it this time! I don't know that one yet!"

"Then who—"

I cut off to flatten against the stalagmite, allowing a rock the size of my head to splash down in the maelstrom between us.

"You go home," one shaggy thing yelled down at us. "You go home now!"

And, okay, I thought I could guess.

"Would you like to explain how?" Pritkin yelled, gesturing at the torrent spilling through the door.

The only answer was more rocks, everything from fist to boulder-sized. One hit my stalagmite's shiny dome, shearing it off into the flood and scattering shrapnel-like hunks everywhere. Including down onto me.

"It seems he would mind!" Pritkin told me. And then he gauged the distance and made a flying leap across the narrow straight that separated us, landing on a jutting piece of my rock. It was tiny and mostly underwater, and I would have been impressed if I hadn't been so damned freaked-out.

"How do we get out of here?" I yelled, because the roar around us was still deafening, even this close.

"I was hoping you'd have an idea!"

I stared at him. "You don't have a *plan*?"

"Plans are overrated!" said the man who never made a move without one. He looked up. "And I wouldn't worry about the *unintelligible*. They can't hit the side of a barn—"

"The what?"

"A small type of forest-dwelling troll! The spell doesn't translate proper names, Ohshit!"

I closed my eyes and leaned my forehead against the rock's remaining bit of dome as half a river tore past on either side. I was not here; I was not hearing this; I was not, I was *not*. "Forest-dwelling *trolls*?"

I opened my eyes to see Pritkin looking slightly apologetic. "Earlier, we came through a . . . a type of doorway. And now we're in, well, perhaps you've heard stories—"

"We're in *faerie*!" I yelled, flailing my arms and almost falling off my rock. "I know that! What I don't know is how we get out!"

"You know that?" Pritkin blinked, although that might have been from all the spray flying around. "I suppose I should have realized. You're too soft for a peasant girl!"

I glared at him.

"I meant that in a good way!" he assured me.

I closed my eyes again; I don't know why. It never helped. But I preferred it to what I saw when I opened them.

"—not so bad, once you get used to them. Just very territorial," Pritkin was bellowing, before another rock splashed down, missing his shoulder by inches.

It landed on the bottom of the stalagmite, splintering off some more shrapnel, but this time I didn't even flinch. I was too busy staring at something in the gloom back the way we'd come. Something that looked like a bunch of people carrying flashlights that were reflecting off the walls.

Only flashlights were usually golden, weren't they?

And these burned pure, cold silver.

Of course, I thought dully. Because a raging river, a bunch of rock-wielding savages, and a nonexistent power stream weren't enough. That would be easy mode. And somewhere along the line I'd transitioned over to expert. Which would have been fine if I had as many lives as a video game character.

But I had only one.

Which I was about to lose.

"—then again," Pritkin shouted, because he was *still talking*, "there's a slight chance they may not have had time to absorb my particular brand of charm on my last visit—"

"You don't have any charm," I snarled, and shoved him off the rock.

Chapter Forty-two

I jumped in after him, just as two more spears flashed toward us, almost invisible in the cascade of light from above.

And when I came up, spluttering, a few moments later, it was only to have to duck back down to avoid another volley that tore by my head. I heard it hit, the massive crack deafening even underwater, and felt the tremors that shook the cave like an earthquake. And that must have knocked some more rocks loose, because, suddenly, they were raining down everywhere.

"Get down!" Pritkin yelled. "Get down! Get—"

"You get down!" I yelled back, because a spear had just shattered a huge stalagmite, with a bang like a mountaintop had been sheared off. Which wasn't far from the case, with what looked like half the ceiling cracking and shifting and then spearing down—straight at him. "Pritkin!" I screamed, before remembering that he didn't know that name.

And then the outer edge of the wave hit, and I was going under, too.

But that actually turned out to be a good thing, considering the rocks and shards and what looked like whole trees pelting down from above. A rock slammed into the water a moment later, right beside me, big enough to have ripped my arm off. Except that the water broke some of the impact, so it just *felt* like it was being ripped off. And then the current caught me before I had a chance to wonder how I was supposed to swim with only one arm.

And forced me to start worrying about how not to drown with one instead.

For the next few minutes, my head stayed mostly underwater. But I was almost grateful for that, since every time I came up, I regretted it.

The first time I surfaced, I glimpsed Pritkin up ahead and swimming hard, which was a huge relief. And being hotly pursued by a bunch of silver fey, which was not. Especially since they weren't having to battle the water like we were.

In fact, they weren't getting wet at all. I wasn't sure there was a word for what they *were* doing, but it might have been called rock climbing if it was done at a sprint and sideways. The best I could figure out in between waves slapping me in the face, they were leaping from tiny outcropping to minute shelf to half-inch-wide protrusion on the walls, all wet, all slippery, all at full speed ahead, and all while throwing those damned energy spears at us.

Suddenly, Pritkin's little jump wasn't looking so impressive anymore.

Of course, neither was the fey's aim, which was being affected by their mad chase, by the fact that they were trying to hit wildly bobbing targets in bad light, and by the small matter of them being targeted themselves.

Because they had been. By the hairy nuggets. Who I was starting to feel a whole lot warmer toward, suddenly.

And the small fey seemed to have a big problem with their latest guests. More than they did with us. Like, way more. We'd been yelled at and threatened and had some rocks lobbed in our general direction, but that was nothing compared to the reaction caused by the silver fey's appearance. I didn't know what the little guys were saying, because I guess the translation spell didn't do profanity, either. But they were yelling down something that sounded truly vicious accompanied by an absolute avalanche of rocks.

And it looked like Pritkin had been wrong.

They could aim, after all.

Either that, or they got lucky, because one of the fey suddenly took a bath, courtesy of a hundred-pound boulder crushing his skull.

A red plume stained the water before the current swirled it away, and I thought for a moment that one of his companions was going to jump in after him. But instead he grabbed a low-hanging vine, using it to swing to an upper one. And a second after that, three small fey were jerked through a hole in the ceiling and thrown down onto the rocks below.

I didn't hear them land, for which I was grateful.

I also didn't see them, for which I was less grateful, because it had to do with the cave floor suddenly giving way onto a waterfall that had me screaming down into darkness.

The second time I came up for air, I saw that, waterfall or not, we hadn't lost our pursuers. Specifically, Pritkin hadn't, because the silver fey seemed to be a lot more interested in him than in me. And a dozen fey warriors on one not-yet-a-war-mage weren't good odds.

I jerked Rosier's bag off my back and started trying to dig through it.

But if it had been hard to see before, it was all but impossible now. The waterfall had dumped us into what I guessed was an underground river, but I couldn't be sure because there were no convenient skylights anymore. Just a vast, dark, echoing space, with the only light a rapidly dimming haze from behind and a few patches of phosphorescent lichen in the water. And the fey, glowing like beacons in the darkness up ahead. Or like deadly silver flashes as they leapt from rock to rock to rock, trying to catch up with Pritkin's darker form.

They were doing a good job. They were doing a damn good job, since there were also patches of sandy bank that flashed by, here and there, making their weird parkour act that much easier. They were gaining, while I was facing the fact that Rosier had brought a lot of pills and potions, probably to help knock out his son, but damned little that looked like a weapon.

Other than the gun, which I couldn't use here. And even if I could, there were more fey than bullets! And that was assuming that the damned thing still worked after being drowned and if I could get close enough to fire and if they didn't catch Pritkin in the meantime—

And they didn't.

But only because he suddenly sped up, I didn't know how.

And disappeared; I didn't know why.

Until I was grabbed and yanked ahead by something that was probably a current but felt more like a maelstrom. And I realized: that thing I'd thought was a waterfall? Was the bunny slope.

And we'd just hit the Olympic run.

The third time I came up, I could see fine, thanks to the glowing silver light spilling out from a single fey. He was only a few yards away, but he didn't see me, being too busy battling a small, hairy creature that I vaguely recognized as the guard I'd seen by the portal. He'd found a boat somewhere, maybe pulled up onto one of the banks, I didn't know. But he had, and had been using it to rescue his buddies who had been thrown down by the fey.

Only rescue was a debatable point, since one passenger was slumped in the bow, as lifeless as a corpse, and another was about to be.

And this one wasn't fey.

The silver warrior landed a savage blow on a second little troll that caused him to fall back, almost into the water. And that caused his appearance to change and blur and—

Pritkin, I thought, realizing what had happened at the same time that his opponent did.

The fey lunged after his formerly disguised enemy, in order to finish the job, and probably would have succeeded because Pritkin looked dazed from the blow. But the first troll took that moment to counterattack, tripping up the fey. And a second later, he found himself fighting a desperate battle against a much larger, faster, stronger foe on a barely-bigger-than-a-rowboat craft that started rocking madly back and forth as I tried to grab the side.

I managed, somehow, but didn't even try to pull myself up since I didn't have the strength. Instead I pulled the only option I had and tried to aim it, while the little guard went into berserker mode, stabbing around with his spear so fast that it was almost invisible. And the silver fey started bobbing and ducking and weaving worthy of Muhammad Ali, and my hands were shaking from the cold of the water, and I was aiming the gun with my left arm because of course it was my right that had been injured, and the damned fey was shining so brightly in the darkness that he was almost blinding.

But not enough that I couldn't see it when the troll guard was knocked aside, brutally hard. And when the fey lunged at Pritkin, who had ended up over by me, shaking his head to try to clear it. But it was too little, too late, with no more time and no more help and a silver blur shooting right at us.

And then shooting right back the other way, because it looked like a .44 Magnum worked just as well on the fey as on everything else.

And that included my shoulder.

The fey warrior staggered back, his face blooming red, and fell off the front of the boat. And my arm seized up from the recoil, dropping me off the back. Only I wasn't sure it had seized up as much as broken.

Because now I couldn't use it at all.

My head went under, the current being hard enough to fight even with two arms, and this time, it stayed that way. I got turned around, which is easy when everything is dark. And when your shoulder is a pulse of agony and doesn't work. And when your waterlogged dress wraps around you, hampering what little movement you had left.

And when you realize that you can't hear anything but a deafening echo.

Suddenly, all I saw around me was darkness.

Suddenly, all I felt was cold.

I stopped thrashing, hoping to see the direction the bubbles were heading when I let out a breath, only to find that I didn't have one. And muscles, it turns out, don't work so well with no oxygen. I stared around at nothing, just more dark, dark water, and panic stopped my throat.

I'd fought my way back up three times—third time's a charm; wasn't that the saying? Only I never wondered before, what about the fourth? Why didn't they ever say what happened if you needed a fourth?

I was beginning to think I knew.

And then someone grabbed me.

I was jerked up with an arm around my waist, hard enough to almost cut me in two. Things went hazy for a minute as I tried to figure out which way was up. And failed, because I broke the surface in a totally different direction from the one I'd been heading, with my head reeling and my stomach roiling and somebody yelling something I couldn't understand, because right then, I couldn't understand anything.

But I felt it when I was hauled over the side of the boat. And fell into the slimy bottom, just a cocoon of wet wool and clammy skin and silent panic. Because I still couldn't *breathe*.

I lay there, gasping uselessly, like a beached fish. Trying to suck oxygen into lungs already full of something else. There was more yelling, and somebody turned me over, and somebody else started beating me on the back with arms like Schwarzenegger, but I was too busy throwing up a bucketful of icy water to care.

It felt like I expelled an ocean. It felt like I vomited the world. But at the end, I was breathing—sort of—in ragged, thankful gasps that were so clear, so cold, and so sweet that this, just this, just air had me tearing up from the sheer wonderfulness of it.

And then a light speared my eyes, right in my face, which had me gasping and flailing and knocking it back—

Before I realized that it was an oil lamp and not a fey.

"Don't speak." Pritkin's arm went around me from behind, his voice barely audible even with his lips almost touching my ear. "They may be able to tell where it's coming from."

How? I thought, staring at a hundred little lights, like a cave filled with fireflies.

Or, more accurately, like a cave filled with boats, hundreds of them. All bobbing about the cavernous space, stuffed with two tiny fey, a war-mage-to-be and a drowned rat hanging onto the side, gaping. At what, I finally realized, was a flotilla of mirror images of our motley crew, which now filled the river almost shore to shore.

And yeah, I thought dizzily, Pritkin might not be able to fight them, but he could still confuse the hell out of them, couldn't he? And it was *working*.

The fey who had disappeared down the river must have doubled back, probably at the sound of the gunshot. Because there was a bunch of them here now. Including the one who leapt from a sandbar to an outcropping of rock just ahead. He looked like something straight out of myth, with shiny black armor that ran with the light of all those little lamps, which also tinted his long, silver hair and gleamed in his eyes as he scanned the cave. And kept on scanning.

Because he couldn't find us.

I started grinning and raised my hand to push a sodden mass of hair out of my eyes. And then froze when all the Cassies on all the other boats did the same. It was so bizarre, like looking into a fun-house mirror, only far more realistic. The silver fey's eyes flickered here and there, watching a few hundred repetitions of the same small movement. But his eyes didn't stay on us any longer than on any of the others.

We floated gently past, not moving, barely breathing. And our silent host went along like a ghostly flotilla, bobbing at a good pace now, making time. We're getting away, I thought, hand clenching on Pritkin's thigh. We're getting away!

And then the fey started singing.

I guess they were actually talking to each other, but the voices were lilting, sonorous, almost musical. They carried in the clear, cool air of the cave and echoed off the walls, giving an impromptu concert that I couldn't understand but didn't like. "What are they saying?" I whispered to Pritkin, but this time, it didn't look like he knew, either.

And it didn't look like the translation spell worked with this particular group of fey, because all I heard was chanting. Although there might be a reason for that, I thought, as a massive energy spear flashed into the hand of the fey on the outcropping. And then shot upward, toward the ceiling, where it burst into a thousand twinkling lights like falling stars.

Beautiful, I thought again, mesmerized in spite of myself.

Until I realized: these stars burned.

Glowing embers started to fall like rain, hissing off the water and sparking off the rocks. But they didn't hurt the crowd in the boats—no, they didn't hurt them at all. Because they were just illusions.

But we weren't.

And now the falling embers were falling down on us.

The guard started making a terrifying screech and stomping on a bunch of rags that had just flared up. And that turned out to be the body of a third troll, who I guess wasn't dead after all. Because he began moaning and thrashing and then hitting back and trying to put himself out.

Which actually worked great, since there was plenty of water in the bottom of the boat to help.

Because one of the embers had just burned a hole in it.

Pritkin plunged a hand down into the spouting geyser, and it suddenly wasn't spouting anymore. Or even flowing. More like pausing. And squelching. And then shifting and spreading out in the bottom of the boat in an odd, gelatinous way, as if the water had suddenly grown a skin.

Which would have been great if another current hadn't grabbed us a second later, sending us spinning and plunging and sinking and tumbling into a tunnel and down what would probably have been a terrifying stretch of underground rapids if I'd been able to see them.

I mostly couldn't.

But I didn't need to.

Because I could hear: the massive roar and crash and hiss of what had to be thousands of gallons of water, all plunging down, down, down into darkness somewhere in the distance up ahead.

"Oh, come on!" I screamed, not that it mattered, and not that anyone could hear me, including myself. Not over all the water in the world falling off the side of it. We're dead, I thought blankly as the boat kicked into high gear. We're so very, very dead.

And that appeared to be the consensus, including among the trolls. The little guys stopped yelling and started rowing, but even their massive arms didn't do much to slow us down. We were too close. And it wouldn't have helped anyway, since the fey were still in pursuit, like splashes of silver on the cave walls behind us as they struggled to catch up to the raging current.

So it was death by waterfall or death by drowning or death by fey, and the fact that the operative word in all those was "death" had me grabbing Pritkin by the leg, which was the only thing I could reach.

"Yellow," I gasped.

"What?"

"Yellow! Yellow!" I screamed, and really hope he heard me, because the translation spell didn't change the way mouths worked. So lip-reading was out. But when I tried to drag my now-fifty pounds of sodden wool over the trolls to get at Rosier's bag, and the little yellow patches inside, it seemed he got the idea. And grabbed it and started rooting around in it.

And holding up a lot of useless junk that had probably cost Rosier a pretty penny but was about to be flotsam, along with what remained of our bodies if we didn't—

"There!" I screeched, spotting Rosier's little yellow levitation patches, still in their plastic containers. "There! There! There!"

Pritkin mouthed something I couldn't hear, and I suddenly realized that he didn't understand how to get them open. And I had one hand and no nails and damn child-resistant packaging; I always knew they were going to kill me someday. And it looked like that was today.

Because when I glanced up, there was nothing in front of us but wind and mist and a whole lot of air.

Chapter Forty-three

We hit the turbulence at the edge of the cliff a second later, where thousands of gallons of water were all trying to be first over the rocks, and throwing up huge amounts of spray in the process. It was like being shot at by water cannons from multiple directions, and for a long moment I couldn't even tell if we were right side up anymore, couldn't see, couldn't hear, could barely breathe, because of stark terror and because Pritkin was about to crush me in two. But it didn't matter, not when I was out of ideas and we were plunging to our doom and—

And—

And—

And it was taking a damned long time for us to go over already.

I'd closed my eyes, but now I opened them to see a world gone white, with thunderous crashes and equally massive amounts of water being tossed around, like giants at play. And it just kept coming, soaking me and slapping me and threatening to drown me while I was still in the air, or at least on a boat stuck dangling over a hell of a lot of it. But not falling, not crashing—not yet, because the trolls, those wonderful, awesome, incredible little trolls, had wedged the boat's oars in between two of the rocks that dotted the lip of the fall.

And trapped us behind them.

For the moment, anyway, but the oars were as old as the boat and I didn't need to see them clearly to know they were straining. My heart skipped a beat, then another, and then felt like it stopped altogether as I realized that I had a reprieve I hadn't earned and a hand clutching a lifeline if only I could get it open. And I *got it open*, biting and tearing and then staring around for somewhere to put the little patch, because these things activated *fast*.

But everything was wet—everything, even the boards passing for seats. Which were getting hit with just as much spray as I was and which had already been damp from soaked clothing and soggy derrieres to the point that there wasn't a single dry spot left, not even underneath. So I slapped it down on a wet one, shielding it with my body and praying.

Only to have it float up like lunch on the space station, and how freaking stupid was *that*?

"They couldn't make these waterproof?" I screamed at Pritkin, who didn't understand me.

But he was looking at the little thing with renewed interest. And then at the nearest troll. And then back at me. And then—

"Oh, holy *shit*!"

But there was no time for debate; there was no time for anything. Except plunging over the side a moment later, when an oar broke and Pritkin grabbed me and I grabbed the boat and the bigger troll grabbed his buddy. Who wasn't grabbing anything because we'd just stuffed him under the seats.

And yes, I was going to hell, because we'd shoved the patch down his throat first. But I'd been to hell, and it beat the shit out of faerie. So that wasn't the problem. The problem was that the patch that was supposed to work, that had *just been working, damn it,* wasn't working now.

Because the only thing that caught us as we spun into the void was gravity.

For a moment, everything stopped. I didn't see my life flash before my eyes because I couldn't see much of anything. Just the spray crashing into the rocks behind us, bursting into the air above us, and then leaping out into the vast void ahead. And then we were following the droplets, arcing and dipping and falling and screaming—

And hitting something and spinning and tumbling and catching.

And then juddering and plunging and *shooting* ahead, like on a flume ride at the world's most sadistic fair. Somebody was still screaming, but I didn't think it was me this time since I couldn't even seem to breathe. Or to think, except to wonder where all the water had suddenly gone.

Because it had, like the world's biggest faucet had just been turned off.

Only no, I realized, shoving a mass of soaked hair out of my face and gasping for air.

Not turned off.

Just out of reach. Because the enormous fall of water—and God, it was freaking *enormous*—was still boiling away near enough to keep on soaking us, but too far away to keep on killing us, because we were watching it from a vantage point out in the void. A vantage point made up of a tiny island of smoking wood and screaming trolls, because the patch, the goddamned wonderful patch, had worked!

The boat turned lazily, wafted about by the air gusts coming off all that spray, and I realized that I was about to snap Pritkin in two, girly arms or not. But he didn't seem to mind; he didn't even seem to *notice*, maybe because he was busy noticing something else. And then so was I. And oh. My. God.

I twisted around to get a better view. And then just sat there, wide-eyed and shaking. And staring at something that would have cost half a blockbuster's budget to fake.

But it wasn't fake; it was just *fantastic*.

The waterfall made up one side of a cavern that the term "humongous" might have been coined for. The other sides were dark rock spotted with patches of crystals and more waterfalls, small only in comparison to the mammoth we'd just fallen over. Some tumbled across rocky ledges fifteen, maybe twenty stories above our heads, so tall that they evaporated into the mist that was spawning rainbows in the air all around us before they could hope to hit down. Others started far below, spilling their water into something I couldn't see, because there was some light leaking in from far above, but the bottom of the cavern disappeared into darkness.

It was beautiful.

It was *beautiful.*

And breathtaking, not that I had any left. But I'd get it back. I'd get it back because we were alive—alive, alive, alive, and everything was beautiful!

I looked up at Pritkin, who was standing just behind me in the prow of the ship. He looked pretty beat up, but a second ago, it hadn't mattered. He'd been staring around with the same awe I felt, like a man who'd just stared death in the face and seen it shrug. But now the light had drained out of his face, and he wasn't even looking at the cave anymore.

He was looking at the waterfall.

And the gleaming warrior that had just appeared on top of it.

The fey was standing on one of the largest boulders, spray shooting up all around him, his long, too-white hair whipping wildly around his face. I didn't know how he got there, because the rock was almost smack in the middle of the waterfall, not near any convenient stepping-stones. But I knew what he was doing.

Because of course he was. Of *course* he was. Anybody else would have assumed that the fall would have killed us, but not the fey. No, they'd had to see what happened for themselves.

And they were.

Because our little flotilla was nowhere in sight.

I craned my head around, but there wasn't a single other beat-up boat anywhere. Damage, I suddenly remembered. The illusions Pritkin used didn't hold up to damage. That must have been what the firestorm was for.

And I guess falling over Niagara hadn't helped.

"I'm sorry," Pritkin said, his hand clenching on my shoulder.

"Don't apologize," I said, my voice shaking. "Don't you dare."

"I involved you in this. They were chasing me, not you. I didn't think, and I didn't protect—"

"I got myself into this. And I don't need protection."

I looked back up at the fey. They never showed that nonexpression in the fairy-tale books, even the ones I'd had as a child, which had contained the grimmer version of the Brothers Grimm. They always had the—suitably ugly—

villains snarling or glowering or slavering, filled with hate
or malice. When the truth was, most of the ones I'd met
were like the guy who mugged you in an alley and shot you
even though it was too dark to see his face.

Because why take the chance?

As if in answer, another spear flashed into the fey's hand,
but this time, for the first time, it didn't make me afraid.

It made me furious.

"You *want* this?" I grabbed the staff out from under the
smaller fey's butt, where it had somehow ended up. And
then stood back up and screamed across the void, *"You
want this?"*

"You can't mean to give it back to them," Pritkin said,
his voice tight. "They'll kill us anyway—"

"Like hell I'm giving it back!" I yelled, not because I
expected pointy ears to hear me. I could barely hear myself
over the crash and roar of the falls. But right then I couldn't
seem to do anything else. "I'm thinking maybe I'll just
break it. Is that what we want to have *happen* here?"

And I guessed not. Because the fey suddenly found
something else to do with that energy spear, which melted
back into his skin. His eyes met mine across the void, completely expressionless. But then they slowly slid over to the
staff.

And, oh yeah. He wanted it all right. He wanted it bad.

So picking us off wasn't going to work with one of us
holding it. Not unless he was willing to lose it, too. And it
didn't look like he was.

"It's mine now," I told him. "Consider it compensation
for what you assholes have put me through!"

"Ohshit," Pritkin said urgently, like maybe that wasn't
how you were supposed to talk to mighty fey warriors.

And no, I thought, probably not. And then I thought,
fuck the fey. What were they going to do? Kill me twice?

I suddenly felt like laughing. "Everybody wants to kill
me!" I told them. "Every-damned-body I know, for *years*.
But, oh, look. Still here! *Guess I must be doing something
right, huh?"*

Pritkin was starting to look concerned, like he thought
maybe I'd been hitting the bottle earlier. And it sort of felt
like that, too. Giddy and strange and terrified and brazen, all
at the same time. A whole craploch of fey warriors had been

chasing a powerless Pythia and a not-ready-for-prime-time mage for what, most of an hour? So why weren't we dead?

"You *suck*!" I yelled, suddenly laughing, because why the hell not? "I know vampires who would have had me dead and drained and my scalp on their goddamned *belt* by now, and what are you doing? *Nothing*. You're doing nothing! Because you know, don't you?" I held the precious stick over the edge of the boat, just to watch the fey flinch. "If I let go, think you'll ever find it again?"

"Oh shit." Pritkin sounded strangled. "That is *priceless*. And unique. And completely, completely irreplaceable."

"Guess that means he just lost, then, doesn't it?" I said, watching the fey. Whose eyes had never left the stick but whose fist suddenly clenched.

Aaaaaand okay, maybe those ears worked better than I'd thought. Because a whole line of fey suddenly appeared on the rocks, like they'd condensed out of the mist. And then broke, with no command I could hear, half of them staying put so we couldn't go back the way we'd come, and half moving like lightning for the rocky cliff beside the fall.

Because there was one, black as obsidian and worn mostly smooth from years of rivulets and constant fine spray. It looked like a death trap to me, but the parkour kings seemed to be navigating it like the rock wall at the gym.

The kiddie wall.

And it looked like we had ourselves a race, boys and girls. Which would have been fine, since it beat like hell being barbecued in place. There was just one small problem.

The fey on the waterfall started lobbing spears at us.

Okay, two small problems.

And then we fell.

Pritkin grabbed me, I grabbed the nearest troll, and he grabbed his buddy, who was still caught underneath the slats that formed the seats. Caught, but not liking it, not liking it one bit, and looking like he wanted to be anywhere else but here, which, yeah. And he was thrashing and we were falling and then the fey's spear flashed by overhead, almost setting my hair on fire.

Well, at least I know how to get down now, I thought insanely, right before we caught again.

The trapped troll froze, halfway through a punch, and

looked around, his eyes huge. And then got very, very still, as if he understood that he'd done something to screw with the spell. But he obviously didn't know what. And that meant he couldn't control it, which was a problem since the fey clearly thought we could.

That explained the barrage, which was falling on the far side of us like a glowing cage, to keep us from escaping and to drive us closer to the cliff. They weren't trying to hit us; they couldn't afford to hit us. But maybe that wasn't entirely apparent to someone without a great vantage point.

Like a guy stuffed under a seat, for instance.

Another volley came streaming overhead, bright as fireworks in the gloom, the little troll screamed, and we fell. And this time, I didn't think we were going to catch at all. We plummeted six, maybe seven stories, and then caught lopsided and slung around and almost turned over.

Because our little floatation device was trying to make a run for it.

It was kind of hard to blame him. He'd been ripped down from the roof, beaten and battered and almost drowned, and then forced to power our clumsy escape attempt. And now his friend had just started wailing on him.

"Stop hitting him!" Pritkin was yelling, trying to prize one little guard off the other. *"Stop hitting—"*

"If I stop hitting him, he leave," the other guard panted. "He say, he not need us. He say, we can all go to earth for all he cares!"

"That's what we're trying to do!"

Pritkin grabbed the bigger guy's arm, but not before he'd gotten a few good thumps in, and the little guard's outrage at the attack made him forget about everything else for a moment. He swung at his friend, red faced and furious, and our ride abruptly evened out, became smooth even. I stared around, but I hadn't imagined it. The little troll couldn't freak out and fight at the same time, and if his nervous system wasn't overloading, we weren't falling.

Which was a problem, because the guys up top had stopped firing.

Maybe they'd figured that out, too. Or maybe they were just afraid of hitting their buddies. Because they were gaining.

I sat there in awe, watching them practically run down

the damned cliff face. They were moving as fast or faster than someone could rappel, but they didn't have stakes or rope or any equipment at all. And they didn't need it. Because the rock itself was helping them.

I hadn't been able to see what they were doing along the riverbank; it had been too dark. But it was lighter in here and I was closer and there was no doubt about it. Fissures and cracks were opening up wherever they needed them, little lips were bulging out from solid rock under their feet or sinking in for handholds. One stumbled and a whole ledge shot out of nowhere to catch him.

It was as if the whole damned rock face was putty that re-formed itself to whatever configuration they needed, as malleable for them as the water had been for Pritkin. And as bad for us. I grabbed Pritkin's arm. "Do you know any fey insults?"

"What?"

"Insults. Abuse." I shook him one-handed. *"Can you swear in their language?"*

"Why?"

"We need them to *fire*." I looked pointedly at the trolls, who were back at it again.

And young or not, Pritkin had never been exactly slow. He glanced at me for a second, then at them. And then started yelling something at the fey above us that the spell wouldn't even try to translate.

But I guess it must have been pretty bad, because the two trolls stopped midpunch to gape at him. And then at the barrage of lightning bolts being hurled down at us again like we'd managed to piss off Zeus. Give me time, I thought hysterically, as we dropped again.

And caught.

And dropped.

And caught.

Our little pontoon was starting to look pretty beat-up, but it was nothing to how bad things were going to be if we didn't hurry up. Because we'd never fully straightened out from that initial tumble, and had been drifting closer to the rocks every time we stopped. And when I turned around again, the cliff face was—

Right in front of me.

Like the guy with half a face perched on top of it.

Chapter Forty-four

I stared at the fey from the river in horror, not understanding why he wasn't dead. I *had* shot him. Two gaping wounds, one under his chin and one in his forehead, were a testament to that. Along with the blood and gore that matted his hair and splattered his chest. And the powder burns that covered half his face, starkly black and ugly against the otherworldly pallor of his skin.

He looked like an accident victim; he looked like a corpse. He should have *been* a corpse, because the angle of one of those bullets had to have taken it straight through his brain. A senior-level master might have been able to come back from something like that, but nothing else I knew.

Nothing else until now.

Because instead of keeling over, he was leaping maybe twelve feet straight out, from a tiny outcropping onto the end of our boat. And sending us hurtling backward from the impact, almost into the hail of spears from above. And then slamming right back into the cliff again, like a pendulum on a clock, when Pritkin and the guard threw themselves forward in an attempt to knock him off.

It didn't knock him off.

It did crush him against the rock, though, but not hard enough. Not with the damned stuff churning and moving behind him like wet clay. And then re-forming around his body, to the point that he left a fey-shaped hole behind when he lunged at us again, batted aside the broken oar Pritkin had grabbed, and jumped into our failing ride.

And promptly helped it fail some more.

Pritkin and the silver fey landed in the bottom of the boat, kicking and fighting, and we went into freefall. The little guard started wailing on his buddy again, but this time, it didn't help. And I grabbed the side of the burning boat and braced for impact.

Which didn't come.

Not because we caught again. But because Pritkin had grabbed the stick—or the staff or whatever the hell—and tried to get it against the fey's neck. I think the idea was to throttle him between it and the bottom of the boat. But the creature was too strong, throwing him off and back into me, and then grabbing his end of the staff like he intended to punch it through both our chests.

But he didn't.

Because it punched through his instead.

I sat there, seeing but not understanding. Unlike with a gun, there had been no recoil, and no sound that I could hear over everything else. And the whole fight had taken all of a few seconds. It literally took longer to tell about it than it did to watch, and humans aren't built to comprehend things that fast; we're barely built to *see* them.

Which is why I was almost as surprised as the fey when he looked down at the gory cavity that had been his chest.

And saw nothing there.

He toppled off the craft, spinning out into the void on a rush of wind, but not disappearing, not dropping. Or rather he was, but we were, too. And just as fast.

Until Pritkin slammed the staff through the watery patch he'd placed over the hole in the bottom, which was still sort of holding. And did something with the staff—I didn't see what. But I felt it.

Because, suddenly, instead of being feet away from crashing into the base of the falls, we were airborne again.

Very airborne.

Like, whoa, airborne, I thought, completely incoherent while clinging to Pritkin and staring at the line of fey on top of the waterfall, who were staring at us as we rocketed past.

Going the other way.

Which would have been good, which would have been great, if there wasn't a ceiling, like, right there and ceiling, ceiling, *ceiling*!

And I guess Pritkin saw it, too, although I hadn't had time to actually form the words. Because he pulled the staff to the right and we banked—a little too abruptly. Make that a lot too abruptly, slinging us on circuit around the cave while being almost completely sideways. And would have sent us tumbling to our doom except that all of us were already bracing under the seats with our feet and holding on to the sides with our hands and generally had our butts clenched on the seats in cold, hard terror.

Which only increased when we sped by the rock wall and another fey *jumped on.*

I got a heel to his forehead, but I wasn't wearing shoes and it didn't help. Unlike the air screaming through a hole in the hull, which was hitting him in the face hard enough to blow his lips back from his teeth. And the broken edge of the paddle the guard was now wielding, which seemed to be doing some damage until the fey ripped it away from him and tried to impale him on it.

That left the fey hanging on to the boat one-handed, with his body flapping out behind him almost horizontally, which would have spelled doom to anyone who was remotely normal. He just proceeded to stab at the guard again, who was saved only by boiled leather armor and a sidestep. Which turned almost balletic when he rotated in a flash of motion—

And brought a thick-soled boot down on the fey's remaining hand.

"Yes! Yes! Yes!" I screamed, although no one could hear me. I couldn't even hear myself, with the wind ripping the words away before they were out of my mouth. Like the fey, who suddenly went flying.

Right into the sheer cliff face that was jutting out just ahead of us. We missed it thanks to a quick swerve by Pritkin, but that cost us half a second. Which was all the fey needed to twist, get his feet under him, and catapult *back onto the boat* as we rocketed past.

And abruptly the little guard flew backward off his feet. The fey had almost missed the boat—literally—falling against the outer hull instead of inside, and had snagged the guard's neck to save himself and to try to strangle him at the same time. But the guard had other ideas, snagging the underside of a seat with his boot and using one of his oversized fists to wail on the side of the fey's head.

But it wasn't working, and we were out of weapons—even the broken paddles had fallen out by now. And the fey had the guard in a headlock, so even if I figured out some way to send him flying, the guard was likely to go, too. But he was going to anyway if I didn't do something, so I grabbed the little guy's belt and *pulled*.

I wasn't crazy enough to think I could overpower a fey warrior, but I hoped to tip the balance enough for the guard to do the rest. But I had only the one arm that worked, and even with both, the fey was stronger than me. A lot stronger. Hell, it felt like one of his *fingers* might have outdone me, because it didn't seem like I was making a damned bit of difference at all.

And Pritkin was fighting to tame the power of a hurricane and couldn't help, and the seat the little troll was using to brace with was coming loose, the bolts holding mostly through rust at this point, and a pair of tiny black eyes were meeting mine—

Not to plead for help, because I didn't have any more to give. But to tell me it was all right, that I'd done my best, that it was okay, when it *wasn't* okay. When nothing about it was okay! The black eyes swam before my gaze, turning older and dimmer and bluer—to those of another man I hadn't been able to save. And like the other, this one was slipping through my fingers, and I couldn't hold, couldn't hold—

And then I was using both hands and screaming because my shoulder felt like it was being ripped off my body, but it still wasn't enough, and there was no one to help—

Except for the fey themselves.

Because we'd just completed a full circuit of the vast cavern, coming back to where we'd begun in front of the falls. And the spears the fey had been lobbing, which had been missing us because of the distance, were suddenly at point-blank range. And I guess the leader had decided that if he couldn't have the staff, nobody could. Because a volley of fire tore through the air, straight for us.

And this time, it connected. One glowing spear shattered the prow, exploding the high carved finial into dust and sending us slinging around like a top. Another ripped through the bottom of the boat at almost the same time, right where I'd just been sitting before being thrown into the floor. And a third—

And a fourth and a fifth slammed into their own man, who was sprawled across half the hull, still stubbornly clinging to his prize.

The little troll tore away, falling over by me, and the energy blasts lit up all that black armor like lightning bolts. They didn't penetrate; they didn't have to. The shiny black became red became yellow became white, and the fey screamed, screamed while he was cooked like a lobster in its shell, screamed as he began to smoke, screamed until his face turned black, and yet he was still clinging to the ship because he'd *melted there*—

And then the troll's boot smashed through charred wood and fey, too, and he fell, spinning off into the void.

And I was screaming, too, because they were about to throw again and we couldn't outrun them, not in time, and there was nothing to serve as a shield and no way to keep the bolts from landing—

Except the obvious, which I'd somehow managed not to think of at all. But I didn't feel too bad because it looked like the fey hadn't, either. They threw, launching an enormous volley like a line of fire stretching across the void. And Pritkin jerked up the staff, sending us tumbling into the floor as the boat went completely sideways and the wave of wind went straight at the fey.

Whose lightning reflexes weren't quite lightning enough when their own volley boomeranged right back at them.

It was like the shooting gallery at the fair, I thought blankly. I'd been caught halfway through a scream with my mouth hanging open as I watched through the hole-riddled hull as half the lineup suddenly disappeared, while a few others dove for cover. And the rest—

Didn't do anything.

They didn't get blown backward by the gale, as I would have expected if I could have expected anything right then. They also didn't fall forward. I suddenly realized that they were trapped in between the huge amount of air the river was churning up on the one side, as all that water came barreling down from above, and the rush of power that Pritkin was sending on the other. Like bugs between two slides of glass, they just hung there for a long moment, along with the water that was getting blown back into the mouth of the falls.

A lot of water. Almost all of the water, in fact, which was being vaporized and sent back, in long white flowing streamers, like the fey's hair. More and more of it, until I couldn't see anything anymore, not the fey, not the rocks, not the mouth of the falls. Nothing except a wall of white where a moment ago there had been a tremendous torrent.

And suddenly was again.

Pritkin yelled something that I guess was *hold on*, although there was no way in hell to tell. But a second later the whole ragtag little craft swung around, with those of us who remained scurrying to find new handholds in punctures in the hull and on what remained of the seats and on the bare bones of the craft, which is all we were about to have left since more boards were falling away every moment.

And then we dove.

I had a split second to see the boiling wall of white collapse, to see a bunch of half-drowned fey collapse with it, to see the whole screwed-up mess plunge over the falls in a tsunami's worth of water. And then we were racing the deluge for the ground, the mighty blast of air coming from the end of the crappy little stick sending us shooting back down just as fast as we'd come up. And this time, there were no energy bolts to have to worry about, even from the guys on the cliff, who were far too busy avoiding the water smashing and crashing and sending sideways waves flooding over them to care about us.

And anyway, you can't hit a speeding bullet. And that's what it felt like we were, with the wind almost blinding us and a hurricane howling in our ears and the river rushing up to meet us. And then the spray churning at the bottom of the falls slicing up on either side of us as we curved and skimmed and *shot* ahead, just before the whole thing was obscured by the vast torrent from above.

I looked over and saw Pritkin backlit by the sparkling, crashing deluge, laughing like a madman, while the hairy little guy who'd ended up under my arm was waving his fists around and whooping, and the other guy stuck in the hold was staring around with eyes three times bigger than normal, which almost made them regular-sized—

And suddenly I started whooping, too, because *still alive, fuckers, still alive.*

And then the ceiling started to fall in.

Not just part of it—all of it.

The long stretch of underground river ahead started boiling and jumping and whipping up, with waves splashing twenty feet into the air to grab at us as we flew past. The giant waves were caused by equally giant boulders that were slamming down all around us. And massive cracks were running in the ceiling ahead, showing lines where even bigger sections were about to break away. Because the corridor, the huge, rock-cut corridor, wasn't just cracking, it was collapsing.

The fey were bringing a mountain down on our heads.

But not fast enough.

Because a second later, we were swerving hard at the far wall, and then into a crack all of five feet across and limestone slick and going straight down.

"Augghhhhh!" someone said, but it wasn't me that time. I couldn't say anything, thanks to the little guard who had just grabbed me around the neck.

"Aughhh, aughhh!" the guard screamed, as the floor rose up to meet us, because I'd been wrong, it wasn't straight down. It was a slalom course of turns and twists and dips, in between collapsed heaps of ceiling for us to run into and wide fissures for us to fall into and no way to avoid them except by throwing our body weight one way or the other.

Which might have worked better if we'd been touching the floor more than half the time.

"Bring us down! Bring us down!" the little guard was yelling as we scraped across the ceiling. But we didn't come down until he let go of my neck to smack the board over his friend's chest. Which was the last straw for our charmed, trapped fey, who punched him right in the jaw.

They started fighting, and we started dropping, and rising, and dropping, and rising, and slamming and ricocheting back and forth between floor and ceiling, and banking and almost flipping, and screaming our way down, down, down, until I was sure the damned thing would never end—

And then it did.

Because we burst out of the side of a cliff, on a waterfall that was no longer there. Just an opening onto sunlight and air and a river that could best be described as way the hell too far below. Especially after our little patch decided to take that moment to finally give up the ghost.

"Oh, *shiiiiiiit*!"

"Is that really your name?" Pritkin demanded as we crawled up onto the shore some time later.

I staggered onto a pebble-lined stretch of sand, heaving and sniffling and making strange little shock-y sounds that I'd probably be embarrassed about later if I survived long enough. I flopped down, rolled over onto my back, and watched the smoke rise from a completely destroyed stretch of mountainside. Trees, bushes, and streams had all been swallowed by a scar that had to be a mile long. Had to be.

I lay there, too exhausted to even gasp and too shaken to freak out. Even when the smaller troll started doing it for me, emitting a terrible, ululating cry at decibel levels not meant for human ears. Luckily, mine were too full of water to burst. And then he ran off, the sound of tiny running feet and an answering cry echoing back to us from somewhere nearby.

Pritkin dropped down beside me, breathing heavily. The remaining troll started cursing weakly. Another piece of mountainside collapsed, like a soufflé somebody had taken out of the oven at the wrong time, loud enough, even at a distance, to make me cringe.

"Ohshit?"

"It's more the story of my life," I said miserably.

And then I passed out.

Chapter Forty-five

Two hours later, I was sitting on top of a platform perched high in a tree, while a tiny Wookie barred the only exit. The platform was connected to a lot of other platforms on a lot of other trees by rope bridges, swinging vines, and weighted boards that went up and down and sometimes around via a complicated system I was too tired to figure out.

Especially since I wasn't likely to be using it.

The tiny Wookie regarded me steadily out of a wildly bearded face. Ewoks, I thought. The little ones had been called Ewoks. Only this version wasn't quite *that* hairy, and there was human intelligence in those dark eyes. And human-ish features under all that hair.

Well, except for the nose, which managed to make even Pritkin's look petite. And the large, gnarled hands. And the beard, which was black and bushy and big enough to have hidden anything, including more of the weapons he had draped around everywhere. And the teeth, which were more canine pointed than human blunt ...

On second thought, I didn't think Lucas would have cast these guys, after all.

I told myself to get a grip already. Only it didn't work so well since I didn't know where Pritkin was, and that went double for his father. And I didn't know where to find another, preferably nonflooded, portal to take us back to earth. And I couldn't have reached it even if I had known because there was an Ewok in front of the only bridge out of here.

Who was starting to look a little worried, maybe because I was now glaring at him.

I turned around and glared at the scene beneath me, instead.

It was pretty. The sun had set about an hour ago and the stars were out. But they were hard to see because of the thickness of the leafy canopy overhead, and because of all the light scattered around below. There were fires burning among the trees, cheery campfires and twinkling torches and a big bonfire-type thing just below us, where a bunch of tiny, hairy men were trying to wrestle something onto a huge spit.

They hadn't managed it yet, but other scents were starting to drift through the air, making my stomach growl and my mouth water. But there was nothing to do but sit and salivate. And scratch. Because what had once looked like an unfortunate Muppet had degenerated into a large, hairy wart after being soaked and dried.

But nobody else was wearing shorts, so I'd thought it best to keep it on.

"You know, they gave Leia a new dress," I told the guard, over my shoulder.

He didn't feel it necessary to reply, maybe because I didn't have any PowerBars to share.

God, I thought fervently, PowerBars. Or jerky. Or really anything, anything at all. They never showed this part in the movies, how adventures mean you're constantly filthy and beat-up and exhausted and *starving*. No, Leia had been pristine with perfect hair, and her dress—her nice, soft, flattering dress—had been well pressed and she hadn't looked like she was getting ready to start gnawing the boards off the damn platform!

Of course, Han and Luke had almost been roasted alive in that same scene, so I supposed it could be worse. And they were treating me pretty well if they planned an execution. I'd woken up to see some guy with a bone through his nose and feathers in his hair who looked like he should be shaking a chicken at me, but who instead had been dressing my shoulder with a pot of salve. It smelled like a bear had made love to a skunk, but it had numbed the pain nicely.

And now I had a jug of water and a pile of furs on the boards behind me, in case I wanted to sleep, I supposed.

But I didn't.

I wanted to *go*. I wanted to find Pritkin. I wanted to get him to Rosier. I wanted to get that damned curse off him and get us back where we belonged and *end this*. . . .

Only that wasn't happening, was it? Not with Chewbacca over there, watching my every move. I sat and chewed on my lip.

If I couldn't get to Rosier, then I had to bring him to me. Somehow. And I had to do it soon, in case the crazy fey time stream sped things up, and the cursed soul showed up, thanks to my colossal screw-up, and—

And get a *grip*, Cassie!

I could do this. It was just another shift. And, yes, I was in faerie and Rosier was on earth, and my power didn't work well here, if at all, but we were *right by a portal*. Before it got dark, I'd been able to see the river glistening through the trees. And the portal was in the river. And Rosier was just on the other side of the portal—at least he'd better be, because if he'd run off somewhere, I'd wring his demonic *neck*.

Right. So. A shift. Rosier from the other side of the portal to me, and then us to wherever Pritkin was. I didn't see him, but he couldn't have gone too far, and they weren't spitting him down below, so I assumed he was okay. They'd probably separated us so we couldn't collude or something, and shut up, shut up, shut *up*, just get his bastard of a father *here*.

I closed my eyes and reached for my power.

Not surprisingly, it didn't come. But it wasn't gone. The power went where I did now; whether I shifted in body or not, whether I shifted in time or not, it was like a great golden shadow, following, shimmering, beckoning . . . just . . . out of . . . reach—

Concentrate!

I took a deep breath, because I was short of it for some reason, and tried again. It felt almost exactly like trying to reach for something high on a shelf, when you're not quite tall enough. Reaching hard, like I was straining and stretching and my fingertips could touch it but not grab it, like it was *right there, right there, right there,* but I couldn't . . . quite . . . *Damn it!*

I stopped, panting and sweating and swearing under my breath, because I'd almost had it that time. Only for a second, and only like a fleeting touch, but I'd felt it, pure and beautiful and powerful. All the power I could ever need or hope to use like a shimmering sea spreading out all around me ...

I paused for a minute, because that was exactly what it was. Spread out, like a vast ocean on all sides, crashing and beating and battering at the barrier that separated us. Like it didn't like this arrangement any more than I did. But I still couldn't touch it, not directly, not here, any more than I could reach the bottom of the river when on top of Pritkin's elastic water trick.

In fact, that was really a better analogy, because a shelf doesn't move. But my power did, ebbing and flowing like water, sometimes closer, sometimes farther away, but always coming back. It was like I was on some kind of metaphysical pool float that I couldn't get off of, and wanted something over by the deck that I couldn't reach.

But the water could, if I displaced enough of it. So I started mentally wiggling and squirming and jumping, trying to figure out this new way of controlling power that I couldn't actually touch. And it worked—sort of.

I was doing something, anyway, something that made the float I wasn't on rise and fall more and more, until it felt like I was sitting on a boat in the high seas instead of on a platform waiting for the fey to decide to come and cook me.

And, okay, maybe this hadn't been such a good idea, I thought, playing with that much power, as the waves started striking harder, and things started getting a little out of control, and then more than a little. But I didn't stop; I wasn't sure I could stop. I just concentrated on Rosier, got an image in my head of that annoying, smug pain in the ass, and—

And—

And *pulled*.

I fell backward, although not from the snap of the power. That hit and absorbed, radiating shock waves through me, feeling weird and exhilarating and sort of good and bad all at the same time. Like when the little car rolls to a stop after a roller coaster and you're left wondering if you really had a good time or not and clutching your chest.

And something else.

I sat up, realizing that I'd fallen backward because something had hit me. Something that I didn't understand at first, because it wasn't a pissed-off demon lord. Well, not entirely, I thought, as I examined a piece of homespun-looking cloth, mud-splattered in places and rumpled, like someone had slept in it.

Because someone had.

It was a cloak, the kind that probably half the people in Britain were wearing right now. But it didn't belong to any of them. That was Rosier's little circular pin holding it at the throat, the one concession to vanity he hadn't been able to deny himself, despite the fact that the pretty pewter item didn't go with the rough material.

It was Rosier's cloak. I sat there, clutching it for a moment in slight disbelief, feeling dirty wool under my fingers and a huge grin breaking out over my face because I'd done it! I'd shifted a cloak!

I decided to try for the owner next.

Or I would have, if someone hadn't gotten nosy.

Literally. I felt a touch on my shoulder, and looked around to find myself nostril to nostril with something the size of an eight-year-old's foot. And a pair of beady black eyes on the long stretch behind it, regarding me narrowly. "What you do?"

"Nothing."

The eyes dropped to my prize. "What that?"

"A cloak—what does it look like?"

"Where from? You no have before—"

"I did."

"Did not."

"Did, too."

The eyes dropped from squinting at me to squint at the cloak instead. They didn't seem to see very well, which wasn't surprising with all that hair in the way. But then the inhaling started. And I should have known: a nose like that had to be good for something.

A gnarled hand grabbed a fold of wool. "It no smell like you."

"I—I borrowed it from a friend."

"Not smell like him, either."

"Not that friend! Another friend. Well, sort of, and give it back!"

"What you do?" he demanded again. And then said some other stuff that sounded like *chicken-tex-dump-stick* but probably wasn't.

Trust me to get the spell version of Babelfish, I thought, and snatched my cloak back.

"I'm not doing anything with it," I told him, trying for indignation. "What does somebody usually do with a cloak?"

The suspicion did not subside. "Why you need?"

"It's getting cold! See?" I rubbed my arms.

He didn't look like he bought that, maybe because it was a balmy evening without even a touch of the chilly nighttime temperatures of Wales. But I guess he decided that maybe humans were strange, cold-blooded creatures and needed more warmth, because he finally let go. I promptly threw on the cloak, which seemed to satisfy him, and he ambled back to his post.

I waited awhile, my back to him, sweating under two layers of wool. And trying to be as boring as possible while doing it. And I guess I hit the mark, because the next time I risked a glance over my shoulder, he was watching something off the other side of the platform, and sniffing the air like he liked the scents that were wafting everywhere, too.

I closed my eyes, drew my cloak around me, and tried again.

It was harder this time, a *lot* harder, and for a moment I didn't think it was going to work at all. But then I got something. Something that didn't want to come through, like it was stuck somehow, or like someone was playing tug-of-war on the other side. But I tugged harder, pulling and heaving and yanking—

And getting slapped in the face with something nasty for my trouble.

It was sweat-smeared and weed-stained, with holes in what I finally identified as the knees, and dirt splattered halfway up the calves. Trousers, I realized, with a sinking feeling. I looked around quickly, and then shoved them underneath my cloak.

Rosier probably hadn't been anywhere he needed them.

Or the lone surviving shoe, which landed in my lap next. Or the belt that showed up after that. And then something I didn't immediately recognize, something small and white and limp, and frankly a little bit funky, that—

Ewww! I dropped the pair of tighty-whities I'd just pulled out of the ether and sat there, panting and exhausted, and glaring at a heap of Rosier's nasty clothes, but no Rosier. And with no strength to try again when I could barely sit up.

I put a hand down to support myself and just breathed for a while.

Wonderful.

Now what?

That had been my one big idea, all alone and stuck up in a tree in faerie, and now I was fresh out. And shifting was my best thing; it was what I'd always been *good* at— even Agnes had said so. So if I couldn't do that, what was left?

Except to bundle the nasty stuff up and weight it with the shoe. And drop it off the side of the platform. And try not to hit anybody in the head with it on the way down, although another little guard far below grabbed his spear and leapt around wildly when it landed in a patch of weeds behind him.

But he didn't find it, and I breathed a sigh of relief, peering into the darkness and wondering what Salvatore would think if he knew where one of his loafers had ended up.

And then the Ewok started making some sort of noise behind me.

I turned to look at him again, but he hadn't come back over. He also hadn't moved, like, even to blink. I'd have thought him a hairy statue except for the firelight glinting in those black, black eyes. Or the way the chest under the layers of rags rose and fell, a little more quickly now. Or the way his hand clenched on his spear.

Looked like he wasn't a fan of human magic.

Like, really not. He didn't move, but the whites of his eyes were showing. And flickering around as he looked from me to the side of the platform to me again, and yeah. He had no way of knowing what I'd just conjured up, did he? Or what I'd thrown down into the middle of his buddies, and on reflection, maybe I should have just lived with the litter because there was such a thing as being *too* tidy, and now he was making those sounds again.

And taking a step toward me.

And no, they really weren't cute enough for Lucas, I thought, scrambling back. They weren't cute at all, and while I'd assumed there were humanlike features under there, I didn't really know that, did I? I didn't really know anything and I wasn't anywhere even close to home and I was out of juice and, for all I knew, maybe Pritkin and I *were* on the menu, because it wasn't like the dark fey at Dante's had been particularly picky, and—

And then what I could see of the guard's face changed, and crumpled, like maybe I'd done something to piss him off. Only how could you tell when all you could see was a couple inches of skin? But said skin was looking a little flushed suddenly, like I'd been staring too long, and maybe that was an insult in their culture, because what I could see of the face wasn't looking happy.

And that was doubly true when I jumped to my feet and took a step backward, hands raised, trying to look as non-threatening as possible.

Only maybe that didn't mean the same thing in their culture, either, because he was looking seriously flushed now, something that didn't change even when I took another step back. Like maybe I was showing weakness and *that* was pissing him off, only what were my options here? And he was making those sounds again, more like screeches, and they didn't make sense, maybe because the translation spell was wearing off or maybe because he was cursing at me— who the hell knew?

I stumbled back and he started waving his arms, including the one with the spear in it, and then rushing at me, and I gave a cry and tried to retreat again, only this time, there was nothing under my foot but air.

I screamed and the guard screeched and he lunged and I started to fall and the canopy of trees swirled sickeningly above me—

And then stopped just as abruptly.

But not because he had caught me.

But because someone else had.

"Do you always get in this much trouble?" Pritkin asked from behind me.

I craned my neck around to see him standing on one of the little swinging platforms, holding a basket in one hand and me in the other.

"Mostly," I breathed.

"You know, I've noticed that about you," he told me. And then he kissed me.

Chapter Forty-six

"Guard," I gasped, jerking back.

"What?"

"There's a guard!"

Pritkin looked confused. "Yes?"

He glanced over his shoulder, and then so did I. And the guard who had been about to kill me was suddenly looking like the third wheel at a junior high school dance: awkward and uncomfortable and slightly embarrassed. He had been examining the toe of his boot, but he glanced up when Pritkin said something in a language the spell didn't know. But the guard must have, because he abruptly turned and booked it down the rope bridge at a sprint.

I looked at Pritkin in shock. "What did you *say*?"

"I relieved him. And I think he *was* relieved. Poor man; he was afraid you were about to put a hex on him!"

"I don't do hexes."

"Well, you did something," Pritkin said. "That Svarestri warrior didn't collapse from a heart attack."

"Which one?" I asked miserably, and sat back down. And put my head in my hands, because I couldn't avoid the elephant in the room forever, could I?

Not when I'd just trashed the hell out of the time line.

I sat there for a moment, listening to him spread out a picnic I no longer wanted, the sinking feeling in my stomach filling it instead of food. I'd been mad at Rosier just for

bringing a gun along he knew we couldn't use, and what
had I done? I *knew* better. I knew that anything I did this
far back might have disastrous consequences, that it could
mess up time in a way I couldn't fix, that I was supposed to
be guarding the time line, not trashing it myself!

If I had trashed it.

But it sure as hell seemed like I had. We'd killed another
fey—that much I was certain about. And maybe more than
one, because despite their scary resiliency, that had been a
damned long drop onto damned hard rocks, and sure,
maybe I'd gotten lucky and maybe some of them had made
it, but I couldn't believe that all of them had.

I couldn't believe *most* of them had.

So how did that not trash time? Did the fey time line
not *count*? Were all of them slated for heart attacks in the
next few days? What?

I didn't know, because I hadn't received any sort of
warning like Rhea had said I would. I hadn't gotten anything at all, despite being in my right mind this time and
looking for it. And I still wasn't.

My power hummed along, a warm background energy,
dimmer than on earth, but as I'd just demonstrated, still
here on some level. But maybe it wasn't enough of a level?
Maybe it couldn't talk to me here? Or maybe I just didn't
know how to listen.

Yeah, I was kind of betting on that last one. Which
meant who knew how much I'd just screwed up? And for
one man.

Maybe this was why Pythias weren't supposed to
have . . . people, I thought miserably. Maybe that was why
Agnes had lived in that sterile museum of an apartment, all
alone. People interfered with things, complicated them,
messed with your head.

Agnes would have let Pritkin die, if it came down to it. I
had no doubt of that. She'd have done the right thing and
stayed home and just accepted that this was how things
were now.

And if it had been Jonas? a little voice asked. Or someone else she cared about? Would she have done the right
thing then?

I thought about that picture, the one Rhea and I had
found. They'd looked so happy. Just two middle-aged peo-

ple at a beach, with sand on their skin and the start of a
burn across their cheeks and greasy food in their stomachs
that would probably give them indigestion the next day
instead of the hangovers their younger selves might have
had. But they wouldn't care about that. Because they'd stolen a day from the job, and the responsibilities, and the
never-ending in-box, and they'd lived a little.

But what about the next day? What about when they
went back to the job? Because they had.

What had happened then?

I didn't know. But I knew what *hadn't* happened. Agnes
hadn't trashed the hell out of the time line! Maybe she'd
never been faced with the choice I had; maybe she would
have failed it, too. I didn't know that, either. I just knew one
thing.

She'd expect me to fix it.

Somehow.

I felt a finger under my chin and looked up to see bright
green eyes looking into mine. "Why the long face? We
won."

I laughed. It wasn't a particularly nice one, but it was the
best I could do under the circumstances. "We *survived*."

"Against the Svarestri, that counts," Pritkin told me seriously. And then he grinned, a bright, open expression that
had my breath catching, because he never looked like that.
"And that's worth celebrating, isn't it? We survived!" He
yelled it, and half a dozen voices yelled it back, along with
hoisting their mugs.

One of which was slapped in my hand the next second
by a smiling, half-naked baby war-mage. "Time to enjoy
life!"

"Enjoy." I refrained from rolling my eyes—just.

"You sound like that's a word you're not familiar with."

"I'm familiar with it. Just not on a first-name basis."

He grinned again and shook his head. And went back to
unpacking the basket while I investigated my mug. Beer.
Strong. But not bad, and my empty stomach accepted it eagerly.

"What do you mean, you relieved him?" I asked after
draining half of it.

"I mean, I told him to go get dinner. They're roasting an
ox in your honor and everyone's very excited. They mostly

live off fish now, since they were run off their lands, but nobody really likes it."

There were a lot of things wrong with that sentence, but my stomach only focused on one. "That's . . . ox?"

I peered into the basket, and just the smell made my mouth start to water again. And my stomach to grumble. Suddenly, it felt like I could eat a whole damned ox by myself.

"No, it's not ready yet. But I thought you might be hungry, so I told them we'd take whatever they had." He looked at me sternly. "If they bring an eye up later, eat it. It's considered a delicacy, and you'll offend them if you don't."

"And . . . and what'll they do if I offend them?" I asked nervously.

"Probably pout. For *years*. No one has a memory like the fey."

He pushed the furs closer to the tree so he wouldn't get food on them, and finished laying out our feast. I watched him work for a moment, trying to shift gears. And to catch up, although nothing was making any damned sense. "In my honor?" I finally said.

"Mmhm."

"But a little while ago they were throwing rocks at my head and trying to *stab* me. . . ."

"That was before."

"Before what?"

"Before you helped saved the lives of two of their warriors. And before they knew about the blessing." He paused, cutting the bread long enough to narrow green eyes at me. "You might have mentioned that."

"Mentioned what?"

"You don't know?"

"Know *what*?" I demanded, tired and anxious and hungry.

And then startled, when he suddenly shoved the knife at me, fast enough to make me gasp and flinch back. And then to flinch again as what sounded like a cascade of bells pealed in the air all around me. And before I'd recovered from *that*, a half-dozen spears appeared, as if by magic, all big, all shiny, all in the hands of a bunch of pissed-off-looking guards.

And all pointed at Pritkin's throat.

For a moment, we just stayed there, the spears, the guards, and the two of us in the middle of the deadly circle, not even breathing. Anyway, I wasn't. Pritkin looked cautious, but not nearly as alarmed as he should have been with a bunch of knife-edged blades centimeters from his jugular.

But he was very deliberate in his movements as he slowly set the bread knife down. "Just checking," he told them as one of them quickly snatched the blade away. "But as long as you're here, can we get more beer?"

The guards gave him the look that he deserved, gave me the once-over, and left just as quickly as they'd come. Nobody offered more beer. But I suddenly felt better anyway.

A lot better.

Not being on the menu can do that for a person.

"So . . . they're not going to hurt us?" I asked, crawling on the edge of the platform to watch them swing back down again. And to watch counterloads swing back up and then around, because a single makeshift elevator seemed to serve a number of trees. One portly-looking female was giggling and laughing as she swung in a big arc, smacking oversized mugs into eager, reaching hands around the circle of trees, like some kind of manic beer fairy.

Damn, that looked like fun.

"Hurt us? You're Fey Friend," Pritkin said, his voice giving it capitals. "They'd . . . well, probably not die for you; it's not their mark. But at some point, you did a great service to a member of one of the dark fey clans, and therefore can expect consideration from all of them."

It took me a minute. It took several, actually, while I stared at occasional sparks from below, a few of which were starting to fly up into the air as far as the edge of our platform. And then I remembered.

"Radella."

"What?" He looked up from slopping something into a bowl.

"A fey. A pixie. I gave her . . . a rune. . . ." Pritkin looked puzzled. "A thing to help with fertility."

"Ah. No wonder you were named Friend. I'm surprised they didn't adopt you!"

"I don't think I'd have fit in the house."

He laughed, and as usual, it made me jump. "No, I suppose not."

I crawled back over and picked up my beer. "What does 'consideration' mean?" I asked, after draining the rest of it.

"I wouldn't push it too far," he warned, handing me the bowl. "And only with the dark fey. The light won't honor their marks, and in fact may make things worse for you if they find one. And any dark clans who are on the outs with the one who marked you . . . well, they probably wouldn't hurt you, but they might try to ransom you back."

Yeah, that would go well, considering Radella might not even have been born yet.

"But, on the other hand, it does give you free passage through the dark fey lands," Pritkin added. "You have a right to be here. You're known to be friendly. And you have protectors. It is not a small gift."

Thank you, Radella, I thought fervently.

"Then why did I have a guard?" I asked.

"He was an honor guard, the brother of one of the trolls you helped. And a guide, in case you wanted to go anywhere."

"Go? Then we can *leave*?"

Pritkin cocked an eyebrow. "Tomorrow."

"What's wrong with tonight?"

"The fact that it is night?" he said, filling his own bowl. "Travel along the dark fey border is not easy even in the day, when you can see what is about to eat you. And I, for one, am tired. Aren't you?"

Hell yes, I was, but I had a job to do, and it wasn't getting done sitting here. But it also wasn't getting done without Pritkin, and he didn't look interested in budging. And I kind of doubted my ability to carry him.

"Besides, you'd miss the celebration," he added.

"What celebration? What are they doing?" I asked, craning my neck to look over the edge of the platform.

"What's happening?" Pritkin asked, because he was too far back to see for himself.

"A bunch of old guys—old trolls—with white beards. They're gathering near the ox. They've got two guards with them. I think they're the ones that were on the boat with us."

Pritkin grinned. "Sounds like the entertainment's about to begin."

"What entertainment?"

"You'll see. Come eat."

I crawled over with every intention of getting some answers to the questions crowding my brain. But the food looked enticing, and Pritkin wasn't listening to me anyway. A band had struck up in a not-too-distant tree, and he was tapping his fingers and nodding his head and scarfing bread and beer and some weird roasted meat stuff that . . . that, well, that smelled really good, actually.

I stuck my nose in my own bowl. *Really* good. I started looking around for a spoon.

And ended up polishing off most of the not-small-sized bowl before I realized it. And damn, it *was* good, some kind of venison-y stew-y something with roasted veggies and a thick brown gravy. I licked the spoon.

And looked up to find Pritkin watching me, looking amused, I didn't know why. Maybe because I was eating like Scarlett O'Hara at the barbecue instead of like a proper, dainty little woman. Fiddle dee dee, I thought, and ripped off another hunk of bread.

"I can go get more," he told me, openly laughing now.

"You stay put!" I pointed the bread at him. "I have some questions."

"Such as?"

"Such as what would you have done if I hadn't been there?"

"There?"

"At the mill. What would you have done if you hadn't . . . seen me?"

He thought about it for a moment. "Had a bath?"

"I'm serious!"

"So am I." He picked up a bowl of little smoked fish and offered it to me, but I shook my head. I have a problem eating anything that is able to watch me do it. Pritkin apparently didn't have that issue, crunching bones and all with apparent relish.

"Those damned fey ran me across half a mountain range!" he told me in between bites. "And used me for target practice besides. I finally lost them and made my way to the nearest source of water. It's my element, and boosts spell casting. I had every intention of blending in and hiding out until I was sure they'd left. Sorry if that disappoints you," he added, "but I had no intention of fighting them."

"Hiding out is good," I told him fervently.

He nodded. "Just my luck they were coming the same way."

"Didn't you expect them to be? There can't be that many portals to faerie scattered around. If they were trying to get back—"

"They weren't."

"How do you know that?"

"When I met them, they were headed toward the city, not coming away from it."

"The city? You mean . . . they were going to court?"

"Possibly."

"*Arthur's* court?"

Pritkin looked confused for a minute, and then he grinned. "Oh, Arth Aur."

"That's different?"

"It means 'Golden Bear,' in our language. It's his nickname. He doesn't like it much, but it fits him. Big and blustering and golden-haired—and dangerous. But a good man overall."

"A good man who hangs out with the Svarestri?"

Pritkin shook his head. "That's just it: he doesn't. He has an alliance with another of the major fey houses, and you don't get two of those!"

"But they were going to his court."

"Probably."

"With a weapon."

"Definitely."

"You think they planned to hurt him?"

"I have no idea what they planned," Pritkin said. "I have no idea what they were even doing on earth. Rumor is that they despise the place, and everyone in it. I'd never even seen one of them before today."

"Then how did you know who they were?"

He shrugged. "The way they looked."

"They looked like men."

"Did they?"

I stopped and thought about it for a minute. The answer was no, not really. I'd never seen a member of the light fey before, but I'd known without question that that's what they were. The bone structure, the way they moved—a hundred different things had given it away. They hadn't just looked different; they'd looked *alien*, like the kind of villains Lucas would have put in that movie if he'd really wanted to scare the crap out of everyone.

"Interbreeding," Pritkin said, before I could ask. "The other major houses have bred with humans through the years, and therefore look more like us. The Svarestri haven't. I knew what they were as soon as I saw them."

"And stole their stick."

"Staff," Pritkin corrected. "And I didn't steal it. I retrieved it."

"Retrieved it? Then it's yours?"

He shook his head, pawing around in the basket for something. And finally coming up with a small pot of what looked like mustard that he proceeded to dunk the fish heads in. And to grin at me when I shuddered.

"No, a contact of mine among the fey asked me to be on the lookout for it, said it had been stolen. He didn't sound like he thought it likely to come to earth, but was taking all possible precautions. He was . . . more upset than I've ever seen him. He claimed a war might break out if it wasn't returned."

"A war? Over a wizard's staff?"

Pritkin swallowed fish. "Not a wizard's—a king's. The Staff of the Winds is the Sky King's own weapon, which is why it caused such an uproar when it went missing."

"The . . . Sky King?"

"Leader of the Blarestri. You probably know them as the Blue Fey. Or possibly not; they don't come to earth that often, either. But more so than the Svarestri, who never come at all. Well, until now."

"With a stolen staff."

He nodded. "And that's what's odd."

"That they came to earth or that they stole the staff?"

"Both. Either." He flipped the hand that wasn't holding the fish bowl. "The Svarestri have reason to want to put the Sky Lords' noses out of joint; they've been enemies for years. But it is interesting that they would risk so much for so little gain."

"Little? That thing seemed pretty powerful to me!"

"It is—in the king's hand. It's said he can raise a storm large enough to wipe out a whole army with it. But that's him. He's the most powerful of the Blue Fey, possibly the most powerful being in all faerie, and his element is air. The staff in the hand of someone else ..." Pritkin shrugged. "Useful, yes. Worth risking a war for? No."

I frowned, and slathered butter on bread with a spoon because we were out of knives. "So a group of people who never come to earth were taking a staff they aren't supposed to have and can't use, to the court of a guy who doesn't want anything to do with them?"

Pritkin nodded.

"That doesn't make any sense!"

He nodded again, because he had his mouth full.

"What did you do with it anyway?" I asked, because he obviously didn't have it on him.

He stared up at the canopy of trees, where little sparks were flying around from the bonfire below, like fireflies. "Do?"

"Yes, where did you put it?"

"Put what?"

"The *staff.*"

"Oh, that. The elders have it."

It was nonchalant.

"You just gave it to them?" I didn't bother to keep the skepticism out of my voice.

"They didn't ask. They're arguing over what to do with it right now."

"What to—you mean they're planning to keep it?" I chewed my lip some more, because that ... that probably wasn't good.

I didn't know how things had originally played out, before Calamity Cassie got involved, but I doubted it was with the little guys making out like bandits. They kind of reminded me of me, and our lives didn't work like that. When pennies dropped from heaven, they were usually in five-hundred-pound sacks that crushed our skulls.

"That's what they're arguing over," Pritkin said, watching me with a curious expression. "Some want to keep the staff and find a way to use it. They lost most of their lands, except for this strip by the river, a few years ago to the Green Fey, and the staff is the sort of thing that might be able to win at least some of them back."

"Green Fey?"

"The Water Lords." He tilted his head. "You know, the ones who usually come to earth?"

"Oh, right. Those Green Fey."

"You probably know them as Alorestri, but that just means 'They Who Wear the Green' in their language, and either way, it's meaningless. Just a name they give themselves so they won't have to give us their real one."

"Do you know their real one?"

Pritkin nodded. And then a liquid series of syllables came out of his mouth that sounded almost like singing—a whole song, because it lasted, like, a full minute. "That's . . . beautiful," I said, because it was.

"I memorized it as a child. Took me a whole week."

"As a child?"

"And then there's the second camp," he said. "The ones who want to return the staff to the Blarestri and plead their case there. But others say it's unlikely that the Sky King is going to fight the Lady of Lakes and Oceans—whom he used to be married to, mind you—for nothing more than the return of a piece of his own property. Which, for all he knows, they stole in the first place!"

"I—what?" I was having trouble keeping up. The fey had too damned many names!

"And then there's the third camp, who want to give it back to us and send us on our way, effectively washing their hands of the whole thing—"

I brightened.

"—and who are in the minority. The others say they have it now, and any group who comes looking for it is likely to hold them accountable."

"Then . . . then we've put them in danger?" I couldn't believe I hadn't thought of it before. God, I was an *idiot*.

"The Svarestri put them in danger," Pritkin said, gripping my arm as I struggled to get to my feet. "They came into their lands, violating a treaty in the process of chasing us."

"But what about now? What if they come *back*?"

"We're well protected here."

I stared at him. "Did you *see* those things?"

"Yes, and I've seen what our hosts can do on their home ground. They've fought off the Green Fey for years now.

This place is well warded. They wouldn't have brought us here otherwise."

I felt myself relax slightly.

And then a screaming arrow came shooting directly at my head.

Chapter Forty-seven

I shrieked and Pritkin pulled me over by the tree, onto the pile of rugs. And the arrow disintegrated in a sparkling haze just beyond the edge of the platform, sending a few translucent bits of ash fluttering our way. "Looks like it's time for the entertainment," he told me.

"Entertainment?"

He nodded, grinning, because he was a bastard. He had always been a bastard, and youth had obviously not changed a goddamned *thing*—

"You can't leave," he told me as I struggled to get up carrying fifty pounds of freaking wool.

"Watch me!"

"But you're being honored tonight, too. We all are."

"You call this 'honored'?"

"Please," he said, seriously enough to stop me. "They need this. They haven't had many victories lately, if any at all, and tonight—they *need* this."

"What is 'this'?"

He nodded at the open space between the circle of trees. "Watch."

And a second later, I was. I was watching us, along with our two stalwart companions, bobbing along an underground river, only this one was made out of sparks. The great fire was throwing them up from below, and somehow the fey were turning them into a shimmering monochrome movie that glowed and flowed and gleamed in the air and had everyone's rapt attention.

I crawled to the edge of the platform and stared down into a vortex of fire, painting radiant, moving pictures in midair. And felt myself relax again as awe overtook out-rage. And I wasn't alone.

All around us, people were gathering in the trees, crowd-ing the platforms and sitting along the sturdier branches, seeking a better vantage point. There were geriatric grand-mothers with long gray braids, children with bright black eyes and noses that had yet to fulfill their true potential, and solid, hairy men with rough hands and battle scars, draped with enough weapons to fight a war. Yet they were staring at the lights with just as much rapt fascination as the kids.

And no wonder. The movie in the air pretty much filled the whole open space, with 3-D graphics Hollywood might have envied. The long rush of river showered down from above on a cascade of sparks, the jagged points of the rocks were picked out in bursts of stars among the tree limbs, and the leaping Svarestri were painted in quick flashes of light amid it all, throwing even quicker bursts at the wildly bob-bing heads below.

"This is how they tell stories?" I whispered.

"This is how they tell stories," Pritkin agreed. "I used to hide in the trees and watch them—from a distance. They showed me remarkable things, battles long over, heroes long dead, great cities turned to dust. But not really gone. Not as long as their people remember them."

"And now they'll remember us?" It was almost over-whelming to think of being part of someone's history, even in a small way. To be remembered . . . Stupidly, I felt my eyes get wet.

"Oh, they'll remember us," Pritkin said, sounding amused. "After a fashion."

I looked back at him. "What does that mean?"

"That," he said, as fire-me came speeding by the plat-form, the shower of sparks somehow managing to convey goggling eyes, flailing limbs, and a comically wide-open mouth silently screaming its head off.

I frowned at my unflattering doppelganger. "I thought you said we were being honored!"

"We are. But you know who decides the histories."

"Who?"

"Whoever's telling them!" He laughed and pulled me back, as fire-me looked around frantically, made an oh-shit face, and ducked under the fiery river—right before a spear burst into sparks that scattered almost as far as my real toes. I quickly pulled them back under the edge of the fur.

But the surrounding crowd didn't seem to hold my cowardice against me. On the contrary, a new flagon of beer almost bopped me in the head a moment later, having been lowered from a platform above by a couple of cackling old women. And several bright-eyed kids were spying on us through the foliage off to the right, apparently finding us more interesting than the show.

I waved at them before realizing that they might not know what it meant. But then a small hand raised, with nails like dark-tipped talons. And slowly moved up and down as one waved back.

We grinned at each other, both feeling absurdly pleased for some reason. And Pritkin liberated the beer and refilled our mugs, because why the hell not? And the rock throwing and light fey cursing continued, with enthusiastic participation from the crowd.

Very enthusiastic, I thought, as the sparks rippled and swirled and genuine weapons were thrown at Svarestri heads.

I hoped someone had thought to cover the ox.

"I don't remember this part taking so long," I said after several more minutes.

"It didn't. But the people here *hate* the Svarestri."

"I thought it was the Green Fey who took over their lands."

"It was," Pritkin agreed. "But it was in response to the Svarestri doing as much to them, and seizing most of the fertile land on their northern border. The Svarestri lands are said to be rocky and cold, rich in minerals but not much else."

"So they take what they need from others."

He nodded. "And then the Green Fey take replacements from the Dark. But there's damned little left to take these days, at least along the border. And there's no way for these people to cross it, not with more powerful factions ready to destroy them as soon as they do. They've been left between a hammer and an anvil, courtesy of the Svarestri expansion and the Green Fey callousness. If they choose to enjoy the satisfaction of pelting their enemies for a few minutes, believe me, they deserve it."

An edge had crept into his voice. He was watching the light shimmer and change, and his face changed along with it, from cheerful engagement to fierce satisfaction, depending on what shadows the spectacle was throwing. But either way, it looked like he was enjoying the prolonged beating as much as the trolls were.

"I don't know what will happen when they run out of room entirely," he said after a moment.

I didn't answer, although I could have told him. Because the dark fey had been coming to earth in ever-increasing numbers in my day. And congregating in enclaves under glamouries, those who couldn't pass as human, because there was nowhere else for them to go.

I wondered what it must be like to lose not only your home but your entire world, except for the handful of family or friends you brought with you. Of course, immigrants had been doing that for years, but immigrants could always go home again, or work to integrate into their new society. Most of the fey couldn't. They would be forever strangers in a strange land, and that suddenly struck me as terribly cruel.

"Why do the Svarestri need so much land?" I asked. "I thought they didn't marry humans."

He snorted. "They don't."

"Then shouldn't their birth rate be low?"

"It should be. But the rumor is, they've made marriage compulsory, along with childbearing. They're trying to build up their numbers."

"For what?"

Pritkin shook his head. "No one knows."

And then the crowd gasped, a collective inhalation of breath, as the battle on the boat commenced.

"Here's your big scene," I told Pritkin. And then I noticed: the fight had been subtly altered to focus on the little guard's jabs at the fey, which in this version became a prolonged, heroic battle à la David and Goliath. Which it sort of had been, since the guard was maybe a third the size of his opponent. But it shortchanged Pritkin, who was left standing to the side, looking on admiringly.

"That's not how it happened!" I said indignantly.

He just grinned.

"Don't you care?"

"Care? I'm being immortalized in poetry and song," he said, referring to the low-voiced chanting the graybeards had been doing. "A thousand years after my death, they'll still sing of my heroic nonparticipation—and yours," he added, as my wide-open mouth—damn it, did they ever show it closed?—shrieked by again.

"Can't they edit me out?" I asked hopefully.

He laughed. "You may as well get used to it. This is how we will forever be remembered by generations of young trolls."

Wonderful.

And then there was another collective gasp, because fire-me had finally got her shit together and shot the Svarestri warrior. Only, in this version, I'd cursed him, because apparently no one had equated the little thing in my hand to his sudden lack of face. He fell backward and the crowd went wild, screaming and yelling and stamping on platforms, to the point that I was afraid some of them were about to come crashing down.

But I guess they were sturdier than they looked, because none did. Even when a thousand voices shook the treetops, and a couple dozen real spears shot through the air, the crowd doing their best to kill him all over again. And I was laughing, because it was impossible not to be affected by their mood, which was bordering on gleeful.

And then everyone oohed, including me, when the huge area among the trees was suddenly lit by a hundred little boats made of stars. And, somehow, the elders had even managed to conjure up what looked like mirror images in the water, with showers of thinner sparks that glittered and gleamed like shimmering reflections. And lit the faces of the watchers with flickering fairy light.

And I'd been wrong; it had to be two, three thousand people staring out through the trees, faces awash with light and wonder.

"You said there were stronger dark fey clans?" I asked suddenly.

Pritkin nodded.

"Couldn't they unite? Push the Svarestri back?"

"It . . . would be difficult."

"Why?" It seemed to me that they had damned good reason. The enemy of my enemy might not be a friend, but I'd find a way to put up with him if it meant *not dying*. I thought most people would.

And then I thought about the Circle and Senate. Or the Circle and the covens. Or the whole damned supernatural community, for that matter, which seemed impossibly divided. And too busy squabbling and bickering and fighting each other to worry about the greater threat.

I guess maybe I couldn't say anything to the fey, after all, could I?

"Because of their past," Pritkin said, looking around, his face alight with wonder. And then he glanced at me. "Don't you know how the fey were made?"

I shook my head.

"They're all the same, really. Even the lordly Svarestri, although they'd likely string up anyone who said so. But it's true."

"What's true?" I asked, watching fire-me now scream my way down a raging river. At least they were consistent.

"That they were all born of the gods."

It took me a second. The big plunge over the falls was coming up, and I'd been tensing like everyone else, despite the fact that I knew we didn't die. And then what he'd said sank in.

And I tensed up some more.

"What?" I twisted around to look at Pritkin. His face had gone back into shadow, as the darkened tunnel scene tempered the light somewhat, but his eyes still shone with reflected sparks. And with the enjoyment of telling me something I obviously didn't know.

"The old gods," he repeated. "The ones out of legend. It's said they came from another world, or worlds, far away. They discovered faerie first, before earth. And when they did, they sought to make servants for themselves, but none of the then-fey would do. And you know the gods . . ."

"Randy little bastards," I said blankly.

He nodded. "They inbred with some of the inhabitants who were already here—most of them, in fact. In some cases, that resulted in what they viewed as positive changes. Proper servants to cater to their every whim. But in others . . ."

"They got monsters," I said, recalling a few of the creatures that had attacked me.

"Or what they viewed that way, yes. The dark fey, as they became known, were forced out of the cities and into the hinterlands, to make their own way or starve. Many starved. But a few survived and bred with each other, and with the remaining original inhabitants, and with the occasional member of the so-called privileged races. . . . The result is the huge variety you see today."

I stared around, suddenly remembering my mythology. And all the stories about the gods siring monsters as well as heroes. For every Perseus there was a Medusa; for every Odysseus a Cyclops. But it had never really occurred to me to wonder why.

I guess I'd always assumed, if I thought of it at all, that the monsters were just some sort of demon. And maybe some of them were; the gods had certainly had monstrous opponents, said to be from the Underworld. But that ignored the monsters who were *on their side.* Where had they come from? Why get a Theseus one time, and a giant the next?

Maybe because of who you slept with.

"But that doesn't explain why they can't unite," I said. "If anything, what you just said should give them more in common."

"It might have," Pritkin agreed. "But resources were scarce, and new groups were arriving all the time to contest for them. And whenever several groups did band together and begin to gain power, the gods intervened, starting wars and disputes to keep them disunited."

"I'm surprised they didn't wipe them out entirely!"

"They might have, but they had discovered earth by then and become distracted. And some of the dark fey were useful for doing jobs their lighter counterparts wouldn't touch. Thus, they survived, until the day the gods disappeared, vanishing as quickly as they had come. And the world changed."

"There was a war." I didn't even have to guess.

Pritkin nodded. "One so terrible, they don't even sing about it. Some things, no one wants to remember."

"And the dark fey were part of it?"

"Everyone was. But the main combatants were the two leading light fey families, the ones favored by the different groups of gods."

"Different groups?"

"The Æsir, gods of battle, and the Vanir, gods of nature, who were at each other's throats more often than not. The Æsir were worshipped by the Svarestri, who remain as martial as their forebears. The Vanir were worshipped by the Blarestri, which is why the Sky Lords' lands are said to bloom like a garden, despite being high in the mountain fastnesses."

"And once their masters left . . ."

"Their servants took up the old conflicts as if nothing had changed, using the weapons their former masters had left behind to savage each other almost to obliteration. And dragged the rest of faerie into their quarrel."

"Why? What was the *point*? If the gods were gone—"

"What is the point of any war?" He shrugged. "I assume it was to see which family would lead. The Blarestri won—barely—and continue to be the most powerful clan to this day. But it was not so much a victory as both sides fighting to exhaustion, leaving them with little choice but to make peace. They did so, but the groups they'd dragged into their conflict continue to hate each other."

"That's ridiculous!"

But Pritkin was shaking his head. "Put yourself in their place. Unwanted, despised, treated as nothing your whole existence, with no dignity, no power, no pride allowed to you. Until, one day, a war breaks out about which you know little, but which suddenly has the great ones that you have envied and hated and secretly admired for as long as you can remember, coming to speak . . . to you."

"Because they wanted something!"

"Of course. When else do the powerful notice the rest of us? But it didn't matter to the tribes of dark fey, who suddenly found themselves decked in the colors of the great houses, with golden chains around their necks and important-sounding titles before their names. They who had been nothing were now valued auxiliaries, and in some cases, even front-line troops—"

"Cannon fodder!"

"What?"

"Nothing." I guess they didn't have cannons yet. "They put them out to absorb casualties, to save the light fey numbers."

"Yes, and the dark knew this. But they thought if they fought hard enough, did well enough, proved their worth, their families would be honored. Be given lands to live on, titles to hold, be able to hold their heads up among any in the land . . ."

"And when the war was over?"

He sat back against the tree. "What do you think? What do you *see*?"

I looked back at the spectacle and the ring of watching faces and didn't answer.

"But the scars didn't heal," he told me. "The dark fey clans who were on different sides in the fighting still despise each other. For old wounds, for older resentments, and because they cannot fight the ones who were really the cause of their suffering. The light fey are too strong, and the gods . . ."

"Have a lot to answer for. So do their servants!"

Their children, I thought, looking around. Yes, the percentage of godly blood might be small now, might be minuscule even, but once, these had been their sons and daughters. How did you throw away your own flesh and blood? How did you look at a tiny child and call it a monster?

"If it's different from you, it's not so difficult," Pritkin said softly, because I must have spoken aloud without realizing it.

"I couldn't do it."

"No, I don't believe you could. But you aren't fey. And the light fey . . . aren't like us."

I glanced back at him, because there had been something in his voice. And discovered that there was something in his face, too. And this time, I didn't need a translation.

I'd seen the same expression often enough, in the mirror.

It looked like the dark fey weren't the only ones who had felt abandoned.

Chapter Forty-eight

The crowd was rapt, watching their two heroes courageously battle to keep us from going over the rocks, while showers of sparks sprayed around like fireworks. Or like massive waves of water, suffocating even in the air. All of a sudden, I was finding it hard to breathe.

I sat back against the tree trunk and concentrated on my beer.

"I never knew my parents," I told Pritkin. "They had ... an accident ... early, and I was left with a guardian who ... didn't like me much."

He waited, but I didn't elaborate. I wasn't sure how much I could tell him, how much he'd remember later. We'd shared some pretty memorable events already, but let's face it, the sixth century was the sixth century. I'd probably end up just some crazy witch he met, a crazy witch named Ohshit. I stifled a half-hysterical laugh with my mug, because he was looking fairly serious for once, but it fit. Oh, God help me, but it did.

"Mine didn't like me, either," he finally said.

"You had guardians?" I hadn't known that. Although I supposed I should have guessed. Rosier wouldn't go to all this trouble for a child without seeing that he grew up.

Pritkin nodded. "An old farmer and his wife. My mother was part fey, but she died, and my father ... I suppose he didn't want the burden of raising a child alone. He told the old couple that he would come back for me someday, but the woman told me not to expect it."

"Why not?"

"Part-fey children sometimes turn out . . . strangely. She used to watch me; I think she was waiting for me to sprout a tail or grow donkey ears or some such! I never did, but she never stopped checking my ears, on the pretext of washing them. I think she was disappointed that they weren't even pointed. She said my father was probably relieved to be rid of me."

"Charming."

Pritkin shook his head. "She was all right. Just superstitious and fearful. They both were. The world was changing, and they didn't know how, or where, or if they'd fit into the new one. I think that's why she didn't like me. She could tell I wasn't afraid."

"Of what?"

"Of everything. According to her, the whole world was a danger, especially to a child. Venture too far into the marshes, and the will-o'-the-wisp would lead you to your doom. Wander into the forest, and the monster Afang would drag you back to his cave, littered with the bones of disobedient little boys and girls. Go swimming, and the mermaids would lure you into dark water until you drowned. And then there was always the bwgan, who would get you for almost anything else!"

"But you weren't worried?"

He shook his head. "I was . . . intrigued. The stories were supposed to keep children safe by giving them reason to avoid dangerous areas. But they had the opposite effect on me. I wanted to see if the mermaids were as beautiful as everyone said. To find the Afang and see the fabled spikes on its hide. To follow a will-o'-the-wisp, in case it would lead me into faerie . . .

"I listened to her stories, the most frightening ones she knew, and then asked for more. Why not? They were the most exciting things about my life! And most of them were about faerie, where I wanted to go more than anything."

"To find your mother's people."

He nodded. "I didn't know why they'd left me. Just that the fey were different; you never knew why they did what they did. But everyone always said the same thing: they would come for me someday. They always came back for their children."

But they hadn't. Pritkin had repeatedly shown a lot of knowledge about faerie, even going to negotiate with the dark fey king, or the guy calling himself that, in my day. He'd also made a later visit to find out some information about a would-be assassin. But neither of those trips had exactly gone the way I'd have expected for someone who had spent the majority of his childhood among the fey.

Instead of, say, slipping through whatever portals he could find and running amok until they threw him out.

"I was six years old the first time I ran away," he told me, "six and convinced I had outgrown that sorry place. I recall packing my small belongings—not too difficult—and being on my way several times. To be honest, I am surprised they didn't let me go."

I wasn't.

I'd met his father.

"But they always brought me back, before I'd had a chance to see anything. They said it was for my own good, and of course they were right. I'd have likely died of exposure or been picked up by slavers or worse on my own. But I didn't understand that. All I knew was that nothing ever happened on that farm. Every day was exactly the same: a list of chores, a bowl of soup, a cuff on the ear—or two. I was a terrible child."

"I don't believe that."

"Oh, I was. I asked a thousand questions and fair drove the old woman mad. The old man simply ignored me. I think he was half deaf, something for which he was doubtless grateful!"

"Asking questions doesn't make you a bad child."

"No, but running away does. And disobedience and defiance. I knew they didn't want me, that I didn't belong there, but they wouldn't let me leave. Money came every year for my upkeep, money they desperately needed, and it felt as if they were keeping me prisoner because of it. I was too young to look at it from the other side, to see that they might feel trapped, too. As if they had no choice but to house a monster—"

"You weren't a monster!"

"—a potential monster," he amended, "because of their poverty."

"They were the adults, not you. It wasn't up to you to make excuses for them!"

"Well, I didn't. I resented the hell out of them and caused them no end of trouble." His head tilted. "You didn't feel like that?"

"No."

"No anger at all?" His brow furrowed, like he couldn't understand that. And I supposed not. Anger had always come naturally to Pritkin.

"No." I drew my knees up. They made a good table for my massive mug of beer. They also provided a barrier, but Pritkin didn't take the hint.

"Fear, resentment, bitterness, envy?" he persisted.

"No."

"You must have felt *something*. It's impossible to just feel nothing."

"No. It really isn't."

He sat back and looked at me, and it was that look. That here's-something-interesting-that-I-don't-understand-but-I'm-going-to look. Only he wasn't, not this time, and not merely because I couldn't explain.

But because he wouldn't get it anyway.

You learn some things when you grow up in the house-hold of a psychotic vampire. Like not to interrupt a feed, unless you want to be dessert. And not to touch the boys' gun collection, unless you want to play William Tell with real bullets. And that when Tony slammed through the house in that one particular way, it was probably time to go find a closet to hang out in for a while.

And how to be small, which helped with everything else.

Not physically so much, although I had tended to skulk around in corners, according to one of Tony's gals, and I couldn't argue with her. And not mentally, because if there was one thing you needed around Tony's, it was to keep your eyes open. Just small.

To the point of being able to walk across a room and have nobody notice. To the point of being able to practi-cally blend in with the furniture and have people forget I was there. To the point that sometimes, I'd started to wonder if I *was* really there, or if maybe I could see ghosts because I was one, too.

I'd eventually decided that anyone with as many scraped knees as me was probably human, but I'd never forgotten how to be small. In fact, I'd sometimes thought that the main reason I'd been able to avoid Tony's guys for so long after I ran away was that I'd practically spent my life practicing for it. And in a household of creatures who read emotions almost as well as actual words.

Vamps wouldn't like the comparison, but they were like dogs in how tuned in they were to their surroundings. The extra-sharp senses helped with that, but it was more than just better eyesight or whatever. It was the need of a predator to tell who is vulnerable and who is not. Who will make a good victim, and who will fuck your shit up. Vamps don't make those kind of mistakes often, especially vamps who work as the foot soldiers for a vampire mobster.

Tony's boys were good.

But so was I. And I'd figured out that a major part of staying small was being able to detach your emotions from your surroundings, to flip a switch and just go dim, there but not there in some vitally important way. Vamps didn't notice me a lot of the time, because I didn't fall into the category of either predator or prey. I wasn't dangerous, but I wasn't afraid, either. So I was invisible, or as close as anyone could be to creatures with that kind of eyesight.

I thought of Pritkin, that curious, stubborn, angry little boy at Tony's, and shuddered.

And looked up to find him watching me.

"If I didn't react, they didn't notice me as much," I said. "It was . . . easier . . . not to be seen."

He looked away, at the still-running spectacle, and his jaw tightened. The changing orange-red light limned his profile and lit his hair. For a moment, he almost looked like his fire-self: a glowing sprite thrumming with barely repressed energy. Then he suddenly looked back at me. "I see you."

You always did, I thought, watching sparks dance in his eyes.

And then I drank beer. "Did you ever find any fey?"

Pritkin looked frustrated, like he wasn't ready for a

change of topic yet. But in the end, he went with it. He sat back.

"No. But it didn't matter. When they were ready, they found me."

"What?" My head came up.

He nodded. "I was young, but I remember it perfectly. A group of them, dressed in fine clothes, like nobles, but with no horses. I thought that was odd. How did they get around with no horses?"

"How did they?"

"I found out later that there was a portal in the woods, not far from the house. They'd left their horses on the other side. It seems that, every time they brought them into our world, some damn human stole them."

I grinned in spite of myself. "I'd have liked to see that. The mighty fey, sloshing through the mud."

"There wasn't any that day, I'm afraid. But you should have seen the Svarestri this morning. They'd found some old mule and loaded it up as part of their disguise. But it was having none of it. It's why I gave them a second glance: a too-tall group standing around in too-fine clothes in the middle of the road, cursing a mangy old mule."

"Did it help?"

"Quite the opposite. The creature had stopped to eat some weeds, but when they began cursing it, and then striking it, it bucked and reared, almost hitting one in the teeth."

"Too bad it missed."

He nodded agreement. "After which it ran off, and they didn't bother to chase it, despite the fact that it supposedly held all their goods. And I became . . . curious."

"You're always curious."

"How would you know?"

"You . . . come across that way."

"That's strange. I can't figure you out at all."

"Don't try."

"But I want to try. A woman who wears peasant garb but carries a fortune in magic. Who travels alone, without guards, which many men would hesitate to do these days. Who knows about portals and recognizes faerie, but doesn't know who the Green Fey are."

Damn it.

"Who calls me by a name that isn't mine, but who seems to know me . . . and to care what happens to me."

I always forgot how smart Pritkin was, and it always bit me on the ass. "Tell me about the fey," I persisted. "You said they came to your house?"

He regarded me solemnly for a moment, and for the first time, I thought he might not answer. I wasn't exactly being forthcoming myself. But he surprised me again.

"They showed up one morning, out of the blue. The old people were cowering inside, afraid to even speak to them, just praying they'd go away. I doubt they'd seen any fey before, but they'd heard the stories; they thought they were going to be abducted. And I . . . hoped to be."

"What did the fey want?"

"To ask about my mother, my father, what I remembered. But I couldn't tell them anything. I'd been too young when I came to the farm. It was all I'd ever known.

"Then they wanted me to do some magic for them, but I barely even knew what it was. Magic was something out of the fables, and far less interesting than the monsters and the heroes who slayed them. Or the cauldrons that gave unlimited food. Or the great battles fought with mythical weapons. Magic was something for potty old wizards; I wasn't interested in magic."

I smiled.

"But they insisted, and seemed annoyed by my confusion. Finally, one of them showed me something." Pritkin's eyes grew distant. "He was blond, not dark like the others. And wearing plain gray instead of green. He raised a leaf from the ground without touching it, asked me to do the same. I didn't know what he meant at first; I kept picking it up and handing it to him."

I bit my lip in sympathy.

"I was only seven, and they were so tall, and they were all looking at me. One of the others smirked and said something I didn't understand. But the one in gray was patient. He told me not to think of the leaf but of the breeze. To call it to me."

"And did you?"

"I didn't know how. I just remember getting angry. I'd wanted the fey to come for so long, so very long, and now they were there, but instead of taking me away, they were asking me to do this impossible thing. This thing that no one could do, but that I wished I could. I wished the leaves would rise up and swallow us, so I wouldn't have to see their smug faces anymore . . .

"And then they did.

"A little breeze blew up, all of a sudden. And the leaves—it was autumn, and they were everywhere— whirled up all around us, like a miniature storm. First a few and then more and more, until I couldn't see the fey anymore, until I couldn't see anything."

There was still wonder in his face.

"I take it they were impressed?" I asked.

"No."

"No?"

"If anything, they seemed . . . unhappy. There was a discussion. I don't know what was said; I couldn't understand them. But there was a woman there, beautiful but cold, and she kept scowling at me. Looking back, I was probably ragged and dirty and ill-mannered, just a worthless urchin in her eyes, but at the time, I didn't understand that. I just knew she didn't like me, and in the end, they went away."

"They were stupid, then."

He smiled slightly. "Do you know, some of them came back? For several years, they came, by twos and threes, men and women in gray, and stayed for a while in the forest near the house. They didn't invite me to their camp, but they knew I would come, and I have to believe that was why they were there. They taught me things: magic, the lore of their world, even some of their language. But they never took me with them when they left. And they never told me why."

"They were stupid," I said again, more harshly that time, because there had been wistfulness in his voice, and the echo of the confusion and pain of a child who didn't understand why he wasn't good enough. Why nobody wanted him.

"They were fey," he repeated. "They think differently than we do. Although I've never understood their criteria for who they take and who they don't. I've seen them take some who . . ." He cut himself off.

"Be glad they didn't take you," I told him. "You were better off."

"I doubt that."

"I *don't*. You don't know what it's like, growing up around a bunch of people who treat you like an inferior, who see you only as a commodity to be used, who couldn't give a shit about you unless you're benefitting them in some way. . . ." I stopped, biting my lip. "You'd have tried to fit in, done your best to learn about them, to be one of them. But it would never have worked. You'd have always felt like what you were—an outsider. Because you're not like them. You're not . . . like anybody."

I looked up to see his face swimming in front of me.

"Be glad they didn't take you!"

"Someone in your life was stupid, too," he told me. And then he kissed me.

Chapter Forty-nine

The explosions, flickering light, and gasps and oohs from the crowd, all receded into the background. For a second, there was nothing but sensation: warm hands, stubbled jaw, lips that should have been hard, that were always hard, but were suddenly soft and gentle. And a strange feeling in my stomach, something like when we went over the falls.

I don't know why; it wasn't even a particularly passionate kiss. Wasn't like the one on the riverbank, which had been lusty and amused, a payback for my spying on him coupled with a half-serious offer. Or the one after we got here, which had been all happy and relieved and glad to be alive. I wasn't sure what this one was, except that it was tender and sweet and yet somehow more unsettling than the others, a lot more, and—

I broke away, half panicked for no reason I could name, and a wash of noise and light broke over me.

"Look," Pritkin said softly. "It's *your* big moment."

"What?"

I blinked, and looked around in confusion. And then at the big, empty space, which wasn't empty now. Because it was full of an image of me facing off with the Svarestri leader, a tiny, flimsy figure next to the staunch solidity of the trolls or the jagged electricity of the Svarestri.

With, yes, her mouth still open.

But thankfully, my part was mercifully brief. The story

quickly focused on the real hero: the guy under the seats. And it was hard to argue with that logic, since we'd have all been dead without him.

But I thought it was a little unfair that he wasn't shown with a wide-open mouth, too, considering he'd barely shut up the whole time.

"He was very brave," I said loudly, because several trolls in a nearby tree were watching me. Our hosts seemed to agree. Mugs were hoisted, fists were pumped, and grins were exchanged all around. And then gasps and ooohs and claps of sheer delight, as fire-us started tear-assing around the circle of trees, which was standing in for the massive cave.

"They know they can't hold here forever," Pritkin said, watching them. "The light fey are too powerful, too united. But you take your victories where you can get them."

And, suddenly, I was seeing it through their eyes. Because today *had* been a victory, hadn't it? I'd been focused on surviving for so long that sometimes, even the idea of victory, of *winning this*, seemed like a child's dream.

What did I have that could stand up to the kinds of things we faced? Half the time, I didn't even know what they *were*. I might have my mother's blood, but I wasn't my mother. I might be Agnes' heir, but I wasn't Agnes. I was a second-rate, badly trained, mostly clueless Pythia who had been stumbling my way around for three months now, somehow managing not to get killed.

And kind of expecting not to manage it for much longer.

I'd been so focused on that, that I'd forgotten to look at it the other way, the way I had when facing off against the Svarestri leader. Because I *was* still here, wasn't I? Despite the attempts of everybody from the Silver Circle to the Black, from my own acolytes to myths and monsters and freaking gods, the bumbling, stumbling, you've-got-to-be-kidding-me Pythia had not only survived but had *beaten them*. Had beaten the whole damned bunch of them, and suddenly I was yelling, too. And crawling to the edge of the platform to scream along with everyone else as the great Svarestri warriors fired and fired. But kept. Missing. The target.

"You can't shoot your way out of a paper bag," I yelled,

despite the fact that no one here knew what that was. "A paper *bag*!"

The crowd agreed. They roared as the whole crazy spectacle ended with sparks raining down from above, like falling boulders, and fire-us zooming out of the cliff side and then on a victory lap around the tree line, through scores of reaching hands that didn't care if they got a little singed as long as they were part of it.

And for a second, they were, we all were, all the little guys who never figured in anyone's plans, because we weren't worth worrying about, weren't worth thinking about, except to be stepped on and passed over and killed in someone else's wars. Because the ones with the power thought we didn't matter, that we were only fit for slaves. Yet today we had proved them wrong. Today we had *beaten them*.

The show ended with a firework of sparks that lit up the treetops and caused a few unintended blazes here and there that had to be quickly put out. But nobody seemed to mind. The band had struck up again, and everyone was busy drinking and dancing, and leaping back and forth between platforms to gossip with their friends, and to swing by to give us beer, so much beer that Pritkin was laughing and turning it away before long, before we both ended up drunk out of our minds.

I already felt like that a little, grabbing a new mug somebody had put in my hand, somebody with bright eyes and lots of face fuzz and grinning sharp teeth that didn't look so scary anymore. And watching Pritkin, who was sitting cross-legged, prying the stopper out of a bottle somebody had given him. That held something a lot stronger than beer, by the smell of it.

A *lot* stronger. He offered it to me, but merely the fumes were enough to singe my eyebrows. But the beer was good and the trees were bright with lights and laughter and songs I didn't know but that had my toes tapping anyway.

And then I was being pulled to my feet, beer in hand.

And swung off the platform onto a speeding circle of wood already filled with revelers. That deposited us a heart-stopping moment later onto the next tree in line, amid a crowd of laughing faces and grasping hands. And then we were laughing, too, and running across the boards, ducking and dodging and in some cases leaping over the crowd, to catch another passing swing by the skin of our teeth.

"What are we *doing*?" I asked breathlessly as the trees and the bonfire and the crowd of faces swirled around me.

"Troll dancing!"

"Troll dancing?"

Pritkin nodded, gleeful.

"What the heck is that?"

He didn't answer. But the next second, I was being pulled from our swing onto the edge of a larger one that had been passing us in midair as we whooshed the other way, only now we were going its way, held on by the grasping hands of a lot of grinning people. And then deposited onto a platform a story or so higher up, after a heart-stopping leap—

Into the middle of a line of revelers on a race around and through and in some cases over the trees.

I just went with it. Rope bridges swayed under my feet, platforms appeared in front of me, above me, on every side, giving glimpses through the foliage of parties taking place everywhere. Swings were caught before I even noticed them being there, stairs appeared out of nowhere, barrels and boxes and in some cases reaching hands substituted for stairs when there weren't any, and eating, drinking, singing people kept my mug full as we ran past, doing whatever we were doing.

And then Pritkin stopped and pulled me out of the mad stampede into a corner of a platform.

A blond eyebrow raised. I usually couldn't see his at any distance at all, but the slight tan made them stand out more. Made him look different, strange. Of course, the easy smiles and casual nudity were already doing that. It was like the guy I knew had been replaced by a happy satyr with leaves in his hair and a glint in his eye and wickedly curving lips.

Which lowered to my ear to say: "Race you."

And then he was off before I'd even registered what he'd said, catching a passing swing one-handed and zipping away, almost before I could blink. I looked around, a little frantic, and spied a rope ladder going up. I took it to the next platform built onto the tree, a small one with just a couple very drunk guys sitting on it, swinging their legs over the side.

I ran over and knelt beside them, and pulled some branches out of the way so I could see. I didn't have to ask where Pritkin was headed. There was a tiny platform, like the crow's nest on a ship, near the top of a huge tree, the tallest in the area. He was looking up at it as he hit a platform on the other side of the open space, and then he paused to look back over his shoulder at me. And grin.

And, oh, it was on.

I grabbed the shoulder of the nearest troll. "I have to get to the top." I pointed up. "Fast!"

He appeared to be pretty drunk, but the second, who had been draining his mug, finished a few moments later. And let out an appreciative belch that threatened to rupture an eardrum. And pointed.

I followed the unsteady finger upward, to a rope nailed to the trunk above my head. A rope with a loop on the end, like for the size of one foot. And that was it; no platform, not even one of the individual models like the beer fairy had been using. No handhold other than the rope itself. No anything but a noose for the foot of a crazy person, because that was the only kind who would even consider using such an obvious death trap and—

And he was almost there.

I looked out over the clearing and saw Pritkin rapidly ascending a rope ladder, the only thing left between him and his goal. He had less than a couple stories to go, and if there was another way up, I didn't have time to find it. So, obviously, he was going to win. I should just sit down and drink my beer and wait for him to get back and brag about it, and why was I reaching for the noose?

Which I belatedly realized had been tied down due to tension, and once released—

Was basically a slingshot.

Or maybe a bungee in reverse would be better, because I was jerked up and then across the big open space, before I'd even had a chance to get a good handhold, slipping and floundering and grabbing the rope in front of me with both arms as I tore through a shower of sparks and a haze of wood smoke and ash from the spectacle, which was still fluttering down everywhere, including into my mouth as I kept going up, up, up. And then I caught on something above the crow's nest, something I couldn't see but that must have

been high, so high, because it jerked me up again and over
the edge of the platform and into Pritkin, who was about to
step off the ladder. And sent us both falling and rolling and
grabbing for the rope balustrade on the far edge, which was
the only thing between us and a whole lot of air.

"Are you crazy?" Pritkin was asking, shaking me. "Are
you *crazy*?"

Yes, I thought but couldn't say because I was laughing
too hard. I'd ended up on the bottom, and I stared up into
his face and laughed and laughed, I don't know why. But I
couldn't seem to stop, and I frankly didn't try too hard.

"You *are* crazy," he told me, shaking his head.

"But I won!" I gasped. "I won, I won, I won!"

"By a moment only!"

"It still counts!" I grinned up at him. "So what do I get?"

He didn't answer. But his lips curved in another of those
disturbing smiles, even while his eyes burned. And for a
moment, I swear I felt the earth move.

And then I was sure of it, as the platform began to shake
underneath us. And a cascade of leaves rained down all
around us. And, for a moment, I thought that maybe some
new entertainment was starting up, because trolls really
knew how to party.

But then the tree actually *tilted*, almost sending us the
rest of the way off the side before Pritkin caught me, pushing me up the now-slanted platform. I grabbed the top and
pulled myself the rest of the way up. And looked over and
saw—

Something impossible.

The center of the big open space, which a moment ago
had been filled with revelers, tables groaning with beer, and
a big ox roasting over an even bigger fire, was now a churning, boiling mass of dirt and flaming logs and debris. It
looked like the people had managed to jump free, running
into the forest or swinging up into the trees, but the feast
was gone. And in its place—

"They bypassed the wards by coming up through the
ground," Pritkin said, as silver-haired devils started emerg-
ing from the cauldron of earth. "The dark fey's element is
fire. Their wards are smothered by earth—"

"Stop telling me how they got in and tell me what we do
about it!" I said.

And then I saw her. A small, dark-eyed girl like the one who had waved at me, standing all alone on what had once been a tabletop but was now a piece of flotsam on a dirt sea. The Svarestri weren't targeting her, didn't even seem to notice her, but it wouldn't matter. Because in a minute they'd be targeting everyone, destroying the last of her people over a weapon they probably couldn't even use.

A weapon we had brought here.

"Pritkin—" I said, my lips numb.

But he was no longer there. And a second later, neither was I, as an arm swooped down from above. And pulled me up and over the tilted platform, and onto a joist still clinging to the tree.

I didn't have a chance to ask what was going on, because he was yelling, but not at me.

"Up here!" he bellowed down at the running, screaming, chaotic scene below. The words must have been magically enhanced, because they tore through the forest like he was speaking through a bullhorn, loud and echoing. "Are you deaf? *We're up here!*"

And no, I thought, it didn't look like the Svarestri were deaf. Because he hadn't even finished speaking when they jerked their heads up, all at once, like they were on a string. And focused. And threw.

The huge tree exploded in a fireball that consumed half a dozen others in the vicinity, like Roman candles. But didn't consume us, because we weren't there anymore. A familiar wrenching jerk tore us away right before the bolts landed, sending us sailing through the air back toward the tree I'd come from.

Only we didn't end up there. Because Pritkin grabbed another rope halfway, one I hadn't even seen against the dark sky. And a second after that, some sort of pulley system jerked us up even higher, and then—

"What the hell?" I screamed as we started *flying* forward, skimming through a tunnel of branches barely below the treetops.

"Quick line through forest; it's their escape route," Pritkin said breathlessly. "It'll draw the Svarestri away from the village."

And then what? I thought but didn't say. Because it didn't look like that would be a problem. It didn't look like that would be a problem at all, with trees exploding all around us as bolt after bolt shot up from the forest floor.

They must have been running and firing, and they were running *fast*.

"Hold on!" Pritkin told me as a spear exploded just to our left, scattering burning debris and a firestorm of leaves everywhere.

"I am holding on! Holding on is not the problem!" I shrieked, which probably wasn't helpful, but what would be?

And then I found out.

"*You* had it?" I yelled as a familiar stick appeared out of nowhere.

"I glamouried a substitute on the way here," Pritkin told me a second before he activated the staff. And it may as well have been a booster rocket attached to our asses. Because our flight through the treetops suddenly became an express train straight to hell.

We went hurtling through a storm of burning branches and falling leaves, with the forest turning into one long line of fire as bolts hit above, below, and to the side of us. I couldn't see with a forest's worth of branches slapping me in the face and smoke and shrapnel flying everywhere and the wind strong enough to make my eyes water without all of that. But that was okay; that was all right.

Because the damned Svarestri couldn't see us, either. Not hidden by all the foliage and with a firestorm billowing up behind us. The staff fanned the flames into a whirlwind and then what looked like a solid wall of fire as we left the fey in the freaking *dust*.

There was only one small problem.

Namely the lifeline above our head. Which wasn't a second later, when a burning tree fell in the wrong direction and toppled over right on top of it. And sent us flying again, only this time, headed straight for the forest floor.

Chapter Fifty

We landed in a bunch of prickly bushes I didn't feel because there was something in between us. Something that snapped the next second and sent us tumbling to the ground as whatever shield Pritkin had been able to throw up gave out. We hit hard, because even the bushes were more like little trees around here, and high off the ground. But the next second we were rolling back to our feet, and running.

Because they were coming.

I knew that, even though I couldn't hear anything. Except for the crackling of a not-so-distant fire and the sounds of scurrying animals diving for cover and a random bird overhead, tweeting a confused note. But I knew they were coming anyway, because I knew *them*.

And really wished I didn't.

And then we slammed back into the hollow of a tree, and a hand went over my mouth that I didn't need, because my throat had already closed in terror at the sight of a silver-blond head passing by just outside.

I froze in place, more out of instinct than sense, because he had to see us; he *had* to. We were almost close enough to touch. And then we were close enough, as he backed almost into the tree, to give himself the widest possible field of vision over a deep, dark forest filled with flickering flame light, and then flickering fey light as several more ghostly

Svarestri ran by. And then he was running, too, following them as they moved deeper into the forest, searching for a prey they'd already found but for some reason hadn't noticed.

We didn't move. And a moment later I realized why, as several more Svarestri passed us, silent as ghosts in the night. And then several more. And then what looked like a whole damned battalion.

There hadn't been this many before, had there? I wondered, but not for long. Because the last group had barely passed when we were stumbling out of the tree as well. I turned to Pritkin to ask what the plan was, and then stopped. And suddenly understood why the fey hadn't seen us.

Because, for a second there, neither did I.

I was holding his hand; I could feel it, hard and strong and clenching around my palm. He was there—he was *right there*—but he wasn't. And then he moved, and I saw a faint shimmer against the night, one that ran with reflected flame around the edges, like a man wearing some kind of mirror suit.

Damn, those fey had taught him well, I thought, right before he collapsed.

I grabbed him, but he only went to one knee, and stayed there gasping against my shoulder. A shoulder that I could suddenly see as well as I could see the rest of him, because the reflective camouflage coating was draining away like water. Until it reached our feet and vanished entirely, leaving me looking at a corpse-pale man who was shaking from effort.

And was all too visible even to human eyes.

I glanced around, my heart thudding, but the fey weren't there. They weren't there. But they'd be back and we needed to be gone when they did, but gone where?

We couldn't go back to the village. It looked like we'd managed to draw them away from the trolls, and we couldn't lead them back. Even if the guards could help us, there were children, old people . : . and the Svarestri hadn't seemed to care who they hurt. Their entrance alone might have killed dozens, if these people didn't have reflexes like cats and the paranoia to create a system for flying through the trees.

No, we couldn't go back there. We couldn't go anywhere

and be safe, not in faerie. And anyway, I didn't want us in faerie, I wanted us—

I grabbed Pritkin's shoulder. "You said we could go home."

He nodded, looking a bit dazed still, but less like he was about to fall over.

"Then there's a portal near here. There must be!"

He nodded again. "There's—" He stopped and licked his lips. "There's one just over the border."

"How far?"

"A few minutes, but that—" He broke off. And looked around as if he was trying to see a solution in the trees, one that didn't appear, because when he looked back at me, his eyes were as dark as I'd ever seen them. "That won't help us."

"Why not?" I asked, right before we froze in place, undergrowth covering us more than the night, as several more Svarestri picked their way through the brush, going the other way. They were already starting to circle back around, to establish a perimeter, to begin closing in.

Whatever we were going to do, it had to be now.

"That's where the Svarestri are," he whispered as the fey moved in the opposite direction. "It's one of their portals. And they'll expect us to try for it; there's no alternative at this point—"

"We could hide. What you did before—"

He shook his head, still breathing hard. "I can't keep it up long enough, not this far from water. And there will be guards on the portal who'll sense us if we try to slip past. Even with the spell, we're visible when we move. And we can't fight them using the staff. A hurricane in the midst of a wood would kill us as surely as it would them." He looked around again, but it didn't seem to help any more than it had last time. And then he grabbed me by the upper arms.

"Don't even," I told him, because I knew him, too.

"I can distract them, not for long, but for long enough—"

"Long enough for nothing!"

"You can go back to the village. You're Fey Friend. They'll hide you—"

"I'm not running off and leaving you here!"

"This is my fault! I got you into this—"

"We've had this discussion—"

"Then we'll have it again!"

"You can have it whenever the hell you want," I snapped. "But you'll be talking to hear yourself, because I won't—*damn it*!"

That last was because he'd just gone invisible again, or as close to it as the spell allowed. But I'd halfway expected that, because I knew him, too, and a lot better than the fey. I grabbed him as he rose, sending us both toppling back to the ground. And then latched on as he tried to get away, wrapping myself around something I couldn't see but that couldn't budge me, because he was already close to exhausted and I was hanging on like someone's life depended on it, because it did.

And then he stopped. "Wait! What was that?"

"What was what?" I jerked my head up.

And then had it snapped backward by a certain someone's fist or elbow or possibly heel. How could I tell? I just knew it broke my hold for a second, and a second was all he needed. He scrambled off, invisible in the night except for a few twitching tree limbs, and then not even that, and there was no way, no way in hell I was going to be able to find him, probably not at all and certainly not before he freaking martyred himself.

I sat there for a split second, debating options.

And then I started screaming.

A couple of seconds later I was tackled by a suddenly visible mage who grabbed me and shook me and, okay, this part was like old times. "Are you *insane*?"

"I thought . . . we'd already . . . established that," I said breathlessly as several other cries echoed through the forest.

Pritkin heard them, too, and shook me again. "Don't you *understand*? If we stay, they'll find us; if we run, they'll find us! And I won't be able to protect you when they do, not in faerie, not from this many—"

"I told you, I don't need protection."

"Well, then I hope you can protect me!" he said wildly as footsteps nobody was bothering to conceal thundered our way.

I hope I can, too, I thought.

"Just hide us for as long as you can," I told him. "And get us as close as you can to that portal. I'll do the rest."

And then we were running, full out, my heart pounding a little fast—okay, a lot fast—because this really might be the craziest damned thing I'd ever done. But it's not a gamble when it's the only chance you have, and we *did* have a chance. Not a great one, but right now, I'd take it.

And then we were slamming back against a tree again, as half a dozen Svarestri burst into the open, right in front of us.

And there was no hope they didn't see us this time, no hope at all, because three of them were holding torches. One of which was thrust into our faces a second later. I held my breath, sure I'd just killed us both—

And then I knew I had, because the fey surrounded us. One of them said something, but not to me. And not to Pritkin, either. Or if he was, it was a little weird, because he was looking about six inches above his head.

I'd have thought he was looking at me, because I'd ended up standing on some tree roots when I backed up, trying to merge with the trunk. But no, he was definitely staring at the wood above Pritkin's head. For a second there, I actually thought he was talking to the *tree*, which would have been nuts except *faerie*, but then Pritkin answered him back. And then another fey shoved something in my face.

I shrank back, but he wasn't hitting me with it. Maybe because it wasn't a weapon, I realized. It was . . . a torch.

I stared at it, but that's unquestionably what it was. The blunt end of an unlit torch. Which he seemed to expect me to take.

So I did. And then he lit it from his. It flared to life, and must have illuminated my face, but he still didn't react. And finally, I noticed my reflection in his armor and understood why.

The hand I had wrapped around the torch was mine—small, stubby-fingered, with the chipped remains of the last manicure I'd given myself glittering under the torchlight. But in the armor . . . in the armor, the hand gripping the wooden torch was slim and long-fingered, and as pale as the hair falling over my shoulder. My suddenly very masculine shoulder, which was encased in shiny black armor that ran with the flames I was now holding.

The fey was still looking at me. I nodded, and the masculine face in his armor looked grave and cold, instead of girly and freaked out. He stepped back.

I glanced to my left, where Pritkin still looked like a soot-covered woodland sprite to me, or Tarzan after a really bad day. But he was listening and nodding and then saying something to the leader of the fey cohort, who said something in reply as another dozen ghostly figures joined us. The translation spell was having real trouble with the language, but I guess Pritkin wasn't, because the leader started snapping orders, and small groups started breaking off, heading in all directions. And then we were, too, taking our torch and moving off to search for ourselves.

"This way," Pritkin hissed, still furious, like the fingers biting into my arm hadn't already told me that.

I didn't care. I so very much didn't care that it was all I could do to stop an extremely stupid grin from taking over my face, which probably looked really creepy on a fey and also didn't make sense because we weren't out of it yet. But I was biting my lip anyway, and shaking from relief, and ducking my head because inappropriate, Cassie, seriously inappropriate. But some part of me had finally had enough and wasn't listening.

Fortunately, no one was near enough to us to notice, and I managed to have today's nervous breakdown quietly.

It didn't last long anyway, not after I looked up and saw what was ahead.

Pritkin jerked me into the shadow of a stone gateway, which was pretty much all that remained of whatever wall it had been part of. It was dark red and gleamed in the light the torch was shedding, before I half buried the thing in the dirt. And then stayed down on my haunches, burning pitch in my nostrils and the gate of hell staring me in the face.

And that's exactly what it looked like: a big, red, swirly portal framed by the arch, and maybe half a football field away. And Pritkin had been right—it was guarded by a dozen Svarestri. Or maybe more for all I knew, since I couldn't see all of it, could only see about a third of it, since there were half walls and tumbled columns and decorative pieces of stone in the way. But no greenery. It was like the forest didn't like this place, either, because no vines were eating into the stones, and no undergrowth disturbed the flat red clay under our feet.

I glanced behind me, and the soil of the forest was dark, either rich brown or black—I couldn't tell in the light. But not rusty, not red. This stuff looked like somebody had lifted it straight out of Red Rock Canyon in Vegas.

But I didn't get an explanation. I didn't get anything at all, maybe because we were too close to risk talking. Or maybe because of Pritkin's state of mind, which clearly wasn't good. He was gripping the staff in one hand, tight enough to turn his hand white, which matched his pale, strained face.

The Pritkin of my day might enjoy this sort of thing, but I didn't think this one did.

And that was before the damn portal activated, with a sound like nails on a chalkboard, and a line of black-clad warriors started spilling out. And, okay, wherever that portal went, I didn't want to go. "I thought you said there was a portal *to earth*," I whispered.

Pritkin still didn't say anything, but he nodded. At something I couldn't see because the side of the arch was in the way. I went to my hands and knees and crawled forward, and sure enough, there was another portal, in a clear, light blue color that would have been soothing.

Except that that was where all those new soldiers were going.

"That goes to *earth*?" I twisted my head around to ask.

Pritkin nodded grimly and pulled me back.

"But what are the Svarestri doing on—"

"I don't know. This isn't supposed to be here."

"What isn't?"

"*Any* of it. Other than the portal—the one to earth. It's always been here, as far as I know. But the other, this whole thing"—he gestured around at the patch of livid red ruins—"this wasn't here a few months ago."

"Then why is it here now?"

I didn't get a reply. Because the fey soldier Pritkin had been talking to earlier took that moment to burst out of the trees, moving almost too fast to see. But not fast enough to outrun the spear that took him full in the back.

His armor exploded along with it, shattering and all but leaping off his body but leaving him relatively unscathed. Unlike the whirlwind that caught him a second later. He started yelling something, and then screaming it, something I couldn't understand but didn't really need to. Because a moment after it picked him up, the wind twisted him in ways a body wasn't supposed to bend, and then *ripped him apart*, sending pieces flying in all directions, including ours.

One landed in the dust outside the archway, but I didn't look at it. I was looking at Pritkin, who was staring at the remains with the shell-shocked look of a guy who hasn't seen that sort of thing before and would be okay with not seeing it again. And then he was grabbing me and I was tackling him back, because no, no, no, the forest was not where we needed to go.

"The portal," I gasped, because he wasn't underestimating me this time, and tired or not, he was stronger.

"We're never going to get to the portal!" he yelled, not bothering to lower his voice this time, because the wind was already so wild, it didn't matter anymore.

And then neither did Pritkin's escape attempt, which was suddenly moot in a major way. The whirlwind that had destroyed the fey had spread out, ripping through the forest as it began circling the old stones like a cyclone and moving inward. It was like being at the eye of a hurricane, or more likely, the center of a noose that was quickly tightening.

Somebody else didn't like the Svarestri going to earth, and they weren't playing.

I tightened my grip on Pritkin, who had jerked us back inside the arch, the only cover available. But it wouldn't make a difference in a minute, and his expression said he knew that. He was staring in disbelief at the wind, which was already uprooting huge trees and turning them into flying shrapnel, which was sending the outlying boulders bouncing around like pebbles, which was turning the whole perimeter of the ruins into a whirl of black and green and, increasingly, red.

"Hold on!" I said as dust rose up like clouds to choke us.

Pritkin didn't reply. I doubted he heard. I couldn't even hear myself. But I could feel my power reaching for me, as desperate to touch me as I was to go to it, but not quite able to make it. But that didn't matter as much anymore, because I knew the score now. I knew that, in faerie, I couldn't touch it, but I could ride the ripples caused by trying.

I just didn't know if I could do it fast enough and take someone else along for the ride.

But it was the only shot we had, and the one I'd been playing for ever since I made that scream, because I wasn't leaving him behind. I wasn't, even though my new trick didn't seem to be working this time, the waves it generated not strong enough to lift two. But it was *going* to lift two; it was going to if it ripped me apart in the process, and it kind of felt like it might. The strain had me gasping and panting and then screaming in pain, to the point that I barely understood that we were moving again, that Pritkin was dragging me even as I did my best to drag him. Only he was taking me somewhere physically and I was trying to access the metaphysical tide that wouldn't . . . freaking . . . *come—*

And there were Svarestri now, running all around us. I noticed them the way you'd notice a nurse entering a room where you're being operated on without anesthetic. They didn't matter . . . didn't matter. And I guess they felt the same way about us, maybe because the storm was hard on our heels.

But it didn't matter, either. Nothing did except for that portal, but if it was where Pritkin was trying to take us, it wasn't going to work. Because the Svarestri had the same idea and were crowding against it, a mass of formerly rigidly controlled creatures who had suddenly become a thrashing, tearing, yelling mob. And we weren't getting past that; we just weren't.

And we didn't.

We went through it.

A second before the storm ripped us to pieces, another sort of storm grabbed us. And I wasn't sure it was much of an improvement, because my power had ceased to be ripples in a swimming pool and was now lashing at the barrier between worlds like twenty-foot seas in a typhoon in response to my increasingly frantic calls. I didn't know if I could control it anymore, was pretty sure I couldn't, in fact, but it was too late because it *had* us—

And then I lost it.

I lost it, and we fell to the ground.

Or maybe *into* the ground would be more like it, as a tsunami of dirt was suddenly thrown up like a wall, all on one side. I looked around desperately for the portal but didn't see it. I suddenly couldn't see anything except another wall of dirt erupting from the ground, like a mountain being created out of nothing.

Only it wasn't nothing. It was the debris from a crack in the earth big enough to drive a car through. It was trying to swallow us while another mountain was trying to bury us and we were sliding and climbing and running and falling and getting back up, because the crack was gaining.

Someone screamed as he was swallowed, just behind us. Someone else went flying through the air as a cyclone grabbed him. And the wind was roaring and dust was flying and I couldn't see anything, not anything—until another dirt wall shot up, blocking our path. Or it would have, except we were already on top of the ground it seemed to want, and we shot up along with it.

For a second, we were flying, the sheer force of the swell flinging us up and then over before we hit back down, hard enough to leave me rattled. But Pritkin pulled me to my feet and we ran some more, blind and choking and with no idea, no idea—

Until we suddenly cleared the cloud and I saw it, out of whatever was left of my vision. I smeared a mountain's worth of dirt across my face to stare at it in disbelief, before Pritkin all but threw me down the grassy incline and into—

Water.

Sweet, cool, familiar.

Because there was the bank and there were the trees and there was the goddamned *mill* I'd honestly never thought to see again and—

And it had worked.

It had worked!

We were back.

Chapter Fifty-one

The water ran over my filthy hands, like something out of a dream, clear and cold and almost miraculous after the pound of dirt I'd just swallowed. I just sat there a minute, listening to Armageddon taking place somewhere in the distance and looking at Pritkin looking back at me. He'd gone from forest sprite to commando: blackened face and body and hair slick with the mud we'd made when our dirt-covered selves hit the water.

I probably wasn't any better, and my shoulder hurt like hell again, probably because I'd hit it a few dozen times. And it felt like my left ankle might be sprained or possibly broken. And my lip was swelling up, like I must have bitten it at some point, and it was hard to breathe.

And I didn't care.

I grinned tremulously at Pritkin and got a flash of white teeth in return.

The moon was full and visible through a haze of dust, filtering down on an incongruously peaceful scene. We couldn't see over the high bank, but it sounded like the battle was trending away from us. And the water felt like balm on my bruised body. And I still couldn't quite believe it.

It seemed like a miracle.

Well, sort of a miracle, I thought, as a Svarestri leapt down the bank at us.

And, before I could blink, was torn off his trajectory and

slammed into a nearby tree, still burning from the bolt through his heart.

But I didn't let out the breath I'd been holding, because someone else was there a second later. Someone new. Someone with golden armor incised with designs I didn't know, and golden hair, and a face more human than the other fey's, so human it might have fooled me except for an otherworldly beauty so great that even here, even now, it made me stop and stare in wonder.

Sharp green eyes played over the riverbank where Pritkin and I lay, motionless. Pritkin's hand clenched on my thigh, but I didn't need it. My hand had been outstretched on the bank in front of me. Had been, but wasn't now, because now we were in water and back on earth and the illusion Pritkin had crafted was so pure, so perfect, that for a second even I didn't believe we were there.

I guess the fey must have agreed, because the next time I blinked, he was gone.

And I collapsed against the bank, gasping for breath.

"Sky Lord," Pritkin whispered, almost inaudible despite being right in front of me.

"No shit!" I whispered back, when I could talk.

And then, slowly, slowly, we crawled to the top of the muddy incline. And peered over the top. And saw . . .

A battle like nothing I'd ever witnessed or dared imagine.

What looked like entire mountains were being ripped out of place and thrown at beings who threw them back, aided by cyclones of power that tore at my hair and threatened to send my body flying, despite the fact that the main battle had to be half a mile away now. Lightning tore at the sky, and then through a column of Svarestri, crackling over armor that, for once, mostly held. Except for one guy at the end, who must have already had his weakened, and who was knocked back twenty feet or more.

But the others kept fighting, and a column of golden warriors suddenly disappeared into a fissure in the earth, which immediately closed over them. But they burst back out of it a moment later, not all of them but most of them, in the middle of miniature cyclones that allowed them to tear through the air and flank the Svarestri. Who were slowly being beaten back, toward the portal hovering in the air where there had once been a hill and was now a blown-out cavern.

The warrior we'd seen a moment before with the fancy armor seemed to be directing the fight, but he kept looking back this way, as if something puzzled him. As if he couldn't see us but nonetheless knew we were there. Pritkin must have gotten the same idea, because his hand tightened on my shoulder, and we started slowly backing down the slope—

Started but stopped, in my case. Because the next second, a boulder the size of a house bounced across the landscape, having been thrown from the fight. And right in front of it, screaming his head off, was—

"Rosier!"

I yelled it before I thought, relief springing the word to my lips before I could clamp them shut, but it shouldn't have mattered. Not with the symphony of destruction taking place all around. But despite the fact that the wind tore my voice away, three heads swiveled instantly toward mine. Rosier abruptly changed course, running hell-bent for leather in our direction; the golden fey, who had just turned to look at the combat again, jerked his head back around; and a woman I hadn't seen, because she was right behind Rosier, lifted her chin and looked straight at me.

And then *was* right at me, pointing finger and flashing eyes and that damned cherry-covered parasol and all—

And then three things happened at once: the golden fey threw an energy bolt, Cherries threw a time spell, and I threw myself at Pritkin and shifted. But not far. Because we had to find Rosier, and where the *hell* was—

Shit!

I shifted again as another bolt slammed down where we'd been standing. And then another, and another, like the damned fey could *feel* us or something. We'd no more materialized somewhere than he swiveled and threw again, deadly accurate and so fast that I was dizzy in seconds, just trying not to die. And then—

And then I wasn't fast enough.

We slammed into existence on the hillside right next to the mill, because, Rosier or not, I was trying to get farther from beautiful death over there. But whether through chance or some kind of weird fey ability I didn't know about, a bolt was there almost before we were. I had a chance to see it flash, to feel the heat, to think—*no*.

And then to think, *oh, crap*, because the bolt just stopped, frozen in the air, inches away from my eyes. Which would have made me fairly close to ecstatic, except that I hadn't done it. And the person who had was just behind it.

"I—I can explain—" I told Cherries, whose face was currently almost as red as her favorite fruit.

"Explain?"

Okay, maybe not. And then a time wave tore through the air, which didn't make much sense, because if she wanted me dead, she'd just had a perfect opportunity. But I shifted anyway, before it could hit, and a second later we rematerialized on the roof. Because I needed a goddamned vantage point.

"Who are you?" Pritkin asked, voice full of wonder. *"What* are you?"

"Fucked, if you don't shut up!" I said shrilly.

He shut up. But his eyes were wide and he was drinking in the whole scene, from the battle still raging in the background, to the half dozen girls in white fanning out in all directions, to the half-naked demon lord headed this way, until he saw the girls. And abruptly turned and pelted the other way instead, flashing pasty buns as his speed kicked up his shirttail behind him.

And the golden fey, who was suddenly right on top of us.

The only hint I had was a flash of gold to the left, but my nerves were so keyed up that it might as well have been a neon sign. I rolled and threw at the same time, and froze one of those damned energy bolts three inches from my chest. And then tried to scramble out from under it and almost fell off the roof.

Pritkin caught me, his mouth hanging open in shock, and God, this wasn't the plan, this wasn't the plan, this wasn't the goddamned plan! It also wasn't the sort of thing you just forgot, sixth century or no. But dealing with what Pritkin had seen was going to have to wait because I was having a crisis and couldn't seem to breathe, and then I was gasping and choking, and scrambling back, away from the damned flaming spear and the bastard who had thrown it and even Pritkin, because fuck this! Fuck *all* this!

I grabbed the decorative curlicue on the front of the roof, and held on, my chest heaving. I honestly thought I might be having a heart attack.

Pritkin reached out for me again, after a moment, but I batted his hand away. Which was stupid; we might have to shift again, assuming I was able, which frankly didn't feel too likely right now, but sooner or later somebody was going to look up. The only reason we hadn't been found already was the amount of magic flying around, which was raising my hair like electricity and shaking the air around me and making my little contribution seem almost irrelevant.

Or maybe I was the one that was shaking. I couldn't tell; I couldn't tell. Reaction was setting in, and no, no, no, Cassie! You don't get to do this yet. You get to do this *after*. But my nerves had decided to take a vacation early and, oh yeah, now I was shaking. And crying, not for any reason, not because I was hurt—well, that badly—but because I had to do something and that was what my body seemed to have decided on.

I bit my lip and looked away from Pritkin, who seemed kind of at a loss, which, yeah. And stared around, tears making tracks in the dirt on my face and splashing onto the dirt on my hands and God, now my nose was running. I put up a hand to wipe away that indignity at least, all while telling myself to think, to think, to get it together and *think*—

And then I stopped.

Not frozen, not spelled, but feeling sort of like it.

Because the golden fey was watching me.

I stared at him, and he stared back. I thought at first that it was just a trick of the light, the golden glow of his frozen spear gleaming in his eyes. But no. The pupils expanded as he looked at me, and then *they slid over to the side* and looked at Pritkin.

And no. No, he didn't get to *do* that. I'd just frozen him, and in my panic I'd thrown everything I had, which was a lot, which was a whole lot, because I was still hyped up on an entire bottle of the world's rarest potion. That was why I was sitting here shaking with fear and exhaustion and bawling like a baby. It was the reaction that usually came with freezing time, times a couple of exponential points because of *my life*. But while that little trick might wipe me out, it does something else, too, and *stops goddamned time*.

So how was he looking at me?

And then he wasn't just looking.

A finger twitched.

I stared at it, trying to convince myself that I was seeing things, that it was a trick of the light being reflected off the burning trees.

But then it happened again.

"G-give him the staff," I told Pritkin.

But Pritkin was shaking his head.

"Give him the damned staff!"

"I can't."

"Just *give* it to him, and maybe this will all be over. Maybe . . . he'll let us go?"

I made the last into a question, and looked back at the fey, who was definitely following this. But he couldn't move, not yet, so I didn't know if he agreed or was just waiting for another chance to kill us. But I knew how I voted, 'cause all the light fey seemed to be crazy, murdering bastards, but it was still worth a shot.

Only Pritkin didn't seem to think so.

"I can't," he repeated, his fingers closing on it.

"Would you like to explain why?" I asked pleasantly.

Pritkin swallowed. But his eyes were steady on mine when he replied, "The Svarestri were taking this to court. They must have been. There's no other reason they would have been on that road."

"So?"

"So I have to find out why—"

"No, you don't," I said, still pleasantly. And that was despite the fact that I hadn't been hallucinating. The fey's finger had just twitched again.

But my nerves did not appear to be responding this time. I wasn't even crying anymore. I thought maybe they'd burned out.

Which, all things considered, would be kind of a plus right now.

"The Svarestri were taking it to court, the *king's court*," Pritkin repeated, like maybe I hadn't heard him the first time.

"I know that."

"Then you know they must have had a plan for it. I have to find out what that plan was—"

"So find out without the staff."

"I need the staff to draw out whoever they were planning to meet. Nobody is going to pay any attention to me without it. I won't be able to find out anything—"

"You'll live!"

"But the king may not! We've discussed this. What if they plan to hurt him—"

"Hurt him?" I asked, and, okay, maybe my nerves weren't as dead as I'd thought. "Hurt him?" I threw out a hand in the direction of the freaking clash of the Titans over there. "Do they look like they need any *help*?"

"Listen to me," he said urgently, taking my hand. "That just shows how much of a risk they took stealing the staff in the first place. They didn't do it on a whim; they *need* it for something—"

"And you don't think that the . . . these other guys . . ." I waved a hand at golden boy, because I couldn't remember all these names and alternate names and damn the fey and all their freaking names!

"The Blarestri," Pritkin said helpfully. "Also known as the Blue Fey, or the Sky Lords, or the—"

"Whatever! You don't think these Sky Lords are able to find out what their counterparts are up to? They're all fey—let them sort it out!"

"If they were in faerie, I would," Pritkin said earnestly. "But they don't know earth well; even the Green Fey are rarely here and don't know as much about us as they think they do. But I *know* the court, and most people in it; I have connections they don't have, an identity already established that will allow me to move about freely, to ask questions without inciting suspicion." He glanced at the frozen fey, and why did I get the feeling he wasn't just talking to me anymore? "I can find out what the Svarestri wanted with this, and then convey the information to the Sky Lords, who can deal with it."

"And with you!" I said, openly glaring at the fey. "You've seen what they're like—all your life. They left you to rot before; do you really think they'll hesitate to kill you now? If you don't find out anything, they'll kill you out of anger, and if you do, they'll kill you to shut you up, and either way they'll kill you! You can't *trust* them—"

"I don't believe that," Pritkin said, also looking at the fey. "I don't believe they're all the same."

"And if you're wrong? You're gambling with your *life*—"

"—which is my choice, isn't it?" he asked, his voice soft. But I'd heard that tone before, and I'd seen the set of that jaw. Like a hundred times or more, because that was his do-it-or-die face, and God, I didn't need that face right now!

"Give it to me!" I said, suddenly grabbing for it, only to have him scramble back out of reach. And damn it, we didn't have time for this!

"You can come to court with me—" Pritkin offered as I lunged for him again. And missed, because he wasn't encumbered by fifty pounds of freaking wool!

"I don't want to go with you," I told him, hiking up my damn skirts. "I want you to come with *me*—"

"I can't do that right now—"

"Yes, you can!" I grabbed for him again.

"You're not listening to me—"

"I'm listening!" I finally managed to grab the staff and held on. "But there are things"—he twisted it away—"you don't understand"—and jumped back—"that I need to talk to you—damn it!"—because the infuriating man was like quicksilver. "Would you hold still a minute?"

"Will you *listen*?"

"*I am listening!*" And then I lunged.

Which might have worked out okay, because Pritkin was backed against the edge of the roof and had nowhere to go. Although, knowing him, he might have figured something out. Only he didn't have to.

Because the fey did.

The damned creature moved with liquid speed, tripping me up and sending me thudding into the roof thatch. And then *through* it, as the rotten stuff gave way under my weight, plunging a leg through. And then my whole body, as Pritkin tried to grab me and the fey tried to kick me, or, no, I guess he was kicking at the roof.

Which promptly fell the rest of the way in.

Which was bad enough already, but then the damned spear fell, too. And I thought mills were supposed to contain grain, not TNT. But we were halfway to the floor when the whole place *ignited* in billowing red-gold clouds that burst into being everywhere, like the very air was on fire.

And, just as suddenly, froze.

I had been falling butt first, so all I could see was Pritkin's unmoving, desperate face staring down at me, hand still extended, debris from the roof that was in the process of flaring up, and fiery sparks everywhere, like glowing rain.

That began to move, sluggishly, in the air around me as I fought and twisted.

"The grain's on fire," someone said. "Get out!"

"No! She's fighting it off. Grab her!"

But whoever was talking wasn't fast enough. I tore myself out of the spell a second later, landing in a panting heap on some sacks of grain, before rolling off onto a dirt floor. Only to be almost incinerated when the air around me went up like a firestorm.

It was full of floating yellowish dust, the grain in question, I guessed, which ignited like gunpowder. But it didn't burn me, because I'd never stopped moving. I rolled out of the way just as a new time spell boiled through the old one, taking another section of the room back into real time. And sending it up in a boiling column of fire.

And then another one, and another, flared to life all around me, as I ducked and dodged and rolled and looked frantically around for Rosier. And found three different Pythias instead, the power emanating off them almost blinding. There was Gertie, the old one from Amsterdam she'd called Lydia, still all in black, and some young girl in elaborate robes.

And then I spied Rosier, over by the door, frozen among half a dozen acolytes, still staring upward at the Cassie-shaped void in the sparks. The one right beside a stack of grain bags piled up like a pyramid—

Or a staircase.

I grabbed an almost-empty flour bag off the floor and slung it through the mass of sparks in front of me, sending a wave of them flowing at the crowd by the door. And while they were blinded, I ran, weaving through the boiling columns of air, scrambling up the makeshift stairs, my hand reaching out because I had to touch Pritkin to shift him out of someone else's spell. But it wouldn't take much, just a single touch, and then to Rosier, and then we'd be gone and let's see them catch me!

But I'd forgotten about the golden fey, who had remained in place, as still as a statue. But who had apparently shrugged off Gertie's spell as easily as he had mine. And whose hand now moved in a gesture so small I'm not sure the others even saw it, but that sent me flying—

Straight into a time portal that the old Pythia had just opened up.

It was the same kind that she'd used on me in Amsterdam, which had sent me back to my own time before I had a chance to realize what was happening. But I had more experience now, and a whole bottle of Tears under my belt, and this time I fought it, tearing and clawing in front of a swirling black maw that jerked and pulled and twisted, leaving me caught between earth and sky, between two different times, between hope and utter failure.

"Demmed girl's stubborn," she told Gertie, who narrowed blue eyes at me.

"Please," I begged her. "I'm not trying to hurt anything! I'm just trying to remove a spell—"

"There's no spell here that concerns you, girl."

The young Pythia stepped forward, gold-chased robes sending a swirl of sparks into the air. And threw out a hand glinting with jewels. And, immediately, the pull from behind became exponentially stronger.

"No! You don't understand!" I panted, trying to concentrate while putting everything I had into staying put. "I don't want to change time—"

"Then you should be glad to know that you haven't," Gertie told me. "You may have led those fey on a merry chase, but in the end, you only brought them back to where they would have been in any case. Those you killed would have died in the battle anyway."

Lydia nodded. "Time's not so easily undone as all that."

"I don't want to undo it! I want to save him!" I tried to look up at Pritkin, but I couldn't see him anymore. The portal was pulling me back, and all I saw was darkness.

"Save yourself," Gertie advised. "Let go. Or let it rip you apart."

"No—please—just listen for *a minute*—"

But Gertie wasn't listening. Gertie was flinging out a hand.

"Please! I don't have any more Tears! *I can't come back again!"*

"Good," she told me, and threw.

And the next thing I knew, I was hitting the polished floor of my suite's atrium, feeling like I'd been shot out of a cannon. And skidding and rolling and slamming into the wall as if I had been, too. And then landing on the floor, where I sprawled in a battered heap, dazed and disbelieving.

But not as much as when I looked up.

And saw the blond acolyte step out of nothing to stare at me, burn marks still fresh on her skin.

"Let's try this again," she told me viciously, and stabbed something into my thigh.

I had a second to hear the wards blare a warning, to see shadows coalesce in the corners of the room, to see them descend on her and to see her fall, screaming and clutching her head. And then the room tilted and reeled and darkness closed over my own head, so absolute it felt like there would never be light again.

Chapter Fifty-two

"Cassie! Cassie!"

Someone was yelling my name, and someone else was shaking me. Or maybe they were one and the same. I couldn't tell. I also couldn't seem to move, except very sluggishly. And when I did, I *hurt*, all over.

My joints felt like rust had formed around them, old, thick, caked-on rust. My head was pounding, like a happy lunatic with a jackhammer had gotten in there and decided to redecorate. Yet it was managing to whirl around at the same time, despite the fact that I was already lying down with my eyes closed. How do you pass out lying down? I wondered. How do you—

Somebody slapped me.

And damn, that was getting old.

I opened my eyes to see a frantic face hovering over mine that was nothing but a blur, because my eyes weren't working right, either. But I didn't need them. A mixture of perfume and hair oil and cookies hit me before Tami's frantic face swam into view.

Along with the living room, because I was lying on the sofa, in the midst of utter chaos. There were mages everywhere, dark-coated, heavy-booted guys with grim faces, busy freaking out the crying children they had by the hand or in their arms. Jonas was by the door, arguing with a red-faced Rhea; the blond acolyte was in a chair, guarded by no fewer than four mages, and my bodyguards—

Were everywhere.

But not facing off with the Circle. It was a fact that should have made me happy, except that they weren't doing anything else, either. Including standing.

Marco was slumped on the couch beside me. I was having trouble seeing properly, but even I could tell he wasn't moving, wasn't blinking. His eyes were open, but, like mine a minute ago, they weren't focused on anything.

I struggled over and slid a hand inside the latest terrible golf shirt. But while his skin was warm under its coating of fur, there was no heartbeat, no movement of the chest up and down, no anything. And that . . .

Didn't happen.

Vamps didn't go unconscious like humans. They were up and mobile, or they were in a healing trance, or they were dead. Those were pretty much the only options. And yet Marco wasn't up, and he wasn't dead. And if this was a healing trance, whatever had hit him must have hit everyone else, too, because the others weren't any better off.

Rico was slumped in a corner, like a lifeless doll. Roy was lying in a heap by the bar, highball glass still in hand. Half a dozen others were scattered around, looking like they had simply dropped on the spot, or been towed out of the way of traffic and left sprawled in odd positions, like puppets with their strings cut.

"What happened?" I asked, hearing my own voice slur in my ears.

"What didn't happen?" Tami said frantically. "You were out for hours! You got drugged, and the vamps fell out—everyone except for Fred, who ran off like a scared chicken! And Jonas showed up and then he called for his men and—"

"Wait," I told her, trying to keep up while my vision pulsed in and out.

But my life doesn't wait.

"Lady!" Rhea had noticed me awake and strode over, Jonas behind her.

"What's he doing here?" I asked groggily. Because I might be out of it, but I was pretty sure he was not on the guest list.

"I let him in!" she told me, looking no better off than Tami. "I'm sorry, but you were unconscious and Lizzie was here and I didn't know what else to do—"

"Lizzie?"

"She attacked you," Rhea said, looking at the blond acolyte with hatred. "She drugged you and the demons attacked her and I managed to subdue—"

"You managed. What happened to the vampires?" I asked, looking at Marco again. I'd never realized how big of a presence he was, even when he wasn't doing anything. He was the kind of guy you *felt* in a room.

Except for now.

Now I didn't feel anything.

"We don't know," Tami said. "They just fell over, all at the same time, and we couldn't wake them—"

"All at the same time?" I looked at Jonas.

"My people had nothing to do with this," he told me. "I arrived to speak with you—alone—and found your so-called defenders unconscious on the floor. I called for backup, as you and your court had no protection. As I have told you before, you cannot rely—"

He kept talking, but I wasn't listening. It was easy with the roaring in my ears now sounding like an ocean. Or maybe that was my heartbeat. I just know I could barely hear over it as I grabbed the house phone. "Casanova," I told it.

"He's unavailable right now; may I give him a—"

"Put him on the damned phone, David," I said, because I recognized the voice of one of the front desk guys I used to work with, back when Casanova was making me earn my keep. "It's Cassie."

"Oh, sorry." He swallowed. "I didn't check. I'm a little flustered—"

"What happened?"

"What happened is the boss just keeled over this afternoon, along with half the damned security force! First he's gone for two days, with no warning, and the next he—"

"Were they all vamps?"

"What?"

"The ones who fell out! Were they all vampires?"

"Yes—"

"Of Casanova's line?"

"Um, I think so? I can go check—"

"Never mind," I managed to get out, before I hung up.

"What is it?" Rhea asked, seeing my face.

"Mircea."

I put through a call to his private line, but nothing. I called the number for his court in Washington. Same thing. I stood up and almost fell over, but managed to fall in the direction of the chair where the blonde was sitting, smirking at me. Smirking at me while Mircea lay dying somewhere, either dead or damned close, because that was the only way—the *only* way—this made sense.

A master could pull power from his family in extremis. But first-level masters almost six hundred years old didn't need to do that anymore. First-level masters, even those considerably weaker than Mircea, could power a *city*. So if Mircea had needed to borrow this much power, and with no warning—

My heart twisted, and my breathing stopped. For an instant. Until I grabbed the blonde by the front of her T-shirt. *"What did you do?"*

The smirking intensified.

"We'll see to her interrogation, Cassie," Jonas told me. "But in the meantime—"

The blonde burst out laughing.

For a moment, we just looked at each other.

Why didn't I think we had a meantime?

"Apple," I told Rhea, who ran to get one.

"She will talk, I assure you," Jonas told me.

"I know she will," I said, my eyes not leaving the girl. I don't know what was on my face, but hers was smug, self-assured, cocky. She didn't look like someone who was surrounded by war mages and an angry Pythia. She looked like someone who has already won, and is just waiting for everyone else to catch up.

"Apple," Rhea said breathlessly, handing me one.

"What did you do?" I asked the girl again, bending over her chair.

"If you're trying to threaten me, good luck," she said. "That dart would have taken down a bull elephant. You're out of power. And by the time you get it back . . ." She trailed off, smiling.

I held out the apple, flat on my palm. "One minute."

"A minute is all you have left," she snapped. "In a minute, the master will be back and you'll be dead—"

"But you won't be," I promised. "You will be very much alive."

"You're damned right I—"

She stopped, somewhat abruptly. Because the apple had suddenly blushed a darker shade of red. It took a lot out of me; it took too much. A full bottle of Tears was warring with a hit of knockout drug and a lot of running around. The net result was edging up on zero.

But I had to do this.

I had to know what they'd done.

"I'm not going to kill you," I told her steadily as the fruit began to change color on one side. "I'm going to age you." The red started to brown in spots, and the plump flesh to move oddly, sickeningly, blowing up slightly before starting to deflate. "To the point that no one will be able to tell that you used to have pretty blond hair and smooth skin."

The apple suddenly imploded, one half sinking in, almost to the core, while gray splotches joined the brown. She recoiled, but there was nowhere to go, with the Circle's mages hemming her in on all sides. And me in front, keeping the decaying thing in her face.

"Old people earn their wrinkles," I told her. "They buy them with a lifetime of joy and sadness, triumph and pain. With the sight of their lover's face on their wedding day, the sound of their baby's first cry, the feel of their child's hand in theirs. But *not you*."

And then it was all gray, in between one blink and the next, the once shiny surface of a formerly perfect fruit now fuzzy with mold and leaking nasty-smelling juices onto her nice blue blouse.

"You'll just be old," I said as she stared at the rotting thing. "In the blink of an eye. Too old to be Pythia, if that's what he promised you. Too old to enjoy the triumph your friends will be celebrating. Too old to do anything or be anything or have anything or experience anything. Ever. Again."

Wide, frightened blue eyes met mine, and then they narrowed and her chin raised. "My friends will save me," she spat. "Once the master returns—"

"Your friends? You mean the other acolytes? The ones

in competition with you for his affections? *The ones who sent you here?* Those friends?"

She stared at me, and then looked at Jonas, standing behind me. "You're bluffing. The Circle doesn't allow—"

"But you're not dealing with the Circle, are you?" I asked. "You're not even dealing with a proper Pythia. You're dealing with someone raised by homicidal vampires, and *I don't bluff.*"

"And I'm afraid," Jonas told her mildly, "that the Circle tends to be . . . pragmatic . . . in these cases."

The apple was no longer leaking. It was a piece of desiccated, withered flesh, clinging to a rotten core. I let it fall into her lap. "Once last chance. What are they doing?"

She swallowed. And then tossed her head defiantly. "It doesn't matter. You're too late to stop it—"

"To stop. What?"

"We're attacking the vampire's stronghold in New York. With a whole army!"

"Upstate," Jonas murmured. "The consul's home."

"Why?" I asked her.

"To keep them from invading faerie—they're the only ones who can. They were stupid enough to assemble their leaders all in one place, for some kind of conference. It'll be the last time they—"

"What about Mircea?"

Her lips curled. "He's the one keeping the vampire alliance together, and you know how they are. One Senate won't dare invade if it leaves them vulnerable to attack from the others back home. Break the alliance and no more invasion. Plus our vampire contact didn't want to go up against him, and decided to take him out before—"

"Take him out." I felt the room spin again. "Then he's dead."

She shrugged. "If he's not, he soon will be. Along with the rest when we get the Tears—"

"Tears? You're after . . ." I broke off.

Because of course they were.

Of *course* they were.

"Our contact told us they have two whole bottles," she confirmed. "More than enough for what we need. But he wouldn't get them for us. Said it was too risky. Said they were in some kind of command center with a ton of wards—"

"I know where they are," I said, my lips numb.

"—and that we'd have to wait until the attack started."

"Just like at Lady Phemonoe's," Rhea said, furious. "When you plundered her."

The blonde moved her eyes to Rhea. "You were there to do the same thing. We both want the power; we're just taking different paths to get it. Those of us with any sense chose to align with the *god*. You chose the vampire's whore. So don't tell me—"

Tami decked her.

The girl's head rocked back, the blow hard enough to send her slamming into the mage behind her. Who didn't so much as flinch. But he did catch her when she slumped over and tried to slide off the chair.

I looked at Tami.

"I'm sorry!" she yelled. "I'm out of control! I'm hitting everybody—"

"If you hadn't, I would have," Rhea said, low and vicious.

"But she might have told us more—"

"She told us enough," I said, and started for the hall.

Only to have Jonas grab my arm. "Where are you going?"

"Where do you think?"

"No. I'll have my men—"

"Do what? Drive up to Washington State? Take a ley line?" I shrugged off his grip. "That might get you there in an hour or two, but this is happening *now*, Jonas!"

I made it to the bedroom before he grabbed me again.

"I have men on the ground," he told me quickly. "We always have people watching the Senate. I'll send them—"

"Then send them! And while you're at it, send the demons." I looked around, but if my former protectors were still here, I couldn't see them. And I couldn't command them. "Tell Adra—"

"We don't need the demons," Jonas said. "My people—"

"Can't handle those girls! Not if they get the Tears first, and maybe not if they don't. The demons probably can't, either, but I'll take what help I can get. Tell Adra—"

"All right! I'll tell him—if you agree to stay here!"

The hand tightened on my bicep, and this time, it didn't look like it was budging.

I stared down at it for a moment, and then up at him. And saw him flush, whether with embarrassment or anger, I didn't know. But he didn't move.

"I'm not going to lose you," he told me, low and harsh.

And this is it, I thought. This is how we fail. Not because the other side is better, but because we won't work together. Not even now.

And that was my fault, wasn't it? The Pythia was the great unifier, or she was supposed to be. The one who got everyone to drop their stupid quarrels and work on a common cause. But I didn't have the words, any more than I'd had them with Mircea. I didn't know how to make Jonas let me go, not in a suite full of his mages. I didn't know how to make him understand that we weren't *running* out of time, we *were* out. I didn't know how to get through to him.

"Not going to lose her?" Rhea said, from the doorway. "Like you lost the last Pythia entrusted to your care?"

"Stay out of this," Jonas told her.

But Rhea wasn't staying out. Rhea was already in and coming up beside us. "That's what this is about, isn't it?" she demanded. "Not Lady Cassandra's age—there have been younger Pythias. Or her lack of training, which her blood more than compensates for. Or even her reaching out to the covens, which is far overdue. But *you*. Your grief, your pain, your constant need for—"

"Learn your place, girl!" Jonas snarled, pushing her away when she tried to come between us.

"I know my place!" she said, her voice no kinder than his. "I've always known. But you don't, do you? The Lady didn't tell you—"

"What are you babbling about?"

"—because she knew how you'd react, what you'd do. This! What you always do, trying to control everything, trying to control *her*. But not me. She wasn't going to let you control *me*—"

"This doesn't concern you!"

"My mother's death doesn't concern me?"

And suddenly, everything froze.

It looked like I'd stopped time. Only I could still hear the sound of the clock, see the dust motes floating in the light from the hall, feel the quiet brush of the air-conditioning.

And the sudden clenching of Jonas' hand on my arm.

"Your . . . mother?" he asked, the words surprisingly tone-less.

"My mother," Rhea said, grabbing one of the photo albums, the ones we'd taken from Agnes' safe, the ones I'd never had a chance to look through. And thrust it at him. "It's all there, my whole life. How she had me in secret, how she sent me away as an infant, how I grew up with one of her old initiates, a coven witch, because she knew you had nothing but contempt for the covens, knew you'd never find me there—"

"I would never?" Jonas was looking at the album she was holding out. It was spilling over with photos to the point that they fell out of the side in great clumps. Many of them featured him, usually with Agnes.

But he still didn't get it, I thought.

He didn't get what she was telling him.

"She knew I would test strongly for the power," Rhea said. "Knew I'd be brought back to court soon enough, to be with her. But as an initiate, no one would question my being there. And coming from a coven family, no one would try to use me as a political pawn, or force me into a position I didn't want, just so he could profit—"

"No!" Jonas looked up at her, and I guess I'd been wrong. I guess that had been shock. Because it looked like he did get it, after all. "I would never—"

"But she thought you would," Rhea said, twisting the knife. "And she knew you. She told me once, it was the hardest decision she ever made, and the loneliest. But she knew the number of times you tried to influence her—"

"For the good of the magical community!"

"For the good of the *Circle*—"

"They're the same thing!"

"*They are not the same thing!*" she said, furious. "That is why we have a Pythia, to speak for us—all of us. And Mother knew this, but she loved you, and it tormented her, but she *loved* you—"

"And I loved her!" he rasped. "For fifty years—"

"Then prove it! Prove it and do what she would have wanted. Let Lady Cassandra go, before it's too late. Let her *do* this."

"She can't do this, not without help!"

"Jonas," I said, putting a hand over the one he still had on my arm. "That's what I've been trying to tell you. I *can't* do this. I can't win this war for you on my own. But maybe I can win it *with* you."

He looked from me to Rhea for a long moment, pain and fury and fear all there in his face, clear for anyone to read. He wasn't going to do it. It was like my life lately: too much, too fast. Or maybe not, I thought, as his hand suddenly sprang off my arm. "Go."

I didn't give him a chance to change his mind. I grabbed up the mage's coat, still smelling of nineteenth-century soot, and shifted.

Chapter Fifty-three

I didn't have to ask if they'd found the potion. Marlowe's office door was open, and curls and puddles of lethal substances bloomed bright in the darkness: red and deep purple and orange. A group of war mages, dark ones judging by the lack of insignia, remained frozen in a contorted mass in front of the cabinets, coats swirling and shields half raised as they fought to get away from the dangerous tide. Except for one who had landed in a potion puddle that must have been just outside the spell range.

Because it was busy sizzling through what remained of his flesh.

It looked like somebody had broken through the wards, everyone had rushed forward for a wholesale plunder—and then someone else had thrown down a bunch of lethal substances, catching them all off guard. And then frozen them where they stood.

And that included the competition, I thought, staring at a withered corpse caught halfway to the floor. The limbs were gray and shrunken and desiccated, the face unrecognizable. But the red hair was as vibrant as ever.

So it was the brunette.

I turned and went out of the office.

I didn't have to ask which way she'd gone. The corridor to the right was a frozen tableau, with bolts of spell fire suspended in the air, unmoving. Explosions of plaster hung overhead like clouds, sprays of glass twinkled like stars, and potion bombs had detonated in what looked like tufts of cotton candy.

But I stopped anyway, grasping the door frame, indecision clawing at me.

Because I didn't have to do this. I could shift back in time a day and warn everyone. I could tell Marlowe to move his damned potion. Could tell the Senate to up their security. Could—

Be ignored, disbelieved, and not taken seriously, just like I had been my whole life.

My name wasn't Cassandra for nothing.

And I could almost hear the response, if I told Mircea to move a potion—one he knew I wanted badly—from Marlowe's hands to somewhere less secure. "So that you can access it easier, *dulceata*?"

Plus, even if I could get them to believe me, I didn't know who the acolytes' contact was. A vampire, she'd said. Someone with access. Someone who might learn of the move, and then I'd be no better off—in fact, I'd be worse. Right now, I still had the remains of a full bottle of potion in me. Tomorrow, it might have worn off.

But if I stayed and failed . . .

If you're ever going to talk to me, I told my power silently, help me now. Do I go forward, or do I go back?

For a long moment, there was nothing, except my own gnawing anxiety. But then the corridor behind me dimmed, ever so slightly, or maybe the one ahead brightened. It wasn't a lot of difference, was barely any at all, to the point that I wouldn't have noticed it if I hadn't been looking for it.

But I had been, and it was there.

"So, lousy odds either way, but slightly better ahead?" I asked. But that time, I didn't get a response. Which, judging from past experience, meant I'd gotten it about right.

I swallowed. And then I ducked under a pinkish red cloud, which would probably have eaten my face if it were moving. But it wasn't—nothing in the whole corridor was. Including the line of bullets hanging in the air just ahead, on their way to obliterate a mage's chest.

He was one of the Circle's men, whose failing shield was down to a faint flicker of green in the air around him. I scooped the slugs out of the air and threw them down the empty hall behind me, hearing them explode against the floor once they cleared the area of the spell. They echoed loud in the stillness, but it didn't matter.

She already knew I was coming.

She was waiting for me, she had to be, or we'd already have a vengeful god on our hands. But we didn't. Because two bottles of potion were enough to allow her the luxury of time—all the time in the world. To play her games. To bring him through. And to deal with me.

I, on the other hand, had a seriously depleted power supply and an unknown time frame. Jonas would find Adra, of that I had no doubt, and he would send his people. But while they could take out almost any other adversary around, what could they do against the power of a god? Because that was what she was wielding.

And it looked like she was wielding a lot of it.

There was a row of bodies ahead, half skeletonized, where a time spell had eaten its way through a crowd. Some had died instantly, heads and torsos aged back to bone, or in a few cases to dust. Others ... hadn't been so lucky.

I put an arm over my face and tried to block out the pervasive stench of blood, so much blood, from people unfortunate enough to get only a glancing blow from the spell. One man still moved, slowly, helplessly, sticklike legs protruding from a normal torso. I wanted to help him, but even I could tell he was too far gone. And I didn't have the strength to spare.

I left him there.

The next hallway was even worse, although in a different way. The walls looked like trucks had been driven through them. One explosion had been suspended in the moment it burst out of the walls, the jagged edges leaping out at me like a cluster of knives as I passed. While another, farther down, was exploding over and over again, caught in a time loop like an endlessly running replay, and shaking the floor underneath my feet every few seconds.

It looked like she'd just thrown spells everywhere, with many serving no purpose I could see. A painting on a nearby wall stripped itself back to blank canvas, then repainted itself again and again. A broken water main flooded through a fissure in the floor above, the shimmering veil hanging suspended in midair, like a curtain. A couple of spells had fallen on the same potted plant, causing it to wither and then burst back to life, flowering all over again. And draping the little table on which it sat in flowers, a decade's worth or more, that fell onto the blood-strewn floor below like a funeral spill.

I passed through the glistening strands of the waterfall, only to stop abruptly at the sight of what had to be a hundred spell bolts, all converging on a single spot—mine. It looked like the people in the hall had finally realized they had a common problem, but too late.

The bolts were far too thick to find a way through, so I ducked into a hole someone had thoughtfully blasted in the wall. And into a small set of dimly lit rooms. Where a slow-motion battle was taking place between half a dozen fighting couples as a time spell slowly unraveled.

They looked almost like they were dancing, a dim haze of light from somewhere up ahead setting their shadows to moving on the remaining walls and floor. I threaded my way through, and finally realized why I could see them so clearly. The whole back wall of the last room was missing, allowing me to step out into a wide-open space where the collapse of the upper floor had included a good deal of the ceiling, leaving an area open to the moonlight.

It looked almost like a stadium, only instead of spectators, there were only more combatants, busy killing or dying or both.

And a wild-eyed girl in the center, helping them along and laughing joyously.

"Is this what it's like to be a god?" she called to me from across the field of rubble. "Is this how they feel all the time?"

"I don't know."

"You have to know! Your mother was Artemis—didn't she ever tell you?"

"We don't talk much."

"Why not? You can go back and see her whenever you like. You can do whatever you *like*!"

She threw out a hand, and the flesh of a nearby mage all but flew off his bones. The time spell stripped him of everything in seconds, leaving behind a skeleton in tattered leather that nonetheless continued to menace a leaping vampire. But which would fall apart into the dried-up bones it was as soon as the spell failed.

He was one of her own, one of the dark mages on her side, but she didn't seem to notice. Or to care. The life-or-death battle going on around her had become her playground, the people her toys, the whole bloody mess there for her amusement.

Yes, I thought. That is probably exactly what the gods had felt like.

"Is that what he promised you?" I asked, picking my way through the rubble. "To give you the power of a god? To make you Pythia?"

She laughed again, a genuinely delighted sound. "Pythia. You know, I used to dream of that? Used to lie awake at night, in my narrow little bed, and plan for the day when I'd be in control. Of my life. Of my future. Of *everything*. I'd have the money and the fame and the title, and all those richly dressed people would be coming to see *me*."

"But that didn't happen."

"No. It went to Myra. When the only good idea she ever had was how to get rid of the Lady! I was always better at using the power than her. It came to me easily, when she had to struggle. It liked me, wanted *me*—but Agnes said I was too ambitious. Ambitious!" She laughed again. "What the hell did she think Myra was? What did she think any of us were? What else *was* there?"

"What else? You're true clairvoyants, from wealthy and powerful families—"

"Who don't give a damn about them unless they get the top spot!" she said viciously. "Nobody gives a damn. My parents told me that, right before I left. It's one of my earliest memories. There I was, all of five and clinging to my mother's leg in fear. Before she pulled me off and crouched down, and gave me my first life lesson. 'Do whatever it takes, but become Pythia. There's nothing here for you if you don't.'"

"Your mother was cruel."

"My mother was honest! She knew how the world works. Get power, keep power, or grovel your whole life to those who have it. Like they did to me, when I was named an acolyte. There were only a handful of us, and one of us was going to get it, one of us was going to *be* it. And, oh, how everything changed!"

She flung a spell—at me this time—and she hadn't been wrong. She was fast and deadly. I shifted barely in time, as a wall collapsed into rubble behind me, materializing on her other side—

Where she had already whirled to meet me.

"They sucked up to me," she said, as if nothing had happened. "Fawned and flattered and bought me things, all kinds of pretty things: cars I couldn't drive, clothes and jewelry I wasn't allowed to wear. But I loved it; I loved all of it! Not because of the things, but because of why they bought them. How they hushed when I came into a room, the way their eyes followed me, the way they *crawled*."

I darted out of the way of a spell, and it hit a column just to my left, twining around it like a vine. And sending the plaster and bricks underneath crumbling and crashing and then scattering and dusting to nothingness on the floor beside me.

Apparently, nobody had ever told her that the villain monologues and *then* attacks.

"But Myra got the nod," she said, "and all of a sudden, I was back to being invisible. I was never good enough, no, no. Not for my family, not for the Lady, not for anyone. But now look. Even the master himself, even a *god* waits for *me*."

And before I could dodge, she sent another wash of power at me, one hard and fast enough that I barely had time to counter. The two time spells met in midair, forming a coil that writhed and twisted and seemed to be trying to eat each other. And then abruptly flew apart, into a thousand tiny spheres that sped away in all directions.

We hit the floor, both of us at the same time. Because the air around us was suddenly filled with little floating orbs of death, like mirrored bubbles reflecting the scene. And peppering the remaining walls of the area with holes from the faster-moving ones, like the blast from massive shotgun shells.

"Wow. Never saw that before," she said, sounding awed. And then she threw again.

I scurried behind a group of filing cabinets that rusted apart as I passed, into a doorway that collapsed almost on top of me, and out into a room strewn with papers underfoot and muddy boot prints. Both of which sloughed away into nothingness as the spell ate along the ground behind me.

Until I threw a slow time wave over my shoulder, thick enough to be considered a wall, frantically trying to buy time. And it did—about a second's worth. Until a fast time spell of hers came boiling through the middle like a concentrated dart, or like a missile launched underwater. And then tore out the other side, slamming into the same type of spell I'd just thrown on myself, shattering them both.

And sending me crabbing backward out into a hallway as the remnants of the spells flew over my head, barely missing my face. And then she was there, right there, and I did the only thing I could, the only thing in this whole Pythian arsenal that I'd ever been really good at. And shifted.

But not me.

I shifted a cabinet, old carved walnut by the looks of it, jerking it off one wall and slamming into place right where she'd been standing.

And then just lay there for a moment, panting and exhausted, and hoping like hell that had worked.

And maybe it had. Because dust and bits of flaking wallpaper, now centuries old, fluttered down around me like confetti, but nothing else moved. And the staunch solidity of the cabinet gave me reason to hope that maybe, just maybe, nothing would.

Until the door opened and she stepped daintily out, her little slipper still Pythian white against the filthy floor.

"Good one," she told me. "I barely had time to get up a shield."

"Glad you liked it."

"When we used to duel, that was Victoria's favorite move." She smiled. "Want to see mine?"

No, I thought, and shifted.

And that time I did shift me, because I needed a moment. And ended up on the roof I'd glimpsed earlier through the missing ceiling, since it was the only place I could think of where there weren't other people around. I landed on hands and knees, panting, staring around for a telltale glimmer of white. But there didn't appear to be one.

Which . . . was both good and not. Because I couldn't

risk her tiring of our game and running off to get her reward. But the whole keep-her-talking-until-the-demons-arrive-and-hopefully-shred-her plan did not appear to be working.

At all.

I gulped in cool evening air and tried to think of an alternative. But I wasn't coming up with much. Because of *course* they used to duel. And they must have done it a lot, because she was damned good. Meanwhile, I had gotten my butt kicked by Gertie twice, and had barely managed a draw with the redhead—and that had been with Rhea's help.

But staying up here wasn't going to work. I had to find her again. I had to think of something—

"Pretty, isn't it?"

I spun around.

And found her looking up at the big silvery moon floating serenely overhead, on a bank of silver-gray clouds. My hand twitched and she looked down, grinning. Like she knew how close to bottoming out I was.

"No offense," she told me. "But I have a hard time believing your mother was a goddess."

"So do I."

She laughed. "I like you. You know, I don't think I'll enjoy killing you much."

"Then don't."

"Can't do that." She shook her head. "The master is waiting—"

"Let him," I said quickly. "Didn't you say you liked that feeling? Because it won't last. Not once you bring him back. Right now, you're the most powerful person in the world. But after? He's a *god*. We're nothing to them—"

"Speak for yourself."

"Aren't you tired of being overlooked? Unnoticed? Aren't you tired of being just that girl in white?"

"You have no idea."

"Then what do you think you'll be to *him*?"

"I think I'll be his queen."

"That's what he promised you?"

She nodded. "A contest: winner take all. Whoever brought him back first would be his consort and a goddess. Whoever failed . . ." She shrugged.

"And you won."

"Of course. Victoria tried to sell us on the idea of working together and sharing his favor. Share. Like she ever shared anything. But in the end, she wasn't a problem at all."

"And your other competition?"

"Jo's off on a wild-goose chase, looking for some old relic." She rolled her eyes.

"Relic?"

"One she thinks is strong enough to blast through the barrier. I told her she was wasting her time. If she ever finds it, the fey will kill her. They don't let go of their toys easily."

I swallowed. "No. No, they don't."

"And Lizzie—poor, dumb thing—still thinks she's going to be Pythia. She doesn't get it; we won't need a Pythia anymore. First thing on the list is to get rid of all magic users, so no more threat of banishment. Afterward, the only ones with magic will be us—"

"And the other gods, once he lets them in."

She laughed delightedly. "Who says he's letting them in?"

"He's planning to keep earth for himself."

"And faerie, and the hells," she agreed. "Why remove your mother's spell when it would just let everyone back in, the whole greedy lot of them? He doesn't need everyone. He doesn't need anyone. He can take it all, and be master of it all. Just him and me and the children we'll have . . . which is why I'm afraid you have to go."

"He'll kill me for you when he comes back."

"Probably," she agreed. "But I can't take that chance, can I? Leaving him with a choice between a demigoddess child of Artemis and me?"

And I suddenly realized why she'd been willing to play this little game.

"I don't want him," I said fervently.

She grinned. "I don't think you'd have an option. And I—I've been second once too often. What did they say in *Blade Runner*? 'Time to die.'"

"Never saw that movie," I said, and kicked out. And while I may suck at time duels, Pritkin had been teaching me all sorts of dirty fighting tricks. If I'd been in boots, I might have shattered her kneecap. But even in tennis shoes, she went down.

Only to get kicked in the chin when she looked back up, snarling.

"You know, being queen doesn't sound so bad," I told her. And shifted to the lower floor where I'd come in. Because I might not be a great fighter, but I was a pro at running away. I could teach *classes* on running away.

Or I could have—if she hadn't followed right on my heels.

I whirled around at a sound behind me, and she sent a time wave that I somehow shifted away from, but not before it turned a clump of my hair old and brittle enough to crumble when I rematerialized. And threw out a hand. And shifted her—into the wall.

Literally.

I'd accidentally done something similar to myself once, getting stuck in a fireplace because I was shifting too fast to pay attention. It had taken ten minutes and a huge amount of magic from Jonas to get me out. She managed it alone and in seconds.

"You really are good with the power," I told her.

"Thank you," she said. And froze me.

It happened so fast, I never even saw her move. In fact, I don't think she did. I'd always made some sort of gesture when shifting, even if it was only a small one. But maybe that was just me, the human part of me, who felt a need to *move* when I was moving.

But I guess it wasn't technically necessary, because she never even twitched.

But something else did.

The frozen curtain of water behind her was not so frozen anymore. It glimmered softly in the light, like a fey waterfall, cascading sluggishly toward the floor. And behind it, just visible through the slowly moving stream, was every color of the rainbow.

Or at least the lethal, warmer shades of the aggressive spells war mages used.

I gazed at them as my rigid body tottered and threatened to fall. And remembered all those spells, that corridor's worth of spells, the very last spells that all those dying mages had thrown. The ones she'd avoided once—but not this time.

And no, it turns out that you really don't need to move to throw a spell, after all.

Epilogue

Half an hour later, I was sitting on what I guessed had once been a balcony, overlooking what might once have been a great hall. It was hard to tell, since it was mostly rubble now, but it looked like the consul liked to live well. You could still see touches of it here and there: the gleam of inlaid marble under heaps of collapsed walls, rich fabrics threading through mountains of broken furniture, the glint of what remained of a wall of mirrors shining in the firelight, because something over to the left was still burning.

Instead of the seat of vampire power on earth, it finally looked like what it was: a war zone.

But the fighting was over for the moment, and everybody was busy picking up. And licking their wounds. And planning their next move.

A vampire came by in dirty, wrinkled clothing, with a smear of blood on his nice, white tunic. But his silk sash was still straight, and he'd paused at some point to wipe the dust off his highly polished shoes. He had a tray with him—silver, of course—containing cups of coffee. I took one but declined the blanket he also offered, from a group draped over his arm.

He moved on.

I sat and thought about power. Specifically mine. Because maybe it *had* been talking to me, after all. Or at least listening. And I hadn't been asking for one thing, had I?

I'd been asking for two.

All week, practically every thought had been about two things: finding Pritkin and trying to locate a weapon to fight the gods. What if my power, which wasn't human and didn't think like us, had decided to take a shortcut? What if it had decided to take me back to the one place and time . . . where I would find both?

I heard again Fred's voice asking, "How did they fight each other?" Felt once more the smooth old surface of a staff of unbelievable power. Heard the brunette saying that my last rogue acolyte was after "an ancient relic" that could challenge the power of a god.

Maybe because it had been made by one.

Everyone had been looking for a weapon against Ares: Jonas thought I was one; Mircea wanted me to make him one. Everyone was looking for answers, but what if the ones we needed weren't here? What if they were fifteen hundred years in the past, at a court still shrouded in myth and legend? What if the story of an ancient king's return to save us at humanity's darkest hour was truer than anyone had ever realized?

My hand clenched on the pitted surface of a tiny bottle. It was the one the acolyte had dropped when she hit the wall, the one she'd never had a chance to retrieve. It was the last one, the last full bottle of the rarest potion on earth, and my last chance.

To rescue Pritkin.

To find the answers we desperately needed.

And, possibly, to save a world.

But I had an errand to do first.

The hallways of the consul's stately home looked a little different now, which wasn't surprising since nothing had happened yet. The attack would be tonight, and when it came, a lot of people were going to die. Some of them would be ours, good people whose deaths I could easily prevent, except for the warning clanging in my mind.

I wasn't sure why; I didn't get details. Just that the battle, terrible though it had been, had had a purpose. But I could guess.

The little knots I'd seen of vamps and weres and mages, all battling together, were unprecedented. They didn't fight alongside each other; they ignored each other or killed each other—except for last night. Which had caught them unawares, with very little backup, and with a mutual enemy that was threatening all their lives. It was the war in miniature, and taught the lesson far better than I ever could.

But it was still terrible, knowing that I could prevent it all, by a single warning. . . .

And in the process, leave us as divided as ever. Facing an enemy that was still hammering at the gates, trying to get in. Who wanted to kill us all.

And so I walked the halls silently, the weight of all those lives on my shoulders, and wondered what really aged the Pythias. Channeling the power of a god when we weren't one, or this? Knowing things we could never say, seeing sights we could never talk about, keeping secrets our whole lives.

Like Agnes.

I didn't doubt that Jonas had really loved her; the expression on his face had been eloquent. But I also didn't doubt that he'd exploited their relationship as much as she'd allow. To the point that she'd hidden their child away, to keep him from doing the same thing to her.

Because she knew: it isn't easy to say no, and to keep saying no, to someone you love.

Maybe that was why so many of the Pythias hadn't seemed to have long-term lovers. Maybe that was why even those that had, like Agnes, had been forced to hide them away, to keep people from suspecting that they were being influenced. Maybe that was why so many had seemed to live so alone.

I didn't plan to be alone for the rest of my life. But I also wasn't going to be Agnes to anyone's Jonas. I wasn't going to have that kind of relationship, and any man in my life was going to have to understand that. *Any* man, I thought, and pulled open the door to the room where I'd been told I'd find Mircea.

And I did.

But I found someone else, too.

I stopped dead at the sight of Mircea, insensate on a bed, being guarded by a gorgeous brunette.

No, not *a* gorgeous brunette. *The* gorgeous brunette,

from the painting I hadn't remembered to ask him about. And not sitting. *Lying.* Under a thin sheet that did little to hide the ample, naked curves beneath.

She looked at me out of sloe dark eyes, and her mouth took on a contemptuous twist. "He doesn't need you," she told me dismissively.

"What?"

"He's sleeping," she said, as if I'd somehow missed that. "And I can give him what he needs."

I bet, I thought, feeling my blood pressure start to rise.

"You can go," she repeated impatiently. "Vamoose, am-scray, make like a tree. Do you get it?"

"Yeah. I got it," I told her, and reached for my power. And slid a question along one shimmering strand, receiving back an instant reply.

And laughed at the irony.

I could save this one.

Of course I could.

So I did. But I sent her to a pasture in the middle of no-where, a particularly dung-filled pasture, because power has to be good for something, right? And then I gathered Mircea up in my arms. And I swear I saw a glimmer of dark fire under those too-thick-for-a-man lashes.

"We are going to have a long talk when you wake up," I told him grimly.

And I shifted.

Look for Karen Chance's next thrilling
adventure in the Cassie Palmer series,

RIDE THE STORM

Coming Spring 2016 from Signet

COMING SOON FROM
NEW YORK TIMES BESTSELLING AUTHOR

Karen Chance

RIDE THE STORM

Ever since being stuck with the job of pythia, the chief seer
of the supernatural world, Cassie Palmer has been playing
catch up. Catch up to the lifetime's worth of training she
missed being raised by a psychotic vampire instead of at the
fabled pythian court. Catch up to the powerful, and sometimes seductive, forces trying to mold her to their will. It's
been a trial by fire that has left her more than a little burned.

But now she realizes that all that was just the warm up for
the real race. Ancient forces that once terrorized the world
are trying to return, and Cassie is the only one who
can stop them...

AVAILABLE APRIL 2016

Available wherever books are sold or at
penguin.com

NEW YORK TIMES AND *USA TODAY*
BESTSELLING AUTHOR

Karen Chance

THE CASSIE PALMER SERIES

Touch the Dark

Claimed by Shadow

Embrace the Night

Curse the Dawn

Hunt the Moon

Tempt the Stars

Reap the Wind

"One of my favorite reads."
—#1 *New York Times* bestselling author
Charlaine Harris

Available wherever books are sold or at
penguin.com

facebook.com/projectparanormalbooks

Also available from
New York Times and *USA Today*
bestselling author

Karen Chance

MIDNIGHT'S DAUGHTER

Dorina Basarab is a dhampir—half-human, half-vampire.
Unlike most dhampirs, though, Dory has managed to
maintain her sanity. Now Dory's vampire father has
come to her for help—again. Her Uncle Dracula
(yes, *the* Dracula), cruelest among vampires, has escaped
his prison. And her father wants Dory to work with
gorgeous master vampire Louis-Cesare to put
him back there.

Although Dory prefers to work alone, Dracula is the only
thing that truly scares her—and when she has to face
him, she'll take all the help she can get…

Available wherever books are sold or at
penguin.com

facebook.com/projectparanormalbooks